Lead With Your Left

• • •

The Best That Ever Did It

by Ed Lacy

Introduction by Bud Elder

Stark House Press • Eureka California

LEAD WITH YOUR LEFT / THE BEST THAT EVER DID IT

Published by Stark House Press
1315 H Street
Eureka, CA 95501, USA
griffinskye3@sbcglobal.net
www.starkhousepress.com

LEAD WITH YOUR LEFT
Originally published by Harper & Brothers, New York, and copyright ©
1957 by Ed Lacy. Reprinted in paperback by Permabooks, New York, 1957.
A shorter version published as "Keep an Eye on the Body" by Mercury
Mystery Book Magazine, 1956.

THE BEST THAT EVER DID IT
Originally published by Harper & Brothers, New York, and
copyright © 1955 by Ed Lacy. Reprinted in paperback as
Visa to Death by Permabooks, New York, 1956.

ISBN-13: 978-1-944520-71-7

Book design by Mark Shepard, SHEPGRAPHICS.COM
Cover art by Robert Maguire from *Visa to Death*

First Stark House Press Edition: January 2019

FIRST EDITION

LEAD WITH YOUR LEFT

Dave Wintino is the youngest homicide cop on the force, and is constantly getting ribbed for it.   When an ex-cop named Owens is found murdered while delivering some for a bond company, no one takes Wintino seriously when he suggests it could be more than just a random burglary. He starts investigating on his own, and discovers that Owens and his old partner were still working together. Could an 30-year-old case involving a bootleg still and a gangland killing have anything to do with Owens' death? When Owens' partner is found murdered as well, Wintino knows that there is more than coincidence at work here—if only he can get someone to take him seriously.

THE BEST THAT EVER DID IT

Two men are murdered on a New York City street. One is a guy who just won a thousand dollars in a slogan contest. The other is a cop. The wife of the cop hires Barney Harris to find the killer. But what possible motive could there be for the killing of these two total strangers? Of course, the cops are already on this one, but Barney gets lucky, and stumbles across a clue in a neighborhood bar. He finds a prostitute the two men had in common. But he still can't figure out why a killer would go after them both. What linked these two men? And what kind of scheme prompts a gunman to go after a guy so squeaky clean that the boldest act of his life is planning a trip to Europe with his contest winnings?

Sunday Punched

By Bud Elder

"With these new additions, there may be revealed murderous admissions otherwise concealed"
– Rupert Holmes, *The Mystery of Edwin Drood*

How do they do it?

How do the notes swirling around Louis Armstrong's head manifest themselves through his trumpet?

How does Woody Allen make a fresh, essential film a year?

How does the gourmet chef at George's Happy Hog BBQ in Oklahoma City keep finding new, mouth burning, rib rubs?

And how did one Ed Lacy, who authored the two books in this volume, consistently find a well that gushed enough new voices and engaging plots to fill around 30 novels and several hundred short stories?

Who wouldn't eat a bug to have even a fraction of these talents?

You'll not see Ed Lacy's name in any chain bookstore's "Mystery" section, but in the real world you probably should. Like any overachieving pulp writer, he loves his characters and keeps the clichés to a dull roar. And what turns of phrase.

Like:

 "Rough Oscar" – a tough guy

"Everyone treats this like a big yak" – the joke's on you.

Ed Lacy, Leonard S. Zinberg, was born into affluence and died in a laundromat near Harlem. He was Jewish and a leftist and believed in racial equality to a level that he created the first fictional black detective. He had heart issues and looked like Alan Arkin in *The Russians Are Coming*. He lived near a police station so he could hear the rumpus in cop speak.

Like:

"Fit like grape skin" - quite tight

"Sunday punched" – hit while not paying attention

Lacy won an Edgar, a sort of Academy award for scribblers, and breathed the rarefied air of a paperback writer whose work was deemed substantially sound enough to be bound in hard.

Like:

"Showed my buzzer" – to pull a badge

"Bullslop" – decorum prevents

Whoever, whether it was Lacy himself or his editors, wrote titles for the author's books gets a C+.

It was no secret that Lacy was a boxing fan himself. His first novel, *Walk Hard Talk Loud*, (again, titles?) centered on an African American pugilist, so it would be an easy assumption to think *Lead With Your Left* might be another story with gloves attached. Instead, this 1957 book, in which, granted, the lead is an ex boxer, couples the dogged determination of an Ed McBain procedural with Hammett's *Maltese Falcon* eternal edict "When a man's partner is killed you have to do something about it. When one of your organization gets killed it's bad business to let the killer get away with it."

Early on in the book it becomes clear that rookie Detective David Wintino is on edge over the death of a retired policeman he has never known.

"The wrong angle his body made said he had to be dead. Who dropped the newspaper over his face, the headlines and pictures about the ball game? Why don't they want anyone to see a dead face? Or maybe the dead don't want to see us live jokers."

Wintino is distracted from solving this first case, plus others down the line, by a pretentious, materialistic wife and a lovely lady researcher, a stalking victim, whose dilemma connects the dots. Mystery solved and everybody is happy, which makes *Lead With Your Left* an able character study and pretty straight whodunnit.

Like:

Run your gums – talking out of school

I bagged a hard up jerk on his first two bit job – a loser got arrested.

Here again we go with the titles - included here is *The Best That Ever Did It*, which makes absolutely zero sense, the title, not the book.

However, check out Lacy's writing, straight out of 50s Noir 101.

"It was like an old fashioned saloon, although it only dated back to 1923. (During Prohibition it was called the Grand Café Ice Cream Parlour and happily sold needle beer and very little ice cream.) It was called a bar, rarely a café, a joint, a gin mill, a dive and a dump. Strangely enough nobody ever called the place what it really was...home."

Like:

Needle beer - that which is low in alcohol

Outside this den of doom two murders occur at the same time, one victim a policeman, the other a just announced lottery winner. What do they have in common? What gat-bearing bad guy gave them the ratatatat?

Hired to find the culprit is Barney Harris, a 250-pound auto mechanic/PI whose code of the street would have Mike Hammer in tears.

"I'm telling you up front, I don't go in for shootings or any rough stuff, all that movie slop."

One wonders throughout the reading of *The Best That Ever Did It* why Ed Lacy and Hollywood never shook hands. Lacy has more unique and very well described characters—from a blind barfly to the hooker that might just, somewhere deep down inside, have a heart of gold—than any studio programmers.

While Lacy was obviously popular with the public during his career, he had the rare achievement of catching the eye of highbrow critics as well. Ed Gorman said "There is a lyricism, almost poetry, to the writing that touched not only the powerful melancholy storyline but also the elegant and evocative place descriptions."

There must surely be a special place in heaven for those pulp writers who were worker bees, whose names always meant less than their paperback creations' lurid covers and provocative titles.

Should that be true, ring that bell, Ed Lacy has his wings.

Like:

Everything was a boot to watch

Old mousey duck

Readers will now be left to decipher these two phrases on their own. Just like in a mystery.

—October 2018
Oklahoma City, OK

Lead With Your Left
Ed Lacy

Author's Note

This is entirely a work of fiction; all names, characters, and incidents are purely imaginary. While I hope the people in the book seem like real people, they are not intended to represent any specific person or persons, living, dead, or about to be born.

E.L.

Tuesday Night

It was a few minutes before eleven when I unlocked our door. The dumb lamp we had in the two-by-four "foyer" was on. The lamp looked like a drippy flower and cost fifty-seven bucks strictly because it was imported from Denmark. If all their lamps are like this job they must be blind over there. I could just about make out the couch opened as a bed, was surprised Mary was in the hay so early. I called out softly, "Babes?" She didn't answer.

I took off my coat and tie, then my shoulder holster, went through my pockets and put everything on the table beside the lamp. I dropped my suit on the floor; it was due for the cleaner's anyway and we only had one closet and no room for soiled clothes. I went to the john and washed, afraid I'd wake Mary if I moved the Chinese screen in front of our "kitchenette" for a snack. For a hundred and twenty bucks a month you'd think we'd have room enough to move around. But not at this "good" address on East Sixty-ninth Street. Still I couldn't entirely blame Mary, I got some kicks out of living in a swank joint, and all the modern nutty furniture we were in hock for. And yesterday almost all my pay check went for old bills. What kicks.

But the old railroad flat in the Bronx had its features too. Like now I could go way up to the front room and get the news on TV, see who'd won the fight as I worked on an apple. But no TV watching in a one-room apartment, not even a swank one. Turning out the damn light I carefully threaded my way through the furniture and climbed into the sack.

Bed felt great. I'd been going since eight in the morning. Staring up at the darkness I wondered if Ed Owens had lived in a hundred-and-twenty-buck apartment. I saw Owens in the alley again. The wrong angle his body made said he had to be dead. Who dropped the newspaper over his face, the headline and pictures about the ball game? Why don't they want anybody to see a dead face? Or maybe the dead don't want to see us live jokers.

Mary had a heavy way of breathing, almost a light snore. I didn't hear it so she wasn't asleep, just laying there sore as a boil at me. I reached under the cover for her hips. She wasn't wearing one of my old shirts, but those damn ski-pajamas she bought to spite me. When my fingers found her she pulled away. I said, "Look, honey, I did try to call—at six—but you weren't home. I got stuck on a big case."

"Sure, you put in overtime, four to eleven, seven hours—a day's work on a normal job. What did you get, time and a half or double time, for it?"

She had that nasty shrillness to her voice that reminded me of Mom when she was steamed, way she sounded when she knew I was out boxing. The shrillness that meant—with both Mary and Mom—that talking was a waste of time. But I was so full of it I had to talk. "Look, Babes, this is real big. I was in on the killing of an ex-cop. Guy named Ed Owens was shot down right in—"

"I'm not interested!"

"Mary, this was one of these dumb killings where a—"

"I couldn't care less!"

I sat up in bed. "A man who'd been a good cop, gave almost thirty years of his life to protecting people, was shot down in an alley. Sure, you're not interested, nobody is. That's the trouble today, nobody gives a fat damn about anything or—"

Mary turned over, faced me in the darkness. "Dave, you came home seven goddam hours late, *seven hours,* so I'm hardly in the mood for any of your childish speeches."

She said "childish" to steam me but I said evenly, "Maybe Owens' wife doesn't think it's a speech. Maybe she's wondering what the hell living is all about when a retired cop has to work as a twenty-five-buck-a-week messenger and gets killed in the bargain. Some bargain!"

"Is that what I have to look forward to, Dave, you lying dead in the street some night? My God, what do you think was going through my head when you didn't come home?"

I found her shoulder in the darkness, held it when she tried to turn away. "Babes, I said I tried to phone you. That was the only time I was near a phone. Had the big brass from downtown with me, couldn't get away even for a moment. Another thing, this is why I'm so interested in this case, I kept thinking if this was going to be me, working as a lousy messenger when I'm too old to be a cop. Nothing makes sense about the killing, no motive, no—"

"You're too old to be a cop now! Dave, I can't take this much longer."

"Now Mary, let's not start that."

"Why not?" she asked loudly and I knew her mouth was a hard line the way it always got when she was angry. When I first met her I thought that hard line was cute, used to tease her just to see the red lips fade into a line and finally burst into a big smile. "I come home and make supper, sit around jumping out of my skin wondering what's happened to you. And at eleven o'clock my husband comes home and makes some small talk about his job—he talks about a killing!"

"*Small* talk? Damnit, an ex-cop was killed this afternoon!"

"I don't want to hear about it!"

"It concerns you, concerns everybody. *A cop was killed!*"

"Davie, the boy do-gooder! I don't want it to concern me. And let go of my shoulder, or is this the loving touch, the third degree?"

"That's dumb talk," I said, letting go of her. "And don't start crying." I reached out and snapped on the indirect lights that ran along the back of the studio couch. Even in the middle of the night Mary always looked sharp, her blonde hair tidy, the curves of her breasts trim even in the damn pajamas. I reached for one of the curves and she slapped at my hand and missed.

Anyway she wasn't going to bawl. When she's real mad Mary gets into a cold rage like she was about to spit ice. I looked at the hard line of her mouth and knew she wasn't going to cry at all: she was going to talk.

"A husband and wife can usually talk over what happened to them during the day, the office gossip and jokes, but what am I supposed to ask you? Who you caught robbing? What pimp you hit? And when can we ever talk? You work these crazy hours, nights, days, middle of the days, Saturdays, Sundays. You're off Thursday and Friday this week—a big week end ahead for me! Dave, what kind of a life do we have? I want to go out and see people, take in a movie on a Saturday night, but you're only off one week end a month. I get up in the morning and see my husband getting his tools ready for the day—a gun and a blackjack. And for what? I'm just a steno in the agency yet my take-home pay is larger than yours."

"In a little while I'll be making full salary. And I'll be eligible for retirement when I'm forty-one," I said and kept seeing Owens' puffy dead face. What kind of job could I get after twenty years as a cop? A store cop, guard, messenger? Why should a guy need a job when he retired? What was the point in retiring? "Babes, be reasonable, I'm doing okay. What the hell, I've no trade, only one year of college—you want me to be a forty-buck-a-week stock clerk?"

"Yes. You're an eager beaver. Start out as a stock clerk and in time you could be a sales manager or—"

"Or/and own the firm. Stop talking like a movie. Last year when I was sweating in that five and dime for thirty-eight bucks a week, they gave me a movie title—I was one of the 'assistant managers' instead of stock boy. Mary, you were all for me taking Civil Service exams: okay, now I'm a cop, I have—"

"Of course I wanted you to take the exams and get out of that horrible store basement. But if I'd known the risks you take as a cop, the crazy hours, the way it would shake up our life, I would have been against it then."

"The point is I did take the exam and I'm a cop now, I have a trade. I've only been working five or six months at it. In time I'll be making a decent salary, take other exams and maybe become a captain. Give me a chance."

She shook her head and most of her trim body under the pajamas shook too. "Don't try to sell me, I know the pitch—you're David Wintino, the youngest detective on the force. Want me to take out the newspaper picture of the Commissioner shaking your hand?" She paused. "And I wasn't talking like a movie before. Some people do get ahead. Clerks do become executives—when they have somebody behind them. Uncle Frank called me at the office, asked why you haven't been down to see him."

"I thought there was something beside my coming home late. How's his ulcer?"

"Very funny!"

"Babes, I'm not interested in the freight business or in being the boss's pet relation."

"You were interested when he used his influence to keep you off the Youth Squad, or the times you got into trouble socking other cops—you didn't worry about his ulcer then! Dave, I said I can't take much more of this and I mean it. I'll be jittery as a sick cat in the office tomorrow and you know the way things are there—I goof once and I can forget about ever becoming Mr. Jackman's secretary. You're just selfish, you're always against everything I want. You didn't want to live in a decent apartment, you argued about the furniture, you don't like my friends—I've taken enough from you!"

"I know, now tell me how you stood up to your hundred and fifty per cent all-American family when they found they were getting a Jew and an Italian in the family, all in one package."

Her mouth opened wide now and her pug nose quivered and her eyes went big as she gasped, "David! That's a dirty, horrible, lousy thing to say!"

"Yeah, it was. Sorry, Babes. I'm on edge."

She got under the cover, turned her back to me. I put out the light. After a moment I could hear her weeping. I rolled her over, kissed her, her hair so soft and her skin cool where it wasn't wet with tears. I held her tight, a little proud that this beautiful chick was mine. For a moment that was all that mattered. "Honey," I whispered, "I don't mean to make you cry. We'll work things out."

"Will we, Davie?" she said in my ear, her lips warm.

"Of course we will. Okay, I'll go have a talk with your uncle."

"And nothing will come of it. You like being a detective."

"Babes, you want me to soft-talk you? All right, I like the job."

Mary rolled out of my arms, said to the darkness, "Know why you like it? Because you're cocky, a know-it-all, and being a detective makes you feel good, you like authority, bossing people. You and your pretty face, you like that part of it too. You even enjoy looking like a seventeen-year-old sharpie—you eat up the amazed look when people finally believe you *are* a real cop, a detective."

"Lay off me. Somebody has to be a cop," I said weakly.

"Somebody doesn't have to be *my* husband!"

"And if anything happened you'd break your back screaming for the police. You're like all the other fine law-abiding citizens."

"That's it exactly, whenever I need a cop I'll call for one. That's much different from being a cop's wife."

"How do you know, you never tried being a cop's wife."

She shrilled, "Go ahead, say you resent my working. You'd like me to mope around the house like a glorified maid, thinking up ways of cooking supper for my big strong provider, whenever he decides to give the little lady a break and come home. Wise up. That corn went out with silent pictures. If I ever find myself doing that I'll give you a fine supper each night—right in your face!"

I pulled her to me again, held her when she pushed me away, my hands going over all the curves I knew so well. "Listen to me, Mary, I—"

"I won't listen."

"Yes, you will. This is you and me talking in bed, not a couple of strangers shacking up for the night. You want to work, a career—great. I never asked or wanted you to spend all your time handling a dust mop or a frying pan. I never tell you to change your job. Why can't you understand that being a cop is my work, something I think is important? That's what I mean by being a cop's wife. Honey, before you get too set up in this advertising business, let's have a kid."

"What?"

"I want a baby," I said, not really sure if I wanted one so soon. "We have a child now, by the time he's fifteen, we'll only be thirty-six, we'll all be pals. Have your career but let's make a baby first. And in a year—you'll only be twenty-two or -three by then—we'll get somebody to look after the baby and you can go back to the agency business again. I don't know, maybe that's what we need to settle us. Don't you want a kid?"

"Not this way. I want my baby to have a father not a lousy posthumous medal. No, Davie." She started pushing again and I let go of her.

"What's this add up to, the kiss-off, Mary?"

"You know now where I stand. As to how it's going to add, that's for you to decide, Dave. Are you married to me or to your badge? I told you, I mean it. And I do, really."

That was a wallop that shook all the tiredness out of me. "You realize what the hell you're saying?"

"I certainly do because I know what fun it was before you got on the force. Even when we were living in that crummy room and watching our pennies. It was fun then. It isn't now. Good night, David."

"Good night, Mary." I turned toward the windows. Outside a car went by now and then, in the distance a horn sounded, then the small scream of brakes. We ever got the furniture paid up, we could get on rubber ourselves, a good secondhand heap—although Mary would want a new car. Our marriage was getting to be one of those deals where everything had to be her way. And I'm selfish! Didn't matter whether I *wanted* to work for Uncle Frank or not. Uncle Frank, what a case. Him and his silly wife and those fat-assed kids who acted like a couple of fags.

But what had happened to us? Babes was right, it had been great in the beginning. Even when I was a soldier and Mary had to sneak out of her house to see me. Maybe I was her way of getting to New York City, a one-way ticket from the hick town? Naw, that wasn't fair, Babes was the best at times. Maybe it was her job: ever since she'd gone on this Madison Avenue kick she'd been rough. Trouble was, lately I felt as if I'd married Mom and… damn, hadn't phoned the folks in a couple of days, not since last Friday.

For no reason I suddenly saw the old flat, Mom shrilling, "You're trying to kill my baby!" Her gray hair all wild-looking and her face so pale.

She had to say "baby." And Dom Franzino rubbing his bald head, embarrassed as he said, "But Mrs. Wintino, he ain't no baby. He's a natural welter and going on eighteen. Ten amateur fights with nine kayos. Nine kayos, Mrs. Wintino. Dave can take a man out with his left. Fans go for a puncher, go nuts over a left-hook artist. And his baby puss won't hurt none. He'll make a fortune, a—"

"Killing my baby," Mom moaned, wringing her hands, her face looking as if it was coming apart at the wrinkles. "No… never!"

Dom stared at me as if asking what the hell I'd got him into. Then Pop coughed slightly, said in Italian, "Mr. Franzino, my wife is becoming sick. We will talk this over, let you know our decision."

I grinned at the darkness. Two weeks later I was in the army. Mom used to cry about me getting drafted, now she was relieved. My left screwed up the army for me, never left the States—spent all my time on a service boxing team in Salt Lake City, fighting a few bootleg pro bouts for the hell of it.

I turned over again and got comfortable. Mary was really sleeping now. I told myself, okay, stop feeling sorry for yourself. Boxers like Robinson, the Kid, Olson, would have cut you to pieces. Of course if you ever managed to hit them, just one real clout… That's over, never was. And in the morning Mary will feel better. I should have phoned her, could have done it easily enough. Forget all this wind. All I should be thinking about is finding who killed Ed Owens. Think about that and only that.

It was a little after two in the afternoon. Danny Hayes and I had returned to the precinct house from talking to a shop owner who claimed a couple of blouses had been lifted from his counters. He was a big help, all he could say was, "It was a couple of tall women. They came in while

I was busy and walked out again. All I remember is they were tall." He didn't expect us to do anything, was merely reporting it for his insurance claim. We'd just parked in front of the station house when Lieutenant Reed, in charge of the Detective Squad, and Captain Lampkin, the boss of the precinct, came running down the old brick steps, jumped into our squad car as Lampkin said, "Killing. West End and Seventy-eighth. Stick-up. Get the siren working." Lampkin was a big sloppy square who always talked like a teletype message.

Danny was driving and it was kind of cool for May so he was wearing the dirty trench coat that showed off his thick shoulders—made him look like something off a TV screen, except they never have colored detectives on TV. He made it pretty fast but Danny can't wheel a car like I can.

There were two radio cars plus the usual afternoon crowd of curious housewives when we got there. It was one of these old but still ritzy big houses, seven- and eight-room apartments. The body was at the entrance to the delivery alley that led to the back of the house, a plump man in a worn suit, the frayed collar on his white shirt and the dirty tie all bloody. One foot was bent far under the body in a position that would have hurt like hell if he'd been alive. He was wearing heavy socks with the ends of gray winter underwear stuck in them, high black shoes that needed resoling. There was the newspaper with the picture of a ball game over his face and above it thick grayish hair and an old sweat-stained brown hat a few feet from his head. When Reed pulled back the paper this puffy face with some red veins in the long nose stared up at us with mild surprise.

All his pockets were turned out, the inside pocket torn. There was a torn wallet, a crumpled pack of butts, keys, a bulky old lighter, and a pack of mints scattered on the cement floor near his body.

The beat cop, an old beerhound, slipped Lampkin a halfhearted salute as he told him, "I found him at six minutes before two, Walter—Captain. Only witness we got so far is this"—he jerked a big thumb at a frightened young colored fellow in work pants and a torn army jacket—who says he was coming out after delivering an order, groceries, when he seen the stiff. He yelled and I come a-running from the corner."

"God is me witness I never saw him before! I know nothing except the man is stretched on the bloody stone!" the delivery man said nervously. He spoke with a kind of British accent.

Lieutenant Reed gave Danny the eye. Danny went over and said softly, "Relax, homie, and tell me exactly what you saw. And don't worry, you're in no trouble. What island you from?"

"Trinidad, and I'm here all legal and—"

"Sure," Dan said gently. "My old man was from Barbados. Let's you and me step over here and talk a little."

Captain Lampkin pushed his cap back as he scratched his head. "Homicide will be here soon, along with the rest of the boys. Touch anything, Buddy?"

"Now, Walter, long as I been a cop. Nobody has touched anything. I just spread the paper over his face. But see under his coat there, on the left side, that's a hip holster. Probably one of them little foreign automatics. Want me to pull the coat back, take his gun?"

"No, we'll wait," Lampkin said, taking off his cap to scratch his fat head. "Yeah, does look like a holster. But I wouldn't pick him for a punk or a hood."

Lieutenant Reed waited politely for Lampkin to stop talking, then quietly told me to get the janitor and start questioning the people in the house. The superintendent was no janitor, he had a regular little office with a typewriter and a desk. He was an old Swede wearing a starched collar and a worn blue suit. He said he was in his office when he heard somebody yelling police and came out to find the beat cop with the delivery man. He'd never seen the stiff before. I got his name down, along with the owners of the building and I was pretty excited—this wasn't the first dead man I'd seen, but it was the first gun killing. I found a couple of maids who'd been using the laundry room and didn't know a thing, but I put them in my notebook.

The alley began to fill up fast as the routine went into full swing. Some big cluck from Homicide was there, looking very important, a heavy-set square whose suit was too small—probably didn't know yet that big men can't buy bargain clothes. He had a fat baby mouth and a necklace of chins. The sonofabitch put me in the mood to pop him, and the rest of the men laughing, when he first saw me and asked, "What you doing here, sonny? The super's son?"

When Reed said, "He's one of my squad, Detective Wintino," this big hunk of blubber did a hammy double-take as he said, "Jeez, he don't look old enough to be a Boy Scout."

In less than fifteen minutes the photographers and lab men had finished. The stiff was Edward Owens, a retired cop—he had his Police Benevolent Association card in his wallet, along with a buck and a Chinese laundry ticket. He was working as a messenger for a brokerage house down on Wall Street. His gun, a .38 Police Special, hadn't been used and he'd been killed with one slug through the heart, fired at fairly close range. Reed had a couple of more detectives working and they hadn't found anybody who had heard the shot or noticed anyone in the service entrance. I thought I was going to be stuck going through the apartment houses across the street looking for witnesses, but Lampkin had called downtown for a detail to go to the brokerage house and have everybody there stand still. The

Homicide clown decided he'd better go down too and Reed said, "Dave will drive you, he's a speed boy."

"Regular hot-rod lad, I bet," Homicide said.

I sirened the car down West End Avenue, then cut over to the West Side Highway. The lump was named Anderson and he chewed on a wad of gum and told me, "All right, Sonny, the guy's long dead, won't make no diff to him if we get downtown in ten minutes or fifty minutes. But it does to me—I want to get there alive."

"Relax, you're still breathing—or are you?"

"Don't know what the force is coming to, punks like you not old enough to have the milk on your mouth dry or—"

"Fatstuff, you already made too many cracks about my being young. You want to guess ages, get a job in Coney Island."

He looked me over like he was alone in the car. "Snotty kid, too. Getting so a man—"

"Want to stop the car and see who's the best man?"

"Jeez, I'm not only more than twice your age, Wintino, but… What kind of a name is that?"

"It's my name and I like it," I said, weaving in and out of the highway traffic. We were doing fifty-five and he was so scared he was holding onto the door with one hand and his chins were dancing. I wasn't doing it just to frighten him. Fast driving gives me a bang.

"… But I could also write you up and—"

"Do that. And you know where you can shove it."

He sighed. "Maybe you're right. Young as you look you must be the mayor's bastard son to be on the force." He sighed again, tried to calm his nerves by working on his gum. "How do you like this Owens working as a messenger? Goddamn papers always so quick to say cops are on the take; they ought to do a piece on Owens. But they won't."

"Probably had a pension of three grand. Hell, I'm only making a couple bucks more than that now."

Anderson shrugged, nearly put his big feet through the floorboard as I cut around a car. "I could take my pension today but with prices so high, what's the use. Pension is okay if you already got your house paid up, the kids set, no sickness. Only how can you ever get that far ahead on our salary? Wintino… You're the rookie who made the big arrest couple months ago. Sure, I remember now, this drunk parked next to a hydrant and he turned out to be the psycho who knocked off all them women. A lucky collar."

"Yeah." Everybody called it pure luck, forgot that if I hadn't been thinking of those four dames with the battered heads all the time, I wouldn't have connected the rusty length of iron pipe in the glove compartment with the women.

I cut across the highway, shot down the ramp to the street as Anderson yelled, "Damnit, you think this has wings?"

There was a radio car parked in front of the office building and as we braked to a stop, the siren still working, a lot of people stopped and I gave my hair a pat as I jumped out. I don't believe in looking sloppy. A well-built, solid-looking cop said to Anderson, "I've been holding an elevator for you. Room 619." It wasn't hard to spot Anderson for a dick.

The brokerage firm was a suite of three large offices with about a half a dozen stenos pounding typewriters. They all stopped talking when we came in. A couple of them were good-looking. A cop was talking to a tall thin guy wearing a dull gray suit and one of these old-fashioned pop-'em bow ties that had to be at least ten years old. At one time the guy must have been lean and in shape, now he looked shrunken and skinny. His eyes were tired and bloodshot, his features thin, and face wide. His hair was a lousy dye job, jet black. He looked about sixty and judging from the patches of stubble around his long jaw he still didn't know how to shave.

Anderson flashed his badge and so did I, but mine was on my belt. May look corny but I like to have both hands free. The cop nodded at the bag of bones, said, "This is Al Wales."

"I'm a retired detective. Fact is Ed and I were partners. If you'll step in here," Wales motioned with his head toward a small office, "I can give you all the dope you need. We'd also appreciate it if you'd remove the officer from the door and let business go on as usual. You know how it is, looks bad for a house dealing in bonds. Whatever happened to Ed, the dirty bastards who did him in had nothing to do with his job here."

"The cop stays," Anderson said. "You in charge here?"

"No, I'm merely a part-time messenger, like Ed is—was. Step into the office and I'll have Mr. Stewart, our manager, join us."

"We can talk here," Anderson told him.

"What's the point in making a show?"

"Get this Stewart," Anderson said, looking around at the stenos. "I'm in a hurry."

"Don't be a horse's ass!" Wales' voice had been tired but now it turned into a kind of whip. And he seemed to pull himself together. I bet he'd been a rough Oscar in his time. Then he added in a lower voice, "Don't be a fool, they'll yell to City Hall—this isn't any two-bit outfit. Told you it looks bad for business."

Anderson stared at Wales, trying to decide what he was going to do about it. He decided to do nothing. "Okay, we'll go in the office. Now get this Stewart guy." He turned to the cop. "But nobody goes out till I tell you."

The office was four plain chairs around a polished oak table with a clean glass ash tray in the center. There were a couple of framed pictures of apartment houses on the walls. Wales called out something to one of the girls as we went in and Anderson planted his large backside on the table. Wales stood by the door and I glanced out the window: we weren't up high enough for a view of the harbor or anything interesting. A plump joker with crew-cut gray hair, expensive brown pin-stripe suit and a sweet tie, strode into the office. I mean strode, he must have practiced it. The walk matched his salesman face. He said, "Gentlemen! I'm Harris Stewart, office manager. Mr. Wyckoff, president of the firm, is in Washington. This is indeed a terrible piece of news about Mr. Owens. Simply incredible—there's absolutely no point to a robbery."

"Where was Owens going?" Anderson asked.

"According to the time sheet he checked out at five after one to deliver bonds to a client, a Mr. Jensen McCarthy who lives at 316 West End Avenue. Mr. Owens never delivered the bonds so we—"

"How do you know he didn't?" I asked as Anderson gave me an annoyed look.

"Mr. McCarthy was waiting for them and he phoned a few minutes before you, that is the police, called to tell us the horrible news. Mr. McCarthy was in a hurry to leave for his house in Westhampton and asked where our messenger was. We must assume it was robbery although I can't understand it. Naturally we have a list of the bonds in my office."

"A guy carrying bonds is robbed and killed," Anderson said. "What's there hard to understand about that?"

"But the bonds are not negotiable, they're worthless except to the owner," Stewart said, waving his manicured hands.

"That's right," this Al Wales put in, "all we carry is mortgages and nonnegotiable general bonds. Of course, assuming this was a robbery and that's what it looks like, whoever killed Ed might have thought he was carrying something worth taking. Must have been an amateur punk."

"We didn't find any bonds on him," Anderson said. "If they were worthless why did you need an armed messenger?"

Stewart's eyebrows shot up. "Armed?"

Anderson nodded. "He was packing a gun, never had a chance to use it. You didn't know he carried a gun?"

"I most certainly did not. The firm never asked or authorized any employee to carry a gun." Stewart turned to Wales. "Did you know about the gun?"

Wales said, "The gun had nothing to do with the job. Most retired cops get a permit to carry a gun. You know that, Anderson. You say he never used his gun. Did it look like Ed was in a fight?"

"No. No bruises. One shot through the heart did it." Anderson turned to Stewart. "Bond messengers have to use the service entrance?"

"No."

"Owens was killed in an alley leading to the service door."

"That don't make sense," Wales said. "He never used any back doors. And Ed was a quick guy with his hands and his gun—when he was younger. Hard to believe he'd be taken without some kind of battle."

"Well, there wasn't any, far as we can tell. Either Owens handed over the bonds like he was told, and was shot; or he was shot before he knew what it was all about. And all over bonds that weren't worth a thin dime—a real dumb killing," Anderson said.

"Does sound like one of those jerky ones," Wales added.

"But his pockets were torn," I chimed in. "Means he was shot first and then searched fast. He never had a chance."

Anderson told Stewart, "Give me a list of the bonds, I'd get them on the wire. And I need a phone, boys at the local precinct will want to talk to this McCarthy right now."

"You can use the phone in my office," Stewart said. "I'll have one of the girls type up several copies of the bonds' serial numbers, and all the other information at once."

Anderson nodded and stood, pulling his pants out of his rear like a slob. At the door he told me, "Stay here and write up Wales."

When they left Wales said, "We might as well sit down. You ever a fighter, young fellow?"

"Amateur. What makes you ask—see me in the ring?"

He shook his head and you wondered how his long scrawny neck bore the strain. "I haven't seen a fight since Louis was knocking them over. You got the right hands for a pug, wide, deep-set knuckles."

"I did okay. Wanted to turn pro but my folks raised too much fuss. So I joined the force."

Wales smiled, he had neat even teeth—and all of them store choppers. "Nothing in the world like being a young cop, the boss of your beat. Or maybe it's just there's nothing like being young. Get old and all you can do is read about things. I read and read. Why my eyes look shot. I don't need glasses, though and… damn, who's going to tell Jane about this?"

"Jane?"

"Ed's wife. They got a daughter working someplace in South America for an oil company. Had a boy who died when he was a kid. This will be rough on Jane."

I got out my notebook, wrote down Wales' full name, home address, last precinct squad he worked on, the Owens' home address. "How long you been working here, Mr. Wales?"

"About three years. Ed needed the dough but I'm all alone. I work to keep busy. My wife passed away back in '49, right after I retired from the force. When Ed started working here he got me on. Five hours a day, a way of passing time."

"You two the only messengers?"

"Yeah. I come on at nine and Ed came in at noon."

"If the bonds you carried were worthless why—"

"They're not worthless but nonnegotiable: there's a big difference."

"Sure. But if they weren't worth anything except to the owners, why did the firm only hire former policemen?"

"Because they know we're bondable, in good physical condition for our age, and only a fellow with a pension can fool around with a part-time job."

"You in the office when Mr. Owens was killed?"

"No. I left at eleven-thirty to take some bonds to a customer up on the Grand Concourse. He wasn't in so I came back here—about twenty minutes before the police arrived. You say Ed's pockets were torn. Was his receipt book missing too?"

"All we found was a torn wallet, identification cards, some change, pack of butts, mints and a lighter. Receipt book mean anything?"

Wales shook his head again. "No. It's of no value. Shows some jerky kid must have done the job."

I wiggled on the chair. "I don't think so. A jerk doesn't follow a messenger all the way uptown. And if it was a jerky lad in an on-the-spot stick-up, he would have taken the change, Owens' gun."

"Maybe. And maybe when the punk saw the gun he figured Owens for a cop and got scared. Could be a nut. And if Ed wasn't tailed why would anybody rob him? Ed never dressed like money from home."

"Did he carry much cash?"

"Ed? Lucky to have a buck floating around his pockets. Every extra dime went on the ponies. Not that Ed was a real gambler, but a few bucks here and there every week. On that little pension they give us you don't raise any hell."

"Did Mr. Owens have any enemies? Perhaps some character he once collared?"

Wales shrugged, a tired motion. "No. At least none I ever heard of. We were just run-of-the-mill detectives, the usual arrests. We had one big collar, got a killer in a gang war. But that was a long time ago and he went up in smoke in the chair. Of course Ed stayed on the force a couple of years after I left. He was a little younger. But he liked to talk, and he would have told me if he thought somebody was after him."

"We'll have to dig into his arrest record."

Wales smiled sadly. "Dig, dig, clear every little detail, that's a detective's life. A crime is like an iceberg, one-tenth showing and nine-tenths hidden."

"Iceberg—neat way of putting it. That's what they drilled into me at the academy: whenever you're stuck start digging into the case all over again."

Wales nodded as he licked his thin lips. "They're right, only most times you never get the time. New cases always coming…"

Anderson came in. "Got everything, kid?"

I closed my notebook. "Think so."

"Come on, Lampkin wants us back at the precinct house. Nothing more for us here."

As I stood up Wales climbed to his feet. "Mind if I ride up with you? I'd like to look around. Me and Ed—I mean, well, wouldn't hurt none."

"Come along. The captain probably wants to talk to you anyway."

Wales left the office and met us at the elevator, wearing an old battered plastic rain hat. I brushed against him as we stepped into the elevator; he wasn't carrying a gun. Wales said, "That's okay, I'm clean." There was a fresh odor of whisky on his words.

Wales sat in the back seat and I got the siren going and shot up Broadway to Chambers Street, then wheeled over to the highway. Anderson said, "You ain't got your leather jacket on and this ain't no motorcycle, so quit making like a speed king, kid."

"Close your eyes if you can't take it," I said, doing more cutting through the uptown traffic than necessary.

Anderson turned and asked Wales, "Ever see anything like this before? Makes a good collar while a rookie and he's an acting detective third grade before he can get corns on his feet. Me, I was a harness bull for over seven years."

"Probably make a good dick, it's the last thing he looks like."

Anderson laughed, a real jackass chuckle. "Got something there. He looks like he got his badge with a cereal box top. And *not* looking like a cop is one way of stopping a slug or a handful of knuckles. Me, I'm glad I look like what I am."

Wales said, "Force is changing, lots of college boys on it now. I like the way this young fellow speaks, calls people mister. He'll be real good once he stops talking so much."

"What's that mean?" I asked, glancing at him in the windshield mirror.

Wales gave me his tired smile before he said, "You got to learn to ask questions, not hand out information. Doesn't make any difference in this case, but why tell Mr. Stewart and myself Ed's pockets were torn? Sometimes a little thing like that can trap a man."

"Damn right," Anderson said, "you have to—"

"You shoot your gums off too," Wales said dryly. "Right off the bat you told me the bonds were missing and that Ed was packing a gun."

"That was part of my questioning you. This is just an ordinary stick-up, let's not make a big case out of it."

"It isn't ordinary, an ex-cop was killed," I said. The car on my left got panicky at the sound of the siren and stupidly tried to cut to the right. I made the brakes scream, shaking us all up, then raced around the car as Anderson cursed, swallowed his gum, and finally yelled, "Slow down! And that's a goddamn order!"

At the station house Lieutenant Reed sent Hayes and me out to finish interviewing the people in the surrounding apartment houses. They were all large houses, seventy to a hundred apartments. They'd borrowed some dicks from another squad and had over a dozen men working the houses. It was dull routine and we ended up with nothing; not a soul had seen or heard a thing. There were the usual crackpots who "thought I heard several shots around four o'clock…. Oh, he was shot at two…?"

By nine I was punchy and glad when Reed called us in. By the time I finished my paper work and had a bite with Hayes it was after ten. As I left the station house I saw Al Wales sitting in the muster room, his back against the crummy dirty green-colored wall. He sure had a bulge in his pocket now—a pint. His bleary eyes were open, staring at nothing. As I waved at him he mumbled, "Find the bottom of the iceberg yet?" He spoke like a man full of dull pain.

I turned over in bed, kicked the sheet up from my feet. My toes touched Mary's ankle. I stroked it with my big toe and she broke her heavy breathing with something that sounded like a whimper.

Everybody so certain it was a dumb hold-up, and those are the hardest to solve, dead ends where nothing makes sense. Two retired cops. Never know what Owens was like but Wales was okay, never once called me a runt or a kid. I was in bed, so was Danny Hayes and probably Anderson and the rest of the squad. Reed might still be up, waiting to hear what his stoolies knew, maybe had a man going over the nightly round-up of "undesirables." We were all safe in bed, doing nothing, while one of us was on a slab in the morgue.

I touched Mary's ankle again. Maybe she was right. A cop, an ex-cop, was dead and nobody really gave a damn. Just another stick-up victim, as if he hadn't spent most of his life trying to protect people. Hell, who was an ex-cop to get any more consideration than an ordinary murdered citizen?

I thought he should get a damn sight more consideration.

I suddenly smiled at the darkness. Dave Wintino, the boy Dick Tracy! I didn't have a thing to go on but a hunch—like the feeling I had about the lead pipe in my big pinch. Maybe it was dumb to play a hunch… but *somehow* I was sure Ed Owens hadn't been killed in a stick-up.

Wednesday Morning

At exactly 6 a.m. I awoke as though an alarm had gone off. I can always do that. It was light outside already and looked like a good warm day. I slipped out of bed easily and Mary didn't move. She was sleeping half outside the blanket, curled like a cat, and for a moment I admired the full curve of her hips in the ski pajamas. Then I shut the bathroom door and ran the electric razor over my face and took a shower, thinking how odd it is with women. I mean Mary actually had a straight up-and-down figure, even a bit on the skinny side, yet in certain positions—like that one on the bed or sometimes when she sits with one leg under and I get a flash of her thigh—what curves. I sometimes wonder where they come from.

And maybe Ed Owens' wife had curves he liked to watch too.

I was getting fresh shorts out of the desk drawer when Mary sat up, coming wide-awake fast as she always does, and said, "Are you getting up or going to bed? What time is it?"

"Sixteen after six. Have coffee with me?"

Mary yawned and stretched her arms over her head, her breasts pushing out. "Guess so. Sixteen after six, what a time to get up."

"My last day on this tour. Starting Saturday I—"

"I know, I know, you start working at midnight. Lovely!"

"Let's not begin the day arguing. Go back to sleep and leave me alone."

"Sleep—some chance!"

"If we had a bigger apartment instead of a correct address, I could get up without waking you."

She sat up in bed, got a cigarette working. "Dave, why must you always make excuses for the job? If you were going to work at 9 a.m. like most husbands, we… oh, nuts, I feel too beat to argue."

She puffed on her cigarette slowly, watching me as I got out my tropical gray suit, a white shirt, cuff links, a heavy T-shirt, and a striped pink and hard gray tie. I went into the can and rubbed some hair conditioner on my noggin, then gave it a stiff workout with a brush and comb, getting it just right—the pomp in front raised and with a good curl. Understand, I don't see any sense in looking sloppy. I put on my shorts and socks and shoes, was giving the shoes a fast shine with yesterday's shirt when Mary got out of bed. She tossed her butt in the john and jabbed a sharp little finger in my gut. She said, "Davie, I'm queer for those ridges of muscle."

"I go for your tummy too," I said, pulling her to me, kissing her. Her lips had a stale tobacco taste.

She rubbed up against me for a moment, said, "Keep this up and you'll be late."

"Man's expected to be late once in a while," I said, playing with her soft blonde hair, wishing she didn't use such a bright rinse.

"And let law and order go to hell?" she said, the light sarcasm in her voice teasing me.

"Put the coffee on." I was like the others, forgetting a cop had been killed.

"'Put the coffee on,' my lover says in a sexy tone."

"Babes, I have a lot of work to do. Look, you go back to bed and I'll stop someplace for coffee and juice."

She poked my gut again as she drew away. "I'll make you coffee soon as I wash up. You know how I am, once I'm awake."

I dressed while she was in the kitchenette. She had the radio on to an early morning record jockey and the music was hot. When I sat down for my java Mary said, "Honest, Dave, you belong on Madison Avenue. You have a flair for wearing clothes. You look the part."

"I've been on Madison Avenue, had a fixed post there during a strike. Madison Avenue and 114th Street."

"Oh, stop talking about your awful job. I bet even the Commissioner forgets his work when he's home."

"I was kidding. Getting warm fast, we'll be able to go to the beach soon."

"I can picture us. When are you getting your vacation, in November?"

"Stop riding me, you know I'm junior man," I said, sipping my coffee, thinking that if she didn't have her job we'd have plenty of time for the beach on my fifty-six-hour swing every week.

Mary kept stirring her cup. "Don't know how you can take coffee so hot. Dave, will you get in touch with Uncle Frank? At least be polite enough to see what he wants."

"Okay. Tomorrow, when I'm off."

Her face came alive. "Really?"

"As you said, at least I can be polite." Frank wasn't a bad guy, good for laughs—long as he remained Uncle Frank and not bossman Frank.

"That's a promise now," Mary said, coming around the tiny table and hugging me as she sat on my lap. I wanted to tell her she was pretty but not *that* pretty. Instead I held her against me with my left hand, finished the coffee with my right.

She suddenly said, "Ouch!" and sat up, rubbing her shoulder. "That damn holster is going to leave me black and blue yet."

I damn near spilled the coffee on my pants. I tickled her bottom, making her jump to her feet with a gasp. I stood up and kissed her, said, "See you for supper—I hope," and picked up my wrinkled suit from the floor on the way out.

Waiting for the elevator I checked my pockets again: badge, wallet, keys, pens, notebook, extra shells, touched the gun in its shoulder holster, and ran a hand over my hair. I left the suit at the corner tailor shop, bought the morning papers, and dropped into the first coffee pot I hit to have a slow cup of the junk and see what they had to say about Ed Owens. Not that it mattered what the papers said.

There was a picture of Owens in the alleyway and just a caption in the *News*. The *Times* surprised me by giving him a whole column. After a sentence saying he'd been shot in a hold-up while carrying nonnegotiable bonds, they went on to say Owens and Wales had solved the murder of a Boots Brenner back in 1930. I never heard of the joker but the paper claimed he was well on his way to becoming the Al Capone of New York City when he was found in a vacant Brooklyn lot full of lead. "Within 24 hours, through brilliant detective work" Owens and Wales arrested a small-time bootlegger named Sal Kahn who was running a still near the lot where Brenner's body was found. Kahn had a record of several arrests for making and selling booze. He admitted killing Boots when the gangster tried to muscle in on an electric still Kahn was running. The still was an "amazing work of scientific ingenuity" and although Kahn pleaded self-defense, he died in the chair without revealing the name of his partner, who had built the still. Both Wales and Owens had been cited by the mayor for their fast work.

I gathered the politicians had been busting a "crime wave" and had used the death of a strong-arm goon to crow about how safe the city was.

I finished breakfast with a piece of candy, took the subway over to the precinct house, paying my fare. Seems dumb to me to advertise every day that you're a detective. I walked into the detective room a few minutes before eight. Danny Hayes was already there, breezing with a sleepy-looking fat slob named Ace who has a terrific memory for faces. I picked up the daily report sheet, read the arrests. There wasn't anything of interest except they had collared a clown named Hanson up on Washington Heights trying to pass a stiff check in a drugstore. Seems Hanson had bounced a check in the same store a few months ago. Most crooks are dumb as hell.

I said hello to Danny as I put the report sheet down. "How about this paperhanger Hanson, think he could be the phony doctor dropping rubber around here? He was working a drugstore."

"We're going to check," Danny said.

Ace waved a heavy hand at me and yawned. "Now I can go home and sleep in peace, the younger generation has things in hand. Will you look at that outfit. Where'd you spend the night, Dave, between the covers of *Esquire?*"

"Momma, who's the funny mans in the baggy suit and soiled sport shirt?" I said, thumbing my nose at him. "Gowan home, brawn, and let the brains take over. What's on the Owen's deal?"

"You still got seven minutes before your tour starts," Ace said. "What you bucking for, Reed's job? Hate to have you in charge of the squad—you'd be a ballbreaker."

"Cut the wisecracks, Ace. An ex-cop's been killed."

Ace stood up, like a tent coming erect, and favored me with a belch. "Got special news for you, kid. The cemeteries are full of ex-cops. When our number comes up we go with the wagon too. There's nothing new on Owens, not a lead—one of those great big blank walls."

"Lab come up with anything?"

"Nothing except he was killed with a .38." Ace stretched and for some reason I suddenly thought of Mary.

"Ace, you married?"

He turned to stare at me, heavy arms still in mid-air, a dopey look on his fat face. "Sure I'm married. Now what the devil brought that brainstorm on? I was married before your pop told your ma, 'Let's try and make a David.' Why do you ask?"

"Nothing. Just … uh … thinking about cops' wives. Like this Owens' wife. What did she have to say?" I wanted to ask how Ace's wife felt about his being a cop—maybe they all complained like Mary—but he'd think I was flipping if I ever asked. I couldn't ask Danny: he was separated from his schoolteacher wife, but not because of the force—she caught him with another woman.

"I think Homicide talked to Mrs. Owens," Ace said. "Gather they didn't have a chance to talk to her much, the shock had her on the ropes."

"Anybody else questioned?"

Ace gave me a fat grin. "Being as I'm just a detective on the night tour Captain Lampkin hasn't time to go over all the details with me. Of course if I was young and with waves in my hair and on the day shift, why I could sit down and tell him how to work."

"Everybody treats this as a big yak. We ought to spend a lot of time with Mrs. Owens, and with Wales, and dig into their past arrests. Plenty of work to do," I said.

"There certainly is, Wintino, and you can start by getting me a buttered roll and a container of coffee—light. Too tired to eat this morning," a voice said behind me.

I turned and Lieutenant Reed was standing in the doorway kind of stooped as though afraid of bumping his bald dome. He had tired circles under his eyes and needed a shave. I said, "Certainly, Lieutenant," and took the two bits he held out.

Downstairs they were turning out the platoon and I waited a moment till that was over, then ran across the street to the delicatessen. I didn't like the idea of Reed using me as coffee boy but then he had the other members of the squad hustling java for him too, sometimes. And it was about time he learned coffee and a buttered roll was thirty-two cents.

I had to wait till a fresh pot was brewed and I returned to find a tall, well-set-up guy, about thirty-seven, sitting with Reed. The guy had a brown gabardine suit that had to be custom-made the way it fitted like a grape skin. He looked real sharp in a tab collar and a narrow dark brown tie. His hair was combed slick, he had one of these large rugged faces, and his gut was so flat he was probably wearing a girdle.

As I put the bag on the desk Reed said, "This is Detective Austin from Homicide. You've met Detective Hayes; this is his partner, Detective Wintino. They were the first of my squad to reach Owens."

Austin nodded at me and said, "You must have shrunk since you took the physical. Never figured you for five eight." He had a booming clear voice that went with his beefy good looks.

"I was wearing elevator shoes at the time. They send you up here to check my height?" I asked.

Austin winked at Reed. "Rough little stud."

"Tries to be, anyway. And at times he is. Captain Lampkin wants you to have a talk with Mrs. Owens. That's about the only angle we haven't covered thoroughly. I suggest you go over to her flat now. I'm sending Hayes downtown to the line-up to look over a rubber check artist we're interested in, so take Wintino with you." Reed glanced at the wall clock. "Unless she gives you something, be back here around ten."

"Anything you say, Lieutenant. Frankly I don't believe it will get us anywheres, but it will make the old lady feel we're on the job," Austin said, getting to his feet.

He wasn't so big, it was just the sharp fit of the suit and his big face. He picked up a pork pie hat I would have liked—if I ever wore a hat. I whispered to Danny, "You're lucky, I'm stuck with glamour boy. Dresses like this is the FBI."

Danny smiled, showing his stubby teeth. "Glamour boy? Didn't you look in the mirror this morning? I ought to be back from downtown by noon, Dave. Maybe we'll have Chinese food for lunch."

I got a car downstairs and drove Austin up to the Bronx. He said, "Getting warm. I don't like heat unless I'm in a bathing suit. Reed say that colored boy was your partner?"

"Yeah."

"That's rough. I always say they should—"

"What's rough about it?" I cut in, knowing what was coming. "Danny's a hard worker and smart—that's all I ask of a partner. Have you seen Owens' old partner, Al Wales?"

"No, but I hear he looks like a creep."

"Seems they made an important collar back in 1930. Got a guy who killed a hot-shot goon named Boots Brenner. Ever hear of Brenner?"

Austin nodded as he took out a pack of butts, offered me one. "I remember reading about Brenner someplace. Punk who wanted to be a second Vince Coll, tougher than tough stuff. Want a smoke?"

"I don't smoke. Thanks."

"You must have made a fortune when you were in the army. Or weren't you old enough to be in during the war?"

"I did my time after the war. What about this Boots Brenner?" I asked, a little steamed.

"Like I told you, a punk. Started to cut into the big pie but got himself killed before the big boys took much notice of him. What's he got to do with Owens?"

"I don't know, yet. I'd like to have another talk with Wales. Of course the guy they rapped for killing Boots sat in the chair, but I have a feeling we ought to dig deeper into their arrest record," I said turning into 145th Street and stopping for a light. I didn't have the siren on.

I wouldn't have minded so much if Austin had laughed. He *chuckled.* "Don't go off the deep end, shortie. This wasn't any revenge killing, it was a stick-up and a lousy one. If anybody had merely wanted to plug Owens they wouldn't have bothered walking him into an alley on West End Avenue."

"If it was a stick-up Owens would have put up a fight and he didn't."

"How do we know he would have?"

"Wales says Owens was handy with a gun and his hands."

Austin chuckled again. "Maybe years ago, but yesterday Owens was an old man. And no matter how tough a guy is, a jittery stick-up character may squeeze the trigger first and talk later. Tell you the truth, we're only going through the motions. Know when this will be solved? In a year or two or three we'll pick up some junkie or a loony on another charge, probably another killing, and in the course of grilling him he'll confess to killing Owens. Cases like this follow a pattern."

"No. I have a … a … feeling this was more than a hold-up. The worthless bonds, the torn pockets, for example, make me uneasy."

Austin let me have the chuckle again. "You sound like a song, 'that old feeling.' Better gag than anything I've seen on TV this week. Keep your feelings for your girl friends."

I shut up. When we reached Third Avenue I turned downtown and then east again and we were in a neighborhood of run-down wooden private houses, most of them with tiny lawns bordered by a struggling bush or even flowers. It was like a couple of blocks of some hick town set down in New

York City. I pulled up before one that had a few busted chairs on the porch, chairs that had been left out all winter, a lot of winters. It was a squat two-family house, badly in need of paint and new shingles. I said, "This is it."

"Some dump." Austin took out his notebook, checking the address. "Imagine a guy ever wanting to *buy* one of these joints? Let's get it over with."

The Owens apartment was the bottom one and the woman who opened the door was dressed in a clean worn house dress that looked too heavy for May. She was plump, lots of veins in her fat legs, and her moon-shaped flabby face was topped with dirty gray hair braided around her head. Her eyes were red and the skin around them looked raw. Austin took off his hat as he asked, "Mrs. Edward Owens?"

"Yes, but if you're reporters I—"

"I'm Detective Austin and this is Detective… Winston."

"Wintino, David Wintino, Mrs. Owens," I told her.

"I know you've been under a terrific strain, an ordeal, but we're on police business and would appreciate it if you would answer a few questions." The sugar in Austin's voice sounded phony as hell.

"I understand. I'm sorry I wasn't able to talk much last night. Last night… God, I still can't believe it. Step inside, please," Mrs. Owens said, holding the door open. Her hands were short and covered with spots like large freckles.

We walked into an old-fashioned neat living room: a clumsy big radio set with a million dials that probably still ran on A and B batteries, an old seven-inch TV set in a large cabinet, an upright piano, two leather chairs, a couple of plain ones, and a couch that looked hard. Atop the piano there was a picture of a plain-faced girl with fat cheeks, about eighteen, and a cracked picture in a gold frame of a towheaded boy of about twelve.

Mrs. Owens pointed to the leather chairs and we put it down and she sat on the couch and said, "I suppose you want to know about Ed." She spoke in a faraway voice.

"As a police officer's wife, you know we need all the information we can get to help us track down your husband's killer," Austin said like an idiot, as though he was selling something. "Do you live here alone, Mrs. Owens?"

"I do now. The Sarasohns who live upstairs have been most helpful, they did all they could for me last night. I even slept up there. My daughter Susan is down in Venezuela. She's wired she's flying up for the funeral. Our son, Edward Junior," she nodded toward the picture on the piano, "was taken from us many years ago. Now Ed… I just can't seem to think straight or believe it. He is dead, isn't he?"

"Yes, he is. I understand what you're going through and I'll try to make the questioning brief as possible. Now…"

"That's all right. I can talk about things. Only at times… Well, when Junior died it was bad but Ed was at my side. Now without Ed I feel lost, alone… kind of empty." She looked around the room helplessly. "I was in the kitchen when you rang. You know his garden tools are still beside the tub where he left them yesterday morning. Said he might use them in the evening before it got too dark."

"What gardening tools?" Austin asked.

"A spade and a rake. We have a nice little back yard and Ed loved to raise flowers and things. It's time for planting. Ed always had a green thumb. That's what he dreamt about, retiring to a place in California where he could really grow things."

"We all want a house in the country," Austin said. "Now about—"

"But we've been dreaming about it for so many years," Mrs. Owens said, as if talking to herself. "From way back when Ed was first appointed. Then the children came. We put money aside for their education but that went for Junior's burial, although Susan finished business school. But children, payments on the house, not much left out of a policeman's salary. Not that I complained but… I'm sorry, all this is no concern of yours. Ed always joked about my chattering too much. What is it you want to ask me?"

"A few routine questions. We're sure Mr. Owens was the victim of a nervous stick-up punk but we're not overlooking any other possibilities, of course. Did your husband have any enemies? Did he seem worried?"

"You wouldn't ask that if you'd known my Ed. He was always an easygoing man. His only troubles were financial and he never let them get him down. If anything he was in better spirits than ever lately. A few weeks ago he came home and started dancing me around. 'Janie,' he says, 'we have that California cottage, be raising oranges soon.' He's—was—in a gay mood all the time lately."

"About this cottage, do you think he came into some money?" I asked, although as junior man it was up to Austin to do the questioning.

"No. You see Ed had one vice, he loved to play the horses. I didn't mind, a person has to relax some way, I say. Whenever he had a spare dollar or two he would make a bet. Naturally most times he lost but whenever he won, maybe five or ten dollars, he was like a small boy who thinks he has the world by the tail. I imagine Ed must have made himself a few dollars and was talking big. That's all it was."

Austin asked, "Is it possible Mr. Owens was playing the races big and might have gotten in over his head with a gambling mob?"

The old lady stroked her coiled braids. "I hope I haven't given you a bad impression of Ed. He wasn't a gambler. He merely played a few dollars now and then like I play bingo or even put a few pennies on a number if I have a dream."

"Did he drink much?"

"No, sir, beer was all my Ed touched and not much of that. I never saw Edward Owens drunk except once, when sickness took our Junior. Now Al—Mr. Wales—he began to drink something frightful and Ed was always on him to stop it. That was after his dear wife died of cancer back in nineteen and forty-nine. Al's a good man but a strange one. He never seemed too emotional about things but he went to pieces when Dora passed on. That was one reason why Ed got him to work at the brokerage house. Did Al a world of good, although he still goes off on toots at times. Poor Al, he talked to me on the phone last night and actually cried."

"About this brokerage house, did your husband like the job? Was he happy there?"

Mrs. Owens tried to smile. "He liked the job very much. I think Ed liked most the idea that he didn't have to work. We needed the few dollars he made but we could have gotten along without them, too. It was more like it gave him something to do. He was always nosy and liked going to these big offices, the rich houses."

"Why did he carry a gun?"

She looked puzzled. "My goodness, Ed's worn a gun every day for as long as I can remember. Be like asking why he wore pants."

"Did your husband usually drop into any bars around here, for a beer, and perhaps talk about the bonds he was carrying, some of the rich homes he'd been to?"

She shook her head. "No, sir, not Ed. Did his beer drinking right here while watching the TV. In the mornings he'd fool around in his garden. When he came home from work we'd have supper and watch TV, maybe play rummy, or he'd get out his books and booklets and try to figure a winner in the races. He was strictly a homebody, always was."

"Do you know where he placed his bets?"

"No. Some cigar stand downtown. I imagine Al Wales could tell you, although Al never gambled."

"Now, Mrs. Owens, think carefully: was there anybody who had any reason, no matter how slight, to be angry at your husband? Or was Mr. Owens mad at anybody?"

"Not a soul."

Austin stood up. "I think that's all. Thank you for your time, Mrs. Owens. And don't worry, we'll get the rats who did this."

"Yes, I suppose you will. But that won't bring Ed back to me. Everyplace I look I see something of his, his tools, his clothes, his beers in the icebox," Mrs. Owens said, getting up. "Would you like to see his garden?"

"Best we run...."

"I'd like very much to see it," I said. Austin looked at me as if to say, "Shut up."

We followed her down a short hallway with two bedrooms opening off it, through a large clean kitchen, out to a back yard that was about twenty feet wide and maybe thirty feet long. Except for something growing under two old windows, it was just a lot of dirt to me.

She pointed to the windows which were about six inches off the ground and walled in with loose bricks. "This is Ed's hothouse. I think he has some tulip bulbs growing there now. By the end of July he'll have this whole yard full of pansies and other flowers, maybe a few rows of carrots and some tomato vines. Once, he even raised some good corn here. One summer he spelled out 'Owens' across the yard in red, white and blue flowers. They had a picture of that in the Bronx *Home News.*"

There was a moment of silence till I asked, "Mrs. Owens, did you like being a policeman's wife? The changing hours, little pay, the danger?"

She looked astonished. "Why, of course I liked it, young man, it was my husband's job. Sometimes I worried a little about Ed but he could take care of himself. As for the pay, it wasn't much, but then what job pays enough? Best thing was it being steady, no lay-off. My father was a house painter and always working crazy hours. And near every winter there would be months when he didn't work and we'd be worried sick. Why do you ask?"

"Just wondering," I said stupidly.

"Nice seeing your garden, Mrs. Owens, but we have to leave," Austin said.

"I don't want to keep you. The force has certainly changed, you two all dressed so smartly. And this young man who looks like he's a college student. Yes indeed, I liked Ed being a policeman, I felt he was helping people. Of course sometimes there were dirty jobs and long hours, but like I say, no job is all good. Wouldn't be a job if it was."

When we were in the car Austin asked, "What are you conducting, a lonely hearts column for cops' wives? 'Mrs. *Owens, did you like being a policeman's wife?*' For crying out loud, Winstein, you're a prize dummy."

"The name is Wintino. What's so dumb about it? Everybody keeps yapping Owens was killed by a goon, a stick-up punk. Maybe. But he was in an alley and never went for his gun so it might have been with somebody he was friendly, like another woman."

Austin shook his head. "Naw, you and me might be lovers, but not the Owens type. How long you been on the force?"

"Less than a year. So what?"

"You'll learn we haven't time to investigate every cockeyed angle to a case. Most times the common-sense angles are the right ones. Owens was held up, and by an amateur, that's the common-sense angle. Look, by this afternoon I'll be off the case and it will be left in the open files. They'll let it stand till we get a break. You want to speculate, a guy in a flying saucer might have dropped down and knocked off Owens?"

"Are you satisfied with the case?"

He gave me his superior smile. "Satisfied? This isn't a restaurant, it's a job. Not up to me to be satisfied or not satisfied. We do the best we can and that's the way the ball bounces."

"Okay, so if I'm not satisfied I keep digging till I come up with something that fits."

"Make sense, Winston. You can keep digging for the next three years. We haven't the time. In a few hours you'll be looking into a forced entry case, a mugging, something like that. And I'll be working on another killing."

"Maybe. But I'm going to keep sifting this one. When an ex-cop is killed it makes you think."

"It does? About what?"

"About myself. I'll be retired like Owens was someday and I don't want to end up in an alley." Nor in a run-down flat with an ancient radio and the same furniture I had when I first moved in, I thought. Although Mom and Pa, their place is like the Owens', the inside of a poor museum. Wonder what a guy has to do to make a good buck in this crazy world without being a bastard. "You married?" I asked Austin.

"You starting on me? Sure I'm married."

"Wife like your job?"

"I never asked her. What's with you, Watson?"

"Nothing. My wife isn't hot about my job."

He chuckled. "Wives need a slap across the teeth now and then. That's my best advice."

I didn't bother telling this dope where to stick his advice. As we waited for a light on the Concourse I considered shooting up to Ogden Avenue for a second, seeing Mom. Might have done it if I was alone or with Danny. Been near a month since I'd been up there. I didn't like to go up without Mary because that was an admission on my part she wasn't comfortable around my folks.

There was another reason too. The old neighborhood gave me a funny feeling. Guys I'd been pals with since we were old enough to play hide and seek, guys who couldn't wait to slap me on the back when I won a fight, now treating me with that cold politeness most citizens reserve for cops. The cagey distrustful look, as if they expected me to belt them over the head with a night stick any minute. Still, I'd better go up and put away one of Mom's big Friday night meals before the summer heat hit us.

We passed the Yankee Stadium and Austin talked baseball all the way back to the precinct. I didn't listen. I kept seeing Owens' place, old and falling apart. As I parked the car I stared at the station house for a moment, a short ugly building that must be a hundred years old. A firetrap that was like ice in the winter, full of mice and bugs. Everything about the job seemed old, stagnant, so—

"Asleep at the wheel, wonder boy?"

Austin was standing outside the car, smiling at me—if you can call a sneer a smile. I got out, followed him up the worn steps, nodded at the desk lieutenant, the sergeant at the switchboard listening to the calls from the post cops and the guys driving on radio motor patrol.

A former cop was shot dead and everything went as usual in this old building.

Austin went to the john and I went up to the detective room. A quiet joker named Larson was at the desk, doing some paper work. He was a giant, a real mister six by six, one of these strong silent guys who keep to themselves. He told me, "Dave, your wife called. Wants you to ring her at her office. Called about ten minutes ago."

I said thanks and dialed the agency. Mary said in the low voice you have to use in a crowded office, trying not to make it sound like a whisper, "Dave? Don Tills is having two tables of bridge tonight and he's asked us over. I told you about him, one of our top copywriters, the golden boy of the office. Be a great help to me if I get in with his crowd."

"I don't mind some bridge. That all you wanted to tell me?"

"Yes and be sure to be home on time. They're counting on us to be there at nine sharp."

"You know I always come home when I'm done here."

"Just be 'done' by five so we can eat together like normal married people and get dressed and go out together, for a change."

"Okay, we'll be normal married people. See you for supper, Babes."

As I hung up I saw Larson grinning at me as he bent over his desk. I said, "Tough for a wife to take our hours. Your wife complain much?"

"Sometimes. She's a nurse and her shifts are almost as bad as ours. But then when we do get some time together we enjoy it more."

"Anything new?"

He shook his big head. "Quiet. The lieutenant is down in Captain Lampkin's office. Stolen auto reported over on the avenue. I just came back from a busted store window on Adams Street. That's about all. Get anything from Mrs. Owens?"

"Nope." It was seven after ten; Mom wouldn't be out shopping yet—not till the crappy soap operas she listened to every morning were over. I dialed her and we asked each other how we were and how was Pop and how was Mary? Could they come to our place this Sunday? Mom said after all Mary worked hard all week, no sense in her cooking for them. Could we come up this Friday? I said maybe but I was pretty busy. I'd check with Mary and call back. Mom said she would have fresh gefüllte fish, chopped chicken liver, and her best lasagna. I told her she was making my mouth drool at the mention of her lasagna and gefüllte fish but I'd have to see how I was fixed for time, check with Mary. Give Pop my love and I'll call Friday morning before ten.

I hung up and Austin was standing at the table, the big grin on his big puss. He asked, "What's your name again?"

"You got a hell of a memory for a detective. Get it straight for once. Dave Wintino."

"Thought I heard right, gefüllte and lasagna! No wonder you're a jerk—a Jewboy and a Wop, what a—"

Without getting up I turned on the chair and planted a left hook next to the middle button of his sharp suit. His grin became a frantic O as he gulped for air, clutched his gut and bent double, then sat down hard on the floor.

I glanced at Larson who was still busy with his paper work, but from the way his big feet were set he was ready to jump up. I asked Austin, "Want to sample more of my mother's cooking?"

His face was still screwed up with pain and he was fighting for air as he gasped, "You… little… bastard… Sunday-punched… me."

"Maybe I did, the way you caught me unawares with your crack about my folks."

"I'll have your badge for this!" he mumbled, sweat starting down his agonized face.

"Think you can get it? I got pull backing me too. Or maybe you mean… Look, lardass, you have a few inches in height on me and at least thirty pounds but I don't think you're big enough to take my badge. But let's step outside and try it. I'd like to spread your nose and—"

Larson was at my side, a heavy strong arm lightly on my shoulder. He said softly, "Cut it, Dave. This is a police station, not a street corner or a gym."

He was in a middle spot, not knowing how much pull Austin might have down at Centre Street and if he took sides he could find himself pounding a country beat, a harness cop again.

"I was merely showing this stuffed clown how strong my mother's lasagna made me and—"

"Go over and sit at my desk, Dave," Larson said. "Don't give me a hard time."

"But… sure, Larson." I walked over and sat on the corner of his desk, ran my hand over my hair: it wasn't mussed. He helped Austin to his feet.

He still couldn't stand straight, an unexpected belt in the gut is rugged. Austin said, "I'll beat the living slop out of—"

"You two want to fight, go outside and on your own time. Sit down and relax." Larson actually lifted Austin off the floor and carried him to the nearest chair. Then he came back to his desk, told me, "Get your can off my desk, Dave. You relax too."

I wasn't sore at Larson and anyway I'd have to be stupid-mad to ever tangle with him—if you didn't take him out with the first punch those arms could crush you like big snakes. As I stood up Lieutenant Reed came in, looked at Austin holding his middle, his face pale. Then he glared at me and asked, "What the hell's going on here?"

I realized he was talking over me, to Larson. I said quickly, "I had to explain my name to Detective Austin, sort of straighten him out. He didn't like the way it sounded."

"Wintino, this isn't any goddamn boys club, this is an overworked office. But seems you don't have enough work, you have time to showboat."

"I—"

"The Owens file is on my desk. Read through it, see if you can use your hands for something constructive, like giving me an intelligent summary of the reports, before you go out to lunch."

There wasn't any point in arguing with Reed. I said, "Yes, Lieutenant," went into his office and took the file into a drab-looking room down the hall where we sometimes questioned suspects. I blew dust off the table and chair, sat down.

At lunch I'd have to call Mary's uncle, have him get in touch with his big-shot politician friend, protect me in case there was a beef and Austin really had influence. If they ever stuck me back in uniform there'd be no living with Mary.

I took off my coat and went to work on the file. Most of it was the reports of the various precinct men who'd worked on the case, all the people they'd interviewed, the few leads they'd run down—everything negative. There was a copy of Owens' arrest record, almost all of the collars made with Wales. They had been hard workers, over sixteen hundred cases. I went through the list fast, checking off those arrests where they'd used force, that would be the sort of stuff to make a joker want revenge. Like Austin must feel now.

Back in '37 they had "subdued" a man named Dundus who was terrorizing a bar with a butcher knife. They must have worked the guy over good: Wales had received minor cuts and Owens had busted Dundus' nose with a sap. Dundus had been sent to Bellevue for observation and then to an institution. That was back in '37. He could have spent ten or fifteen years in a padded cell, then been released. I wondered where he was now.

There was a detailed report on the arrest of Sal Kahn for the shooting of Boots Brenner. They had roped Sal into confessing, Owens posing as a "witness who positively identified" Sal as the man who had dumped Brenner's body in the lot. The lot was right next to an empty garage they were using for a still so I wondered why all the praise for Wales and Owens—they couldn't help but stumble on the still and the obvious solution.

Sal must have been one of these cool cats. He never gave them the name of his partner, although through stoolies he was known to be working with somebody known by the snappy title of The Bird. There was over a grand in electrical equipment in the "shop" but Sal didn't know a thing about electricity. It was a damn good thing Kahn signed a confession. They never recovered the actual murder gun—Kahn claimed he had tossed it into a garbage can. Kahn died seventeen months later in the chair, still clammouthed. He had forty dollars and change on his person when arrested and not a penny was found in his room. He used a court-appointed lawyer claiming he was broke, although as Wales pointed out in one of his reports, "Kahn and his partner must have been selling a lot of alcohol to interest a gangster like Brenner. It must be assumed the missing partner fled with all the money made from the still."

I jotted down the address of the still, along with that of Kahn's sole relative, his mother, and the data on Dundus.

The rest were all routine arrests: rape, assault, burglary, disorderly conduct, etc. For the few years Owens worked after Wales retired he must have had an inside job—he only had three collars, including picking up some joker named Frederick X. Rowland III, for smoking in the subway.

As I was finishing the summary, Danny Hayes came in puffing on a new cigarette. I asked, "The guy at the line-up our paperhanger?"

"Nope. This one just blew into town yesterday. Hear you snapped your stack. When you going to grow up, Dave?"

"The bastard called me a Jewboy and a Wop. Am I supposed to be grown up when I take that?"

"I don't know. But sometimes people say things without meaning real harm. Just been raised ignorantly." He scratched his brown nose. "Hell, I run into that all the time but you can't take on the world."

"Naw, Austin meant it the way he said it. And when I start taking crap you can pull a headstone over me."

"I don't make you all the time, Dave. Would you have slugged him if he had used the names and you didn't happen to be Italian and Jewish?"

"Who knows? Look, I have enough trouble taking care of myself. When a guy low-rates me I try to slug him. All set for some Chinese chow?"

"Reed wants you."

"Going to be a stink about my clipping Austin?"

Hayes shrugged. "Didn't sound like it, but I don't really know. He's sending me out to look at a stolen car, and I think he wants you for another call."

I got the file together and the few notes I'd made, went through the squad room to Reed's office, told him, "There isn't much here, Lieutenant, and—"

"Forget it, for now. Go over and see what this is all about." He shoved a slip of paper across his desk that had an address and the name Rose Henderson scrawled on it. Reed always wrote as if his pen was a barbell. "She's called in twice about being followed, men pushing her around. Sounds like some old maid crackpot."

"I'll go right over. Lieutenant, in checking Owens' arrest record you'll notice that in 1937 he and Wales brought in a nut who was flashing a big knife in a bar. They sent him away, no trial. They must have worked the guy over, Owens busted his nose while taking the knife and Wales was cut up. Name is Dundus. If he's a psycho he could be our man, discounting the robbery angle, which I've never bought."

"This squad is off the Owens case."

"What? Why?"

"Mainly because it's a dead end, we're just going around in circles, getting no place."

"Well, I'd still like to check, see if this guy is out of the hatch, and if so, where he is and—"

Reed held up a large thin hand. "I'll have a check made. And forget about the Owens case and listen to me: Wintino, this is the third man you've belted in this station house. I calmed down this Homicide man, told him you were a hotheaded kid with—"

"Instead of calming him down, Lieutenant, why didn't you tell him to watch his fat tongue?"

"How do you know I didn't tell him that too? That's the trouble with you, Dave, at times you are a hot-headed kid. But I'm not running any free-for-all here. Start another fight and you'll be back in uniform. By God, if you had pounded a beat for a brace of years you'd know how to handle people."

"Lieutenant Reed, when a clown insults my family background, what am I supposed to do, make a complaint through channels?"

"Technically, yes." He leaned back in his chair, his long body looking cramped, his big nose like a dagger in his face. "You're a kid, Wintino, and a cocky one. But I like you because you never goof off. I'll admit you work hard and get results. I'm going to tell you this once and remember it because

I don't go in for any fatherly advice crap. There's always somebody around you have to say sir to. I don't care how important or tough you are, be at least one man who's more important or tougher. Get used to the idea. Actually, Dave, you've been lucky, you're too small to be so hard."

I said slowly, "I understand what you mean but I'll never eat crow for any bigoted knucklehead who makes cracks about my race or religion. I don't think you'd want any man to take that—*sir*."

Reed brought his chair down hard, waved his long arms. "Another thing, you talk too damn much. Gowan, get going before this old maid calls up about a mouse getting into her."

I wasn't sure if Reed was smiling or not.

Wednesday Afternoon

It sure was getting muggy. I stopped for a soda and a hunk of pie, finished up with a couple of hamburgers. I was surprised I could eat I was so angry. I mean this crap about closing the Owens case—that's what it amounted to—and having me off seeing this nutty old maid, Danny working on a stolen car. How important were they compared to that murder?

The address Reed gave me was near the southern end of the precinct, one of these old sections where some of the houses had been remodeled, a mixture of high and low rents.

As I walked down the block I passed this fancy Jaguar sedan. I don't especially care for foreign heaps but what attracted me was this real sharp sport jacket hanging from a side window. It was something: shaggy imported tweed with side pleats and patch pockets. It was a honey, strictly from a swank shop and made to order. I tried to see the label but couldn't make it. Anyway, I was spending too much on clothes as it was.

The house I wanted was a former six-story tenement that had been made over into small apartments. The mailbox name-plate read HENDERSON-HONDURA. I rang the bell and when I got an answering buzz walked up to the third floor and rang 3C. There was one of those one-way peephole deals and I heard it opening on the other side and a woman's voice asked, "What do you want?"

"Are you Miss Rose Henderson?"

"Yes."

"You called the police a little while ago. I'm Detective Wintino," I said, watching my face in the peephole and feeling like a sitting duck. My damn collar looked wilted already.

There was a long moment of hesitation, then: "Please show me your credentials." The voice was deep.

I was off the Owens case for a loony like this! I took out my buzzer and nearly shoved it through the peep mirror. "That do it, lady? My name is Dave Wintino, Detective Third Grade, 201st Precinct. I'm assigned to your case. Now do you think you might open the door and let me get to work?"

As I was putting my shield back in my wallet the door opened. I was off balance: this short girl standing there with very dark close-cut hair hugging a warm and pretty face. The lips were thick and red and she wore a loose plain blue smock showing off one of these built-up-from-the-ground solid figures, almost heavy legs. I must have been giving her bug eyes for she glanced down at herself, then asked, "What's wrong?"

"Nothing. You're a surprise. Had you pegged for an old maid crackpot."

"My, the frank policeman. This must be a new technique. You're a bit of a shock yourself, more like a college magazine salesman. Let me see that badge again, if you don't mind."

"As you wish, citizen," I said, flashing my tin. She grabbed my wrist and studied the badge for a moment, then said, "I'm sorry but I've been on the ragged edge these last few days. Please come in, Mr....?" She had a good grip.

"Wintino, David Wintino, Miss Henderson," I said, stepping by her. She was using a nice mild perfume. I thought our apartment was small but it was Madison Square Garden compared to this cell. There was just room for a narrow foam rubber couch against one wall, a desk with a typewriter between two small windows, one of those red canvas African camp chairs in front of an unpainted bookcase stuffed with books, a coffee table piled with magazines and old newspapers, a battered file cabinet, then the door to the john, a closet you'd have to enter sideways, and what had to be the world's smallest combination sink, stove and refrigerator. There was a small radio on a shelf, a framed diploma from Barnard and a couple of very bright paintings of tropical scenes on the walls, and some sort of weird mobile hanging from the tricky ceiling light.

Closing the door she put her hands on her hips, asked, "Thinking of buying my place?"

"Give me claustrophobia, Miss Henderson. Where do you want me to sit?"

She pointed at the couch which was covered with a coarse deep red material. I sat and she curled up in the camp chair, her rear making a wonderful curve toward the polished floor. She lit a cigarette and I shook my head before she could offer me one. It was crazy, pretty as she was, I had to keep staring at her stomach. She had this tiny belly making a flat, silly curve as it filled out her dress—and why that excited me I didn't know. And why I was even thinking about *that* instead of Owens?

She said, "I do wish you'd stop inspecting me—it makes me feel as if I have two heads. Wintino? Are you of Spanish descent? You look Latin. As you may have guessed, I'm Puerto Rican—Hondura is my real name."

"I'm part Italian. Now Miss Henderson, what's your trouble?"

"Since the beginning of last week my phone has been ringing at odd hours of the night and either nobody answers or a man's voice goes into the most obscene sex talk. Various men have been to the superintendent downstairs, making ridiculous inquiries about me. They've also been to my neighbors. I know I'm being followed on the street. In fact on Monday, Tuesday and this morning when I went to the library—and later when I was shopping—I have been jostled by several different men," she said through the smoke of her cigarette.

"What do you mean by jostled?"

"Exactly what the word means—tripped, elbowed, pushed around."

The last thing she looked like was a neurotic babe. "Having any trouble with your boy friends?"

"No, this isn't any so-called boy friend trouble, as you put it. I know exactly why all this is being done."

"Okay, why?" I asked, watching that wonderful full curve move a little every time she breathed.

"Have you ever read the *Weekly Spectator?* I suppose not."

"You suppose right. I hardly ever get my noggin up out of a comic book."

She gave me a warm smile. "Sorry, I was rude. Mr. Wintino, I'm a free-lance writer and at the moment working on an article for the *Spectator—this* is a weekly liberal magazine sort of like the *Nation, Harper's,* the *Atlantic,* except it deals entirely with economic subjects. My article exposes a newly formed monopoly in the electronics business. I'm certain the firms I'm writing about are trying to stop the article by making me a nervous wreck."

I wanted to tell her she had a head start on the nervous wreck angle but instead I got out my notebook, saw my notes taken from the Owens file, said wearily, "Let me get this straight. You're doing an article for a magazine called the *Weekly Spectator* and you claim that because of this article you're being annoyed on the street and your sleep is being knocked out of whack by mysterious phone calls—and all this is being done, you think, by some of the business firms you're writing about. Is that correct?"

"Yes. Don't forget the men snooping around the apartment house, and ringing my bell at odd hours of the night, and nobody there when I answer."

I nodded, and wrote in my book, "This chick is in a bad way," as I asked, "What makes you think these business companies are back of this?"

"Because this all started last week when they learned from a *Spectator* query I was writing the article."

"You were never bothered like this before?"

"Never."

"Can you give me the names of these firms?"

"Of course: Modern Electric, Wren & Company, Popular Electronics, and Twentieth Century Power, Inc. Two weeks ago I finished working, for over three months, as a typist for Modern Electric, to confirm my material and secure data. The magazine approved an outline and last week I started my final research and a rough draft."

"Can you identify the men who've molested you as working for any of these outfits you mentioned?"

"Certainly not," she said impatiently. "They're obviously hiring… uh… private detectives, I suppose, to do this."

"When do you leave the house every day? Any set time?"

She waved her cigarette as if it was a baton. "No special time. Usually in the morning, sometimes in the afternoon. Depends upon when I get up."

"Miss Henderson, you're saying they have at least one man, and most likely two, shadowing you all day, not to mention a guy working nights on your phone and doorbell. An all-day shadow job costs about seventy-five bucks per man, which means somebody is spending over two hundred dollars a day to make you—nervous. You claim this has been going on for a week and a half, ten days, over two grand. Lot of money for a—"

She crushed her butt with an angry gesture. "Are you implying this is all my imagination?"

"Yes and no," I said carefully, thinking it would be exciting to see her breathe fire, and she looked like she could do it easily. "Let's examine your statement calmly. Those sexy phone calls may not mean a thing; it's fairly common for perverts to get their kicks by picking a woman's name out of the phone book, telling her things they'd never have nerve enough to say to her face. Then you say people have been around here asking about you. Could be you applied for a job some weeks ago, or opened a charge account, and they're simply making a routine check on—"

"But I haven't applied for a job or opened any accounts recently. And they ask if I'm a whore, a dope addict!"

"As for being shadowed on the street," I went on, "many people say that. They see the same man or woman a few times during the course of the day and become convinced they're being followed. And being pushed about, jostled, that happens all the time too—a guy is rushing for a bus and bunks into—"

"Are you supposed to protect my rights or explain them away!"

"Miss Henderson, I have to look at things objectively. I'm not calling you a liar, merely trying to show you there might be other explanations for the things you complain about. For example, let's get back to a boy friend who could be sore enough to phone—"

"Will you stop jabbering about a *boy friend!*" she snapped, jumping to her feet. "I haven't been on a date in months, I've been too busy. I told you I was working as a stenographer and in the evenings I did my writing. Matter of fact while I was working I finished a children's book. I don't understand your attitude, why don't you believe me?"

"I haven't said I didn't, only I can't quite see anybody spending a couple of thousand bucks a week to upset you. Suppose you finish this article and the magazine runs it, what happens?"

"Let me give you a picture of these firms. They aren't the biggest, like General Electric, but they do a good business manufacturing small electrical devices—doorbells, buzzers, switches. For the last year there have been rumors of something revolutionary in the business, what might be termed a liquid wire that can be painted on. This would cut the production cost of thousands of gadgets by at least half—do away with wiring, screws and wireholders, as a small example. A patent has already been issued to a California scientist on this. However, a certain type of crushed metal is needed to make the paint conductive and the four companies I mentioned have cornered the market on this metal. In brief, they constitute a monopoly, plan to squeeze everybody else out."

"I still don't see why they should get so excited about your article."

"It should bring Washington down on them for violating the antitrust laws. The least it will do is force them to open up the field to others, and thus the public will benefit from the low cost."

"A bunch of doorbell manufacturers are spending, two grand a week to stop your article? Hardly seems worth all—"

"This 'bunch of doorbell manufacturers' figure not only to split some three millions in profit in the first two years, but there are untold uses for this wire paint. When perfected it might do away with all wiring in cars, for example. Don't you understand, once they control this, they'll be in a position to drive competitors out and in time send prices sky-high."

"And the magazine, this *Spectator,* what are they doing about your troubles?"

"At the moment I'm not involving them. They can only do what I've done—call in the police. After all, I'm just a free-lancer and the magazine hasn't the money to fight these companies. The *Spectator* is lucky to break even each month."

"What are you getting for the article?"

"Two hundred dollars."

"Why don't these outfits spend a few grand in advertising and buy off the magazine?"

"Because it isn't that type of magazine. Any more questions?"

"You're not getting much pay for all the work you're doing on this. What's in it for you?"

"Partly I do it because they're breaking the law, rooking the public, and I'm part of the public. Also I'll benefit in other ways. The publicity if the article makes enough noise will get me other assignments. Now, do you think I might get some protection from the police instead of a grilling?"

"I wasn't grilling you, we have to check all sides of a story. I'll report this back to my boss, Lieutenant Reed. We've been busy on a murder and I doubt if he can spare a man to guard you twenty-four hours a day. But he might put a tap on your phone, try and trace those calls. I'll let you know what we can do," I told her, getting up, heading for the door, a little high from her perfume.

"When will you let me know what will be done?"

"Probably late this afternoon. I'm not sure: I don't run the department."

She shrugged and everything that moved was a boot to watch. "At least you still don't think there's some love-struck idiot after me."

"I haven't ruled that out."

"What?" she said loudly. "Can't you see that these—"

"Sure, I can see and I don't rule out a nutty boy friend because... Miss Henderson, let's not fence for compliments, every time you look into a mirror you see an exciting young woman. You certainly know that." I tried to sound casual but I blurted the words like a schoolboy.

Her face was a slow blush, then came this warm, almost tickling laughter. "I suppose I should say thank you. Thank you, Mr...."

"Wintino, Dave Wintino." I took out an assignment slip, wrote my name and precinct phone number on it. "Next time you're pushed around on the street, if you're *sure* it was deliberate, tell the nearest cop to hold the man and have the cop call me. Show him this card."

"Thanks. I won't leave the house till I hear from you."

"Miss Henderson, the Police Department is understaffed so I can't promise we'll give you an escort, but even reporting this, having it on the precinct record, is some protection. And don't worry, well keep an eye on you, perhaps have the beat cop stop by now and then."

We said good-day and I walked down to the basement, keeping an eye out for mutts, and found the super. He was an old mousey duck in dirty overalls and I asked, "Been any men around inquiring about Miss Henderson up in 3C?"

"You another one? I'm too busy to be answering questions all the time." He had a weak voice and some kind of mild accent. Eating would be a problem for him, he only had a couple of mossy teeth in his mouth.

"Another one? How many men have been here asking about her?"

"Don't rightly recall. I'd say five, six. They come late at night or early in the morning, get me out of my bed to ask about her. And I need my sleep, I work hard."

"What do they ask?"

"All kinds of things. One asked did I know she was Spanish, a greasy Spick he called her. Guess you saw her name, Hondura, on the mailbox. She's Puerto Rican, and uses the name Henderson to write under. Does she entertain men, these men ask, does she have meetings in her flat, is she a Red? Was one creepy old man yesterday about scared the living life out of me just to see him, he wanted to know if I thought she was selling dope. I understand they been asking some of the tenants too, getting them out of bed. I told them I knew was she was a quiet girl who kept to herself and paid her rent on time."

"Any of these men give you their names, say what they were?"

"Nope. They just fired questions at me."

"Can you describe them, would you recognize any of them again?"

"Nope. Except for the creepy one they was all well-dressed, classy-looking men. I told you I ain't got time to be answering a lot of questions."

"But you have time to shoot your big mouth off. Why didn't you ask who I was before you talked to me?"

"See here, don't you raise your voice to me, young man. Well, who are you?"

I showed him my badge. "Detective Wintino, 201st Squad."

"A cop. Say, Miss Henderson done anything crooked?"

"No. She complained about some jerks annoying her." I took out my notebook. "What's your name? How long you been employed here?"

"Heitman. Teddy's the first name. Been here going on fourteen years this August. What you writing me down for? I don't want no trouble."

"Relax, Mr. Heitman. Have a phone here?"

"Yes, sir."

"Here's my name and police phone number on this slip. Keep it handy. Next time anybody comes asking around about Miss Henderson before you tell them a thing, ask to see their credentials, write down their name and address. Even if they say they're police or government men ask for—'"

"You'll get me into trouble."

"You can get into trouble by talking too damn much. Know who you're talking to before you run your gums. I want you to do me a favor, phone me as soon as anybody asks about Miss Henderson. Leave your name if I'm not in and I'll call you back. Don't make a fuss about it but try to get the name of whoever asks about her, ask to see their credentials or badge, then phone me. Got that?"

"Yes, sir," he said, clutching my card. "I never had no run-in with the police, never. I don't want no trouble. No, sir."

"Aw, stop drooling about trouble. And don't be so ready to give out information about your tenants: tell 'em to go ask the tenant. Remember, if they ask about Miss Henderson, phone me soon as you can."

"I'll do that."

"Fine," I said, walking away, knowing he was too scared to do anything. I walked up the basement steps and the humidity was like a blanket. I stopped to run a comb through my hair, glanced up and down the street, trying to make her tail.

The street was empty, so were the parked cars. Little ways up the block there was a tall guy of about twenty-five wearing dungarees and a shabby black leather jacket leaning against one of the buildings. What made me forget about my hair was the crumpled wire coat hanger he was toying with in his right hand.

I slipped my badge on my belt as he glanced around like a ham actor, crossed the sidewalk to the Jaguar and shielding the hanger with his body, started working the wire into the rubber lining of the front window. He was less than two hundred feet from me and having a rough time with the window.

I edged up toward him, ready to sprint if he saw me, but he was too busy and I was behind him and on his left side when I asked, "Lost your keys?"

He spun around, one of these jokers with eyes too large for his long thin face. He nodded, tried to smile as he said, 'Yeah, misplaced them." Looking me over, he turned back to the window.

"How you going to start the car if you haven't any keys?"

"Get lost, buddy. Mind your business."

"I'm a police officer. Keep your hands in sight and face me!"

He turned quickly, his narrow face frightened pale. I opened my coat with my right hand so he could see my badge, part of my shoulder holster. I told him, "Drop the hanger—do it slow and easy."

He dropped it.

"Turn around and place both your hands on top of the car. Now keep them there. And spread your feet."

He spread-eagled his big feet. He was sweating badly as he stuttered, "Give me a b-break, b-buddy. This is my first t-time."

"Quiet, punk. You'd bust a car open to get a jacket you couldn't hock for more than a few lousy bucks," I said, frisking him. He was clean. At least he had good taste, he was after the tweed sport coat I'd liked. "Don't move till I tell you or you'll get hurt." I got out my notebook, put down the time, the license number of the car, the nearest building address. Across the street I saw the excited face of a fat old lady at the window, then she disappeared. She was probably calling the police. I put my notebook away, told him, "Stay the way you are and don't try anything."

"Please, give me a chance. I swear I'll never—"

"Bullslop. A chance to do what, bust into another car, give me more work making the rounds of the hock shops looking for a damn stolen jacket? Keep your trap shut and don't move." The busybody was back at the window, her face eager.

A car passed us, then another. I saw a cab coming. I called, "Taxi," and when it stopped I flashed my badge, told him, "I'm a police officer taking a suspect to—"

A radio car turned into the street—fast. The old gal hadn't wasted a second. I told the cabby to drive on and he went, looking relieved. When the radio car stopped both cops came out on the run. They were a couple of middle-aged guys I knew—only by sight. The first one asked, "What's up, Junior?"

"Caught this clown breaking into a car. One of you stay here and see if you can locate the owner of this foreign heap. The other take us up to the station."

One of the cops gave me a mock slam-salute. "I'll stay. Some car, Al, you ride them up and don't be all afternoon coming back for me—hot in this sun." He jabbed the punk in the ribs with his night stick. "You, get in the car and don't try nothing stupid."

I picked up the coat hanger.

At the precinct house I took him right up to the squad room. Reed was there. I had the guy empty his pockets. An old wallet with one buck in it said his name was Henry Moorepark, that he lived on East Fourth Street. He said he was a dye worker, unemployed since last February, gave me the name and address of the last concern he'd worked for. Besides the wallet he had a single key, a plastic case with his Social Security card on one side, a snap of a potty-looking babe on the other, two hock shop tickets dated five and eight days ago, and a busted cigar holder. He said he was unmarried, lived with his folks, had never served time. I had him roll up his shirt sleeves and pants legs—he wasn't a junkie. He said again, "Like I told you, I found this hanger and was trying to straighten it out against the car, figured I could take it home."

"What you doing this far uptown?" I asked.

"Just walking around."

"And you found this hanger and were busy straightening it out, and busting the rubber on the car window, when I saw you. That your story?"

"Yes."

"You expect me to buy that?" I said, putting force in my voice. "If I did you'd be the most surprised guy in this room. Come on, give me a straight story."

"I just found the… the hanger and was going to get… get it straightened so…" His narrow face seemed to grow longer and tighter, then it fell apart, went slack as he whispered, "I need money bad, I was trying to get the coat and whatever else there was in there."

I took him down to the desk and booked him, put him in a cell and phoned down to his precinct to check his address, notify his folks. Then I called BCI to find if there was a record on the guy and went back upstairs to the squad room. Reed asked, "Call downtown for a yellow sheet on this cheap slob?"

I nodded. "'He was telling the truth, no record."

Reed shook his head. "Another miserable bastard gone wrong. These cheap cases get me angry, doing it for a few lousy bucks. Nice work, Wintino."

"A big deal, I bagged a hard-up jerk on his first two-bit job," I said, thinking how we were all wasting time. Hell, I should be asking Wales about Sal Kahn.

Reed said, "You prevented a crime, that's supposed to be half our job. And there's no such animal as a 'small' crime. Suppose this punk had a knife on him and panicked when the car owner found him, it could easily have been a murder. What I like is your working by reflex, instinctively. That's being a good cop. Have lunch yet?"

"No, sir," I lied: it never hurts to build things up a little. "Speaking of instinct, I feel I should talk to Wales about—"

"Grab a sandwich, then finish the report on Owens and write up this case. Forget Wales. I called the brokerage office to check with him on that Dundus fellow. Wales hadn't shown up for work today. Must be off drowning his sorrows. Doesn't matter, I checked with the institution. Dundus died there. What's with this Henderson nut?"

"She isn't a nut. She's a writer. She's being rough-shadowed and annoyed by phone calls to make her so jittery she won't be able to finish an article exposing some electrical companies hogging a new invention. I thought she was a crackpot till I talked to the janitor. Somebody has been trying to throw a scare into her."

"Has she any idea who's doing this?"

"No, but she thinks the men who jostled her must be private clowns hired by the electrical concerns. I told her we'd have the post cop and the radio car keep an eye on her house for any suspicious characters. And she wants an escort when she goes out this afternoon."

Reed rubbed his big nose. "Escort? Hell, I got a busy house here."

"But you see she hasn't any set hours, goes to the library whenever she has to look up stuff. I figured if we tailed her once, we'd nail the jokers who've been roughing her up. She's waiting on a call from me as to what we plan to do."

Reed stared at his hand as if he expected to see part of his nose there. "All right, if she's a writer we don't want her knocking the department. Tell her about the beat man looking in. Find out what time she'll leave her flat in the morning, I'll be able to give her a man then. It's two-twenty now. Take off after you finish your paperwork. You'll have to take that car-punk to Night Court."

"My wife is going to love that," I said, almost to myself. I'd forgotten about the damn Night Court.

"Your wife isn't working for me. Cop's wife should expect him when she sees him," Reed said as he went into his office.

When I got Rose Henderson on the phone she blew up. "Tomorrow morning? I'm waiting now to go out shopping, not to mention some research I need."

"I'm sorry but we can't spare a man now. I told you that might happen. I checked with your super, I believe your story."

"That's nice of you. I suppose I won't be killed going to the corner grocery. But I will see you tomorrow, about ten then?"

"A detective will be there by ten. He'll call you first," I said, wondering how the devil I was going to tell Mary I might not make her bridge game. I'd better call her uncle, that might cool her off.

As I hung up I started to dial Mary, then changed my mind. I felt crummy. Why should I have to crawl before my wife, act like I was doing something wrong? Still I was spoiling her evening. But what did they expect me to do, close my eyes to a sad sack robbing a car? I laughed—to and at myself. Whenever I get sore I'm always blaming things on "they" or "them," a kind of blanket name for everybody who's against me. And that was dumb too. Mary wasn't against me, she just didn't understand what being a cop's wife meant. Perhaps she was even right; because I liked the job didn't mean she had to.

I went out for an ice cream cone and dialed Uncle Frank. It took time for the girl who answered to find him—he was always jumping around his joint, bossing everybody. Finally I heard him pant over the phone, "Dave?"

"Yeah. How's things, Uncle Frank?"

"Terrible, lad. Lousy truckman circles the block twice and can't find a parking place so he takes off like a scared rabbit. Two hundred and thirty-one pieces of express freight, dress goods, miss the afternoon train. They won't get to Miami in time for Saturday's business and there'll be a kickback in my face. You downtown, Davie my boy?"

"No. Mary tells me you want to see me."

"Yes, yes. We have to have a talk. This place is getting too much for me. I'll be here till seven, maybe later. When will you be down?"

"I have to go to Night Court. But I'm off tomorrow and Friday. I'll drop in to see you then. Okay?"

"Fine. Always know where to find me. Tell Mary to drag you over for supper, Anna and the kids keep asking for you and… Hey you, go back and shut that goddamn door, we've lost enough items!… Sorry, Dave, shouting at one of the idiots here. I'll see you tomorrow. Good-by, got to rush."

I came back to the squad room and started typing my reports. Reed called out from his desk, "Wintino, you know you change tours?"

"Yes, sir. I report on Saturday midnight."

Reed nodded. "Maybe we'll have a little peace and quiet around here for the next fifty-six hours. Finish that typing and go home and unwind."

I was done by three-thirty. As I was leaving Danny Hayes came into the locker room and said, "I think I'll sleep all day tomorrow. Remember that assault case, the two refugees? It comes up in court Monday. Never seen it to fail, every time we're on the midnight tour we have to be in court in the morning."

"We're just lucky," I said, waving at him from the doorway.

I reached the apartment before four-thirty and took a shower and changed my shirt. I turned on the TV and went from a shoot-'em-up cowboy movie to a con man selling window screens to some spy movie that must have been made in 1910 to a kid's program. I turned the set off for some jazz from the table radio. I had a glass of milk and read the sport pages, wondered what Jane Owens would say if she saw our place with the high rent and all the modern furniture. What did Owens have in mind saying he might get a California farm soon?

I got out the phone book but Al Wales didn't have a phone. I sat in a large straw and iron chair and thought of Rose Henderson curled up in her red African camp chair. Mary was all set to buy a pigskin one but changed her mind for this basket job—she said everybody had African camp chairs. Crazy thing, style—what diff did it make if everybody had them? Although I wouldn't buy a gray flannel suit for the same reason. Henderson-Hondura. Puerto Rican. That fine belly curve… interesting face. Chick like that living alone till some lucky clown stumbles over her. Handled that sloppy, maybe she wasn't alone. Might be an ex-husband around, although she didn't look over twenty-five or -six. I should have checked on her family. Spanish don't let their girls live alone. That could be the string to the case, a husband, or the family, trying to scare her to come back home…. Nuts, they'd hardly go to all that trouble and expense.

Wonder if they'll let Moorepark off with a suspended sentence and will it do any good? I might get him a job at Uncle Frank's. Hell, I'm wearing a badge not a halo. Another cheap crook on his way. I sound like Reed, way he always says "cheap" as if it's a curse word. Seems to hate an amateur crook worse than a real thug. But then with a pro you know what you're up against, it's cut out for you. Petty thieves don't make sense. Lucky if he got a fin for that coat. Didn't look my size but I'd sure give twenty bucks for a secondhand jacket like that one.

I ought to go over to Wales' rooming house but Mary would raise the roof if she didn't find me home. So I sit here stewing about what Mary will say like a kid who'd busted the cookie jar. Never even asked if I wanted to play cards, just made the date. Got that fast new Mexican featherweight on TV tonight too. Damn, I haven't worked out in weeks. Don't have time for anything lately.

Goddamn Night Court, I'd like to play some bridge. Mary will blow her top, eat my—

Mary opened the door, a couple of bags in her arms. She looked fine in a neat gray suit that was the right contrast for her bright blond hair.

She blew a kiss at me as she said, "Hello, hon," dropped the packages on the couch, then took off her coat and high heels, pushed the Chinese screen out of the way and started things cooking. "I've had a hard day. Did you get a chance to call Uncle Frank?"

"Aha. Probably see him tomorrow."

"Swell." She got another pot working, then sat down on the couch and began to undress. I liked to see her walk without high heels. "It's so sticky. I hope this isn't the start of a bad summer. All I could think about this afternoon was a shower. Are you starved? I want a quick shower first."

"I'm not starved but I want to eat soon."

"Don will probably have a lot of stuff to eat. He's always talking about picking up foreign snacks at Charles. I got chopped meat and peas for supper. How is Uncle Frank?" She stuck out one long leg, rolled off a stocking.

"Bouncing as usual. Babes, I… I have to take a punk to Night Court for arraignment. With any luck I'll be at the bridge game by nine-thirty. I'll take a cab." I waited for the explosion.

Her voice wasn't quite shrill as she said, "Oh, damnit, Dave, I told you they were having exactly eight and now."

I went over and helped take off the other stocking. "Honey, I didn't plan it this way. One of those things." I pulled her to her feet, kissed her. "Babes, you look like money from home in those panties and bra—really stacked."

"Am I?" She kissed me quickly. "Now Dave, supper is on and I'm hungry and sweaty and—"

"I've been hungry for the last week," I said, running my hands over her, hard.

Mary suddenly giggled in my ear, nibbled at it. Then she started unbuttoning my shirt. "Be careful of the couch spread. I like it best when it's a surprise. Oh, Davie, I would have been terribly disappointed if you had let me take my shower first."

I undressed with the speed of a fireman. Surprise? I was as astonished as a guy suddenly finding he has it made.

Wednesday Evening

I got a break in Night Court. We were called early and since my boy had confessed, the arraignment went through fast. This Don Tills lived down in the Village in an old brownstone that had been made over into small apartments. It was still muggy and I got screwed up as always with the Village streets, and all the walking and rushing left me sweating a little.

But I was there shortly after nine and Mary was pleased. The Tills had a couple of high-ceilinged rooms with furniture like ours, only more of it and probably more expensive. Mary was wrong about them having exactly eight people, they had nine—there was a guy with a big belly and a sort of tense face, including a thick black mustache, who was sleeping off a bottle on the couch. I never did get his name or what he was doing there and nobody paid him any mind, except to break into laughter when he'd mutter, "Who's on the gate?" every ten or fifteen minutes.

They had two bridge tables set up, with chairs to match, and all the men looked about the same, between twenty-five and thirty, short haircuts, casual sport clothes, sharp alert faces, and all very sure of themselves. In fact they all sounded the same, like actors talking: good voices. The girls didn't look so much alike but they had the same intense faces and all dressed sharply. There was a portable bar and everybody had a glass and they were telling jokes when I came in—mostly some old dirty jokes with new names added. When I was introduced Mary said quickly, "I'm so glad your business appointment didn't keep you any later. We've been waiting for you before we started playing."

"What kind of a belt would you like, Dave, rye, scotch, gin, vodka, or tequila?" Don asked me.

I was going to say I didn't drink but didn't want to sound like a square so I said, "Too warm for hard stuff. Got a beer handy?"

Grace, Don's wife, who really filled her black and gold slacks, gave me a can of beer and a kind of bottomless cup that fitted over the top of the can. She said, "Now you won't need a glass."

I smiled. "I wouldn't have needed a glass anyway. Thank you."

"This way the flavor of the beer isn't lost by pouring it out of the can," Don told me. Seemed like they'd given a lot of thought to something as simple as beer drinking. Then he told everybody, "Fellow I went to Yale with and who works for a Chicago agency, wrote me one of their clients is working on a paper beer container. Has some kind of keg lining to improve the flavor, I believe."

Everybody except me started talking about this: I was waiting to play bridge. Half the time I didn't even know what they were talking about. They had pet words they all liked to mouth: "the cost-*level*," or something was "sales-*wise*," or had a "*built-in* selling point." Even Mary got into the act, saying, "There's something substantial about a can, gives you a feeling of getting your money's worth that a milk container, for example, doesn't have. Consumer-wise I think it would be a mistake to lose that."

Still they all looked like nice bright people and I sipped my beer, which only made me sweat more, and glanced at myself in a wall mirror to see if my shirt looked wilted, and listened. About a half-hour later they finally got the cards out but at nine-forty-five somebody insisted the TV be turned on to one of "our programs." Most boorish bilge you ever heard. "We wrote several very clever programs but the client, a real corn-ball, chose this tripe."

The "program" was so short it wasn't worth all the talk—a one-minute commercial in which an uncomfortable-looking big league pitcher stumbled through a couple of lines about how he loved to use this brand of paint when he was puttering around his house. When it was over they shut off the set and everybody chattered away, arguing about the damn thing. I kept nursing my beer and keeping my trap shut. Belly-boy on the couch broke things up by mumbling, "Who's on the gate?" between snores and then we started to play cards.

Mary and I were playing against Don and Grace Tills. He turned out to be one of these psychic bidders, bidding on what he thinks his partner should have. He opened with a diamond bid and I was holding five diamonds, ace, queen high. His wife must have had a few, she gave him a boost. He then bid spades and she took him to game in diamonds and Don went down four.

We got good cards and Mary made three no trump and two hands later we took the rubber. Don and his wife kept making tracks to the bar and were getting juiced. Even Mary was sailing a little and she can handle a bottle. Everybody must have been lapping it up waiting for me.

We were on the second rubber when a fellow at the other table stood up and took off his coat, saying, "Does anybody mind? Getting rather warm in here."

"You ass," Don said, "you mean you stood on convention *here?* Hell, anybody feels warm, strip. And that goes for the ladies too." He took off his snappy dark-grained sport coat and opened his yellow waistcoat.

Grace said something about waiting for a buy on a couple of air-conditioning units and when I was dummy I peeled off my coat. As I sat down there was a sudden silence in the room, except for light snores of the lush on the couch. There wasn't even the small noises of the cards. It was sort of a shocked silence. Mary was staring at me, her mouth angry-hard. In fact everybody was looking at me, including the four people at the other table.

I casually glanced down at my pants, at my shirt and tie—nothing was open or dirty. Mary was really burning, her face flushed. Glancing around I asked brightly, "I make a funny noise or something?"

Don pointed a slender finger at my shoulder holster and gun. "Guess this is the first time any of us have seen a setup like that—off a TV screen. I assume that's a real gun?"

"Sure is. I'm a detective."

"Wow—a real private eye!" one of the girls at the other table said with what might have been a giggle.

Mary looked as if she wanted to disappear. "Nope, I'm a cop. Detective third grade, attached to the 201st Squad," I said.

An idiotic grin spread over Don's lean face as he dropped his cards, told Mary, "Why didn't you tell me your husband was a real detective?"

Somebody at the other table said, "This is positively delightful," as one of the girls left the table and asked me, "May I look at your badge?"

"Sure," I said, wondering if I was being kidded. I showed her the buzzer. She touched it as if it was a big jewel. "Just a hunk of tin," I added.

They all crowded around me. I was the center of attraction for everybody except the sleeping drunk and Mary. Grace Tills pointed toward my gun, asked, "Mr…. Dave, why are you wearing that? Expecting some trouble here?"

"A cop is supposed to be armed at all times, off duty and on."

"Certainly the last thing you look like is a policeman," a man said, looking me over like a queer. "Have you made many arrests?"

"Whenever I have to. Like asking do you write much copy. It's my job."

Don said, "This is a novelty, talking to a real cop—on a friendly basis." He gave out a silly little laugh, as if he was nervous. "Wake up, Harold."

Grace said, "Let him sleep, he's so coy when he's loaded." She turned to Mary. "You should have brought Dave over long before this. He's terribly interesting."

Mary's face was back to normal color but her mouth was still a tight line. Then she said, "Dave is the youngest detective on the force. He made a very important arrest a few months ago—you remember that psychopath who had killed several women with a piece of pipe? Dave arrested him and was made a detective." Her voice wasn't shrill, she probably felt better now that I was the center of things.

One of the men said, "I followed that case, I get a morbid kick out of reading… That's right, I do recall now, a rookie cop named Wintino. Never connected that—him—with you, Mary. But I should have, odd name."

The girl who had wanted to see my badge asked, "Tell us the truth, is there really much third-degreeing?"

I dropped my cards and shrugged. "I've seen very little of it. But then I haven't been on the force long. There's over twenty thousand men on the force. I suppose there must be more than a few knuckle-happy cops. And sometimes it can't be helped."

"Surely you don't condone such methods?"

"Well," I said slowly, patting my hair—I always get "condone" and "condemn" mixed up in my mind—"it's like this: we have a lot of laws, many of them stupid and far outdated, but they're still on the books. The more laws, the more lawbreakers, the more work for us. And we're always running short on time. Now most crooks are cowards, at least that's what the older cops tell me. These crooks because they are cowards deal in violence and sometimes that same violence, or the threat of it, is the fastest way of making them talk. From my own experience I'd say there's little rough stuff, mostly because it isn't necessary."

"Now look here, Dave," Don said, freshening his drink, "we all know there's police brutality—you might as well admit it."

"There probably are cops who think with their night sticks," I said, "but as I said, from my own experience, I've seen some impatient cops, but that's all. I wouldn't call it brutality."

"Who's on the gate?" the clown on the couch asked but now nobody laughed, they were paying attention only to me.

"How about corruption?" another guy asked me.

I smiled. "Come off it."

"I'm serious. I've read the reports of the Seabury investigation some twenty years ago and that definitely showed—"

"That was long before my time. I can assure you I'm not the captain's bagman, nor have I ever seen such a collector. Sure, there's small cushion some guys go for—a free meal, a few bucks at Christmas, maybe a new tie or hat. And for all I know there may be big payoffs from the rackets, but I've never seen it. A retired cop was shot yesterday while working as a part-time messenger. Does that sound like a guy with a hand in the cracker barrel?"

"Now we all read about traffic ticket scandals, the business with Harry Gross," the guy said.

I tried not to get sore. "You want me to give you newspaper stories or what I know? Let me put it this way: in the short time I've been a working police officer, I haven't even been offered a free sandwich. And if I had I wouldn't have taken it. Hell, there must be some people in the advertising office who are always looking for free theater tickets or a bottle. That doesn't make the whole agency corrupt. Most of the cops I know have a job to do, protecting society, and they try to do it best they can."

Mary was giving me the eye—maybe to shut up. "Are you really protecting society?" Don asked. "Nobody can solve social problems, deep and complex, merely by passing a law. Crime is only the reflection of the sick state of our society and at best a policeman is only a salve when an operation is needed."

I said, "A salve is better than nothing. Take this afternoon when I collared a man trying to—"

"Dave, nobody is interested in such details," Mary said, her voice a shade on the shrill side.

"Oh, but indeed we are," Grace Tills said with a big smile for me. "This is all so wonderful. What happened this afternoon?"

I winked at her. "Is this so wonderful? This afternoon I picked up a jerk in the process of busting into a parked car, trying to lift a coat. The fellow hasn't a record, he's out of work. The car was a Jaguar and the owner could probably afford to lose the coat and the damage to his window. But I can't worry about the social angles. A cop can't be judge and jury, that's when he goes in for rough stuff. It's only a job to me. Maybe this punk was hungry enough to justify robbery but that isn't for me to decide."

"Come now, Dave," the girl who liked my badge said, studying me with what she must have thought were big eyes, "you can't separate yourself from society by saying 'It's my job,' or 'my duty.'"

"It's more than a job in the sense that I'm doing good by preventing other crimes. I mean if there weren't any cops, well, you know. But it's also strictly for pork chops with me, and with you. Suppose you're pushing some towel ads. You never ask whether the cotton was picked by underpaid migrant workers, made in a sweatshop mill, when you sit in your comfortable office and lay out a slick ad," I said, knowing I wasn't saying what I wanted to or making much sense.

"A philosophical cop," one of the men said. "Wonder of wonders."

"No, it isn't a wonder or philosophical or a damn thing but a job with long hours and—"

"Little pay," Mary cut in bitterly.

"And big risks," I said. "If your boss suddenly told you to get out and clean the office windows you'd refuse because you'd be risking your life. Yet for less salary than you're making I'm expected to face guns, knives and fists every day. But even if the pay was good it wouldn't make it a good job because secretly most people hate cops."

"Exactly," the girl with the big eyes said. "Because you do society's dirty work. This man you arrested this afternoon, his resentment isn't against the economic insecurity that made him seek robbery but against you. We need economic equality not night sticks or—"

"Easy, Janice," Grace Tills cut in, "or you'll fall off your soapbox."

"No, no," Janice said eagerly, "I'm only trying to show him the reality of the situation is that police aren't the answer but—"

"The reality of the situation is," I cut in, "that there's a homicide every forty minutes in the U.S.A., a rape every half-hour, an assault every six minutes, and some form of larceny every twenty-six seconds, and when you're the victim you'll be yelling for the police!"

"Lord," Don said, "are those facts?"

"Of course they are," I told him.

"Sounds fantastic," this Janice began, "but that only proves what I—"

Grace Tills put her fingers in her mouth and whistled. She could whistle real good. She held up her hands. "I think it's time we took Dave off the witness stand. Cards, anybody?"

"Almost eleven," a girl who hadn't said anything before said. "Let's stick to drinking. We have to be home by midnight or our Cinderella baby-sitter will sack us. Put the TV on again, there's a soap jingle due on which I hear is sensational."

They all trooped to the bar except me—I just don't like the taste of beer. Janice hurried back with a drink in her right hand and pointed her left at my holster as she said, "It's like being near a snake, same morbid attraction."

"Not good to get too near guns or snakes," I kidded her, watching Mary down a quickie at the bar.

"You and I should talk this out," she said but the soap jingle came on and everybody started chattering about the sales pitch jammed into the thirty-second jingle. The news followed and the commentator suffered from the occupational disease of his calling—self-importance, as though he was making the news instead of parroting it.

I was the only one trying to hear him: I wanted to know who'd won the fight. The TV screen was filled with film shots of the day's news—another conference in Europe, a factory fire, the President playing golf, then a picture of a small room and uniformed cops carrying out a body. I caught one word over the noises in the room. I shouted, "Shut up!... please."

The smooth voice of the commentator was saying, "... and in this dingy room his landlady found Wales' body when he failed to answer her repeated knocks. Police say the retired detective was killed around noon although the landlady didn't discover the body until late this afternoon. One puzzling aspect of the case was a large amount of cash in the dead man's money belt which was untouched. Now, after a word from my sponsor, I'll have the late sport results and the weather for…"

As I put on my coat I told Mary, "I have to get back to the precinct house. Want me to take you home first?"

"Don't worry about me! I'll go home when I'm ready!" she snapped.

"Babes, I have to—"

Don said, "Aren't you being rather melodramatic, Dave old man? Hear about a murder on TV and go dashing out into the night. You really have to go?"

"Melodramatic?" I repeated. "This isn't any play. Wales' partner was killed yesterday and I was on the case. Good night everybody."

Mary ran after me to the door. I asked, "Got cab fare, Babes?"

"I was never so embarrassed in my life!" she whispered. "You had to show off that lousy gun to startle my friends!"

"I wasn't showing off. How was I to know you hadn't told your boon buddies I was a cop. Way you hid it, you'd think I was in the rackets."

"I know you, you did it on purpose, grandstanding!"

"Stop it," I said, opening the door. "Thought you'd like the idea of me being the big attraction tonight—unless you count the juicehound on the couch."

"Attraction? You fool, they were making fun of you! Now you cap it all by rushing off like a child hearing a fire alarm. You're off duty, they can't get in touch with you here, why the—"

"Damn it, Mary, another ex-cop has been gunned. I'm not only on the case but if I'd followed my hunches, Wales might be alive now. Do you need cab fare?"

"We can't even have a decent evening out," Mary said. She was on the verge of crying but held it in. "Just leave me alone!" She turned back toward the others and I walked out. I listened for a moment outside the door—there wasn't any laughter. Mary was all wrong.

I walked around the corner and found myself at a subway entrance. Riding up to the station house I didn't think much about Mary being sore— all lovey-dovey at 6 p.m. and a hot pistol by 11 p.m. Hell with that—Al Wales was dead! That made a monkey out of the robbery theory in Owens' murder, and murder was what it was. My hunch was the correct one—somebody was out to get both men and that could only mean a collar they'd made. Perhaps the killer did a long stretch and just got out. How else could ex-cops make enemies? Instead of horsing around with the Henderson case or writing up a report, if Reed had let me talk to Wales when I asked, the old guy would still be alive now, probably helping me solve the Owens killing.

I reached the precinct house at twenty to twelve. The midnight tour was in the muster room, studying the post condition board and shooting the breeze. The desk lieutenant was a fat slob who'd never heard about the invention of the comb. As I walked in he cracked, "Hey, sonny, where you going? Oh… it's you, Wintino."

The sonofabitch went through this corny routine every time he saw me, which fortunately wasn't often and the patrolmen in the muster room gave it a big yak-yak.

"I came back to get a Popsicle I didn't finish this afternoon, Lieutenant," I said to show the joker I could go along with a gag, even a cornball one.

There were only two men in the detective squad room, a guy built like a football tackle—named Wilson—and a slim, dapper (if you go for herringbone weaves) gray-haired man who was the senior detective on the squad and in charge when Reed wasn't around. He was Tom Landon, the quiet type who always looks bored and never gets excited. He asked, "Got your tours mixed, Dave? What you doing here?"

"Heard on TV about Al Wales being killed."

"Yeah, quite a thing. Eleven thousand bucks in a money belt wrapped around his gut. Shame a man has to kick the bucket with that kind of dough unspent."

"Where's everybody? Where's Lieutenant Reed?"

Landon leaned back in his chair and ran dental floss through his phony teeth—he was always playing with those false choppers. "Home, I guess. Why? Something go wrong in Night Court?"

"No. I thought with this Wales shooting, I mean it proves Owens wasn't in any stick-up, he was deliberately gunned… figured we'd all be working tonight."

"Sure does throw a different light on the Owens thing," Landon said, starting to work on his uppers. "But Wales wasn't killed in this precinct and anyway, Central Office is handling both killings now. I got my paper work to write up before midnight so… Wintino, you actually came here because…? If we wanted you we would have phoned. Beat it."

"We should be working. These two are former cops!"

Landon held the dental floss up toward the light for inspection, dropped it in the waste basket. "Cops die too, like everybody else. Tell me, what were you doing when you heard about Wales?"

"I was at a card party with my wife."

I heard Wilson snicker behind my back as Landon said, "And you dropped everything and came a-running. Dave, why don't you grow up and stop playing cops and robbers?"

"But I had a hunch on Owens all along and if I'd seen Wales today, as I wanted to…"

Landon shook his little head. "Don't take your job home with you, Dave. Leave it in your locker with your walking shoes. What are you made of,

Dave? You have two days off, take your wife to the movies, get high… young fellow like you should be in bed a lot. And never come a-running, they'll get you out of bed often enough. All an eager beaver gets is tired."

"Cut the eager-beaver bull. Owens and Wales are different than an ordinary case and I thought—"

"Why don't you get drunk with your wife and stop thinking so much?" Landon said, turning back to his desk. "And let me finish my work, I'm going home in a few minutes. You ought to do the same."

"Is that an order?" I asked sarcastically.

Landon looked up quickly. "Don't act the snot-nose around me, Dave. Heard you slugged one of the boys today. Okay, you don't have to prove to me you're young and tough and full of ginger. Me, I'm just tired. Now beat it. And that is an order."

I was so damn mad I waited a second before I asked, "Be okay if I do some looking around on my own—on my off days?"

"It's your time, wear your nose down to the bone. Look, Dave, I'm not eating you out. I'm just busy and in a hurry to get home and get my sleep. Sure, look around if you like, only take it easy, don't get in the hair of those super-sleuths downtown, the glory hounds."

I suddenly felt let down as though all the air had gone out of me. "Sorry I blew up, Tom. Just that… two retired cops… Hell, guy can't help thinking that it could be me, in time."

"Nobody is goofing on the case, so don't worry about it. You got to learn how to unwind, Dave. That's as important as getting steam on."

I started for the door, stopped. "What's the latest dope on Wales?"

"He was shot with a .22 through the right eye, at short range. Whole side of his face has flash burns. Must have used a silencer. There were two other men in the rooming house at the time, one asleep, one reading in bed— they say they didn't hear a thing. Wales hadn't been to work today so he must have been sleeping off a drunk when he got it. Medical Examiner places it around noon. Nothing was touched. Wales was fully dressed, probably passed out in bed. Maybe the killer didn't know about the money belt and the eleven grand. So far, no leads, no prints—nothing. Now go home and let me finish up."

"I suppose they're checking the arrest record and—"

"Central Office boys know their business."

"Hell of a way for a couple of good cops to end," I said, making for the door.

Landon nodded. "Wales was especially good. This isn't out yet, so keep it damn quiet, Dave. They found a .38 Smith & Wesson that belonged to Wales in his room. Ballistics says it's the gun that killed Owens."

Thursday Morning

We had a rough night. Mary came home half-bagged, which didn't help my mood. Then I stupidly told her what had happened at the precinct and she said, "The boy wonder got his prat booted home where it belongs. And you had to dash out like a fool, before my friends."

"Your friends keep up their clever conversation, did they ever find out who was on the gate?" I asked, and we took it from there.

I couldn't even keep up with her, most of my mind was busy trying to figure why Al Wales shot his partner. After a while Mary fell off and I stared at the darkness and nothing made sense. Wales had said a crime was like an iceberg. This one was sure hidden, needed a lot of spadework. Two old coots, friends and partners for nearly a quarter of a century and when they're both hanging around, taking it easy before they die, one kills the other. And Al Wales, dressing like he was warming the buffalo on a nickel and eleven grand in his kick. I went to sleep full of questions—and not a single answer.

Mary was up at eight and had the same record on: namely I was the all-American jerk and she hoped last night would teach me a lesson and be sure and see Uncle Frank today and where in hell were the aspirins.

I didn't get up to have breakfast with her, stayed in bed and thought about a cop killing his partner. What would Danny Hayes have to do for me to kill him? When Mary took off I got up and made the bed back into a couch, had some orange juice. I felt lousy, restless and blue. For no reason I put on old slacks, army shoes, a sweatshirt and a long sport shirt to cover my gun in a belt holster, and decided to do some roadwork. I walked over to Central Park and trotted around the reservoir, throwing punches like a pug. I enjoy exercise and the clean air in my lungs seemed to drive away the blues. But when I reached the west side of the reservoir I suddenly stopped—what the hell was I training for? I wasn't a would-be pug anymore but a detective and I'd already wasted too much time. I was on my own these two days, and could devote all my time to the case. I walked over to Central Park West and took a subway to Brooklyn. I had two addresses I wanted to check.

The first was out in the Fort Hamilton section and I walked past rows of old two-story private houses that reminded me of the Owens dump, till I stopped before a shingle house with a tiny garden and a busted picket fence in front. The house looked pretty seedy—it was clean and recently painted, but soap and paint won't hold a house together. There were two doorbells, two battered old-style mailboxes. Neither had the name Kahn, Sal Kahn's mother. I rang the downstairs bell. A frightful biddy answered the door. A fat sausage wrapped in a dirty pink housecoat, her face powdered a dead white with *zigzag* lightening eyebrows and lipstick an inch wide around her mouth, like a circus clown. Her thin, frizzled hair was too red and the powder on her puss seemed to accent the wrinkles. She had two flashy rings on her fingers and a thin marriage band. Didn't seem possible a guy had ever married this bag. She said, "Yes, sonny?" and smiled.

The smile was the clincher. She didn't have any teeth and when that red smear opened it was a shock—a deep gash across her face. "Are you the owner of the house?"

"All that the mortgage company doesn't own," she said, her small eyes growing cautious. "What's it to you, sonny?" She spoke pretty clearly without teeth.

I didn't mind the "sonny." With a sport shirt and slacks on I did look like a big fifteen. "Can you tell me where I can find a Mrs. Kahn?"

The gash opened wide as she shrieked, "Martha Kahn? The Lord rest her soul, she's been at peace six years now. You related?"

"Yeah, a distant cousin. I'm in New York for a few days with… uh… our school basketball team. Thought I'd look the family up."

"And you didn't know Martha was dead? Why…" The over-red mouth clamped down. "You from the California branch of the family?"

"No, ma'am, from the Michigan branch."

"That's good. When I bought this house from Martha just before she died, while she was so sick, I kept writing them in California to send someone here to look after the old woman. Not a peep out of them. But don't you know, soon as she died they had a lawyer here johnny-on-the-spot claiming the estate. And them acting so snooty to Martha just because of that old trouble."

"You mean about Uncle Sal?" I asked carefully.

"Indeed I do. Like I kept telling poor Martha, what that had to do with her I couldn't see. But those smug sisters of hers out in Los Angeles—well!"

"Of course Uncle Sal was before my time and I'm a distant relation, but I remember hearing about him. Went to jail, didn't he?"

"Died in the electric chair, he did!" the biddy said, her voice full of enjoyment at finding a new listener for old gossip. "Got himself in trouble during Prohibition, but then everybody was making bootleg booze. You can bet I used my tub for something besides taking a bath. Sal was just unlucky, got hisself mixed up with gangsters, had to kill one."

"Did you know Uncle Sal?"

There was a slight drawing up of a lot of flabby bosom. "Me? I did not. Martha didn't buy this house till many years after her son died. But she told me lots about him. Always good to his mother, a fine son."

"I'm not up much on this line of the family. Are there any other members around here?"

"They're all in California, well-off I hear, but wouldn't ever send Martha a Christmas card or nothing, on account of Sal's trouble. She never told me of any family in… where did you say?"

"Michigan. Mother was some kind of cousin to Mr. Kahn's brother-in-law. Pretty complicated. Was Uncle Sal her only child?"

"Sure was, not counting two miscarriages before Sal. Poor Martha, husband dead, son dead, and her sick and alone and those snooty relatives out there in the sunshine never sending her a card. You can bet she always remembered them with cards. Wasn't for the money she got, she'd have starved."

"If she owned this fine house she must have been comfortable."

The gash opened wide. "Hummp! First of every month, regular as the calendar, there was a registered letter with two hundred dollars—always ten twenty-dollar bills. I know. The last few months when the poor woman was confined to her bed and only had me to look after her, she opened the letters and I saw the money. But she never would say who it was from."

"Maybe from California?"

"In a pig's… eye! I did notice the return addresses on the last two letters being I had to sign for them. Different names and addresses and both of them phony. Yes, sir. I was such a decent friend to poor Martha I went over to each address, figuring might be a relation who could look after Martha. First time wasn't no such street number, next time wasn't no such party. I asked Martha and she says she had no idea who did send her the money, it just came regular for years."

"Sounds strange, you'd think she'd know who was sending her money," I said.

Baggy nodded. "Ask me, she once told me Sal had a partner in his business but Sal didn't see no sense involving him in this trouble. Ask me, I'd bet this here partner maybe agreed to look after Martha if Sal didn't talk. Yes, sir."

"Didn't Aunt Martha know who this partner was?"

"Said she never knew."

"The letters stop when Aunt Martha died?"

"Sure, soon as the postman returned the next one as deceased, they stopped."

"Can you recall the two false names and addresses you mentioned? Or the name of Aunt Martha's doctor?"

"Now that was over six years ago and… Say, you ask a lot of questions for a kid." The clown mouth became a rough, heavy line as she stepped back and slammed the door, shouting, "I bet a fat dollar you're the son of one of them California bitches! Scoot before I take a broom to you!"

I walked back toward the subway, stopped for a cup of coffee and toast, picked up a paper and read about Wales. He made the fifth page. There were pictures of him and Owens, taken years ago, and nothing I didn't know in the news story. I had a second cup of java and a hunk of pie which was pretty good.

Two hundred dollars a month, $2,400 a year for Mrs. Kahn, over how many years? Somebody had to be in an awful tight spot or grateful as hell to shell out that kind of dough. And it would have to be a big operator to pay that sort of green. Wales? What would he be grateful for? What could old lady Kahn possibly have on him? Maybe the biddy was only repeating gossip, had the story screwy? I wondered if it was worth while going back and flashing my shield at her. But I had a hunch she'd told me all she knew.

I made some notes in my book, decided against more pie, and left. The other address was the garage where Sal ran his still, where he killed Boots Brenner in 1930. This was in another part of Brooklyn and traveling in Brooklyn is like going over a giant obstacle course. After I'd paid three car-fares I was getting low on money—I'd been so sore at Mary I hadn't asked her for a couple of bills—so I flashed my badge in the last bus. The baldy driver asked, "Young to be a cop, aren't you?"

"See the badge, don't you?" I said, walking by him and sitting down.

So a couple of blocks later this billiard-ball-head stops the bus to call over a beefy beat patrolman. I was embarrassed as hell and stepped off the bus with him rather than cause more of a scene. I showed him my badge and Police Benevolent Association card, pulled back my shirt so he could see my gun. He said, "I don't want to make no mistakes, one way or the other. First off you hand me your gun, butt first, all nice and easy. Then I'll put through a call at my box and we'll see. You do look young and short but no hard feelings if I'm wrong. Understand?"

I handed this big bum my gun, telling him, "Be careful it doesn't go off and you shoot yourself." I gave him a dime and told him to save time by using a regular phone to call my precinct. When he finally got Reed on the phone and described me they must have made some crack because the big dumb ox laughed and said, "Looked more like he'd be packing a zip gun than a badge. Thank you, Lieutenant." I knew the ribbing I was in for when I reported back to duty.

The cop gave me my gun, said he was sorry but I must have stood on my toes when I took the physical.

"That's right. And I borrowed my old man's beard too. Look, maybe you can do me some good for a change. Know how to get to this address?"

"You aren't three blocks from it. Dye plant. On my beat when I'm working radio car. Good people at Christmas.”

"Dye plant? Was it ever a garage?”

"I been in this precinct for five years and it's been a dye plant all that time. New building. I think before that it was an empty lot and a ruin. Tell you, Detective”—he stumbled over the word—"seems to me I heard a kid was hurt playing in the old building years ago and they had to put a watchman in. An old duffer in the neighborhood. Still works as a night watchman for the dye company. Old George Davis. He might be able to tell you about it being a garage. Anything important?”

"Naw, checking a reference. Where's this Davis fellow?”

"When you get to the dye plant keep going a block. You'll see an old brown house that looks like a good wind would carry it away. Can't miss it; same side of the street. Old George lives there. Be working in his garden now. Doesn't hit the sack till noon.”

I said thanks and walked away, knowing the big cluck was staring after me with a puzzled look in his dumb eyes.

The dye plant was one of these one-story efficient-looking buildings, all spick and span. It had glass-brick windows and air conditioning, looked like a big outfit.

The old brown house was exactly that and air-conditioned in a different way. It sat back from the sidewalk with a whitewashed flagpole in the center of a small lawn just starting to look green. I followed a broken walk around the house to a large garden. A plump old gent with a fat nose and a shabby derby on a lot of gray hair was digging up the ground with a pitchfork. He had on a worn flannel shirt and his old work pants were held up by wide fireman's suspenders. He was stinking up the sunshine with a battered pipe.

"Mr. Davis?”

He nodded.

I showed my badge as I told him, "Detective Dave Wintino, 201st Squad. And I've had about all the cracks I want about my looking young. If you can spare a few minutes, I'd like to chat with you.”

"I got plenty of time,” he said and his voice had a kind of whine you find in lots of big old men. "It's a fact you look young. What's this all about?” He leaned on the pitchfork the way a real farmer does—I guess.

"You remember when the dye plant was an empty garage and a vacant lot?”

"Sure do. I was always for raising tomatoes in that lot but between the kids playing ball and the rocky soil I got no place.”

"Were you around when they had the shooting in the lot?”

He patted his crazy hat. "Sure was. I mean I wasn't at the actual shooting or when they found the body, but I was there when the cops were. Now that was way back in nineteen—"

"Nineteen-thirty."

He nodded. "Yep and times was real bad. Garage had been standing empty maybe two, three years when one day I seen two men working in it. Never knew exactly what they was doing, all very quiet. So didn't surprise me none when it turned out they was bootlegging. Sometimes when I'd be working my tomatoes in the lot on Sundays, or late in the afternoons, I'd see them. The one they killed in prison and the other."

"The other—what did he look like?"

Davis re-lit his pipe before he said, "One thing I got to hand you cop fellows, you never give up. Like I told that other detective, it's been a—"

"What other detective?"

"Tall one that was handling the case. Even after they give the fellow the chair and the garage was just an old building with busted windows—them darn kids around here—why, every now and then this dick would still come around and look through the building. Although there wasn't anything to see that I knew of."

"Was the detective named Owens or Wales?"

"Hard to say, I'm not much on names. Fact is, I'm around here a good deal, always have been. Some men like bars and shows, me—give me a hunk of ground. Even while the trial was going on and then when the one man was waiting to go in the chair, many is the time I'd see this detective just sitting in his car, watching the empty garage. Thought to myself, it don't make sense to…"

I opened the paper to the story on Wales' death, showed him the two pictures. He touched Wales' photo with his pipe. "That's him. He used to talk to me a good deal, at first. Kept asking like you just did, what this other bootlegger looked like, the one they never did catch on with. Like I say, they was pretty quiet about what they was doing, so I only saw him maybe a few times. Slim young fellow with dark hair and a thin mustache. Always wearing sunglasses, even when it was a dull day. Of course I ain't so sure of this now—it was twenty-six years ago."

"Yeah, too long ago," I said, trying to think. "How often did Wales come out to look at the garage, or watch it?"

Davis shifted his feet on the pitchfork. "Hard to say. For a time seemed like he was there every time I turned around. Of course now I had a kind of job, so I couldn't say if he was there during the day or not. After a time, a few years, we didn't talk much, just nod at each other. Sometimes he'd ask if I'd seen anybody around searching the place. I never did. That was right before the war when a kid fell through the rotten floor and got hurt, when they took me on as watchman to keep the brats from—"

"Wait a minute," I cut in. "Before the war—you mean Wales was still snooping around here in 1941, almost a dozen years after the killing?"

"Yep, he was around up till the time they tore it down. Not so often, I'd see him one day and maybe not again for a month or more. He'd step inside and tell me to go out and look at my plants. But sometimes I'd watch him through a busted window—he'd be standing in the center of the garage and stare at the walls for a long time. Only looking. After a while he'd go to one wall or corner, start hunting. Was nothing in there, the police took out all the machinery when they made the arrest. Building was torn down in 1946 but on account of the shortage of building materials they couldn't start building again till… oh… I'd say it was 1949, when they put up the dye plant. Took me on as watchman again, fine people to work for too."

"Wales say anything when they took the old garage down?"

"No, sir, he'd given up by then."

"Can you recall when he gave up?"

"Just about. It was early in '46, say around April. I remember because I told him about the building coming down and he slipped me a few bucks, says I should go to the movies, take the day off. He said he'd be there all day. I didn't go to no movie, I went home and went to bed. Like I said, he wasn't the kind of man to talk much. Around six in the evening I come back and he says, 'Now they can knock this wreck down. I'm done.' I says to him, 'You find what you been looking for?' And he give me a blank look and asks, 'Who says I was looking for anything?' One thing, he wasn't carrying a package or anything when he left."

"He could have put a bag in his car while you were in the sack."

"Nope, he didn't have his car that day. Remember because it was raining hard and I watched him walking all the way over to Eastland Avenue to catch a trolley. Tell you the truth, youngster, I kind of poked around myself at times, thought maybe it was money these bootleggers might have hidden. But I gave it up after a couple looks. Like I said, wasn't nothing but four rotten walls. Didn't see the paper today, what's this Wales done now?"

"He was shot to death. Pops, did you ever see the other man, this Owens, poking around here? He was a detective too."

"No, just Wales. Don't recall the other face. 'Course at the time of the shooting, whole block was full of detectives. Trampling all over my tomato plants. Why did Wales shoot hisself?"

"He didn't, he was murdered," I said, jotting down the dates in my notebook.

"Murdered? All you read about these days. I say these teenagers should be given a taste of the strap and then—"

"I want you to do me a favor, don't talk about this. Don't even tell anybody you remember Wales. You see what you've just told me can be nothing, then again it might help us solve Wales' murder."

"I won't say a mumbling word. Don't want to get mixed up in nothing. Not me. Say I sure got to read the morning paper now."

I wanted to tell him to keep his trap shut even if that beat cop happened to ask what I wanted, but that might make the old boy suspicious of me. I wrote my name and the squad phone on a notebook page, gave it to him. "If you think of anything else, even if it doesn't seem important, but anything you haven't told me—*anything*— give me a ring. If I'm not there, leave a number where I can reach you. Got a phone?"

"I only room here, with my grandson, but they got a phone. And you can call me at the dye plant all during the night. I'll think about it, maybe I can recall something. But it was a long time ago."

"Anybody eke around here who might remember the killing?"

He shook his head, almost proudly. "Nope, I'm about the last of the old-timers here. That's because I drink two full glasses of buttermilk every morning before I—"

"Well, thanks for your time. And not a word, not even to your grandson or son."

"My boy was killed in the war. I live with my daughter's boy. Now don't you give it no worry, not a word out of me. And I'll phone you quick if I think of anything. Ain't had nobody to phone in years."

On the subway ride back to the apartment I felt swell. I had a lot of pieces that would fit into one picture damn soon. And then Landon and Reed and the rest of the squad would know who was a snot-nosed kid.

I thought about getting off and taking a look at Wales' room. But downtown would certainly have covered that, and then the way I was dressed—a sweatshirt.

I got home before noon and had some eggs and went over my notes, still thinking of seeing Wales' room.

The gun had never been found in the Brenner killing. Was that what Wales was looking for? But why keep looking for it sixteen years after the shooting? And when he did find it, what? There had been nothing in the arrest record about finding the gun. Did he think the rod might convict Kahn's missing partner, this Bird? Or was Al Wales hunting because he felt Kahn was innocent? But then why keep looking years after Kahn burnt?

It didn't have to be the gun—buried money wasn't a bad angle. Brenner wouldn't have muscled in unless there was plenty of loot, and that would account for the dough Wales had on him. But Wales was a good cop and would have reported the money if... A good cop who shot down his partner!

The thing to do was let what I had jell, maybe dig deeper into Sal Kahn's past. I had the feeling my hunch was hot and in time... The phone rang.

I picked it up, expecting Mary to say she was sorry for being a bitch. "Mr. David Wintino?" It was a woman's voice and vaguely familiar.

"Talking."

"This is Rose Henderson. Hope you don't mind my calling you at home. I looked you up in the book."

"I don't mind. What's up?"

"I waited and then phoned your police station twice for an escort. They tell me they can't spare a man today."

"They're very busy."

"But this will mean the second day I've lost. That's exactly what *they* want. If I miss my deadline the article might be postponed for months. You promised I'd have an escort today and now you—"

"Have any trouble since yesterday?" I asked, in my mind seeing her curled up in the red camp chair, the full curve of her stomach I wanted so much to poke with my little finger. And if I hadn't been bothering with her, I might have seen Wales and saved… No, he was already shot by then.

"Yes, there was a phone call at 2:20 a.m. No answer when I picked up the receiver. This is driving me to a breakdown. I feel like a prisoner. All I need is a few more days of research and I could wind things up. You told me I'd have—"

"Listen to me carefully. It's seven after twelve. I'll be in front of your house at one. Where did you plan to go this afternoon?"

"To the Forty-second Street Library."

"Okay. Exactly at one leave your house. Walk over to Broadway and down to the IRT subway. Get off at Times Square and walk toward the library. Keep on the downtown side of the street. I'll be following you but don't ever look for me—that would tip them off. Even if you're pushed around, unless it's real trouble, I won't step in. Idea is I want to make whoever is shadowing you. Remember, don't act self-conscious and don't look around for me. If you should see me, act as if you don't know me. Got that?"

"I think so. One sharp… IRT… downtown side of the street."

"Now, after you finish at the library, go back to your place the same way—downtown side of Forty-second Street to the IRT. How long do you need in the library?"

"At least four hours."

"That's too long. You stay an hour, at exactly two you leave, side entrance, and wait at home till I either call or drop in. That may not be for a brace of hours. We all set? One o'clock on the nose."

"Yes. And thank you."

I took a fast cold shower and started to dress—tropical suit, open dusty-gray sport shirt, and new socks. I put some oil on my hair and gave it a good brushing, then combed it carefully. I should be looking over Wales' room but I'd only be eaten out by the downtown brass. And unless I took a breather from what I'd found out this morning, I'd get stale on the case. And this would take only a few hours.

I checked my pockets, made sure my hair didn't look oily, and took off. I was planted on her street corner by seven minutes before one. I stopped kidding myself, I should damn well be spending this time working on Wales' background. But I didn't feel too bad about it—I felt swell.

I wanted to see Rose again.

Thursday Afternoon

Exactly at one she came out of her house wearing a neat red suit which wasn't for her—it didn't do much to her chunky figure. She held a large paper folder and a pocketbook under her left arm. I watched the doorways, the parked cars, but couldn't make anybody shadowing her as she slowly walked toward Broadway. I stayed a half a block behind and on the other side of the street. We reached the subway okay and I still didn't see any tail. Rose looked herself over in a gum machine mirror without glancing at me. There were only three other people besides us on the platform and seven people in the subway car. I didn't bother with the people in the car—a good tail wouldn't be riding in the same car. I kept my eyes on Rose, as if I was a stud on the make looking her over… and she looked fine: the dark hair, the sullen hot mouth, the strong figure. Even if nothing happened, it was a good way of killing a few hours. I wondered if Rose's friends would ask if I was a corrupt goon?

We walked along Forty-second Street on opposite sides of the street. Alongside Bryant Park they got her. There was a tall wiry guy who fell in behind her—did it fast then slowed down. He was about thirty-five, wearing a new coconut palm hat and one of these corny gray flannel suits, as if sure it made him look the executive type.

Coming toward her was a lumpy joker built like a fat football player, dressed in an old plain brown suit and no hat on his noggin, baldness giving his thin hair a horseshoe shape.

He seemed to be reading a letter. They were damn good. The guy back of Rose closed in and lumpy in front of her walked into Rose. He knocked her backward against wiry who neatly hit the folder and pocketbook out from under her arm as he caught her. The papers and the pocketbook landed in the gutter which a sanitation truck had sprinkled a few minutes before.

Beefy boy was all apologies while wiry pointed to his ankle, rubbed it, and said something to Rose—probably told her to watch where she was walking. Bully boy even picked up her wet papers, "accidentally" stepping on her purse. He handed the stuff to her, fat puss still full of apology.

I'd read about rough-shadowing but this was the first time I'd ever seen it. A two-hundred-and-fifty pound lump walking into you is a rugged wallop. Rose seemed shaken but not hurt. She continued on to the library while horseshoe head went over toward Broadway. I followed him wishing I'd had Danny with me to tail the wiry joker. But if I'd called Danny on his day off he would have given me a stiff ha-ha.

Bully boy took his time walking up Broadway, window-shopping in a couple of *shlock* stores, stopping for an orange drink. He turned into an office building and we both went into the same elevator. The light panel said there were sixteen floors. When he called out, "Ten," I said, "Eleven."

I walked downstairs to the tenth floor and looked around. There were fourteen offices on the floor but fortunately a big rug outfit took up six doors. I narrowed it down to three offices, two of them without names on the doors, and one with DATA, INC. in small black letters.

I walked into DATA, INC. ready to give them a bull yarn if I was wrong. It was quite an office. I wasn't wrong.

It was narrow with a desk, phone, typewriter and two file cabinets as you entered. Then it opened into two cubbyhole offices—one was a regular office and the other had a work bench, tools and a stack of electrical gadgets.

Bully was hanging up the receiver and he stood up as he asked, "What you want, boy?"

I spread my feet as he stepped toward me, met him with a perfect left hook above his belt buckle. He let out a gasping, hissing scream as he slid to the floor, gave up the orange drink. The wiry character came out of his office on the run, coat off. He led a sucker right: it was a feint and his left banged the side of my face. I missed a left to his gut because his blow knocked me backward, but I blocked another right and kicked him on the knee. He cursed, limped back till he hit a chair, sat down, rubbing his leg.

The side of my face was numb and when I took my hand, away it had blood—the smart bastard was wearing a heavy ring. Fatso was still moaning on the floor. I stepped away from his big feet as wiry gave me a hard look, said, "You're in trouble, kid, I'm a detective."

"What trouble? I came in and before I can open my yap this lump starts pushing and swinging on me."

Wiry reached for his back pocket. It looked too flat for a gun or knife but I told him, "Take it slow or you'll be on the floor too."

He got a wallet out, flashed one of these gold private dick badges the state gives you with your license. He stood up, painfully, still rubbing his knee with his long left hand. "I said trouble and I mean it. You'd better come up with a good story and fast. What you doing here?"

"Maybe working my way through reform school. Put that hunk of gold plate away before you scratch yourself. I have a real one." I pushed my coat back so he could see my badge on my belt, and part of my shoulder holster.

Fatty stopped moaning and stared up at me and then over at his chum, whose expression could best be called thoughtful. He said, "My name is Frank Flatts and I'm a licensed and bonded private investigator. I'm asking you to identify yourself."

"Detective David Wintino, 201st Squad. That okay, investigator? Tell lardass to get up slowly and behave himself."

"I'd like to see your badge again."

"Sure." I held my coat open and he copied down my number on a phone pad, along with my name, asked, "What precinct was that again?"

"Two hundred and first. And this act makes me simply shake in my pants."

"I'm within my legal rights in asking for identification," Flatts said. "Is this an arrest?"

"You certainly are within your legal rights. And deliberately jostling a person might be within your rights too—except it's breaking the Penal Law."

Flatts grinned, maybe he was relieved. He said, "So that's it. Come into my office and let's talk about this."

"Your office is too small for the three of us to be comfortable. Talk here."

Fatty got to his feet and sat down at his desk. Flatts limped over to the workshop, brought out a stool, asked, "Have a seat?"

"Why not? Let's keep things on a polite level," I told him, laughing at myself for sounding like one of last night's bridge players. I sat on the stool and Flatts found a chair. I wiped my cheek with a handkerchief. It wasn't much of a cut but still bleeding.

Flatts said, "Sorry I bruised you, Wintino, but you came busting into my office and—"

"My story is I was pushed before I had a chance to say a word. Baldy is good at pushing."

"This is my associate, Mr. Tasman. I think we should get down to cases, I have a busy afternoon ahead of me."

"More women to jostle?" I asked.

"If you are referring to the young woman, that was an accident. I don't go in for rough stuff."

"You don't? What was that, a feel?"

"Perhaps you don't realize it, few people do, but the modern private investigator is a long way removed from the popular version of the private eye, or even from the old-time investigator. I don't go in for rough stuff, or guard work, and rarely take a criminal case. We are essentially a business service. Our work is in the nature of research, we supply businessmen with information about their competitors. And we use the most advanced scientific methods. Electronics has replaced the gun, the—"

"Too warm for a lecture. What are you trying to sell me, Flatts?"

"Simply that striking you was the first time I've hit anybody since I was a college student. And the first time I've been hit—or rather kicked. I want you to clearly understand you're dealing with respectable businessmen not goons."

"I knew that. That was some very respectable rough-shadowing you did put there."

"Let me also enlighten you about the law. Section 7228 of the Penal Law was passed against pickpockets and specifically defines jostling as a crime only if it is done for the purpose of picking a pocket or purse. As for the young lady, we never saw her before she walked into me. I assumed it was an accident on her—"

"Stop it, you're getting my shoes dirty. You've been annoying her on the phone, making inquiries at her apartment house, and pushing her around on the street. I know all about the article she's writing and the four companies that hired you."

Flatts gave me a cool smile. "I haven't the smallest idea of what you're talking about. Let me remind you again that making inquiries is not breaking any law. And I doubt if you can prove any of your other allegations. There's one more point I didn't reach in my lecture, as you so quaintly termed it. I couldn't operate in my business without a lot of connections. I'm not threatening you, understand, but you do look very young to be a detective. But in a uniform, pounding a beat, I'd say you would look far more natural. Now I'm asking you for the second time, are you here to arrest me?"

"I didn't even say I was here as a police officer. You pulled a badge first. Matter of fact I'm off duty. Let's say I'm here, at the moment, as a citizen who is a friend of Miss Henderson."

Tasman suddenly spoke up, grunted, "Don't you know she's a Spick, her real name is Hondura?"

"Lardy, I don't like my friends called Spicks. And for a girl you claim you never saw before you certainly know a lot about her." I stood up. "Let's stop the chatter. This isn't an official visit, although Miss Henderson has made a complaint with the precinct. If you annoy her once more I'll return and run you both in for disorderly conduct and/or jostling—let a judge determine the law."

"The law states—" Flatts began.

"You've already hit a cop."

"In self-defense," Flatts chimed in fast. "And I have a witness."

"Even in self-defense it might not be healthy for you and your witness around the precinct house. I'm giving it to you straight: Stick to your phone taps and the rest of your 'legitimate' crap. Lay off Miss Henderson or I'll scramble your features." I started for the door.

"Are you threatening me, Wintino?" Flatts called out.

"Yeah. I'm telling you both to stop it or I'll work you over."

Flatts cupped one ear. "What did you say?"

"That I'll beat the slop out of you if you keep annoying Miss Henderson. Did you hear that or do you want a free sample?"

I turned toward him and he flicked his hand at the desk, must have turned on a switch, that cold smile engraved on his wise-guy face. The office was suddenly filled with a playback of our conversation. I was astonished at how shrill my voice sounded. I said loudly, above the recording, "It still goes. You'll be listening to that in a hospital!"

I headed for the door again as Flatts cut the playback, said, "I trust you have strong arches, Wintino."

Tasman got to his feet as I passed him. I put my open hand against his big face and pushed, sending him back into his chair. I told him, "Don't bother to get up," and walked out.

I was so angry I couldn't think straight—falling for a clumsy feint like that right hand. It wasn't two yet so I took the subway down to the moldy-domed monstrosity they call Headquarters Building, went up to Criminal Identification and got a yellow sheet on Sal Kahn. He didn't have much of a record. Collared in a raid on a dice joint in '26 and spent two months on Rikers Island. He'd been pinched once for simple assault, charge dismissed for lack of evidence. In '29 he'd been picked up as the owner of a speedboat riddled during a rum-running chase up the Hudson, but never came up for trial. Of course the last rap was the shooting in 1930.

I walked along Centre Market Place, the narrow block behind Headquarters, window-shopped the gunsmith and police tailor stores in the ground floor of the tenements. Then just to say I'd been there, I went across the street to have coffee and a sandwich in Flanagan's, where the brass eats. There was a beefy-acting lieutenant who'd given us lectures on narcotics at Detective Training School sitting by himself. He motioned for me to come over. I was surprised he remembered my name—I couldn't think of his.

We chewed the fat for a while. I asked what was new on Wales and he said far as he knew nothing, they hadn't been able to pick up a single decent lead or even a thin motive. I asked if he'd ever heard of Data, Inc. and he hadn't. I told him a little about the run-in I had with them, but didn't mention hitting them.

He took a toothpick from his vest pocket and as he jabbed at his teeth he said, "Got to be careful with these birds, Dave. In their line they need pull, and not only around City Hall, but up in Albany and in Washington. You see, there isn't much work in the private snoop racket, so the ones that are able to get something going have to be able to supply all kinds of inside information or close shop. That means they must have connections. But you don't have to worry, the last thing these guys want is publicity. Be different if you belted the guy, but from what you tell me he's bluffing you. What you got there, a boil on your cheek?"

When I left Flanagan's I thought about visiting Uncle Frank, asking him to talk to his "rabbi," as the boys called the club leaders—and I've never been able to figure if the slang name has an anti-Semitic whack or not. But I wasn't in any mood to argue with Frank about his job offer. In fact I didn't know what to do with myself: this Flatts guy made me restless—I had a feeling he might be able to put me back in uniform. My big mouth and that tape recording. Wales said I talked too much.

Wales—I had started out in the morning like a ball of fire and that had petered out. His watching the garage all those years had to mean something but I was stopped. Now if I could really shakedown his room, talk to everybody in the rooming house, I might come up with a lead. Fat chance of downtown letting me stick my nose in. Hell, maybe they hadn't even gone through Owens' house yet. Nuts, who was I to tell Central Bureau how to work? I'd really be acting like a kid.

I took the subway uptown and rang Rose's bell. After giving me the eye through the door peeper she let me in, She was wearing a kind of purple cotton slack outfit that could have passed for pajamas. As always she gave me the feeling of a firecracker waiting for a match. We both sat on the couch and she asked if I'd seen what had happened and I told her about following the guy to Data, Inc., and that I thought she wouldn't be bothered any more. The couch was comfortable and I thought it was nice of Rose to dress for me, wear this faint perfume. And suddenly I felt very tired, all that silly roadwork, then rushing around Brooklyn, then running downtown. My head was tired from worrying so much, about Wales and about Mary and now about my job. I wanted to stop thinking for a while.

Rose fingered the cut on my cheek, her hands light and soothing as she washed it with some stuff. I told her not to bother and I was so comfortable I damn near dozed off. She told me, "Don't ever take chances like that again. You look so small, although I imagine you're tough enough to take care of yourself."

"Don't worry, I can take care of myself."

"I can't tell you how much I appreciate this. I don't know why I called you at home. But I was so angry and when they said you weren't at the police station, why I—"

"This is my day off," I said, closing my eyes. Her perfume made Rose seem very close.

"Oh, I'm sorry. Why didn't you tell me? I never would have asked you to work."

"Doesn't matter, I was stewing around the house anyway, wanted to get out," I said, half-aloud. "Getting so I can't stand our place. My wife is always hitting on me. She doesn't like my being a cop."

"She must be afraid you'll get hurt."

"Guess that's part of it. But she doesn't like the hours, the pay, the kind of work. She wants me to have some hot-air office job. What she doesn't understand is my job has a kind of purpose and value no other job has. Even the cop just standing on the corner is doing something, a symbol, a warning. But maybe she's right, it hasn't a big future. She still thinks if you work hard you get ahead, make the big buck."

Rose laughed. "And as the old joke goes, marry the boss's daughter."

I tried to nod, but it was too much effort. "In my case I've already married the boss's niece. Her uncle has some crummy job for me in his joint. The thing is, Mary and me, we can't even talk about it without clawing. I don't know…" I kept mumbling on and on, sitting there with my head against the wall in a daydream, telling Rose about how I met Mary, her family, and all the rest of it. Must have been something I'd wanted to get off my chest, I talked and talked.

The next thing I knew she was shaking me gently. I sat up and opened my eyes. She was giving me the big eyes, an almost sad smile on her cute face. "Would you like something to drink?"

I shook my head and yawned, reached up to straighten my hair. "Heat must have me. Have I been dozing long?" My coat was wrinkled.

"About ten minutes. I have some beer, or would you rather have orange juice?"

"Orange juice will do the trick. I feel like a slob, spilling my troubles all over you."

She went to her tiny refrigerator and poured two glasses of juice, squeezed a lime in them. "I don't mind. As a writer I'm curious about such problems…. The truth is we all actually enjoy hearing the other person's troubles. That enjoyment is the root of all gossip. I wish I could help you, could give you advice, but I'm hardly the one."

Handing me a glass she sat down again. I said, "I didn't mean to talk about it. Slipped out."

"I'm not married, never have been, yet I can't understand what you told me. I suppose I have naïve and romantic ideas about marriage, but for me a husband and a wife should be a separate little world of their own.

Nothing on the outside should be able to touch that world. I'm not that simple I don't know poverty can shatter anything, but aside from real poverty, I can't picture anything penetrating this inner world of understanding. But to start with it has to be two-sided, a complete sense of give and take."

I drank most of the juice. It was cold and the lime hit me like a shot, woke me up. "I think I get what you mean. And at times I tell myself I am inconsiderate, but then so is she. All boils down to my job. Maybe she's right about it not being the best job in the world for me, maybe I would be a whiz-bang at something else. But still, it's *my* job, it's the only thing I know and I like it. That's what she can't understand: it's more than a job to me, it's something I like. Would *you* care if *your* husband was a cop?"

She shook her head and leaned against the wall, resting the juice glass on that fine curve of her belly. "I wouldn't like him to."

"Why?"

She was looking at me through half-shut eyes as she said, "Let's not go into my reasons now. But that wouldn't matter. This private world of understanding I think of, it would have to be a world of small compromises too. In short, he has to be the only man I want and I must be the only woman he wants, and I truly mean want. For such prizes one must make concessions. No, I wouldn't want my husband to be a hunter of men, a walking club, but if that is what he honestly wants and feels, well… there's that wonderful saying about we all can't be in step and each of us must march to the music he hears."

"What makes you think cops are walking clubs?" I asked, finishing the juice and getting up.

"Let's not talk about that, we'll just get into an argument. I didn't mean it as anything personal—and I hate that stupid phrase. But to a colonial the police usually are…" She stood up and gave me the smile. "I don't want to argue with you. It would be rude; you've been so very nice to me—and nice is another bland word. But I honestly do appreciate all you've done for me."

"I told those Data jerks I was acting as a friend not as a cop. That's for true—and don't think I'm making a pass—we are friends," I said, thinking how much I'd like to make a pass at her.

"Thank you. All peoples should be friends and—"

"All peoples is a crowd, I want to be your friend."

"I hope we will always be friends, truly. Only… I should warn you… life has been simple for you, but for me, raised in a colony, even though I was fortunate enough to be island-rich, my father was the editor of an island newspaper, I am full of many frustrations and deep hatreds you cannot understand or… God, don't let me get started on that. And not with you.

You have been wonderful. Yes, we can be friends."

"Okay. And my first friendly act will be to shove off. I'll keep in touch, and if you have any more trouble, phone me at once."

"All right. And thank you again—my friend." We shook hands at the door. Downstairs I started walking toward the precinct house. I wanted to get the latest dope on Wales, tell Reed the stuff I'd dug up in Brooklyn. I'd slipped Rose this big speech about what a swell deal it was being a cop—and if these Data clowns had pull I could be on my way out as of now. Bet Mary would love it if I *had* to come to Uncle Frank. Forget all that.... Rose, a sweet bundle of fire, living by herself, maybe waiting for a—

"Hey, Junior."

I turned to see a squad car at the curb, Landon and Wilson grinning at me. I didn't realize it was after four already. Walking over I asked, "What's the action?"

"Nothing too much. Crazy storekeeper phoned in he'd been stuck with a couple of queer ones. Stupid bastard never saw one of the old-fashioned, large-size dollar bills before. Somebody must have found an old sock treasure. What happened to your face?"

"Nicked myself while shaving. Anything on Wales new?"

Landon shook his head. "What you shave with, a broken bottle?"

"You mean there's another way to shave? What's on Wales?"

"Nothing new that I've heard of. Seems to be one of those tough ones, no witnesses, just a lot of nothing. Reed's been calling your house."

Wilson said, "I did hear something—the Brooklyn cops don't think you're old enough to shave."

"Must be tough on this heap having to ride your dead weight around." I turned to Landon. "Know what Reed wants?"

"Something to do with Mrs. Owens. We'll drive you to the precinct."

I wasn't going to face any more ribbing on my own time. "I'll phone him, if he's still there."

"He's there," Landon said, giving Wilson the nod to drive on and the big jerk had to call out as a parting shot, "Next time you want to go to Brooklyn, let me know and I'll go along to vouch for your age."

I phoned Reed from a drugstore, told him, "This is Dave Wintino, Lieutenant. Landon says you've been calling my house. Sorry I wasn't there. I've been out—"

"What's to be sorry about? You're off duty, you can be any place you want. Mrs. Owens called, said she wants you to call her."

"Me?"

"That's what she said. Must be something personal. Dave, if you speak to her, don't say anything about Wales' gun having killed her husband.

Central Office Bureau hasn't let that out yet. Landon said he told you."

"I understand. Lieutenant, on the Owens-Wales murders, I was out in Brooklyn and—"

"I know you were out in Brooklyn," Reed said, and I could *feel* the grin on his face.

"The point is, I think if we dig into the Sal Kahn murder rap, we'll find that—"

"Dave," Reed cut in, his voice tired, "Central has the best men on the force, they say so themselves. This is their wagon and they'll know how to pull it, without any free advice."

"Yes, sir."

"Just be careful what you tell Mrs. Owens."

"Yes, sir." I damn near slammed the receiver through the phone. I dialed Mrs. Owens and a crisp female voice asked, "A-ha?"

"Mrs. Owens, please."

"This is Miss Owens, her daughter. Who's this?"

"Detective Wintino. Mrs. Owens called me."

"Oh, yes, Ma wants to see you. It's… uh… rather personal and important. Could you come up to our place, Mr. Wintino, now?"

I glanced at my watch: four-fifty. "Well, I'm due home for supper. Let me check with my wife and call you back," I told her, thinking I must sound like the henpecked husband.

"We'd appreciate it if you could drop over soon as possible. Any time this afternoon or tonight you can make it."

"I'll call you back."

We hung up and I dialed Mary's office, knowing I'd get hell. Still, if I got to the Owens house right away, I might be able to be home by six-thirty or seven. Soon as Mary got on the phone she asked, "Where have you been all afternoon? I've called the house at least half a dozen times."

"Out checking a few things."

"That's ginger-dandy! On your day off you have to—"

"It's my day off so what diff does it make to you if I'm checking, sleeping, taking in a movie, or watching pugs in a gym?" I asked.

"It would be just too bad if you spent a few minutes of the afternoon seeing Uncle Frank. I suppose you were too busy for that."

"You suppose right. I'll see him tomorrow. You alone in the office, talking so loud?"

"Now you see him tomorrow and no more stalling. I'm glad you called. Dave, I have to type up the minutes of a big sales conference. I won't be home till nine. There's enough in the box for your supper."

"I'll manage. Mean you get stuck on your job too?"

"Indeed I do," Mary said in an oversweet voice. "But I get time and a half for it and two dollars for supper money. Drop that in the suggestion box—if your wonderful Police Department has such a thing."

"I'll pass it on to the Commissioner at once—maybe he's on the gate."

"Davie, there really isn't much in the box, just hamburger. Better bring in something for yourself."

"I'll eat," I said, not wanting to tell her I was broke.

"Want me to bring anything in?" Mary's voice was just plain sweet now.

"Some ice cream and ginger ale, Babes. We'll watch TV and have sodas."

"Will do. See you at nine."

She hung up and I counted my change. All the fares and phoning left me with seventy cents. I could go up to the station and maybe borrow a buck, along with a lot of ribbing.

Instead of calling Mrs. Owens back I walked six blocks to the crosstown bus and rode over to the Bronx, then up Third Avenue and walked to their house. It was almost six when I rang their bell after drying my sweaty face and combing my hair and straightening my shirt, using the window of a parked car for a mirror. A tall young woman wearing corny black and gold toreador pants that proved she had thin legs, and an interesting suede beach jacket, opened the door. Her face was tanned and kind of horsey, with brown hair combed straight back and down to her shoulders. Susan Owens didn't look much like the photo I'd seen: her face was still plain but she was paying a lot of attention to it, and there wasn't a trace of plumpness about her. I got the feeling she'd done about the best she could with what she had. There was another change from the picture: everything about her, the eyes, the thin figure, even the clothes and the odd sandals on her big feet gave me a feeling of cunning—a sharpshooter all the way.

I said, "I'm Dave Wintino, Miss Owens."

"Oh—I thought you were going to call. Well, they must be making detectives from a different mold this season. Come on in. Ma, your detective is here."

I grinned at that "your detective" as I followed her into the living room and those long legs sure took big steps. There was a pigskin overnighter covered with plane stickers against one wall. Mrs. Owens' moon face looked a little tense as she came in from the kitchen, drying her hands on her apron. "Mr. Wintino, I hope we didn't put you to no trouble by... What happened to your face?"

"Bruised it horsing around."

"Put a hot piece of raw potato on it soon as you get home. This is my daughter Susan. Came in from South America by plane this morning."

"I recognized her from the picture on the piano," I said politely.

"I hope not," Susan said. "I looked like a freshly stuffed yokel when that damn thing was taken." She had a fast way of talking, like a pitchman.

"Do sit down," Mrs. Owens said. "This has been such a hectic day for me. Susan coming in before daybreak, and then hearing about poor Al. I don't understand it, killed in his own bed. And the papers said he had a large amount of money on him. Do you think it was the same robber?"

"Hard to say. Downtown is handling both cases now." I sat in one of the old leather chairs. Mrs. Owens sat on the couch and the daughter leaned against the wall, studying me. When I looked at her she sort of arched her chest as if to prove she wasn't skinny all over. She said, "That robbery angle sounds like a lot of pure slop to me."

"Susan! I don't know where you've picked up such language. Third time I've had to call you on your speech."

"Ma, stop stalling. You want me to tell him?"

Mrs. Owens rubbed her hands on her apron again. "I thought… that is, you see, Mr. Wintino, a most surprising… well… we…"

"You look like a dancehall john to me, Wintino," Susan cut in, her voice flat and hard, "but you're a detective and so was Pop. And Ma has confidence in you. There's something damn fishy about a pinch-penny like Al Wales having a bankroll on him… and then what we found today. I'm going to be frank with you, because Ma liked your face, she thinks you'll understand."

"What do you want me to understand?"

"It's like this, we don't want to do anything shady, or that might hinder you in finding the killers. At the same time four grand isn't anything to toss away and if it turns out we can keep the dough, I don't want it tied up as evidence for the next hundred years."

"What four—" I began.

"Hold still for a hot second," Susan told me, darting out of the room, and I mean darting: those long stems could move.

Mrs. Owens gave me a sickly smile. "We want to do the right thing, what poor Ed would have wanted us to do. I wanted to take it to the local station house at once, but Susan thought it would be just as well to ask your advice. Goodness, that girl has changed so I hardly knew her, but then, I suppose being away, on her own in a strange country, well, there have to be some changes. She has a smart head about these things and four thousand dollars is quite a sum. We found it this afternoon."

"You found four thousand bucks?" I asked as Susan came bounding into the room carrying a large dresser drawer. It was an old plain one, cracked in several places. She placed it upside-down on the living room table as Mrs. Owens reached over to yank a lace covering out of the way. Susan put a small pile of fifty-dollar bills on the drawer and a savings bankbook with the word "canceled" cut across it. Hunks of dirty white tape were clinging to the bottom of the drawer. I had a feeling they were setting up a show for me.

"I was going through Pop's things, you know, getting them ready to throw out or sell. I had this drawer out too far and it nearly fell. When I grabbed it, I felt the money and bankbook taped to the bottom. I didn't know it was money—it was in a plain white envelope—till I tore the envelope open and saw the green. This is what we want to see you about—four grand and this bankbook. It's a Brooklyn savings bank and in the name of Francis Parker. As you'll see the account was opened this March with five bucks. A week later there was a deposit of ten dollars. On April first there's a withdrawal of four dollars, and on April fifth a deposit of four thousand dollars and seventy-five cents. The entire account was closed out on April twenty-second, about two weeks ago. Take a look at the bankbook."

She handed me the book as she nervously lit a cigarette. I said, "You shouldn't have touched things. Where's the envelope?"

"I got so excited when I saw the money, I tore the envelope open. It was all in pieces, so I threw it away."

"Where did you throw it?"

"In the garbage can. It's gone."

"Great!"

"What's so important about an old envelope? At first I thought it was a letter, but when I saw the bills, well, naturally I ripped it open. Told you the envelope tore. Nothing on it, a plain white envelope."

"I was thinking of prints," I said, opening the book. There was a "ck" next to the $4,000.75 deposit, meaning it had been made by check. It was a downtown Brooklyn bank. "Ever hear of Francis Parker before?"

"Never. Neither has Ma and she's sure Pop never mentioned such a name," Susan said, blowing twin clouds of smoke out of her sharp nose. "Now look, we don't have one idea where this came from and we're not trying to hide anything—that's why you're here. At the same time we don't want this folding money lost in the shuffle. It was found here and possession is nine-tenths' ownership."

She was staring at me with cool eyes. I could see Mrs. Owens mentioning Ed had said something about getting that place in California soon and Susan Owens going to work like a ferret. This fitted in with Wales hunting around the abandoned garage for dough… except that was ten years ago and this account was less than ten weeks old. I asked, "Where's the other bankbooks?"

"This is the only one," Mrs. Owens said. "Except a joint account Ed and I have over on Third Avenue. We have $567 there."

"Mr. Owens have a safe deposit vault, did you see any odd keys about?"

I asked.

"Look, look, Pa rarely had one buck to rub against another. That I know. And I looked carefully, under everything. This is all I found," Susan said.

"I know you did. Mrs. Owens, you told me your husband said he might be able to get a farm in California soon. Are you positive he didn't have any money hidden away, never spoke of any money?"

"He didn't. Why poor Ed could just about make ends meet since he retired and—"

"This might be the string to your husband's killing. I have to know the truth about this money," I said, making my voice hard.

"Do we look like rich people?" the old lady asked, her eyes beginning to water.

"Looks don't mean a thing. Did Ed at any time in the last dozen years talk about striking big money?"

"No. *Never!*" The tears came.

"What you doing to Ma?" Susan barked. "I told—"

"Shut up!" I bent toward Mrs. Owens, said softly, "I'm not trying to be rough, but in light of other things I know about Wales, this can be a real lead. Tell me again that Ed Owens never had or ever mentioned any big money."

"He never did. We were always counting each dollar. Ed never gambled unless he had an extra dollar."

"Sorry I blew up. I believe you," I said. And I did. While she was drying her face with her apron I stared at Susan, who gave it right back to me, eye-to-eye stuff. I asked, "What do you want me to do? Don't expect me to go on the hook, this is evidence and I won't—"

"How do we know if it's evidence or not?" Susan asked evenly. "It may have nothing to do with the case. The only fact we know for sure is we found four grand and a canceled bankbook in Pa's dresser."

"What do you want me to do about it?" I asked.

"I thought you'd—" Mrs. Owens started.

"We're playing it straight with you, Mr. Wintino," Susan cut in. "You were one of the detectives on the case—we're telling you about it. But Ma felt that since you're new and not boiled in oil like some of the old-timers, you'd understand what four grand means to a cop's widow scrimping along on a lousy pension."

"Sure I understand. But I'm not going to hang myself. I have to turn this in."

"Nobody is asking you not to; if you have to turn the money in, you have to. Suppose we hold on to it till tomorrow? I have a list of the bill numbers. You take the bankbook, see what you can find out. For all we know maybe one of Pa's nags finally came in. We're not leaving town—if we didn't want to play straight we could have kept mum about all this. If by tomorrow afternoon you feel this has something to do with the case, we'll hand it over. If you ask for it now, we'll get tough too, force you to get a court order. There, that gives you an out."

I grinned at her with admiration—she was real smart, used her dome for more than growing hair. This could put me in the saddle, if it was the break in the case. It might be what I needed. Not only was I holding out the dope I learned this morning, but those Data clowns might be melting my badge by now. Of course if this turned out to be a wrongo, or if the Owenses were playing me for a sucker… Hell, they could only hang me once.

"What's it going to be?" Susan asked.

"I'll play along till tomorrow afternoon. But I want a list of the bills, the bankbook, and a sample of your father's writing, his signature if you have it handy. I'll have to call the precinct, tell them something. If my lieutenant is there, you're out of luck. If not, I called and covered myself—sort of. You'll have to take that gamble."

"If you want it that way. I'll tell anybody about a court order."

"They won't need a court order," I said, looking around for the phone.

"Out there, on the hall table," Susan said, pointing a skinny finger. "You tell them they'll sure need something good to get this four grand out of my hands. And don't forget the part about I'm not trying to obstruct justice but neither am I going to play potsy with our dough or—"

I told her to shut up again, and dialed the squad room. Landon answered, said Reed was gone for the day. I told him, "I'm over at Mrs. Owens' house. She's found something that might be a lead, a canceled savings bankbook that—"

"Will you never stop playing detective?" Landon asked, I tried not to sound relieved over the phone as I said, "Well, Reed knows I'm here. Tell him I'll check on it in the morning and be in touch with him. It may be important."

"Everything is important to you except your own time. When will you learn this isn't our case anymore?"

"You know Mrs. Owens phoned me. What am I supposed to do, tell her to ask the switchboard to connect her downtown? Just leave a message for Reed that I called and will be in touch tomorrow."

"I'll do that, Mr. Holmes," Landon said, hanging up.

Susan smiled. "What's the matter, the lads afraid they'll overwork themselves?"

"Busy on routine stuff. But I'm not busy, that's why I'm doing this. I'll work it my way. You know I won't be able to move till morning, when the bank opens I'll phone you as soon as I can. If the money is evidence, I don't want any tears or arguments about it."

"I'm a cop's daughter, I wouldn't be so stupid as to beat the law. And if this will help in any way to find who did Pa in, I wouldn't hesitate a second to—"

"I know, you're a doll."

Her eyes seemed to laugh at me as she said, "That's not nice talk, Buster. I might give you a box of cigars if things come out right."

"Now you're talking out of turn. I don't smoke," I said, as we stepped back into the living room. I pocketed the bankbook. "Get me something with Mr. Owens' signature, and the list of bill numbers. Also an envelope. Make it two envelopes."

"Have the list in my room—some job copying them all down," Susan said, dashing out of the living room.

I was about to say it must have been a labor of love but kept my trap shut and asked Mrs. Owens, "Do you remember much about the time Mr. Owens and Mr. Wales arrested Sal Kahn, sent him to the chair?"

"I remember they were promoted for it, made detective second grade. Ed and Al had their pictures in the papers. My, that was a long time ago."

"Yeah. Did Mr. Owens ever mention that collar, say anything at all about it, during the last couple of years?"

She shook her fat head. "No. He rarely talked about police work. Always said a good cop left his work at the station."

Susan came back like a nervous wind, handed me the list of serial numbers and dropped two large envelopes on the table. I picked a couple of fifties from the pile for a spot check as Susan said, "You have a real trusting nature."

"Just careful." The bills checked with the list. "Put the money in one of the envelopes and don't play with it. Speaking of money, Mrs. Owens, did the late Mrs. Wales ever mention money? Did she seem well fixed?"

"Indeed not. They lived on the upper West Side in a cheap apartment house. On the top floor. Not having children they should have been able to live better but Dora Wales was always in poor health. A wonderfully kind woman. She and Al were very happy. He never once complained about her delicate condition or the doctor bills."

"That's a fact," Susan said, picking up the money and giving it a silent count. "She was no bargain, always in bed sick, but they seemed to blend together."

I thought of Rose and her little man-and-wife private world.

"Never saw them have a fight," the old lady went on. "And when poor Dora took real sick back in 1949, Al saw to it she had only the best, even though he knew it was hopeless. They must have saved during the years— like I said they never lived well, and all their savings went for these big doctors."

"Recall the name of any of them?" I asked, keeping an eye on Susan's hands and the money.

Mrs. Owens turned her moon puss toward the ceiling in thought. "Yes, I do. Because I once had to take Dora over to Park Avenue for X-ray treatments when Al was stuck on a case. It was Seventy-ninth and Park and I remember because it was the first time I was ever in that rich section, and the doctor, he had the same name as the ballplayer, Di Maggio."

"You and Mr. Owens and the Waleses were always on good terms, weren't you?"

"Thicker than mud," Susan put in, having finished counting and satisfied I hadn't palmed a bill. She put the money in one of the envelopes. "Only thing ever separated them was distance, we in the Bronx and they downtown."

I took the envelope, sealed it, and wrote across the flap, "Keep this shut and don't finger the money, might still raise prints on the bills." I gave it back to Susan. "I'm not kidding, don't open this envelope and don't lose it." I took the second envelope and using my nails, peeled the remains of the tape from the drawer, dropped them in the envelope and pocketed it. "Might get prints from this too, if you haven't smudged it too much." I took the drawer, looked around, and put it behind the piano, "Leave this here, don't let anybody touch it. More possible prints."

"And whose prints do you expect to find?" Susan asked.

"If I knew I wouldn't bother taking them. Remember, don't touch the money and—"

"You've told us all that," Susan said. She pulled a card from her pocket. "You're so busy being a hot-shot cop, you forgot this. Pa used to be a joiner, this is one of his lodge cards, with his signature."

I said thanks as I put the card in my wallet. There was a moment of awkward silence which the old lady broke with, "I was making supper. We'd love to have you join us, Mr. Wintino."

"Thank you but my wife is waiting supper for me," I said, anxious to get going. "It may be the police will be up tonight or tomorrow, routine questions about Wales. An official visit. If they come, tell them exactly what you told me, give them the money if they want it."

"We certainly will," Mrs. Owens said. "And I'm grateful for your interest in us. So much has happened today, I'll be glad to get supper over with and take to my bed. I'll be able to sleep now, with Susan home."

"I'll see Wintino to the door," Susan told the old lady. At the door she slouched against the wall and was still tall enough to look down at me as she said, "Ma was right about you, you're okay in my book."

"Why, because I told you to shut up?"

"You're the way I like people—hard. If you weren't married I could spend the night telling you about Venezuela. There's a country—all one big angle."

"Maybe some other time," I said, patting her hand as I went out.

On the bus going downtown I kept feeling the bankbook in my pocket like it was uranium, and thinking about Susan Owens. I've never been much of a lover boy. I wasn't shy, but about the time I was old enough to get real interested I was training for the ring, then the army kept me on ice for a couple of years, and then marrying Mary when I was nineteen took me out of circulation. So it was a surprising shock knowing I could spend the night with Susan; even gave me a kind of reverse-English bang… because I didn't want to in the least.

Thursday Night

After a fast shower I put on an old silk ring robe and fried the hamburger, and then had a bowl of cereal because there wasn't anything else to eat in the house. I considered trying to get prints on the hunks of tape, but put the envelope away in my shirt drawer. I'd only mess the tape up and spoil it for the lab. Besides, I knew whose prints I'd find.

I stretched out on the couch and waited for Mary, trying to juggle the pieces of the Owens-Wales puzzle till they made even a hazy picture.

Guess I was damn tired—all I came up with was a headache. Trouble was, nothing made sense. Owens wouldn't tape four grand under a drawer unless there was something wrongo about the money. Or was he merely hiding it from his wife? Hell, it wasn't a few bucks, it was four grand. Where did he get it from? And Wales with eleven grand on him. One thing was certain, the money had to be the key to the murders. Suppose the two of them had a racket? But what kind of a racket would pay off fifteen grand? Could it be hooked up with a man who was electrocuted a quarter of a century ago? With an old garage torn down years ago?

Above all, why would Wales shoot Owens? Or was I screwy on the garage angle: maybe this was some brand-new racket they were working with the bond house? That didn't add, if they were swiping bonds the loss would be known immediately. Could be that Owens was carrying the eleven grand and Wales wanted it. They could have argued over a payoff and Wales gunned Owens when he refused to split? But hell, a payoff for what? Or was there a third joker in the deck who used Wales' gun, maybe without Wales even knowing it? Still, you don't let a guy take your gun like that, even borrow it. But if there was a third party, could Wales have killed Owens and then was shot himself when he brushed off the third guy? Then why was the dough left on Wales—another "amateur" who panicked at the sight of a stiff? Nuts, no "amateur" would come with a silencer. Still, it had to be somebody who knew Wales' habits, knew he'd be sleeping off a toot—or was the killer plain lucky?

Odd the four grand showed up after Susan Owens came home from South America. Maybe it had nothing to do with Owens? Then why was she talking, or was this a front for another deal? A hard doll like Susan with a mind like a knife could be involved in almost anything. Ought to find what she's really doing down in S.A. And there must be more dough around the Owens house. Damn, I couldn't do this alone; somebody should be digging into Owens' past, another team working on anybody and everybody who ever knew Wales, and then there was a check needed on all safe deposit vaults.... If they'd only put the whole force on this we'd have it licked in a day. The big brass downtown in Central hadn't even searched Owens' house!

Wales and his sick wife… must be tough living all your life with a sickly woman. Crazy thing about these murders, seems to be so many loose ends, you'd think if we keep pulling something will give and unravel the whole mess. You'd pass Owens or Wales on the street and you'd never make them for anything but a couple of half-dead codgers waiting for a pine box, and all the time they were hip-deep in something shady. And ex-cops too. Damn, how do I know it was shady? They were cops, why should I judge them? For all I know they might have got some market tips while delivering bonds, made a killing. Have to check that…. But why would Owens keep it from his wife, open a phony account? Round and round we go….

Mary came in. She put the ginger ale and ice cream on the table, turned on the TV as she started to undress. She acted as if I wasn't there, never even asked if I wanted to see TV or not. As she undressed and watched some crummy cowboy movie, she talked.

"Dave, it was kicks to be even typing up the reports of this sales conference. Fantastic the way some people make their minds pay off. This wasn't a routine sales talk, mostly it was concerned with a new promotion idea, and oh so clever—a nationally televised quiz program and in certain boxes of this soap powder there will be parts that form a jigsaw puzzle, which in turn gives a strong clue to the jackpot question on the TV quiz. You see the tie-up, the sensational audience participation level? After the jackpot question is reached, anybody at home can phone in the answer— if they've found the clue in the soap boxes—and win a fortune, a double jackpot. Otherwise the studio audience gets a crack at the jackpot. Make the sodas while I wash up, Dave. There's a show on at nine-thirty I want to catch. Don was talking about it. Very literary."

I made a couple of sodas and she came out of the bathroom and sat beside me. "I was so absorbed in my work, didn't realize how tired I am. What happened to your face, Dave?”

"I was running in the park and slipped.”

"Running in the park! Honestly, Dave, you act like a kid. Think I'll open the bed and we can watch TV laying down. It amazes me how those idea men and women can come up with such wonderful things. Out of thin air they dream up a show that…”

I finished the soda and got the couch into a bed and we stretched out. Mary was still on this cleverness kick. Then she got interested in some junk on TV about a movie star who realizes that despite his thousands of fan letters he's a lonely, lonely man….

About then I dozed off, thoughts flashing through my noggin like a newsreel. I saw Owens dead in the alley, Al Wales sitting shriveled up in the muster room, an empty wreck of a garage in Brooklyn, Susan Owens arching her back as she leaned against the wall, the bankbook waiting like a surprise package, and Rose's faint perfume, the touch of her fingers on my cheek.

Friday Morning

I awoke before Mary, showered and shaved, shook her awake as I put the coffee on. In a one-room apartment the order of getting dressed is important if you have to make time. The cut on my face looked better and I covered it with a Band-Aid.

Toweling herself after her shower Mary called out, "Where are you off to so early?”

"Checking on a few things.”

"Checking, digging, checking! It's your day off. Why don't you go to a movie?”

"Maybe I will. Want any eggs?”

She pinched her belly. "One egg, no toast or bacon—I'm beginning to spread. I suppose during the course of your being a busybody you won't have time to see Uncle Frank? You promised you would.”

"I plan to see him. I've got news for you, I'm a big boy now, know how to handle my off days.”

Mary gave me what could have passed for a tiny sneer. "Are you a *big* boy, Dave?”

I was too interested in the bankbook to get excited. I poured the juice and coffee as she slipped into her underwear and stockings, came over to the bridge table I'd set up. I stopped her, ran my hand over her thin shoulders. "Don't you kiss your husband anymore?”

"I don't see you rushing to kiss your wife. I'm in a hurry.”

"Oh, come on, Mary."

"Oh, for… Stop acting like a jerk," she said, pushing me away. "Grow up."

"Would I be real grown if I invented a transparent box top or a postal-card box top, something to delight your Madison Avenue scouts?"

"Don't start… That postal-card top makes sense, built-in consumer response. Merely tear off and mail in… have to tear off the top of the box anyway. Never heard of it being done before. I'll suggest this the next time we have a box-top campaign."

I gave up: sat down and started eating. I borrowed a couple of bucks from Mary before she left, washed the dishes. Then I dressed, wearing a plain conservative tie. I found Dr. Di Maggio on Park Avenue in the phone book and walked up there.

It was a ground-floor apartment in a swank building. A neat-looking brunette nurse opened the door and said, "Dr. Di Maggio's hours are from eleven to—"

"Is he in?" I asked, flashing my badge.

"Why… uh… please have a seat. He doesn't like to be disturbed now, studying his patients' charts and… One moment." She went into another room, closing the door.

Nothing like a badge to make people jump. The waiting room was like most such rooms: the chairs looking as if too many people had sat on them, the magazines worn from impatient fingering. A few seconds later she motioned me into an inner office.

The doctor was a little man, sort of hunched over, and his thick uncombed gray hair made him look top-heavy. He had heavy features that crowded his big face and there were thick folds of skin running around his bull-neck. His voice was strong and clear, gave me an impression of youth, as he asked, "What does the Police Department want of me?"

"I'm Detective Dave Wintino, 201st Precinct Squad. Perhaps you read in the papers about an Albert Wales being killed two days ago?"

"I don't recall. I haven't time for such news. What has that to do with me, Detective Wintino? Italiano?"

I said in Italian, "Yes, my father is from Bari."

"I like to see young Italians in such jobs," he said. Then he switched to English and asked again, "What has all this to do with me?"

"In 1949 Wales' wife Dora was a patient of yours. I understand she was operated on, received a lot of medical treatment before she died. I'd like to know how much Mr. Wales paid for all this."

"A doctor's records are confidential."

"I know that," I said in Italian. "I assume you wish to cooperate with the police."

Dr. Di Maggio shrugged. "Enough of the old tongue. Of course I wish to help but what would a doctor's bill, assuming she was a patient of mine in 1949, have to do with a murder of several days ago?"

"A large sum of money was found on Wales. I'm interested in knowing if he had a lot of money back in '49."

"I can see no harm. Let me look at my files," the doctor said, crossing the room to a closet door. He was wearing old slippers. The closet was almost as large as Rose's room with several file cabinets against one wall. For a second the doctor turned and stared at me, then opened a file drawer. Maybe he figured me for an income tax snoop.

He said, "Come here, young man. No sense in my taking the file out. Yes, I did have a patient named Mrs. Dora Wales. Started treating her in September, 1948. She had a malignant growth. I gave her a course of X-ray treatments. As to her medical history, she was operated on the following April, sent to a private hospital for—"

"What did all this cost, Doc?" I asked, leaning against the doorway, my notebook out.

"A famous specialist was brought in, at the request of Mr. Wales...." He bent over a card, trying to read something in the dim light, "Ah, yes, I see that Mr. Wales was also a member of the police force. I do recall the case now. Although I told Mr. Wales it was hopeless he insisted upon every possible treatment. The constant hope of the layman. However you are only interested in the costs.... My fees over a period of three months amounted to eleven hundred dollars."

"How about the other expenses, hospitals, specialists, all that?"

"I cannot give you an exact amount. However with the various specialists, the private rooms and nurses, I'd say Mr. Wales spent between five and six thousand dollars."

"Would he have to pay that all at once?"

"Yes. I note here he had Mrs. Wales taken in a private ambulance down to Baltimore for examination. That would be most expensive."

"Thanks, Doc. That's all I wanted to know," I said wondering if downtown had checked the banks for any other accounts Wales may have had. Hell, that would be the first thing they did. I took out the newspaper snap of Wales, showed it to the doc. "This is Mr. Wales. Can you remember anything else about him?"

"Frankly I do not remember the face, but then hundreds of faces pass through my office every month. I'm sorry I can't be of much assistance."

"You've given me exactly what I wanted. Thank you."

As I walked out he said "Good-by" in Italian and waved.

I walked over to Lexington Avenue and took the subway to Brooklyn, excitement mounting in me. It was a small savings bank and the manager looked as if he'd just been plucked from a fireside, a little on the sleepy side. I'd give odds he was wearing one of those old-fashioned, detachable, hard collars. He gave me the usual song and dance about it being most "irregular" to give out the info I wanted. I told him it was also "irregular" to kill ex-cops, and when I showed him the news clippings on the murders, gave him the co-operation pitch, he warmed up. I was in a small sweat that he would call Headquarters to double-check me, but he didn't.

From his records and the code number of the $4,000.75 check on the deposit slip he told me it was drawn on the Capital Exchange Bank & Trust but he had no way of knowing which branch. Without telling them why, I showed both pictures to the tellers and a tall, slick-looking colored woman said she was "pretty sure" Owens was Francis Parker, claimed she remembered him because the amount was "such a large one" when he closed out his account. That didn't mean much, Owens' picture was an old snap.

While I checked the Brooklyn address Francis Parker had given when he opened the account—and found it to be as phony as I expected—the manager compared Parker's signature card with Ed Owens' lodge card. We didn't have to be handwriting experts to see they were the same—a cramped way of writing "a" and "e."

After thanking the manager and asking him to keep it quiet, I went back to downtown Manhattan, to the head office of the Capital Bank & Trust, and ran into trouble. I was bucked from one stuffed shirt official to another, each insisting on a court order or a note from the D.A. But I kept repeating, "The solution of the murders of two police officers may depend upon this information," and finally I landed in the office of the top banana. He was a plump little joker with a butterball face clear as a baby's rear, a pointed waxed mustache, and a good gray wig that took me a lot of minutes to make. I was astonished—he looked like the bankers you see in the movies.

He examined my badge as if it was a work of art, said, "I don't see any harm in helping you, Detective. However if we have such a check, perhaps we'll have to notify the signer that we have given you the information. I'll see what our legal department has to say. First we'll see if there is such a check. Four thousand dollars and seventy-five cents —that's a help, an odd amount, and drawn to a Francis Parker sometime around the first of last month."

"It was deposited on April 5."

"Then we paid out the money on the sixth or seventh. Take some time, at least twenty minutes," he said, getting his secretary on the intercom phone, giving her the information. Then he leaned back in his big chair and gave me a happy look as he said, "As it happens I'm a rabid detective story fan. Read a book a night, best way I know to relax. Only thing I liked about F.D.R., he was a detective fan too. Now I've always wanted to ask a real detective…"

Damn if this character didn't tell me about a dozen screwy plots, asking me this and that as though it was a quiz program. I couldn't come up with a single correct answer and he looked disappointed. Finally I said, "Look, in a book or a movie the crime is rigged because the writer invents all the angles—usually in favor of the crook."

"Nonsense, these books prove crime doesn't pay."

"No, sir, the writer, like most other people, thinks he can outsmart the police. He's showing off, saying this is how I could do the crime if I wanted to—despite the righteous ending tagged on the last page. In a real crime, you have to run down a thousand dead leads, like I'm doing, to get to the one that will break the case."

"But then you have the use of the finest labs, many men, to facilitate your work, whereas the private eye has only his wits," he said as if letting me in on a secret.

I went along with the game, trying not to laugh at this big executive who sounded like a comic book reader. "Let me give you a tip, labs can help but there's still nothing been invented good as a stoolie. This honor among thieves is strictly for the birds—and the books. You'll always find guys anxious to sell out for a ten-buck bill. And to process a clue in the lab takes time, but one word from a stoolie is the fastest short cut to the solution," I said, wondering how soon I'd luck up on a guy or two in the know and out on parole, get me a couple of stools.

"Stoolies?" the bank man said, disgust on his fat face. "That seems an ugly, unfair way to—"

His secretary came in and placed a slip of paper before him. She was one of these tall, classy-looking babes, especially in the legs. Big boy picked up his phone and went into a long conversation with somebody—probably in the legal department. This somebody kept advising him not to give out the information. My detective fan kept countering with, "I'm not questioning your knowledge of the law, Maxwell, but we are helping the police…. Sure, but it's part of the bank's duty to the public…. Of course I don't want a lawsuit. All right, I'll come down to your office."

He stood up as he told me, "Our legal boys lean toward the conservative side, naturally. They say we could find ourselves in a lawsuit and at the wrong end of some publicity by giving you this information. You wait here. I'll be back in five or ten minutes." He gave me a popeyed stare as he walked out.

He was okay, the slip of paper was still on his desk. The check had been dated April 2 and signed by an Edwin Wren of Wren & Company, a depositor in the bank's midtown branch. The name hit a tiny bell and I leafed through my notebook—Wren & Company was one of the electrical companies Rose Henderson was exposing. And my hunch began to grow cold, it was like adding pies and snakes—it couldn't be. What possible connection could there be between Owens and Rose? Yet here it was, unless the bank had made a mistake, and I had to chance that they didn't. Anyway, I sure couldn't ask.

My banker who was having a romance with private eyes waddled back in while I was thinking this over. "Sad news," he said happily, sitting behind his desk. "Our lawyers advise against giving out the information. I'm sorry. I think it's nonsense but I'm not a legal eagle." He raised the slip of paper high, neatly tore it in quarters, and dropped it in his basket, winking at me like a kid as he did so.

"Tough, but rules are rules," I said, rolling with the gag and winking back. "Thank you for your time." I headed for the door.

He called out, "Be sure to tell the department they'll require a court order to secure the information."

I nodded, considered asking if he was sure about the signer of the check, and walked out. Hell, I couldn't put him on a spot.

It was noon when I hit the bricks and the street was jammed. I dropped into a drugstore and found Wren & Company in the phone book—they were in the mid-fifties on the West Side. It was hot and I was thirsty and figured I'd have lunch first, but when I saw the mob scene at the soda counter I took a subway uptown. Could be Mr. Wren didn't go out for lunch till after one.

He had his own remodeled building, three floors high and not very wide. It was smaller than I'd expected, didn't look like money till I got inside. The office was brightly lit and had huge two-tone photos of the N.Y.C. skyline for wallpaper. A large mobile made up of switches, chimes and the other electrical gadgets they manufactured was hanging from the ceiling, turning slowly in the air-conditioned breeze. The receptionist wasn't any Miss America but her expensive suit matched the rest of the office—not loud and in good taste. When I asked if Wren was in she gave me a practiced small smile as she asked, "Have you an appointment?"

I shook my head, told her my name as I flashed my tin.

She didn't get ruffled. "Oh, dear, is this about a traffic ticket or something?"

"It's about something that isn't a traffic ticket. Wren in?"

"I'll see." She had one of these streamlined switchboards on her ebony desk, shaped like a silver airfoil, and she phoned in, then told me, "Mr. Wren will see you in a moment. Have a seat, please."

There were a couple of standard leather chairs and a free-form table made of some shiny metal, a bunch of trade magazines on the table. I sat down and glanced at one of the mags, put it down. The receptionist turned to a typewriter and went on with a letter she was doing. I watched her legs under the table. At first I thought they were fat, but she must have been a dancer—they were solid and strong, something like Rose's.

Legs are legs and what good would they ever do me? Yet I was so intent on them it took me a moment to realize somebody was watching me. There were two doors leading from the reception room and one of them was open and a heavy-set, short guy was staring at me. He was wearing wrinkled gray pants, open white shirt with a dark blue tie hanging loosely around his fat neck. He had a good tan on his face but strictly the kind that comes from a sun lamp. His eyes were sunk in deep dark pockets, a ragged thick gray mustache seemed to support his thin nose, and his head was a polished bald dome rising above a few gray patches over his big ears. He was holding a pencil in one hand and a pair of heavy-framed glasses in the other. He looked more like a working foreman than a boss, yet I knew he was Wren.

We stared at each other for a second and he seemed annoyed. "All right, come in," he said in a weary voice, and walked back into his office, moving with the clumsy grace of a guy who has taken on weight in his middle years.

His office was a sloppy mess—the same modernistic walls and furniture—but his desk was covered with papers and blueprints, and there was another desk at right angles piled high with books and magazines. I shut the door and found him already sitting behind his desk. There was a container of coffee and a half-eaten sandwich in front of him. The coffee had spilled, staining the papers under it. He motioned toward a black leather and chrome chair and as I sat down he started on the sandwich, mumbling, "I never have time for lunch."

"Are you Mr. Edwin Wren?"

He nodded.

"I'm Detective David—"

"I know who you are." He leaned back in his swivel chair, rocking slightly, and watched me as he chewed his sandwich thoroughly. He looked the perfect picture of an overworked small businessman.

I let him work me over with his eyes, then he washed the food down with the cold coffee, tossed the container in the wastebasket, spilling some on the gray rug. He hid his mouth with a pudgy hand as he belched. "Goddamn coffee, worse than the cigarette habit, kills a man's stomach." He brushed crumbs from his mustache, said, "You're just a kid with a badge." His voice wasn't nasty, just weary.

"Which would you rather see, my birth certificate or my badge?"

"Aren't you overdoing things, Mr. Wintino?" he asked, putting on his glasses. They were powerful lenses and made his eyes look large and soft, what they say a cow's eyes look like.

"I don't know, what am I overdoing?"

"I commend your thoroughness in tracing me, but as the Data men told you yesterday, we haven't broken any laws and the whole business of this silly girl writing a—"

"I'm not here about that," I cut in, surprised the Data lads yelled to a client. "I'm here to ask about a $4000.75 check you made out to a Francis Parker on April 2."

The eyes got even bigger behind the glasses. The only sound in the office was the slight squeak of his chair as he rocked. I like catching a guy off balance, watching him rolling a mental log. But when he asked, "And why is the Police Department interested in that?" his voice was almost asleep. He fumbled in a desk drawer, took out a large pipe and a pouch, packed the pipe.

"You tell me, Mr. Wren," I told him, trying to sound just as casual. "I traced the check to you through a bank account under the phony name of Francis Parker. His picture has been in the papers—you certainly know that Parker is a retired cop who was murdered a few days ago."

Wren puffed on his pipe and nodded. The tobacco had a nutty smell that wasn't bad at all. He said, "I barely glance at the papers but I did see a minor headline about a shooting. Still, exactly why are you here, why is a business check of mine official police business?"

"I'm doing this on my own time, Mr. Wren, so I would appreciate if you'd stop fencing. An ex-cop is murdered, we find four thousand in cash in his house and a bankbook. You gave the dead man the four grand. You read about the killing. Why haven't you come forward to tell us about the money, the phony name?"

"Because I had hired this ex-cop to do some work for me. He did it and I paid him. That was some six or seven weeks ago. I still fail to see how that is any concern of the police."

"What sort of work did he do for you?"

Wren lit his pipe again before he said, "Detective work. We'd heard rumors of Miss Henderson's article and we wanted to learn who the author was, where she lived, various details. Frankly at that stage we didn't even want a known private agency on the case. One night I met this retired policeman in a bar, we got to talking over some beers. It occurred to me he was the man for our job. I hired him on the spot."

"He didn't have a license for private work."

Wren smiled. "That didn't seem to upset either of us."

"And he found Miss Henderson for you?"

"Yes."

"You paid him four grand for that? What the hell was the seventy-five cents for?"

Wren puffed hard on his pipe, said over the smoke, "I'm afraid the entire transaction ended on a sour note. Mr. Parker—he insisted he be called and paid under that name, to avoid taxes I suppose, although I never asked him—anyway, Mr. Parker located the writer within a few days. We had agreed upon payment of one thousand dollars plus modest expenses, if any. I then suggested to Mr. Parker he start—let's use the word harass—that he start harassing Miss Henderson. He refused. The truth is he turned about and bluntly threatened me with outright blackmail: he wanted four thousand dollars or he would sell his story to Miss Henderson and this lousy *Weekly Spectator.* I had no choice, I paid." Wren slipped me a quick smile. "Mr. Parker was not without a sense of humor, he insisted seventy-five cents be added for 'expenses'—three subway fares and three phone calls. I am aware what I am telling you leaves me open to more blackmail, but I have confidence in your honest young face."

"Cut the sarcasm. The word 'honest' has a hollow ring coming from you," I said. I didn't know enough about Owens to figure him for blackmail or not. Maybe he saw this as the last chance to dig into the cracker barrel.

Wren stared at me, those large soft eyes behind the glasses twin pictures of pity. "Pretty strong language, young man."

"Your clowns have been giving Miss Henderson a strong pushing around, a real bad time."

"My handling of Miss Henderson may not have been entirely ethical but it wasn't dishonest. You should pay more attention to your choice of words. The young lady is fired with ideals and a chance to make a name for herself. An act is dishonest or 'wrong' only when it is something not being done by the majority. To put it clearer, wrong is perversion and a pervert is somebody out of step. However once he is in step, or the others are in step with him, it ceases to be perversion or wrong. Do you follow me?"

"Should I? What's all this talk add up to?"

"Simply that I take objection to your slur about my honesty. We're businessmen who—"

"Who Miss Henderson says are breaking the law."

He shook his head. "That's her opinion. It's true that by... uh... monopolizing this particular item we will keep the price up, but at the same time we would be able to control the quality, keep that up too."

"Okay, you're public benefactors. What has this to do with the check?"

"Don't be so brash, young man. I want you to see the whole picture, including the check. What we are doing is being done all the time and by the most respected people. To give you a broad example: there's a strict control on diamonds, the supply is kept down to keep prices pegged high. The whole world knows that. If you should discover new diamond mines, be in a position to undersell, and refuse to join the syndicate, they would ruin you. At the risk of sounding cynical let me remind you that most of the people in this syndicate have titles and are considered the height of respectability in their various countries."

"Let's get back to the check."

"This bears upon it indirectly," he said slowly, as if he'd been waiting all day for a good listener. "I'm merely proving Miss Henderson is wrong, that what we are doing is neither criminal nor even wrong. Let me ask you this: suppose tomorrow you hit upon a new soft drink that sweeps the country. You can make this sugar water for a penny, market it for two cents and thus make a neat profit. However since you control it, if you find you can sell it for ten cents, make a 900 per cent profit, which would you do?"

"Sell it for a dime. Mr. Wren, all this talk is getting us away from Parker and why you didn't come to the police."

"On the contrary, if I can make you understand that Miss Henderson is a crackpot, out to make her own type of fast dollar, then you can understand why I had to pay off Mr. Parker. Why I haven't gone to the police and don't want any publicity about the matter, if it can be helped. I had a business deal with a man, weeks later he is shot. That obviously had nothing to do with me. Once I paid off, I was done with the matter, I never saw him again."

"There are three other concerns in this, do they all...?"

"I handled this myself."

"Why?"

Wren lit his pipe again. "A good question. I met up with this former cop, I made the deal. When it turned sour I took full and sole responsibility. There's also the matter of pride. I didn't—and don't—want the others to know I'd been taken in."

"So you shelled out four grand, just like that?"

"Not just like *that,*" he said, pointing his pipe at me. "This goes down as a business expense, taxes will absorb most of the loss. I got the information I wanted but I paid more than I expected. That's it in a nutshell."

"If you report this as a tax loss, what about the phony name of Parker, which he was using to escape taxes?"

Wren shrugged. "I don't fool with taxes. If he wanted to, that was his business."

"Where is this bar and when did you meet him?"

"See here, Detective Wintino, I resent this questioning, as though I was a suspect or something. You're making a mountain out of a mole hill."

"I never said you were a suspect, and a dead man isn't a mole hill. I'm asking you these questions because it may lead to somebody, and so on, until we hit the right one."

"Then I can be of little help. We first met at some bar on Sixth Avenue, I don't remember exactly. I'd dropped in for a quick beer and we started talking about some show we were watching on the TV. I can probably recognize the place if I pass it again. That was around the middle of March. After our first meeting, due to the nature of our business, we thought it best to meet on the street, usually at the corner of Fifty-fourth Street and… As you can see all this has nothing to do with any shooting and it would be darn embarrassing, to say the least, if it came to light. I certainly want to co-operate with the police but I don't wish to make an ass of myself, or to hurt my business. I expect intelligent co-operation from you. If I'm not involved don't drag me in."

"That isn't up to me to decide."

"I believe you said you're doing this on your own time. Same situation when you invaded the Data office. I don't know what you fancy yourself, but common sense has to be a factor in things too. I once had a minor business deal with a man later found dead. That's all there is to it. Period."

"This isn't exactly my own time, a cop is on duty twenty-four hours. A retired cop has been killed; we're not leaving anything to chance."

"Fine, I'm for you. You're a very young man, Detective Wintino, and you must be very capable to have risen so high at your age. But as you grow older, get to be an old coot like me, you'll find there's one basic rule to life—live and let live. I've given you all I know. If this has any bearing on the case I'm glad I could be of help. But if it hasn't I don't want to be dragged through any unnecessary publicity, a headline orgy. Do I make myself clear?"

"I only have a few more questions. What address did Parker give you?"

"Don't recall he ever gave me one."

"A phone number?"

"No. I see what you want—how did we get in touch with each other? He phoned me whenever he had anything. As I told you, the whole thing took a few days, and due to the type of work, it wasn't anything I shouted about or let my office staff in on."

"Did he ever mention any other person, even while making small talk?"

"No. Don't you think you've taken up enough of my time? I'm a busy man." Wren knocked the ashes out of his pipe. "I've given you all the help I can. I'm not sure whether I'd repeat our conversation again, even to your superiors. As I believe the Data people told you, if you become a pest you'll be broken. Now wait, I'm not threatening you, but appealing to your common sense. I thought you were here on this silly Henderson matter and you start questioning me about a murder. I've told you all I know. Please don't put a knife in my business back as a reward."

I stood up. "No need to worry if the department should call you in for further questioning, that doesn't mean the papers will get wind of it. As for Miss Henderson, just keep your dealings with her on a business level—not on a goon level."

Wren got to his feet. "I know when I'm licked. She can publish her damn yarn and the devil with it. We can get around that. Sorry if I sounded as if I was throwing my weight around a second ago, but you must understand my position. The publicity of an article can be handled, but a scandal, being even publicly questioned about a killing—my business would be ruined." He took off his glasses, rubbed his eyes. "I'm under a strain, this new wiring method Miss Henderson must have told you about. I've been going fifteen and sixteen hours a day. That's why I lost my temper before. Well, hope I've been of some help," He held out his hand.

I shook it. "At least we know where Ed Owens got the four grand from."

Wren's tan face went ashen, his eyes seemed to pop, get as large as if he had his glasses on. Then he began coughing as he bent over, kneading his belly with his stubby hands.

"What's the matter?" I asked, stepping back in case he was about to be sick. "Need a pill? Water?"

He shook his head and slowly straightened up, ran a crumpled handkerchief over his sweaty face. He whispered, "Excuse me. These quickie lunches—had a gas pain that seemed to stab at my heart. Thought I was going to faint."

"Ought to have a check-up."

"Yes, I'm past due. Now, what were you saying about Owens?"

"That we now know how and where Owens got the money, the reason for the false name in the bank. Another piece that may fit into a bigger picture, one of two murders. That's police work.'" I pulled out the newspaper pictures. "This your Mr. Parker?"

Wren pointed to Owens' snap. "Yes, although it must have been taken many years ago. Yes, I did see something about the other killing—I only skim through the papers. Well, I've helped you. See what you can do to shield me from any possible notoriety," Wren said, walking me to the door.

"You don't have to worry about that."

"Well, have to be on the safe side when…" His face screwed up with flushed pain again and he mumbled, "I… uh… have to… sounds silly but… good day, Detective Wintino, I have to go!"

I'd thought his coughing and the rest of it was part of an act to get rid of me, most people get nervous when around a cop for any length of time, but Wren actually did run by me, across the reception room and through another door.

The girl at the desk just shook her head, said, "He never listens, his wife keeps telling him to slow down, see a doctor. He'll get himself an ulcer yet."

"An executive-type one, I suppose," I said, walking out.

Friday Afternoon

It was 1:43 p.m. and I was hungry. For a while I didn't want to think of Wren, the frightened businessman, but let my thoughts cook for a few minutes. I had a bright idea: long as I was downtown I might as well see Uncle Frank and stick him for lunch, save some dough. I phoned and he asked, "Davie, you coming to see me?"

"Yes. I'm downtown, thought we might have a bite together." Although if Uncle Frank didn't reach for the tab first, I'd be in a fine spot.

"Who has time for lunch? I just ate a stale sandwich and a bottle of soda. My ulcer will kill me tonight. When will you be over?"

"About a half-hour, I have a few calls to make. Take it easy, Uncle, I just left another man whose blood has turned to coffee. See you soon."

I hung up and dialed the Owens house. Susan's sharp voice asked, "Yes?"

"It isn't yes, it's no."

"What? Who is this?"

"Dave Wintino."

"I've been waiting for your call. What about the money, can we—"

"So far no. Actually I still don't know, so leave the dough alone. I've found the guy who handed out the money but things are still foggy."

"Who's Francis Parker?"

"Your father, on a tax dodge. Remember, don't touch the cash and let me talk to your mother."

"If Parker was Pa then the money should be ours."

"We'll see. I don't know yet that it isn't yours. Put your mother on," I said, hoping I could finish the call without paying an extra nickel.

I heard Susan yell, "Ma, come to the phone," her voice a hard bark. Then she told me, "One thing, if there's any doubt it's going to be in our favor. Not handing out four grand like—"

"Take it slow, we're giving it a try. That's what you wanted. Where's your mother?"

There was a moment of silence and then the old lady said, "This is Mrs. Owens."

"Dave Wintino, Mrs. Owens. During March did Mr. Owens ever mention doing any outside work? I don't mean at the brokerage house, but detective work?"

"Why, I—" Jane Owens began as the operator cut in with, "Five cents for the next three minutes, please."

"What did you say?" Mrs. Owens asked as I told her to hang on, dug out a nickel and put it to work. "Did Ed ever mention doing any private detective work in March?"

"No."

"When he talked about getting the little farm in California soon—about when was that?"

"About two months ago."

"And he didn't say how he expected to get the money for the farm?"

"No. He was just talking big."

"At any time since he retired did he ever talk about doing private detective work?"

"No. He couldn't have done any work like that, he was home till he left for the brokerage office and then he always came right home to work in his garden before it got dark."

"Okay. Thanks. I'll keep in touch." I hung up as she started to ask about the money. I got the manager of the brokerage house on the phone, another fifteen-cent call since I had to wait till he finished talking on another line. He said Owens had never missed a day since he'd worked there. Wales had been sick sometimes. "You know the kind of sickness, he drank too much of his favorite pain-killer," the manager added.

"If you knew he was a lush, why did you hire him?"

"I never said he was a drunk. I wouldn't talk harshly about the departed or—"

"Which way do you think you were talking now about him?" I asked and hung up.

I stopped at a stand for an orange drink and a couple of doughnuts and food reminded me I was supposed to call my folks. I chewed the junk slowly, I usually can do my best thinking when I'm stuffing my mouth. But now I thought about Wren and came up with nothing.

Wren's yarn was crazy enough to be true. The only important angle was it gave a possible motive for killing Owens: Wren was taken for four grand and he paid off with a bullet. Not that he would do the actual killing, but he might hire a goon. But that didn't make sense, a big businessman doesn't go in for punk stuff. And that wouldn't explain Wales' murder. I had an uneasy feeling about things—I was playing it wrong by holding out on Reed and the boys downtown. Trouble was I was in over my head, playing a lone hand when I'd never even been on a murder before, much less a double one. If Reed ever found out I'd look like a kid playing amateur dick. Keep up the way I'm going and I'd end up minus my badge—unless

I could come in with the whole answer.

I decided to give myself a deadline—by tonight I'd tell Reed about the four grand, Wales watching the garage for years, and Owens working for Wren. In the meantime I still had a couple of hours in which to dig. No sense wasting time with Uncle Frank. I got some change and phoned Rose. No answer. I was counting on her for more dope on Wren. I called Ma and she said, "Davie, I've been trying to reach you. I'm cooking, are you and Mary coming up for supper?"

"Well I… uh…"

"Davie, we haven't seen you in two weeks. Papa is so hurt, you mustn't ignore us." Her voice was full of shrill pleading.

"Aw, Ma, I'm not ignoring you. I've been busy. Okay, we'll be up for dinner. Around six-thirty. And Ma, it's hot, don't make nothing heavy."

"Don't you worry about my food, it will stick to your ribs. Don't bring me any candy or other *dreck*. You're not a guest, you're my son."

"Okay, Ma, see you tonight."

The phone company was getting rich off me. I dialed Mary and she blew her top when I told her. "Dave, this is Friday night, I want to go out, see a movie, have a drink."

"We'll see a movie tomorrow. You know how Ma and Pop are, and we haven't been up there for weeks."

"Tomorrow? Sure, you have to be at your lousy job by midnight! Why didn't you go up and see your mother this afternoon?"

"I was busy and she wants us up in the evening when Pop's there. I'm on my way to see Uncle Frank now. Come on, Mary, you know this family stuff, I can't get out of it."

"Dave, it's been a long week for me, I'm tired. I'm definitely not in the mood to eat one of those heavy meals, listen to your folks gab in two different languages or—"

"You mean language-wise you're bored because they don't talk that cocktail drip like the queers in your office?"

There was a heavy silence at the other end till Mary said calmly, "Dave, I'm not going to make a scene. I'll phone and beg off, tell them the truth: I'm tired. You go up and—"

"You bet I'm going!" I said and hung up.

Sore as a boil I tried Rose again and she was still out. I might as well see Uncle Frank and get some peace at home. I took a bus down to his sweatshop. All the time Wales and Owens and the money kept turning over in my mind, like those little steel balls you try to wiggle into holes in hand puzzles—only nothing fitted.

I'd heard a lot about Uncle Frank's joint but I'd never visited the place before. It actually was a beehive of activity, or something. And it really wasn't *his* place, he was a one-third partner. They had the basement and first floor of a large building in the heart of the garment district, and the whole place was a lacework of conveyor belts and endless tracks of rollers with packages moving in a steady stream on top of the rollers.

Uncle Frank looked as though he was made up for laughs—an old pair of dungarees straining to cover his medicine ball gut, a dirty loud plaid shirt, a dead cigar in his mouth like a whistle, and a pair of pince-nez glasses on his fat nose. He looked a little like Mary's father, something about him that still shouted hayseed.

Frank never stood still for a second; walking and running all over the place, taking packages from one conveyor belt to another, or throwing them down a chute, bawling out people, screaming orders. There seemed to be thousands of packages, from thin tie boxes to big crates. At the end of each roller, where the chutes started, there were scales and girls, mostly colored, perched beside the scales and writing down the weights and addresses as men and boys lifted the packages onto the scales, then tossed them down the chutes where they were stacked, or put on skids and pulled out to trucks.

Uncle Frank always was a jerky talker and as he showed me around he would break off a sentence with a nervous yell to somebody about, "Why are you shipping dresses today? It's Friday. All dress goods go express. *Express,* goddamn it!"

He asked me, "Well, how do you like it, Davie? Plenty of action, and this is the start of the slow season. Around November we're busy as crows at seeding time—packages stacked right to the ceilings. The way it should be, we pay rent for space up to and including the ceilings and then…" He stopped to grab a large carton marked "fragile—glass" off a roller and throw it on a pile across the room as he shouted at a kid who didn't look over sixteen, "Where's your eyes, Paddy? That was plainly marked 'air freight.' See that it gets to the last chute and be careful."

He ran a hand over his big lantern jaw and whispered loudly to me, "The breakage these darn kids cause. I don't know, when I was coming up kids were… How do you like it, Davie lad? We go like this from eight in the morning up to ten or eleven at night."

"Sure a lot of movement. What's it all about?" I asked, thinking it was odd about Wren coming across a retired cop in a bar just when he needed one.

"This is a very big operation," Uncle Frank said, blowing up his chest as if making an after-dinner speech. "New York is the style center, the clothing center. Let us suppose you own a shop out in Dayton, Ohio. Well, you have to buy here, either directly or by mail, and you have to pay the shipping costs. Now say you buy a dress for two dollars and plan to retail it at three-fifty. The shipping—hey, you in the blue sweatshirt on the south roller, don't pile those boxes so high, they'll fall and jam the roller. What was I saying, Davie?"

"A dress for three-fifty," I said, watching an old man neatly toss a flat dress box on top of a pile of boxes about ten feet high, tossing it like a basketball player sinking a foul shot. Did the four grand have anything to do with the Owens killing, or was it another blind alley? As a motive it wasn't so hot—why wait, six, seven weeks?

"Oh, yes, you buy the dress for two dollars. If you have it sent parcel post, insured, the postage will amount to, say… about seventy cents. This means you can't retail the dress for under four dollars. A dress weighs about three to four pounds, packed. Suppose you're buying fifty dresses, that's over forty dollars in postage alone. Are you following me?"

"Right behind you." Had Wales and Owens been doing private work all along? That would account for the wad Wales had on him. But the private eye business wasn't that good… unless they were doing blackmail. Then why the crummy messenger jobs? A cover? And why wouldn't Mrs. Owens know? Or had she been lying all the time? No, then she would have kept quiet about the four grand.

"… And so you have *all* your orders delivered to us—the manufacturers deliver free within the city. We wait till you have a hundred pounds of freight and ship by hundred-pound lots, thus cutting your shipping costs in half, including the few cents per item for our service. Handling thousands of packages per day, we make a nice profit, although we carry a terrific overhead and have to… Tom, did you call Westside Motors for another truck? Well what are you waiting for? It's late. Come on, Davie, we'll go up to my office. We'll be able to hear ourselves think there."

We climbed around and over wooden crates, walked through zigzag aisles of packages. I was watching my clothes while Uncle Frank was barking instructions at people as he walked, most of the people not even listening to him. We went up some stairs where a bevy of elderly women were working adding machines fast as typewriters, and into a battered office. Uncle Frank sat down behind his old desk and re-lit his cigar, mouthed a couple of pills as he said, "Always around now, when business is slow, my stomach acts up."

"Is any business worth a nervous gut?" I asked, studying Uncle Frank. I was screwy. He'd never have anything to do with a murder. And neither would Wren, they were businessmen not goons.

"Ulcers, nervous stomach, piles, I've had them all. But I have an appointment in a few minutes, so let me tell you our proposition. I've talked this over with my partners and they agree you're the ideal lad for us."

"I am? What makes me so ideal?"

"Davie, as you saw, we have a very democratic sort of hiring system here, and we're proud of it. We give colored women office jobs, use youngsters just out of school or going to night school as part-time workers. Or we help men out who put in a few hours in the evening to supplement their take-home pay. We even give handicapped people a break, hire deaf and dumb people. You would start in shipping, at the bottom. That would make things look good and also give you a chance to learn the business. With your Italian name nobody will ever suspect you are related to me. Starting pay will only be about thirty-five dollars a week, but within two months I guarantee you will be taking home fifty-five dollars every Friday night."

"That still isn't any hell."

Uncle Frank chewed on his cigar as he tried to smile. "Now, Davie lad, I know all about you policemen; you pay for your gun, for your bullets, money is taken out of every check for your pension, then there's the station house tax, and this and that bite. Mary told me over the phone that you were paid a few days ago and it's gone already. You can't expect to start at the top, or to get rich overnight."

"I don't," I said, wondering if Owens had, in his old age.

"You must look at this as a long-range deal. You saw how I work and I mean physical work—I'm working harder than when I was a youngster at haying time. I'm too old for this, and so are my partners. In time you'll be in charge of the day shift and that means a hundred dollars a week, perhaps a share in the concern. And there's extras to be had—trucking outfits hand out cash Christmas presents. Lad, you have to see this as an opportunity, not merely as a job."

"I certainly appreciate your thinking of me," I said, wondering why I was wasting precious time here, "but I don't know if I'm suited for this...."

"But you are!" Uncle Frank said, bending over the desk and whispering; his breath smelled like last week's food. "You speak Jewish and Italian. You see, we employ a good many Eyeries and Jews here and you would know what was going on all the time. Let's say, if there was any union talk. And although you don't look it, you're tough, an ex-fighter and a cop. Sometimes we have a little trouble—suppose the kids we hire are a little wild, or the old-timers turn out to be drinkers. You could keep them in line. And occasionally there is some theft. Not so much with our employees, although for minimum pay we can't expect the cream, but in this area you find winos, especially at night. They swipe packages if the doors are open, or while the kids are loading a truck."

"I'd be a combination straw boss and cop?"

"Now don't get a wrong slant. We don't have trouble every day or every week, but it does happen, and it jacks up our insurance premiums. Lad, the secret of this business is to knock off every penny of overhead possible, to save every second of—" Uncle Frank pointed to my wrist watch and shot out of his chair as if he was goosed. "Lord, where does time go to! It's three-thirty. I'm late for my appointment. Think it over, my boy, a long-range opportunity. You may be boss of the place by the time you're thirty-five. Phone me here tomorrow."

"Tomorrow is Saturday," I said as Uncle Frank opened a locker, took off his dungarees and shirt, standing in faded pink silk shorts for a second, his legs veined and skinny. Then he changed to a dark brown suit that was sloppy around the shoulders.

"Phone me, I'll be here. Saturdays, Sundays, I'm always here."

I stood up. "I'll think about it but I'm pretty sure this isn't for me. If I'm going to be a cop I want to be a real one, not a store badge."

"My tie straight? Don't make any snap judgment you'll regret. You won't be a 'cop' here, you'll be a junior executive. Talk it over with Mary. When are you two coming over for supper? We have to get together more. Tie straight now?"

I fixed his tie and he grabbed his hat and almost flew out of the office. I stood there for a moment, wondering why I didn't have the guts to tell him to stick his job. Mary and her great ulcer deals.

I used his mirror to comb my hair, take a few specks off my suit, then picked up his phone and told the switchboard operator I wanted an outside line, dialed Rose. She was home and I said I was on my way up.

"I'll be in the rest of the day, working. I haven't had any more trouble, not even a phone call. I'm grateful. What do you want to see me about?"

"A few questions about something else…. I'll be up in a half-hour."

After the bedlam of the freight company the street was practically quiet and the sunlight clean. I wanted to buy Ma a box of candy or some flowers but I had less than a buck on me. On the subway ride uptown I kept thinking of the blackmail angle: Owens and Wales might have been working with a third character, perhaps a licensed private jerk—although what made having a license so important? They got shady jobs—nobody turns to a private dick unless there's a reason why he can't go to the police—and worked small-time blackmail on businessmen like Wren. If they got four or five grand at a clip, made a couple of scores a year, that could account for Wales' money belt—he could have saved eleven grand over a span of half a dozen years easily, the frugal way he lived.

But where was Owens' dough? Or was this their first job and Owens refused to split, that's why Wales gunned him? Couldn't be their first job. Where did Wales' bundle come from?

But I couldn't buy that at all, or any part of it. You don't kill because somebody holds out a grand. Maybe a punk did but not an old time conservative cop like Wales. *Cop*—damnit they were good cops, why should they be doing something crooked in the last years of their lives? Why was everybody so sure Wales had killed his partner? Wasn't for the gun, there wouldn't be any connection between the crimes. But there was the gun. Perhaps the gun had been planted in his room when the killer finished Wales? Or was Wales so dumb as to keep a murder weapon around?

I made a note of that, wondered why I'd overlooked the angle before. A planted gun added, kept Wales in character. Only what kind of character if they were shakedown artists? And to use Wales' gun, then plant it, a guy would have to be a close friend of Wales. That could be the third party, the private dick, perhaps using Wales and Owens without their suspecting? Nuts, they were old hands, they'd know. And they had to know or how did Wales get all the dough, Owens the four grand?

I made another note, as I got off the subway, to have a talk with Data, Inc. Saturday morning. Not impossible Owens had been working for them, or if Wren had wanted to get Owens, he would have arranged it through Data. They could give me the dope on what was cooking in the private eye racket. Be a joy talking to them: when I mentioned murder they'd squirm, forget their toy gadgets!

Rose was barefooted in thin black cotton Chinese pants and a loose red pullover that showed curves whenever and wherever the shirt touched her. A warm smile followed her "Do come in."

The place looked even smaller, maybe because of the piles of papers and open books next to her typewriter. As I sat down on the couch I told her, "Turn around, please."

She spun around, looked puzzled.

"I like the outfit. You look good enough to have for dessert."

She hesitated, smiled and said "Thank you" and added, "Do you want to take off your coat? It's been so muggy."

"I'm okay, won't keep you long. How's the article coming?"

"Fine. I'll be finished in a few days. Want a cool drink? I have an interesting concoction—coconut milk and ginger beer."

"I'll try some. How did you dream that up?"

"Always drank it down in the islands," Rose said, walking to the tiny refrigerator, moving like a dancer. She poured two glasses of what looked like thin milk.

She sat beside me as she handed me a glass, watched my face as I took a cautious sip, then gulped it down. It was cool and spicy. "This is the best. Can you buy coconuts around here?"

"Science marches on. Coconut milk is now canned in Puerto Rico."

"Ought to take a can up to my mother. She's always experimenting on the stove."

"I'll give you a can," Rose said sipping her drink. "I get them on the cuff—I write advertising copy for one of the Spanish-speaking newspapers. Want some more?"

"A little." She poured part of her drink into my glass and I got so excited I was certain I was blushing. It was crazy but the intimacy of it gave me ideas—and the cold drink ended them. I said, "Your buddy, Edwin Wren, must have had this in mind when he told me about a new drink."

"Edwin Wren? What were you talking to him about?"

"He suddenly cropped up in another case. Why I'm here. What do you know about him?"

"Almost everything. He's fifty-seven, an engineer, married, has two daughters—one goes to Smith and the other is married to a doctor out west someplace. His wife is active in the usual middle-class civic organizations. They live in an old duplex apartment on Riverside Drive and Eighty-second Street and he goes in—"

"He lives on Riverside and Eighty-second?" I asked. That was only three blocks from where Owens was killed.

"That's right, lived there for many years. He goes in for modest cars—in fact the Wrens live modestly, although over a five-year period he has averaged $25,000 a year, above taxes. Wren & Company was almost a one-man affair till the war. He landed a couple of big subcontracts, and was able to expand and—"

"Was he ever in any trouble—criminal stuff?"

"Never. This case—what's it all about?"

"I'm working on a double murder and his name popped up in connection with a… check," I said, knowing I was talking too much. Wales had warned me about that. Had he talked too much himself? "Where is Wren from?"

"Born here, graduated into the depression, tried to get a job in South America but—"

"Hold it. What part of South America and when?" I cut in. Susan Owens worked in S.A.

"He never got the job, he lacked experience and in those days a company could get its pick of engineers. He worked on WPA for a few years and along about 1934 opened a small factory in the Bronx, made doorbells and cheap electric chimes. He moved to his present plant in 1949 and has been growing ever since. If they can swing this wire-paint monopoly he'll be in the millionaire bracket. All this of any help to you?"

"He sounds like a solid, aggressive business joker. You sure he's never been in any beef with the law?"

"Not the criminal law."

I must have looked blank for she gave me a full smile and said, "Mr. Detective, let me remind you there are such things as civil laws too and they also can be broken. As my article will prove, Wren and the others are acting in restraint of trade and—"

"Easy there. I'm too tired for a lecture. What I want to know is, was he ever in any lawsuits, jams, anything like that?"

"Plenty," she said going over to a file cabinet and returning with a folder of notes, newspaper clippings and booklets. She sat on the couch, feet under her, stubby painted toes near my hand. Dumping the folder out all over her lap, she said, "He's had the usual manufacturer's lawsuits—suits claiming he had received damaged raw material. Here, in 1939 he was sued on a buzzer patent and won. One of his trucks ran down a man in 1946 and Wren settled out of court for $2,700. In 1949 he sued a bank for $20,000 claiming somebody named Butler had forged his name to a check for that amount and it was the bank's responsibility to check his signature. Handwriting experts agreed it was a forged signature and the bank had to make good to Wren."

"In 1949. What month? You know Butler's full name, if he was ever collared?"

"Collared?"

"Arrested?"

"No. I only have a brief note on it. You said 'he.' I don't recall if Butler was a man or woman. But you can check the '49 papers or a newspaper morgue. Can't you tell me what you're looking for? I might be of more help."

"I'm hunting for that corny needle in the haystack. Fishing blindly, hoping I'll come up with something."

"But how does Wren fit into this 'something'?"

"I'm not sure he does except I don't believe in coincidences and he's beginning to figure in too damn many. But it doesn't add: I'm looking for a killer and he's just a business sharpshooter."

Rose gathered up her notes. "Do I detect a chamber-of-commerce sanctimonious sound when you said 'business'? The bigger the business, the more ruthless the—"

"Hey, get off the soapbox."

"It's true. In the name of business whole islands and countries have been—and are—kept in poverty, strikers have been killed…. Hitler went to war to increase German markets and in my own Puerto Rico the—"

"Honey, I'm looking for a cold-blooded thug who has shot one man, maybe two. Much as you dislike Wren I doubt if you'd call him a murderer, a killer."

She shrugged and the red shirt did a rumba. "No, I doubt if he would use a gun. But remember, a gun and a knife are the more obvious weapons, poverty has killed more people than all the bullets ever made…."

I grabbed one of the catalogues of Wren & Company, made believe I was going to shut her lips with it. "Now don't give me speeches. This killer is the kind who didn't hesitate to use a gun in daytime on the street, in a furnished room with—" I stopped talking, stared at the cover of the catalogue. There was a little brown bird on the corner of the cover. "What's this?"

"An advertising tag Wren used at one time… wren—a small brown bird."

A warm glow started up my spine and then faded away. "You see, another damn coincidence. There was a man involved, after a fashion, in the… Anybody ever call Wren, or was he ever known as, The Bird?" And I thought, I have to take it easy, make a bad collar with Wren as The Bird and I'll sure have to take Uncle Frank's job.

"I never heard him called that. I still don't know what this is all about."

I stood up. "Forget it, I talk too much. I'm keeping you from your writing and I'm due at my mother's for supper and she'll be sore enough without my being late. If you'll let me have that can of coconut milk, I'll scram. And don't worry about Wren ever bothering you again, he told me he's given you up. Tell me, when these calls and the shadowing first started, did you ever notice a plump, middle-aged man asking around about you? Shabby dresser. Have you ever heard the name Francis Parker?"

"No. I never saw anybody except those men who pushed me on the street. First time I didn't see who pushed me. Then the time before you saw them, they had reversed things—the tall one did the jostling. My curiosity is eating me up. What… ?"

"When did the calls first start, when did you first think you were being shadowed?"

"About a week ago."

"Only a week ago?" That could still figure. Once Owens gave him the dope it might have taken Wren time to find the right private eye. Only the woods were full of starving private badges, why should it take him a month to find one? And even if Wren was The Bird, why should he kill Owens and Wales twenty-five years after Sal Kahn burned? Still it was a hell of a lead to look into. I glanced at my watch. "I'm late. Where's my coconut?"

She took a can down from the shelf, even put it in a bag for me. "But you can't leave me hanging like this. What's it all about?"

"Honey, that old saying about what you don't know won't hurt you may be terribly true in this case. We're dealing with a killer. And if I told you the wild idea batting around in my noggin, the least might happen to you would be a rough libel suit. Forget I ran my big mouth. I'll let you know what Ma thinks of this coconut milk. Good-by now." I winked at her and opened the door.

Rose looked astonished, then laughed, deep real laughter. "I never had anybody wink at me before."

"Then you're long due. I'll drop in again." I waved and ran down the steps.

I walked slowly up to the corner, not sure what to do. Crime cases follow set patterns. If it had been a killing done in a moment of anger it could be anybody. But both these were obviously carefully planned killings. And a successful businessman isn't a gun for hire, doesn't go to a man's room and kill him, or gun a guy in an alley. If anything, he hires a goon and a guy like Wren would have to be out of his mind to hire a killer, be paying off the rest of his life. Actually, the only real link Wren had to the case was the job he gave Owens to do on Rose and that wasn't much of a link. As for his being The Bird, the phone book was full of Eagles and Robbinses. And if Wren was involved it sure wasn't a one-man job nailing him down. A dozen men should be digging into his past, his home, his neighbors, his plant should be staked out. And the same thing went for the Owens family. And the Data jerks.

I'd given myself a deadline and it was past that. Although they might hand my head to me on my badge for not reporting all this sooner, I headed for the precinct.

Lieutenant Reed was out but Captain Lampkin was sitting behind his desk, his blue and gold coat open like a drape, his white shirt bunched up over his belt. He was reading a teletype and after a moment he turned his big puss up at me and asked slowly, "You on duty, Wintino?"

"No, sir. But I have something that may help on the Owens-Wales murders," I said, placing the bankbook on his desk. "This was found taped under Owens' dresser drawer by his daughter Susan, along with four thousand dollars in fifty-buck bills. I have a list of the bills, Susan Owens has the money in a sealed envelope. I also have the tape home—might raise some prints. I've checked with the bank and from the signatures, Francis Parker was Ed Owens. The check for $4000.75 was paid to Owens by a manufacturer named Edwin Wren. He claims he agreed to pay Owens a grand for doing some private work in connection with a case our squad is handling: a writer named Rose Henderson is—was—being annoyed by strange phone calls, pushed around and rough-shadowed on the street. She's doing an article that exposes Wren's and several other companies as a monopoly. I took care of that, Wren has agreed to stop it. But he says he hired Owens about six weeks ago and that Owens then blackmailed him for the four grand."

"When did you learn about the money and bankbook?" Lampkin asked, his slow voice reminding me of a funeral-mine.

"Late last night. Mrs. Owens phoned here yesterday that she wanted to see me. She wasn't exactly holding out, but she wanted me to check this morning and see if it was evidence or not…. Four grand isn't carfare."

"And too much to pay for private work."

"Yes, sir. Seems Owens was using a phony name, according to Wren, to avoid paying tax. I figure it might be a motive for Owens' death, although it seems pretty far-fetched. As for Wales, he doesn't fit in, but I have a hunch, a theory, about an old collar Wales and Owens made, that should be looked into. Has some odd angles."

"Seems like both Owens and Wales had something going for themselves."

"That's what I think, Captain. I wasn't trying to solo on this, just wanted to check before I turned it over to you."

"Nice of you to do this on your own time, Wintino. I'll send the dope down to Central Bureau. This Wren in the phone book?"

"Yes sir, Edwin Wren & Company, they make electrical gadgets. I'd like to work with Central on this, or at least talk over my theory with them," I said, almost high with relief. And I wasn't going to let the glory hounds downtown get the credit on this if anything broke.

"When are you due in?"

"Tomorrow midnight."

"This theory of yours, does it require immediate action?"

"I don't think so. You understand, Captain, I'm not sure of anything, just a strong hunch that may blow up."

"They haven't even got a weak hunch working on the Wales killing, so might be worth looking into yours," Lampkin said, picking up his phone. He asked for an inspector at Central Bureau and after they called each other by their first names and asked about the family, Lampkin told him about the bankbook and the inspector must have put on the detective who was handling the case and Lampkin repeated what I'd told him about the bankbook and Wren and that I had a theory about Wales. Then he said, "Dave Wintino, Detective Third Grade… Yeah, yeah, he made that maniac arrest. The Owens family called him last night and told him about the money…. Why? Maybe because he has a trusting face…. What? Come off it, Wally. On his own time he found out who gave Owens the check and why, saved you fellows a lot of legwork…. Yeah, he's a real beaver. You know these young studs—all pistols. Says he has something on Wales, an idea, he wants to talk over…. Midnight tour tomorrow…. Sure, that's okay, he won't mind…. What? You out of your mind? The Giants have it in the bag. You should live that long."

Lampkin hung up and stared at the phone for a moment as if in deep thought, then he looked up at me. "Call Detective Shavers at Central Bureau in the morning, around ten. He'll arrange to meet you. What's the matter with your face? Haven't you outgrown boils yet, or don't you know how to shave right?"

"Why, I… uh… well, sir, I was in a fight."

"I hear you're handy with your dukes. Remember we have several posts here in need of a tough beat cop," Lampkin said, drawing out each word the way he always talked, like it was an effort. He picked up the teletype report.

I started for the door, then asked, "Anything new on Wales?"

He shook his big head. "Nothing, haven't even found anybody to question. Yeah, they found he sometimes got himself one of these expensive young call girls, holed up in a hotel room with her and a couple of bottles, knocked himself out. About every three months. Told the girls he was a buyer from Chicago. A guy his age doing that, don't know where he got the juice. Certainly can't tell about people nowadays."

I said "Yes, sir" and walked out. Downstairs, I remembered I'd left my bag on his desk. I went back to his office, told him, "Excuse me. I left my coconut milk on your desk."

As I picked up the bag he asked slowly, "Your what?"

"Coconut milk," I said, half taking the can out of the bag so he could see.

Lampkin looked sad and when I walked out I heard him mutter, "I'll be a sonofabitch if I know what the world is coming to."

Friday Evening

I was feeling tops when I reached the old apartment. I'd been so damn sure Lampkin was going to bust me for working alone. I don't know why but soon as I kissed Ma and hugged Pa the high feeling left. Then I was sore at myself for being restless in my parents' home.

First it was the fuss Ma made over the cut on my face, crying I was back in the ring again. Then there were the unsaid comments about Mary. She had phoned her excuses, said she had to work late, but both Ma's and Pop's eyes asked me, "What kind of a wife have you got that she is ashamed of us?"

Ma brushed off the can of coconut milk and despite it being a warm night, she gave me the full treatment—minestrone, gefüllte fish, lasagna and boiled chicken. Whenever I said I had enough she would give me another helping as she asked, "You sick, Dave, or don't you like *my* cooking anymore?"

He kept right up with me, even had room to pack away the dessert— noodle pudding in fruit sauce. The old boy looked good. As Ma gave me the latest family gossip Pa, full of his usual sly humor, smoked one of his strong black Italian cigars and made snide remarks about both sides of the family.

I sat and half-listened, my heavy gut making me sleepy, thinking they certainly had the happy little world of their own Rose had talked of. Because of the difference in their religions they hadn't married till they were in their late thirties. When I came along a year later—almost killing Ma—both families made up and had been on fair terms ever since. But it must have been rugged to have been "engaged" for nearly ten years. Did Wales have any family troubles—angry in-laws? That needed checking.

Pop turned on the TV while Ma did the dishes and we sat like a couple of slugs, dozing off at an old movie. Once Pop asked, "Dave, is everything all right with you and Mary?"

"The best. But you know how it is, little fights and… Naw, Pa, guess we aren't making it. She doesn't want me to be a cop. Wants me to take some dull job with her uncle."

"You think Mama and I don't tremble when we see a headline about a policeman hurt or shot? You should understand her view too."

"That isn't it. She has these phony standards—a desk job is good, any other job stinks. She'd rather have me a half-ass 'executive' than a police lieutenant. Know what kind of funky job her Uncle Frank has for me? I should start in at thirty-five a week as a land of strong-arm fink."

Pop sighed. "That is definitely no good. Still you should be patient, see her side."

"Why? Why shouldn't she see *my* side? Pa, I think we should have a kid now, while we're young, but I don't make an issue of the fact she wants to hold on to her gassy job. I—"

Pa held up a skinny finger, pointed toward the kitchen. Ma came in, drying her hands. She put out a bowl of fruit and sat down. "It's after nine, turn to Channel 5, see what has happened to Big White Sing, the Indian Scout."

As Pop changed stations he made a mock bow and told me, "Behold what television does to culture. At her age she must see a cowboy movie every night."

"Shhh!" Mom said.

I sat in the semidarkness, sleepy and full, suddenly thinking of Owens and his wife watching their old TV, another happy home… and him out hustling a four-grand cushion. And a penny-snatcher like Wales spending all his dough on a hopelessly sick wife… how damn lonely he must have been to loosen up and spend a couple of hundred bucks with a call girl. What must it feel like, dressing like a slob, working for twenty-five bucks a week: with eleven grand wrapped around your gut? The—

The phone rang and Pa got it, said, "Yes. He's here. We were sorry you couldn't make it tonight…. Yes, get some rest. The heat takes its toll…. Mama had a wonderful supper. Maybe next Friday… I'll call him."

He put the phone down and came over to me. "Your wife is on the phone, David."

"What does she want?" Ma shrilled.

"Mama!" Poppa scolded softly as I picked up the receiver, asked, "Yeah, Mary?"

"Dave, I feel nervous, scary. I… can you come home right away?"

"Sure. What's the matter?"

"Nothing really, except I have this feeling. Three times in the last hour the phone has rung and each time there wasn't any answer, not a sound."

"Nothing to get excited about. Could be a couple of wrong numbers, or something wrong with the phone."

"Davie, please come home. It may be silly but each time I said hello, the more certain I was that somebody was listening at the other end. The phone was *too* quiet. Please, Davie, I'm jittery."

"Okay, Babes. I'll leave now and be there within an hour. Make you feel better, go visit a neighbor and I'll pick you up there."

"No. Somehow I don't want to leave the apartment. I'm not the kind that goes up in the air but I have this terrible feeling, have it so strong, that something… evil… is waiting outside. Just hurry home."

"Okay, sit tight and don't open the door for anybody but me. Turn up the TV and try to relax. I'm leaving now," I said, hanging up.

When I tried to explain it to Ma she said, "What's the matter, she can't let us have you for a few hours? She's nervous and… David, is she pregnant?"

"Not that I heard. Guess I'd better go." I wondered if the three phone calls were an accident. But it didn't make sense for the Data clowns to start giving me the works. And Wren had said he was calling them off. Maybe she had seen a horror show on TV… and three calls were spooky to a girl home alone. Still, she wasn't the emotional kind… but she might really be tired and upset. I could phone the local precinct to have the beat cop look in, but how would that sound?

Ma hinted that Mary was doing all this on purpose and Pop said, "Such nonsense, Mama. And if his wife is nervous, no matter what the reason, what else should the boy do but rush home? Dave, call us the moment you reach your house."

I said I would and was about to borrow cab fare but didn't want them to know I was broke. I was sounding almost as hysterical as Mary.

I had luck at the subway, an express was just pulling in. Thinking it over on the ride downtown I knew what had happened: Uncle Frank had phoned, said I hadn't gone overboard about the job, and this was Mary's

way of needling me. She'd been mad because I went up to Ma's anyway…
and the last couple of days had just been one long argument. Only if Mary
was sore about something she usually said so.

I made good time, it was a few minutes under ten-fifteen when I ran up
the subway steps and headed toward our place. I didn't even stop to buy
the morning paper. If it was the Data boys, if I found Flatts hanging around
my place, I'd give him a beating he'd sure never forget. But when I reached
our corner, turned into the block, everything looked so quiet and peaceful
I decided to have it out with Mary. If this was her sneaky way of getting
back at me for having supper with the folks it was time we found out where
we stood. In fact that time was long due.

When I'm mad I walk fast and I was rushing into the entrance of our
house when I heard the sudden step behind me, felt a hell of a big gun
shoved in my right side. Then a heavy arm went around my neck, hugging
my shoulders in a hard embrace and Mr. Wren was saying loudly, "No
more talking, not that late. Come on, let's have a last drink."

It was a good act even though nobody was around to see it; looked like
a friendly greeting. His left arm casually around my shoulder while his right
held the gun inside his coat pocket against my side. We were about the same
height and I was looking smack into his eyes, eyes distorted by his thick
glasses. At first I was so completely surprised at seeing Wren—if anybody,
I'd expected the Data clowns—my mind was a blank. But one look at those
eyes and I got scared, but fast.

According to the *Police Manual* I should have gone for my gun. There
wasn't any crowd or bystander to stop a wild shot. Even common sense
should have told me to make a stand, call his bluff. But his eyes told me
the gun in my side wasn't any bluff, it would mean a sure slug in the gut.

He said gently, jovially, "Oh, now, just one last nightcap." Then the
whisper: "Keep your hands in sight. If you're not foolish you may live. Now
walk!"

If he had pushed me, if his gun had left my side for a second, I might have
made my play. But he was smart, waited for me to walk, then moved with
me, like we were a couple of chums. There wasn't a person in sight on the
dimly lit street as we headed toward Second Avenue. Then his left hand
neatly slid inside my coat while his gun, feeling as big and round as a
shotgun barrel, pressed into my kidney as he took my gun from the
shoulder holster. He didn't try to pocket the gun, merely pushed it up his
sleeve and kept walking with his arm around my shoulder.

I was still frightened but mostly I was burning with shame. For a cop to
have his gun lifted is like wearing a coward's badge. I'd never live this down.
I never thought I'd be a complete coward… but I was.

We kept walking slowly toward the lights of Second Avenue. I said,

"You're crazy, Wren, if you think you can get away with this!" And my voice was as shrill as Ma's.

"If I don't you'll never hear about it in the cemetery. Use your head, Wintino. All I want is to have a quiet chat with you."

I told myself that when we reached Second Avenue, or if anybody came along, I'd drop flat and go for his legs. He wouldn't dare pull anything in the light, with people around. But with my gun lost I might as well let him plug me.

We were three stores and a tenement from the avenue. The first store had a FOR RENT sign in the window—it had been a ritzy gift shop till a few months ago. He suddenly steered me into the doorway, looked around quickly, then opened the door and his gun pushed me in.

Closing the door softly he told me, "Clasp the back of your neck with both hands, please," and his gun slid up my side to my neck, like a snake. "Blink your eyes to get used to the darkness, then walk toward the back of the store. A false move, even if you should trip, and I'll be forced to kill you. Walk—slowly."

I walked. I felt lost, beaten. He knew his business, no chance for me to kick backward. The pressure of the gun barrel lessened and then from the sound of his steps and the heat of his body, I knew he was walking an arm's length back of me.

Blinking my eyes I saw the store was empty except for an open arched doorway we were nearing. Wren said, "Walk straight through the center of the opening, turn slowly— when I tell you."

We walked into what must have been a small stockroom. A little door to my right was ajar and outlined by dim light—not a light within the room but coming from outside.

He told me to turn and open the door. The room, the size of a phone booth, was the john with a tiny barred window high up that caught some faint light from Second Avenue. There wasn't room for the two of us. Wren said, "Turn around and sit on the toilet—with your hands in sight. I didn't mean any comical touch but this is the best place I could find for an undisturbed talk. Man's confidence in locks is touching, even in a simple spring lock on a store door."

I sat down as Wren leaned against the doorway, the light giving his glasses a weird smoky look. He was wearing pigskin gloves and the pistol in his hand had a bulky silencer—which was why it had felt big as a shotgun in my back. He said, "I'm sorry to pull a gun on you, and all this hocus-pocus. We may part as friends. I hope so, sincerely I hope that. Killing is a terrible thing, an idiotic gesture that—"

The tightness within me suddenly shot up to my mouth; I had to talk. "You're not going to kill me!" I said, my voice still high. "You're not that much of a fool. I reported my visit to your office, if I'm found dead you'll be number one on the suspect parade!" I sounded hysterical; was surprised I could still wisecrack.

"Don't raise your voice," he said, holding my gun in his left hand as he pocketed his own, then switched my gun to his right hand. The sight of my own rod made me snap out of it.

No matter what happened I had to get my gun back. Wren said, "As for any report, I must doubt that. You are young and cocksure, out to make a name. Very commendable too. After you left, the one thing that remained in my mind was your saying you were working on your own time. I figure you for a glory hunter, a lone hand. Otherwise you would have visited me with your partner. As you see, unfortunately I have some small knowledge of police work."

His voice was still weary and in the deadness of the empty store very clear. "Although I hold a gun on you, Wintino, this is not necessarily an unfriendly conversation. We shall—"

"Sure, you're doing me a big favor. I get knocked off in a store instead of in an alley like Owens got his!" My voice was back to normal.

He smiled, a very tired smile. "Your bravado has returned—fine. Only don't let it go to your head, you'll have need for some clear thinking. As for Owens—I didn't kill him. I wouldn't be here now except I suspected you realized the blunder I made in my office."

"Yeah?" I said, trying to stall for time, to think.

He belched slightly, there was a light odor of whisky. "Whether you are pretending innocence or not doesn't matter now. When you asked about the check, I'd thought all along that Wales had forged it, that's why I had to shoot him. A sad error, perhaps my undoing. I completely misjudged Wales. He was an honest and intelligent man."

I felt as if I'd got a shot in the arm, even the heavy meal in my belly seemed to have digested. One word kept banging in my brain, clearing the cobwebs—*forged*. Wren had sued a bank for a forged check at the time when Wales' wife had run up a big hospital bill. I said, "You mean you thought it was Wales forging a second check?"

He blinked, or something happened behind those foggy glasses. "You are far smarter than I thought. So you know about that. Although Wales didn't forge the check—exactly. I'm going to tell you certain things not because I want to but because I sincerely don't wish to kill you."

"You touch me—Bird!"

Another belch, the hairs of his mustache flying in the breeze. "Don't be stupid-brave, Wintino. That's all I ask of you. Listen to me and think, think like a man not like a kid. In the office I said something about live and let live. Perhaps you didn't pay any attention to it. Concentrate on it now,

Wintino: *live* and *let live*. Keep running it over in your mind. It's a remarkable philosophy, the basic rule of our world. Self-preservation is said to be the first law of life, but we really protect ourselves by following the live-and-let-live rule. I'm not preaching to you, or talking about something abstract. I've found from bitter experience that all that stops our world from being more of a jungle than it is…"

I wasn't listening. Wales had been so right: keep digging. I had never bothered to check Wren's signature on the Parker check. Well, to hell with that now. The bathroom was small and he was in the doorway, less than three feet away. He'd be watching my right hand: by leaning forward I might be able to hook his fat belly with my left. The light was dim, if I fell forward to my right I might belt him fast enough to fall out of the line of fire.

"… So, if I can explain, you'll be able to understand what this is all about. I'm sorry you're so young, an older man would see the logic. Wales did. And Solly Kahn. I'm not a thug or—"

"Some logic! Wales is dead!"

"A rash mistake on my part, as I said. Perhaps that's why I'm talking to you—I don't want to make another mistake. You see, I don't know where one draws the line between criminal and noncriminal, or if there is such a line; when pressed everyone will turn to 'crime.' I'm going far afield, Wintino. The point is I graduated from college at the start of the depression. You work and sweat for an education and it all turns out to be a large zero, a—"

"Get down to facts. Why did you kill Wales?"

He shook his head gently. "Since I have the gun I will do the talking. I'm not trying to bully you, but cut the tough little brat line."

"The big executive mans with a gun calls me a brat," I said leaning toward him.

"Sit back, make yourself comfortable, Wintino. And I know how to use a gun. Now, you never went through a depression. My engineering degree wasn't worth a damn. I was forced to work as a waiter, pearl diver, anything for a meal. While I was living in a cheap boarding house I met Solly Kahn. To you Solly is probably only a man with a record, to me he is a saint. He was a bootlegger and the trouble with bootlegging was the expense and risk of running the stuff in. A still in the city was hard to hide and—"

"And you made an electric one," I cut in, watching the lights on his glasses.

"I did, and an excellent piece of engineering it was, a silent still. Solly and I started making money, big money for those hard times—nearly six thousand dollars." Wren waved my gun in a small arc, as if making a big point. "I was a bootlegger, breaking the law, if you wish, but I'd found laws are a fraud. I lived by a law that said if you work hard you get ahead and if it wasn't for Solly I'd have been selling apples on a corner. I suppose you think you know the rest?"

"Sure I do. Kahn gunned Boots Brenner when he tried to muscle in," I said. I had a sudden uneasy feeling, neither fear nor anger, but kind of as if I was watching something, as if I was seeing myself on a stage.

"The obvious details. Solly shot this thug in self-defense. We were sure he wouldn't get the chair. But the gun was mine, I had a permit for it. When he was caught Solly carefully hid the weapon behind a loose brick in the wall. I was—"

"That's what Wales was searching for all those years," I cut in.

Again that tired smile. "You are more thorough than I imagined. Yes, the gun was hidden and Solly never talked, not even when facing the chair. You see I wasn't around the plant much, I was still seeking that token of respectability and security, a job at my profession. And Solly, who never had been inside a college, demonstrated the highest intelligence, he didn't see any sense in incriminating me. What good would it do? Can you understand that?" He paused, his stomach rumbling. "Tell me, Detective, what good would it have done? Would justice have been served any better? Would anything be gained by ruining me? Tell me, Wintino, what would you have done if you had found the gun?"

"Arrested you as an accessory to the crime. You would have had your day in court."

"My day in court? When there weren't any jobs for engineers what chance would I have had, what future, smeared and with a criminal record? That's the real fact of the matter and Solly realized that. Live and let live. He let me live. It was his money, his and mine, that enabled me to start my factory. Sal Kahn, a true human being. I've never forgotten him."

"I know, that monthly registered letter to his mother."

Wren stared at me, his glasses like two dull headlights. "You're too smart, I certainly didn't make any mistake seeing you, Wintino."

"You still made a mistake," I said, closing my eyes for a second. The light in those thick lenses seemed to hypnotize me. "Pointing a gun at a cop is a big mistake."

"I'm not talking to a cop but to a human being. I trust the gun will never enter our conversation. But let me remind you this is a vacant store and the gun will be your gun. Naturally I have set up an alibi, not to mention the fact that I am a successful manufacturer—we are rarely accused of such things as murder. Now, I don't know how long we may have… uh… privacy here, so let me finish. We both will have an important decision to reach then."

"You have the gun, talk." I relaxed against the tank of the toilet. I still felt I had a chance of belting him but I wanted to hear him talk. I kept my eyes on my gun—away from his glasses.

"Kahn did the human thing, let me live when there was no point in hurting me. The missing gun was a big item at the trial, although it wouldn't have made any difference in the verdict. Al Wales was one of those lucky people who never work—they enjoy their job and hence it ceases to be work. He never gave up searching for the gun in the old building. Naturally I avoided the place although I wondered about the gun too. I had nightmares over it for many years—the serial number would point at me. Well, Wales did find the gun and he was an intelligent man too. He realized I had nothing to do with the actual killing, that I had used the money to build my factory; I had gone straight—to use a trite phrase that has no meaning. So even though he at last had the evidence he had hunted for over many years, he did nothing about it. Live and let live."

"Wales isn't living."

"I've told you I made a stupid error," Wren said, his voice coming alive with anger. "Wales didn't use his evidence because he was a sensible man like Solly who—"

"And they're both dead."

"Wintino, stop talking like a phonograph record. Yes, they are dead and you and I are alive and want to stay that way. In 1949, years after he found the gun, Wales did another intelligent thing. He needed money for an operation on his wife and came to me. Understand, it wasn't blackmail, but live and let live. He needed help in his living. We talked things over, much as we are—"

"You hold a gun on him too?"

"Wales was a mature man, guns weren't necessary. As it happened, I didn't have any cash handy. I'd been expanding rapidly. However, I felt my obligation to Wales so we both hit upon the idea of letting a bank give Wales the money. It was rather a neat idea, one that my business situation made ideal."

There was another tired grin. I looked at his eyes. Then at the street light on the gun barrel. I counted the buttons on his coat, a left beside the last button would kayo him. Even if he shot me, I'd have a chance to grab my gun.

The silence in the coffin-like room was heavy and I glanced at his eyes. The glasses seemed to bore into my eyes. I had this feeling again that I was watching a movie.

Wren said, "I was waiting to see if you had caught on to our scheme— you'd be a genius if you had. I will tell you about it to illustrate how two men under stress can work together in perfect harmony. Wren & Company was doing a large turnover and checks for five, ten, twenty, even thirty thousand dollars cleared through my account fairly often. Wales opened an account in a Bronx bank using an alias and a fake address. Over a two-month period he made a few deposits and withdrawals and in the meantime practiced forging my name—with my help. At the beginning of the third month he forged my name to a check, made out to his alias, for twenty thousand dollars. It was on a regular printed Wren & Company check. He deposited this in his new account. It was truly a foolproof scheme. Banks rarely check signatures but if my bank should question mine, if they called me to verify it, I was to tell them it was my signature but I wanted the check stopped, for business reasons. That would have been the end of it. In that case I would have mortgaged my plant to raise Wales' money. Look at me, Wintino, or doesn't this interest you?"

"Yeah, I'm all ears. The bank let the check go through and in a few weeks Wales closed out his account and the phony name became a dead end."

Wren nodded and the light seemed to make his glasses spin. "Yes, the check went through without a hitch and Wales gave me my old gun, which I destroyed. On the second of the following month, when I received my bank statement, I naturally made a fuss about the forged check. I had three experts testify my signature was a forgery. Legally I had to go through the red tape of suing the bank. Within a few months the suit came up and I won, of course. Wales had his money without any strain on my part. You see what two intelligent men can do when they put their minds to work?"

"I see, you robbed a bank."

"Technically, yes. But who suffered? The bank was insured and as for the insurance companies, perhaps this caused them to raise their rates one-hundredth of one per cent. Being a smart man Wales didn't do anything to arouse suspicion. By that I mean he never put the money in his regular account, nor did he start living big. He played strictly by our rules."

"Is that why he's dead?"

"A mistake. I keep telling you that! A man doesn't reach the top by being soft. I have a family, an industry, a position, to protect. I frankly told Wales he was in a position to keep forging my name. After the lawsuit with the bank I could hardly protest another forgery without giving Wales away, involving myself. I impressed upon him that I had carried out my end of the deal, and if he ever tried blackmailing me in the future, killing would be the only answer. For over seven years I never heard from Wales. Then, several days ago when I received my monthly bank statement and canceled checks I found—"

"A forged check for $4000.75 made out to a Francis Parker," I said getting the complete picture fast. "Wales must have kept things a secret from Owens—till a couple months ago. Wales probably blabbered while juiced and Owens decided to try his luck."

"Precisely, except I was certain it was Wales tapping me again. I can hardly be blamed for assuming that. And the only real answer to blackmail is a bullet. Actually I didn't even read about Owens' death until after I shot Wales and the papers played up both killings. I didn't know a thing about Owens' death but I felt it would benefit me by throwing off any possible suspicion on me."

"You had a wrongo hunch on that."

"Perhaps. It wasn't until you came into my office and said Owens had the money that I realized Owens had got into the game. Undoubtedly Wales killed Owens in the alley to make it look like a robbery. Must have told him to stop and Owens wanted another crack at my jackpot. You can see Wales *had* to kill him, to protect himself. Just as I thought I *had* to kill Wales. I blundered. I shot him while he was in a drunken sleep. He died without pain but I never gave him a chance to explain. I admit it was a terrible blunder, but that's over, nothing we do now can ever bring Wales back to life."

"What's there to do?" I asked, keeping my eyes on his thick mustache.

"That's the point of our talk. I want to live, Wintino. I want to avoid a scandal that will haunt my wife and children forever. Your young, life is ahead of you. I'm in a position to offer you $35,000 in cash. If you spend it wisely and slowly and keep your job it means a comfortable nest egg for the rest of your years and some immediate small pleasures—a new car, a house. Naturally you'll have to keep the money in a safe deposit vault, spend it carefully. Even your wife must never know. If you have children, their education is—"

I sat up straight, pressed the crease in my pants. "No dice."

"Think of something except your pants, damn you. Think! Don't say no before you mull it over. You can quit the department and live like a king in Europe. Or you can hold on to your job, secretly secure, without a money worry. How many young fellows have a chance at life without money worries? Think hard!"

"I'm not buying, Bird. A couple of ex-cops are killed and nobody gives a damn—but I do. You've confessed a murder, I'm going to take you in. If you kill me they'll collar you because I did make a report about my visit to you."

"Boy, don't make me kill you!" Wren said. "Even if you really did make such a report, I can cover the Owens check with the yarn I gave you this afternoon. I've been thinking it over. Even though I did make it up on the spur of the moment, it's good, it will hold. And I have an alibi for every second of the day Wales was killed. If I have to make a run for it, killing you will give me time and as the old saying goes, they can only hang me once. Please think about—"

"There's nothing to think about. You killed Wales. I'm a cop. I have to arrest you." I leaned forward slightly, slowly, wondering if Wren would be amateur enough to try for the head instead of the body.

"God, if only you were older, more mature…! Wintino, listen to me, laws were made not as a punishment but to prevent crimes. I killed Wales but I'm not a killer, a criminal. I *had* to kill, so would you to protect yourself, your family. I'll never kill again, nor commit a crime, so what's the point in arresting me? Can't you understand? It would be your duty to arrest me if you thought that by letting me go you were endangering society. There never will be any reason, any need for me to kill again. If we act intelligently we can both live in peace."

"And when will I get it like Wales did?" I raised my right hand slowly to my head, pretended to scratch my hair.

Wren's gun hand followed my right as he said, "Never, unless you try to blackmail me. Or if I tried to blackmail you, I would expect you to kill me. Wintino, this isn't something to haggle about. I'll go the limit—$45,000 and you get it all by Tuesday."

"Bribing an officer of the law is an additional—"

"*Bribing?* You stupid ass of a kid! You must realize what big money means in this world, what—"

I set my feet and raised my right hand toward my head again. As his eyes and my gun followed, I threw myself forward, on my right shoulder, bringing up as hard a left hook as I could.

The tiny room came alive with thunder and the stink of gunpowder. I felt the punch up to my elbow, my fist ramming into his fat belly. A gut punch is a paralyzer. I saw him sinking to the floor, nothing moving except his mouth, which seemed open in a wide scream of fear.

I reached out and grabbed his right hand, digging my nails into his wrist till he dropped my gun. I picked it up and got to my feet. *He hadn't hit me!*

I wanted to shout a prayer of thanks, and as I stood up a hot wire ripped across my stomach like a burning knife. Everything was pain, searing pain that made me sink to my knees beside him and scream and scream and scream.

I pressed my stomach to hold down the burning and felt blood. The bastard had shot me. The first time my gun was used on a man it had to be me.

I was on my knees, trying not to keel over, almost on top of Wren who lay there, crumpled, not moving, mouth open as far as he could get it. His glasses had half-fallen off his nose and one eye was enlarged by a lens and bright with pain; the other was a small glitter in the dim light. He wasn't out, just stunned by the gut belt.

I tried to move and pain went through my body like a million knives and I screamed again and again… and heard only silence. The store was full of the same old dusty stillness. My mouth was open but I wasn't making a sound. The silence of the empty store had absorbed the brief bark of the gun. It was crazy, nothing had changed—except I'd be dead in another ten minutes, an hour at the longest. And in a few minutes Wren would be able to walk away.

His eyes were mocking me now, at least the one eye covered by his glasses. I looked away, at my gun in my hand, was damn glad I was going out like a real cop. When I raised my gun Wren's eye grew so big with fear I thought it would pop through the thick glass.

I said, "I'm not going to kill you," but the words slid all around my mouth and I chewed on them as the pain throbbed deep in me like a long piston needle going up and down in my guts.

I sent a bullet through his knee cap to anchor him. There wasn't any thunder this time, merely a sharp clear bark and a flash of orange, both swallowed by the darkness of the store, never heard outside.

Wren was on his back, out cold, fainted. I took a deep breath that seemed to smother the pointed burning within me; I pulled his gun out of his pocket, crawled over him. The crawling put my blood on fire and when I reached the archway that opened on the store, I had to let go, sink into the pain.

When I came to, the pain was still throbbing steadily in my stomach, stabbing at my heart and brain now and then. Everything about me seemed wet with blood. There was a dull sound behind me. I had to listen for many seconds before I realized it was Wren moaning, calling for help. I got up on my knees, it was easier to move on my knees than to crawl. I made the left wall of the store, the fire within me soaring higher each time I moved. Resting my shoulder against the wall I tried to see the store-front window. I couldn't focus, things were blurred. I figured I was ten feet away. It didn't matter, I couldn't move another inch. I'd had it.

Holding my gun in my left hand, I took out Wren's. I tried a deep breath: it didn't work, the air came rushing down my throat hot and dry. I had to rest for a few seconds, then pivoting on my left shoulder I heaved Wren's gun in the direction of the window. I heard myself scream this time all right, heard it over the crash of glass. I don't know, but it was me and I was screaming, "*Dad! Dad!*"

I slumped against the wall and waited, each breath tearing my lungs apart with strain and fire. The broken window was a foggy square and for a long long time nothing happened. I had to let go again, fall into the fire inside me.

Opening my eyes was a big job. The window was still foggy… with the pale blur of a face looking in.

Aiming at the ceiling I fired my gun fast as I could. On the third shot it jumped out of my hand. I'd lost my gun again but I had to let go. I had to let go of everything. No flames this time, nothing… I was falling over and over into nothing.

Saturday Afternoon

There was a vase with red roses on the metal table in one corner of the hospital room. The roses were very red. Not many and the cheapest kind—a few dumpy roses with petals open in a big grin. I knew who'd sent them.

The hospital room was small and efficient and crummy, like all hospitals. I shut my eyes again. I'd never felt so pooped. Of course I knew where I was. I'd been semiconscious when the beat cop had knelt beside me, took his gun off me when he found my badge. I'd passed out in the ambulance but came to when a nurse was cutting my clothes off, ruining my suit, just before they gave me a shot that put me to sleep. I awoke for a few seconds when I was getting a transfusion, then dropped off for a long sleep. I vaguely recalled talking to Lieutenant Reed and some hatchet-faced inspector from downtown, the two of them hovering over my bed like a couple of ugly birds. I gave them the dope on Wren and Wales.

I opened my eyes and moved my head. The shade was down but it was bright outside. Looking made me tired and I kept staring straight ahead at the roses—roses from Rose and as red as her mouth. I was probably all over the papers and Rose had come soon as she read about it.

A nurse came in, a long gawky babe who had to look better when out of the white dress, the horrible stockings and white shoes. Over a standard smile she asked, "How do you feel, Mr. Wintino?"

"Okay." Her fingers were firm and cool as she took my pulse. "When did the flowers come?"

"Must have come this morning, before I came on. Shall I find out who they're from?"

"Do that and see if there was any message."

The nurse slipped me what was supposed to be a wise smile. "Your wife is waiting. Feel up to seeing her, for a little while?"

"Sure. Got a mirror and comb?"

"Not yet. You mustn't attempt to sit up or move about."

"Am I going to be stuck in bed long?"

"You ask the doctor about that. I'll send Mrs. Wintino in. The moment you feel tired, stop talking, tell your wife to leave. Sleep is the best medicine you can get at the moment."

The nurse left and my eyelids weighed a ton. I don't know, I thought I opened them a second later but it must have been longer. Mary was sitting beside my bed, looked as if she'd been sitting there a long time. She looked pretty bad, blond hair uncombed, eyes red, face strained, a tired stoop to her shoulders. And the roses on the table behind her seemed to frame her head.

I'd never seen her look so bad. I stared at her face, and the red of the roses, and thought how silly it was for us to keep knocking each other out. This was the right time to settle things. I said, "Hello, Babes."

She must have been daydreaming, she jumped a little. "Dave, Dave, how are you feeling?" She began to cry gently.

"A bit tired. Why the tears? I'm okay. Understand they had to stitch up my guts and I know there's a drain sticking in me someplace…. But in a few days I'll be up and around, out of here."

"Of course you will. I'll try to get a week off at the office, and well go someplace in the country and rest."

"You need a rest. Sure, we'll have a whole week to rest and talk about it."

"Talk about what?"

"Come on, honey, I know you too well, it's all over your face: you can't wait to talk."

"Dave, all I want is for you to get well."

"And then we'll talk?"

"Dave, you're in a hospital, just take it easy and—"

"No, honey, let's talk this out now. I feel like it."

"Dave, you're getting excited, tired. You need sleep and—"

"Babes, I'll be more excited if we don't talk, get things straight. Go ahead, spill it."

"Really, Dave, I don't know what you mean. You go back to sleep and I'll—"

"Mary, let's get this settled. Go ahead, I'll let you know when I'm tired."

"What do you want me to say?" Her voice was a whine.

"All the words you've been saving up for me. Let them go, be the best thing for both of us."

"Well…" She hesitated, her red eyes staring at me. "All right, we'll talk, if you wish."

"That's what I wish."

"Dave, you sound so… I don't know." Her voice became high and thin. "Dave, Dave, listen to me: I can't take this any longer. I can't stand waiting around for my husband to come home, worry myself crazy till the middle of the morning when I'm informed you're in a hospital, nearly dead.

That's no way for us to live…. Oh, Dave! this isn't the time or place, I can't talk about it now."

"Yes, you can, say it." The roses seemed to be laughing at her.

"Dave…" The tears really rolled. "Well, Dave, you either have to give up being a cop or we're done. Dave, I can't take it. I can't!"

"Don't cry, Mary. You want me to be a glorified goon for Uncle Frank at forty a week?"

"Please, Dave, we don't have to talk about this now? We—"

"Yes, we do have to talk about it! Is working for Uncle Frank what you want?"

"All I want is to have you work normal hours, where there's no chance of you ever being shot or beaten up. Is that unreasonable? I don't care what you do, as long as you're not a cop."

"I'm going to remain a cop."

"Why?" she asked loudly, hysterically.

"Because I'm not only the youngest detective on the force, at this moment I'm the *best!* That's important—I could never be the best stock clerk in the city or the best anything else. And because it's *my* job. I…" Talking sure took it out of me: I let the words fade on my lips.

Mary sat up very straight and stiff as she said, "Dave, we're… we're… finished."

"I think so, Babes. Now it's in the open."

She seemed to fall apart as she put her face in her hands, cried into them. "Is that all you can say? Dave, why must you be so tough, so hard?"

"Honey, honey, I'm not being tough. Don't you see, we've been finished for a long time, but we were both afraid to face it. You want a guy you can steer, somebody you can push together with up the same road. All this striving is important to you but not to me." My voice got low and I stopped for a moment, felt strength flowing back into me like a tiny tide.

Mary said through her tears, "Don't talk, Dave, it isn't good for you to—"

"It's great for me. Babes, you want this cocktail dueling, the clever hustle. You wouldn't be satisfied if I was working for Uncle Frank. There'd always be another job and then another—up some imaginary ladder. There's no sense in our hurting each other. Mary honey, you're a nice girl and when you get the right man you'll both hit it off. I'm not that man. I'm a cop."

"*Cop!* You're happy because you're a big hero again, another citation, maybe a medal this time, and you'll be the youngest second-grade detective now. That's what you enjoy, being a cocky wise guy because you think you're something special, something on a stick! It's all your goddamn vanity!"

"And if I do enjoy my job, if I am cocky, where do you come off always trying to change me? Babes, don't you see, it's no good if we have to change each other?"

She ran a handkerchief over her face. "It's a waste of time talking to you, Dave, you're so stubborn."

"It's a waste of time because we see things differently."

She stood up. "Breaking up a marriage isn't pleasant. Dave, I want to give us every chance. Why can't you get a leave from the force and try it my way? I've tried yours and it's made me a nervous wreck."

"Mary, playing catch-up never works. You're young and pretty, you'll get the right guy."

"Made up your mind for a long time now, haven't you?"

"No, but I can say it easily now. I want to put in my hours as a cop and not come home to a night of arguing. That's all."

"Your noble cops! The reporters talked to me, the papers are full of the story. The *good* cops you spent your free time working on, stopped a bullet for, what were they but a couple of cheap chiselers, shakedown artists!"

My eyes were too heavy to keep open. "I was shot bringing in a murderer, what I'm paid to do. Maybe I was a little screwy, put a halo around a badge. From now on it will just be a job to me, but a job I like."

The room was very quiet, reminded me of the stillness of the store. I opened my eyes: Mary was gone. I felt nervous, lousy and relieved. I turned my head to the cool side of the pillow. I ought to sleep, be strong enough to chatter and bull when Danny came… and when Rose came. Not that she liked cops much either. But with her it wouldn't matter too…

The lanky nurse returned. I asked, "What's the message?"

Again the S.O.P. smile. "No message with the flowers. A woman brought them—your mother."

I closed my eyes. "Listen, when my partner, Danny Hayes, comes in, wake me. And if a Miss Henderson should call … well, be sure to wake me. If she visits or phones."

But I knew she wouldn't.

THE END

The Best That Ever Did It

Ed Lacy

For Francis "Down One" Flatts

It was just another ordinary and dreary bar on Amsterdam Avenue in that part of New York City called Washington Heights. Why it was named The Grand Café nobody seems to know. It had neither gaudy neon lights nor air conditioning, and the small screen TV perched in one corner was the same set it had had when TV was a novelty.

It was like an old-fashioned saloon, although it only dated back to 1923. (During Prohibition it was called the Grand Café Ice Cream Parlour and openly sold needle beer and very little ice cream.) It was called a bar, rarely a Café, a joint, a gin-mill, a dive, and a dump. Strangely enough nobody ever called the place what it really was... home.

Certainly not the best of homes, but after a long day at a dull job a man could skip returning to his lonely dingy room and drop into the Grand— which became his living room—for a beer and see the regulars nod at him, hear Jimmy-the bartender-mutter "Hello..." which may have been the only friendly word the man heard all day.

A man could escape—temporarily—the bitterness of tenement poverty that drained his wife's youth and made his children merely pests... by dropping into the bar, which became his den, and watching the ball game or the fights on TV, join in the brassy and meaningless small talk.

In the afternoons a few housewives would come in for a fast beer, to gossip and find out what number was leading. Or just to get a snack, for any time during the day or night you could get a thick hamburger, and it was assumed you wanted a heavy slice of onion and a pickle on it.

In short: in the Grand Café a human could still find a small measure of warmth and dignity in the company of other humans.

On this particular evening, when the men were murdered, the bar was crowded and full of cheer because Lady Luck had gently tickled one of the regulars. His name was Franklin ("But call me Frank") Andersun and he was a thin young man in his late twenties with the kind of face women didn't look at twice, or even once. As befitting the night's celebrity, Andersun was standing at the center of the bar and the others were buying him beers—and he had been trying to make the men's room for the last half hour.

"Tell me, Frankie boy," a newcomer said, shaking his hand and anchoring him to the bar, "how did you work it? I'm reading the paper in the subway and I see your name. Gave me a bang. They really give you a thousand bucks for writing them few words? What was they again?"

"'I eat Nutsy Pudding because I know what I like and I like Nutsy,'" an elderly man repeated, shaking his large head as he talked. "What a way to make a thousand!"

Jimmy the bartender was short and fat, with liver spots on his hands and freckles on his wrinkled face, and all his skin had a preserved, wax-like look to it. Pouring a beer he said, "And that's the trouble with the world, everybody thinks something is easy, after they see it done."

"It was easy, it was the truth," Andersun said. "I'm a fussy eater but I go for that pudding. Eat it like a pig."

"And you're heading for Europe?" the newcomer asked.

"Yeah. But I got to go to the john now or my kidneys will float out of my mouth," Frank said, finally breaking away from the men around him.

"Jimmy, what's he want to go to Europe for?" the newcomer asked the barkeep.

"He just wants to, I guess."

At the end of the bar nearest the door a place was reserved by custom for Danny Macci, whose tremendous shoulders made him look short, although he was well over six feet tall. He had bushy strong hair that was all gray, an ugly face, and a large square chin. Danny had been a professional wrestler back in a TV-less era when wrestling wasn't such a busy profession, and along with a pair of ears thickened like stuffed prunes, Macci had also contracted an eye disease that left him blind. He lived on a monthly relief check and had little trouble cadging beers from the regulars, and even from Jimmy. At the drop of a beer cap Danny would lecture about "Them lousy clowns they call wrestlers today," or show off his muscles. Now he put down his glass of beer, asked, "Why shouldn't the lad go to Europe? Be nice to hear strange sights and people. Wish I was going."

"Had your eyes, you'd be wrestling all over the world today," Jimmy said.

"That's the truth. I'm near sixty but I'm still a wrestler, not an acrobat. Still got my strength." He held up a thick, gnarled hand. "Anybody want to see me crush a beer can?"

"Now, Danny, ain't necessary to do that," Jimmy said. "You got two beers coming up."

Another regular said, "If I was a young man like Frank, I'd open a store with the money."

"Does surprise me," Jimmy said, moving down the bar with three beers (except for strangers, beer was the week-night drink, with a whiskey or two thrown in on Saturday nights), "because Frank used to talk so much about the money to be made if a fellow got a start."

"What's a grand for a business?" somebody chimed in. "Start on a shoestring and you end up hanging yourself with it."

Andersun returned to the bar and thanked another newcomer who had a beer ready for him. The newcomer asked, "Wasn't you in Europe when you were a pilot?"

"I was a waist gunner, not a pilot," Frank told him. "We got to England just when the war was over in Germany and we flew our B-17's back to the States, started training for the Pacific. Never got there either. In flying, you're always looking down at things. Now I want to see what's going on down there."

"Quitting your job?"

Frank nodded. "Sure. I'll be a stock clerk someplace else after I see what makes Paris tick." He finished his beer. "Near eleven. Guess I'll float on home. See you, Jimmy."

"When you leaving?"

"Not for several weeks. Haven't seen about my passport or boat tickets yet. They only told me I won last night."

"And the reporters came right up to see you," Danny added.

"Not a reporter, the company's public-relations man phoned. He planted the story. See you tomorrow."

As Andersun left, the regular who wanted to open a business said, "Soldier is always a soldier, hey, Jimmy? Remember the way we spent our bonus money back in... When was that, '29, '32, '34, or when?"

"I forget the year but it was the only time I was loaded," Jimmy said. "Tell you, soldiers in the second war are different, more serious, like Frank. They were in longer, saw more action."

"But they never faced no gas like we did. I remember the time..."

"Soldiers, soldiers, big bullying heroes!" Danny cut in loudly. In 1917 he only had partial sight and was rejected.

"That's no way to talk."

Danny turned to face the man. "I talk any damn way I want—unless you think you can stop me!"

Even when he was staggering drunk no one ever tangled with Danny, and it wasn't because he was blind—those thick arms could squeeze a man to death.

"Danny, take it slow," Jimmy said softly. "And finish your beer."

The bar quieted down. A woman put a nickel in the ancient juke box and there was the usual small talk. Outside, two brief, sharp clear sounds were made and Danny looked up from his beer, said, "Hear that? They were shots."

"Aw Danny, slow down. A car backfiring," Jimmy said.

"That's right, we heard enough shots in the woods at Verdun to recognize guns, didn't we, Jimmy? I'll never forget..."

A young man came rushing into the bar, full of breathless self-importance at the news he carried. He yelled, "Two guys was shot dead outside! One of them is Frank Andersun!"

Some twenty feet from the corner, where the light from Amsterdam Avenue started to fade into the dimness of the block, a crowd made a rough circle around the bodies. A radio car was parked in the middle of the street *and a cop kept growling, "Stand back. Come on, stand back."*

Franklin Andersun was lying on his side—and what was left of his face—arms and legs flung out at grotesque angles. Further down the block, next to an automobile, was the body of a man about the same age as Andersun but better dressed. He had been shot cleanly in the back and except for his open glassy eyes, lay on the sidewalk as though he was sleeping.

The crowd, growing every second, was quiet—even people leaning out of the surrounding apartment house windows were still. It had taken Danny longer to reach the scene than the others and now he tapped his dirty white cane as he said, "Killed? Told you big soldier heroes they were shots!" There was a high note of almost savage triumph in his ragged voice.

One of the cops said, "Shut up."

"Make me! I'll...!" The words were cut off as Jimmy covered Danny's mouth, whispered, "Cops."

Radio and squad cars converged on the circle of people and a score of detectives went to work. Suddenly one of the detectives bending over the second body called out, "This one, he's got a badge on him!"

The crowd stared at the man shot in the back and an uneasy murmur swelled and burst when somebody shrilled, "Jeez, a cop was knocked off!"

There was surprise, alarm, and a slight trace of enjoyment in the voice, and in the general murmur of the crowd. Then everybody began to talk in whispers.

CHAPTER ONE

Some jerk kept driving his fancy Italian-made sport roadster after a piston ring broke, and of course the motor overheated and got on fire. I was rewiring it, and these low underslung jobs are tough for a guy my size. But it was an interesting car, everything designed for speed, including the high compression cylinders, so narrow I couldn't get my hand into them. As I was wondering why a person would spend so much dough to import a sweet job like this and then not take care of it, Joe—the garage manager—yelled out from the phone booth, "Barney— for you."

It was Cy O'Hara, the real-estate man who shared my midget office. Cy said, "There's a Mrs. Turner to see you. How soon will you be back, Mr. Harris?" Naturally the "Mr." was for the client's benefit.

"I'm busy on this job. I don't know any Mrs. Turner. She say an insurance company sent her? Does she look like money—or is she selling something?"

Cy said, "Why no, Mr. Harris, the insurance company didn't call. As to the other matter you asked me to look into—a rather attractive piece of property and I think the finances are sound. Oh, what about Mrs. Turner?"

"Okay, you corny double-talker. Thanks for calling me. I'll be up in ten minutes," I told Cy, hanging up.

As I was taking off my coveralls, Joe came over and asked, "Got a case, Barney?" He was a big brown heavy-set man bigger than me, with a busted nose: he once tried to be a heavyweight boxer. He also had bad teeth that didn't show up against the deep brown of his face. "Another stolen car?"

"Don't know yet. Any rush on this foreign heap, Joe?"

"Naw. How's it coming?"

"Tricky job, but neat. Need another four or five hours on it," I said.

When I entered the office, Cy went through the sudden-appointment routine, gave me a number where he could be reached—which was the coffeepot downstairs. We had a rule that whenever one of us was busy, the other would take a walk. If we were both busy at the same time, that would be quite a problem, but business had never been that good.

I sat down at my desk and the woman sitting opposite me was about twenty-three, twenty-four, very correctly and expensively dressed in black. She was solidly built, the kind of strong figure the street-corner whistlers call "Built up from the ground." She either had good breasts or a smart bra, and when you got to the face—it didn't belong to either the figure or the clothes; it was a teen-ager's face, very solemn and big-eyed, her dark hair even-cut in bangs. If she wasn't pretty, she was a bit on the cute side.

She asked, "Are you Barney Harris, the private detective?" Her voice was a nervous squeak and I enjoyed that "*the* private detective."

I nodded at my license hanging on the wall. "That says I'm a private detective."

"I'm Mrs. Betsy Turner."

The "Betsy" went with the schoolgirl face and thin voice. I made one of my deductions—she wanted her playboy husband tailed. As usual, as a private eye, I was still a good mechanic, for she said, "My husband is Edward Turner, the detective who was killed in the double shooting up on Amsterdam Avenue ten days ago. You've been recommended to me. What are your rates, Mr. Harris?"

"Thirty dollars a day, plus expenses."

"I'd like to hire you."

"To do what?" I asked politely, trying to comb my wild hair with my left hand.

"To find my husband's killer."

If my mouth wasn't open, it should have been, I was that astonished. "You want to hire me...? Mrs. Turner, I read about the murders, but... a cop has been killed. The police will find the killer."

"The police department isn't acting fast enough for me." Her voice was so frail, almost helpless, it was interesting.

"Mrs. Turner, when one of their own is killed, the police pull out all the stops—they have to for self-protection. Also, despite the 'private eyes' you've seen on TV and in the movies, I've never had a criminal case in my life, never slugged anybody since I was ten, never carried a gun. I don't even do guard work. Mostly cars, skip-tracing, and following two-timing husbands and wives around. What I'm trying to tell you is: I'm just me, and the police are a thousand men with an army of stoolies and equipment. What makes you think I could move faster than they can?"

"You can help."

I tried to keep my laugh down in my belly. "I'd probably be a stumbling block. My advice is let the police..."

"Lieutenant Swan, who was Ed's boss, recommended you."

I sighed—that explained everything. "Mrs. Turner, that... eh... clown is some kind of brother-in-law of mine. Let the police do the job; they can do it much better than any private investigator, believe me."

Those big eyes studied me for a long moment, ran over my bulky body, my cheap suit and worn shirt. Then she said, "I'm impressed with your honesty and frankness, Mr. Harris. I'll hire you."

"It's a waste of money to..."

"Are you working for me?"

"A murder case can run into a lot of days and..."

"Mr. Harris, I want to hire you." A note of firmness crept into her voice.

"Okay, long as you know what you're buying." I'd made my pitch and I certainly could use the money. "Only I'm telling you in front, I don't go in for shootings, or any rough stuff, all that movie slop."

"Mr. Harris, this isn't a movie—it's very real to me. I have a special something I want you to look into, something the police refuse to pay any attention to."

"Like what?" A job like this had to last at least ten days—three hundred bucks would knock off a lot of bills.

"Like—suicide," she said in a whisper, her eyes on the verge of tears.

I must have registered astonishment for the second time. "Something was troubling your husband?" I asked like a real moron.

"I don't know. Edward and I were happy, very much in love," she said quickly. "Ed was courageous and brave. He was cited twice by the department. He was an... well, an aggressive man. Certainly a man like that isn't shot in the back without—they say he never even went for his gun."

"Maybe he never had a chance to get it out?"

"No, they say this other man, this Frank Andersun, was shot first, so Ed must have had a few seconds to get his gun. But somehow, I feel Ed didn't want to fight back, that he wanted to die. That's the only explanation for his being shot in the back. And that's why it's so important for me to learn if he was a suicide, and the only way to do that is to find the person who killed him."

"As his wife, you'd certainly know any reason he had for killing himself, so..."

"I don't know of any reason. I suspect suicide because Ed wasn't the type to be caught with his gun bolstered." Her voice was almost curt.

"The police, what do they think of the suicide theory?"

"They don't think anything of it. That's why I'm hiring you."

I shook my head. "I don't know if I can deliver. All I can promise is to give it a try. Murder is over my head."

"That's all I expect, an honest effort." She stood up, taking a checkbook out of a dainty black leather bag. "I'll give you a retainer of $200." She bent over the desk to write and I had a whiff of her perfume; it may not have been exactly subtle, but she smelled fine. "I live on Riverside Drive, and my address is on the check. I'll expect you at my apartment every night at eight."

"At your apartment? *Every* night? Why?"

"To report what you have found out during the day. It will be more convenient than my coming here."

"Want to be sure you get your money's worth every day."

"Yes, I do," she said quietly. "Anything wrong with that?"

"Mrs. Turner, I don't work from nine to five. I may be busy on the case in the evening. Also, as you probably know from your husband, detective work is mostly waiting around, plodding through a million blind alleys till you stumble—and I mean stumble—upon a lead, a stray clue, that untangles the whole puzzle. Why, I may work for days without coming up with a thing."

"Long as you're working, that's all I ask. It isn't that I don't trust you, Mr. Harris, I can't stand the waiting. I want to feel that something— *anything*—is being done."

"Suppose I report whenever I've some news?"

"I'm sorry, but for my own peace of mind, it must be every night, starting this evening. Is that understood?"

"It's your money."

"I know. I'll see you at eight, tonight. Good day, Mr. Harris." I stood up and she wasn't as short as she seemed—I'm six four and she came up to my shoulders. I walked her to the door, then lit a cigarette and came back to my desk, stared at the check. It was ten minutes to two, plenty of time to make the bank. I looked through the second mail—two ads and a phone bill. No answer from a character who had moved—with a TV set he still owed nine installments on. I looked up his last known address and phone number—he'd been sharing a room with another guy who was very close-mouthed. Locking my phone and desk, I went downstairs and into the coffeepot on the corner. Cy was plying his hobby, trying to make time with Alma the waitress. I told him, "Leaving for the day now. Be able to give you the rent tomorrow."

"Any calls for me?"

I shook my head and Cy made some corny crack to Alma and took off. The place was empty, except for the cook. I laid a dollar on the counter, asked Alma, "Want to make one of those calls for me?"

"Easiest bucks I've ever made," she said, a smile cracking her hard face. I wrote the name and number on the back of an envelope, gave her the pencil and a dime. "Same old routine."

"I know. How's your kid?"

"Swell."

"When you going to invite me over to make supper for her? I love kids."

"One of these days, soon," I lied.

We went over to the wall phone and she dialed, asked in a sexy voice, "Bobby in? This is a friend of his. Had a date with him a couple weeks ago, but I got sick. Oh you, no cracks... all right... all right, you guessed it. Thought I might keep the date tonight. I sound like what? (She winked at me and sneered at the phone.) Sound pretty hot yourself. Sure, I wouldn't mind going out with you, but I got to ask Bobby-boy if it's okay first. What? Oh, met him at a dance hall. Now don't give me a line, honey. How do I know he'll say it's okay? I never two-time my boy friends. A new Ford? That's real gone, honey. Sure I'm free this Saturday, free the whole week end, but got to ask Bobby first. Wouldn't want me to pull that on you, would you? No, no, never mind my number, I have yours and I'm mad about new Fords. Tell you, after I keep my date with Bobby, I'll give you a ring. Not stringing you... don't know what I'd do for a new car. What? (A real giggle.) Fresh thing! Hanging up this minute unless you let me speak to Bobby. What—where did he move to? Honest?"

She wrote a Long Island address on the envelope, handed it to me. There was some more corny talk, then her dime was up and she hung up, said, "What a creep."

I phoned the TV company, told them the new address, added, "Nope, send your own men or the cops. I don't do strong-arm work. Never mind that I'm-built-for-it chatter. Put a ten-dollar check in the mail, please."

As I turned away from the phone, Alma grabbed my arm, said, "Make a muscle for me, Barney."

"Some other time, honey, have to make the bank now. Thanks."

I went over to the garage and got my car. It was a prewar Buick roadmaster and looked shot, but the motor was spotless with a supercharger of my own design, an adult hot rod that would carry me 110 miles an hour any time I wanted. In the summer I took the kid out to Bridgehampton to watch the auto races; sometimes I thought about entering them.

From the bank I drove up St. Nicholas Avenue and parked directly in front of the police precinct, which was built in 1889, according to the date on the cornerstone of the ugly building, and looked every minute of it. I asked the balding desk sergeant if Lieutenant Swan was in, and he nodded. Al's office was painted a bile green and had a minimum of furniture—an old desk and two chairs.

In sharp contrast to his office, Al looked modern and sharp. He was built like a strong middleweight and wore a girdle to keep his stomach flat. His clothes were the kind that said they were expensive, without shouting it, and Al took up a lot of time with his "grooming." He was the lieutenant in charge of the precinct detective squad, and he moved carefully behind his desk, as if afraid he might soil his manicured hands. But there wasn't anything foppish about Al; his fat face had the sullen cast of a fighter and he could be a mean bastard. I got my wide bottom down into the other chair, said, "See you're doing me favors again."

He put down the report he was reading, sat back in his chair—first adjusting the shoulder holster that looked clean and neat against his white-on-white shirt. Al slipped me a tight smile. "Hello, you big slob, expecting you." He had a rasping croak for a voice, claimed he had once stopped a baseball with his Adam's apple when he was a young cop trying to break up a street game. He asked, "Want a drink of ginger beer?"

I hesitated, not sure I wanted a shot so early in the day, or at all. My brother-in-law wasn't a man of imagination and had one practical joke he played over and over—for some reason he got a bang out of spiking everything from milk to water. When you asked for water in his house you usually got straight gin. Maybe it had something to do with the fact he never touched the stuff, not even beer, himself. Although practical jokers ran in his family, Violet would always tell anyone going to the bathroom in our place, "Just mention my name and you'll get a good seat," then get hysterical with laughter, no matter how many times she said it. Bathroom jokes were her specialty, including such corn as toilet paper with gags on it, but otherwise Violet was a most intelligent woman.

"Got sodas in tin cans now," Al said, taking one from a small picnic cooler he kept under his desk. Tossing the can at me, he pointed to an opener on his cluttered desk. I casually glanced at the cap—it didn't seem to have been tampered with.

"How's Ruthie?"

"Fine." I opened the ginger beer, took a cautious sip. It was half rum but

I drank it without showing any reaction and Al looked disappointed. I thought of the time the jerk had put in—carefully opening the can, spiking it, then recapping it with the skill of a precision mechanic.

"When you bringing her out to the house? May and the boy always asking for her. Ought to see my rumpus room now—over a thousand feet of electric track and..."

"We'll be out one of these days. What did you send this Turner woman to me for?" I finished the drink, bent the bottle cap between my thumb and forefinger. Al tried hard not to watch, but could not take his eyes away. I threw the bent cap on his desk.

"She wanted a private dick. You're one, so ..."

"Stop it."

Al picked up the cap gently, looked at it, tried to straighten it, then tossed it into the wastebasket. He grinned at me, showing his neat even teeth. "What's the beef, Barney, throwing away business?"

"You know I don't go in for crime stuff, but..."

"But you took the case?" Al cut in.

I nodded. "But I don't feel right about it."

"Barney, stop knocking yourself out. This Turner broad is a little buggy about her husband's death. She's got his funeral money from the city, some insurance green, and was hell bent on hiring herself a private dick. Honest, I told her she was throwing the dough away, but she insisted—kept getting in our hair—so I figured you'd be the cheapest tin badge she could get. And might as well be you picking up the easy coin."

"Easy?"

"Not a damn thing you can do on this case except stop looking like a bum. Why the hell can't you press that suit, comb your hair?"

"Forget my hair. Al, I'm going to give her an honest day's work every..."

Al waved a manicured hand—his right—the one with the broken knuckle. "Don't. Don't do a thing but sit back and wait for us to crack it. And keep her off our necks. The entire police force is running into stone walls all over this mess, so what can a private jerk do? That's what I kept telling her but she became a pest... and I knew you wouldn't rook her too much on the expense account. Also Mrs. Turner is a sweet-looking number and you need a wife to look after Ruthie— Who knows what will happen?"

I stared at him for a quick moment. Al had this habit of laughing at you with his eyes, mocking you, while the rest of his mug was deadpan. Vi did that too, one of the few things about her that used to annoy me. "Since when did you join the Cupid Union? Trade in your rod for a bow and arrow? Forget my love life. Mrs. Turner thinks it's suicide."

Al laughed loudly—a tearing sandpaper sound. "She gave me a headache with that phonograph record. Look, Ed Turner wasn't the lad to knock himself off. While he was still a probationary cop, a rookie, he made a good pinch—a lucky one—nabbed some clown the Feds wanted. He was made a third-grade detective and after that—gangway for eager-beaver Ed. He was one of these rough young studs who hadn't learned to quiet down—a punk with a badge. Always using his hands instead of his head."

"That include holding his mitts out for dough?"

Al nodded. "Off the record, yes, and clumsy at it too. Transferred once because of his itchy palms. I had to talk to him—get rough a couple of times, before he smartened up. Hell, a little cushion money—that's expected, but this fool tried jazzing the numbers syndicate."

"Maybe they paid him off with lead?"

Al snorted. "Don't be corny. Told you I wised the boy up, told him not to cut in on the big brass's gravy. This case is a weirdie; not an angle makes sense. Got the slug from Andersun—and that's spelled s-*u*-n. Shot by a Luger .38. Turner's went through his body and we can't find it."

"Suppose you searched the streets?"

"'Suppose you searched the streets?'" Al mimicked me. "What the hell you think we did, played games on the block! Damn slug probably stuck in a tire, or some other part of a car, was driven away and lost. All we know is Turner had his car, an old Chevvy, parked and he must have stepped out of the car when he saw Andersun get it. Stopped one himself."

"Without reaching for his gun?"

Al waved his hand. "Yes, and that doesn't add up either. Told you, Turner was one of these ambitious shoot-first lads."

"What about Andersun—with a *u?*"

"Nothing. Local boy, stock clerk, absolutely no record. Just won a slogan contest that day, won himself a grand, celebrating at the bar. Going to take a trip to Europe—it was in all the papers—a publicity plant about his winning. Didn't have the money on him, hadn't even got the check yet. Anyway, this wasn't a robbery. Turner had over a hundred in his wallet. Andersun kid is clean, a hard-working slob, not even a lover boy. Lot of people heard the shots, but nobody saw a damn thing."

I thought for a moment. "Who got second prize in this contest?"

"Barney, take it easy. A sixty-three-year-old grandmother who lives in some hick town in Michigan came in second—never left town in her life," Al said wearily. "Any more questions, Mr. Holmes?"

I took a cigarette from his pack on the desk, lit it. "What was Turner doing there in his car?"

"Now you're getting warm. That can be the jackpot question. He wasn't on duty and that street isn't even in our precinct. His wife has no idea why he was there; people in the street think they have seen him around the block before, but they're not sure. No rackets working in that street, either. By the way, the precinct handling the case is the one below us, and a Lieutenant Franzino is in charge of the detective squad. Told him about you and he isn't too happy about having a private snooper around, but I said you'd stay out of his hair."

"Got anything going yourself—off the record?"

Al smiled with his eyes again. "Got an idea but so far it stinks. But it's the only thing makes sense. Turner and the killer were knocking off Andersun—for some reason—then the killer crossed Turner. That would account for Ed not having his gun out."

"What about this lucky pinch Turner made?"

"Barney, stop making like a detective. We've run through that—guy was a minor dope runner doing five to ten in Lewisburg right now. No gang tie-up. Wasn't an important pinch, but we showed up the FBI, and downtown loves that."

"Wife said he was cited twice?"

Al groaned. "Turner came upon a guy tear-assing out of an apartment house in the early hours of the morning. Said he told the guy to stop, then shot him dead. Seems the guy was merely beating up his gal, but fortunately for Turner they found a gun on the guy—although his gal swore he never had a gun in his life. Could be Ed was smart, in a stupid way; maybe carried an extra gun. Anything else, Mr. Bogart?"

"About your theory—why should Turner be in on killing Andersun?"

Al gave me a belly laugh, then cut it off abruptly. "If we knew that, you'd be out of a job. Look, besides men from both precincts, there's a batch of Homicide guys from downtown working on this, plus men from the detective district. Had a half a dozen men checking on Andersun and his family—drew a zero. The kid worked for a tool company, thirty-eight dollars and fourteen cents take-home pay, lived at home, had a girl friend he wasn't banging, and his big moment was having beers at the corner ginmill. Kid didn't even play cards, or the horses or the numbers."

I stood up—the rum was making me sweat. "How about Turner being shot first and Andersun merely walking into it?"

Al shook his head. He was getting gray above the ears, or maybe he dyed it gray. "Tried that one for size too. Doc got there fast, is positive Andersun died first. And of course this has been through the labs and they come up with same answer."

I said, "The one thing out of the ordinary in Andersun's life was his winning the dough, going to Europe."

Al leaned back in his chair—he never stood up beside me. "That's a terrific deduction—they kill people for talking about taking a trip to Paris these days?"

"Well, I'll look around. Give the family a hello for me."

"Sure, and bring Ruthie out. Barney, remember downtown is running this show—don't get in their way."

I stopped at the door to ask, "Ed Turner—a lover?"

"Not as far as we know, too ambitious to get mixed up with dames. And with a wife stacked like his, what would be the point? When you come out to the house, like you to check my new Caddy."

Guess my face showed things, for Al said, "Don't give me that look. I made some dough in the stock market, show you the brokers' statements that..."

"Who said you didn't make it? I'll keep you informed if I luck up on anything."

"Well, now, thanks, Perry Mason. Don't trip over any bar bells."

I couldn't think of a snappy comeback, so I went out. The rum made me hungry. I looked around for a hamburger joint, had a better idea. I drove down to the Grand Café, and the guy who named it had a sense of humor.

The bartender was a short, egg-shaped old guy, and there was a couple sipping beer in a booth and playing the juke box, and a blind man at the bar. The blind guy had the shoulders and ears of a wrestler. I ordered a hamburger and the barkeep grumbled about cooking so early in the day. The blind man turned his face toward me, said, "Big guy, ain't you?"

"Two hundred and forty-eight pounds."

"Can sort of feel a guy's size. Can't I, Jimmy?" he asked the bartender. He had the cracked voice some men get when they start to grow old.

Jimmy muttered, "Yeah."

I asked, "This the place where they had the two killings?"

"Not in here!" This, Jimmy growled at me. "Never had no trouble in here. Cop, ain'tcha?"

"Private." I flashed my identification card.

"What they need a private goof on a case like this for?" the blind man wanted to know.

"I'm not just sticking my snoot in for kicks, somebody hired me," I said as the bartender put a thick hamburger in front of me, asked, "Beer?"

I nodded. It was a hell of a good burger, old-fashioned one, and when I told Jimmy this, he just scowled, asked, "What did you expect, horse meat? Place may not look like much, but we give you honest value. And you're wasting your time, place has been full of all kinds of cops and dicks. Makes the customers nervous."

"Only doing my job," I said. The bartender kept on, scowling. Usually you can ease things by saying it's a job, or my duty, or my business—as if that meant a damn thing.

There was a lot of silence and the music of the juke box till the blind man asked, "Like to see me crush a can of beer with my hands?"

"Sure would." I was getting no place fast.

Jimmy said, "Now, Danny, what you starting so early for?"

"You heard the man, he's buying me a can of foam," Danny said. He quickly drank the beer, put the empty can in his left hand—which was big as a ham—and crushed it. That was a good stunt for a guy his age. I picked up the beer cap and bent it in half between my fingers, forgetting he couldn't see. I handed it to him and he felt it, asked excitedly, "Jimmy, you see him bend this with his fingers?"

"Aha."

"Didn't press it against the bar or nothing?"

"No, Danny, just his fingers. A strong ox."

Danny turned and ran his hands over me. "Weightlifter?"

"Not for the last year or so."

"What kind of cop are you, no gun?"

I laughed; Danny was sharper than a man with eyes. "Guess I'm not a gunman."

I made a big impression on Danny. We started talking about strong men and Jimmy joined in. They kept bulling about the old-timers: Sandow, Hackenschmidt, Goerner. They had never even heard of John Davis, or Doug Hepburn, Grimek, or Kono. Then Danny started on wrestlers and was breezing about Grotch, Poddoubny, the time he wrestled one of the Zbyszko brothers, and how he had almost pinned Strangler Lewis. Finally, I asked, "This Franklin Andersun, was he a muscleman?"

Danny laughed, filling the air with the smell of beer. "Couldn't lift a toothpick. Boys today got it too soft, cars to take them here and there, elevators and stuff. Everything is done for them, they don't develop no muscles."

"What do you fellows think about the killing? You knew the kid."

The bartender said, "I think it was all a mistake, somebody thought Frank was another guy. He wasn't the kind to be in any trouble."

"That's the truth. If you was picking a guy to be in a mess, Frankie'd be the last guy you'd pick," Danny said, as I glanced at his sightless eyes, caused by trachoma and dirty ring canvas.

"How about Turner, the detective? Ever see him before?"

The blind man said, "I never heard him," and Jimmy added, "That's all the cops been asking me. I keep telling 'em, I only seen him once—out there on the sidewalk, dead."

"Any strangers in here the night of the shootings?"

"You kidding?" Jimmy said, rinsing out a rag, running it over the top of the bar. "Always a few strangers in a bar. But that night, had mostly neighborhood regulars, to hear about Frank winning the dough."

"Brown was in," Danny said suddenly.

"He was?" Jimmy said, rinsing the rag again. "Don't recall seeing him."

"He was in," Danny said. "I remember his voice—never forget his voice."

I motioned for another round of beers, asked, "Who's Brown?"

"Some know-it-all jerk," Jimmy said. "I been living and rooming around this block for the last... well... forty-five years at least."

"Me too, even longer," Danny said.

"Look down the block and you'll see an empty lot across the street. Still got some wide stone steps at the front of it. Used to be a church at one time. That was about 1915, wasn't it, Danny?"

"Right."

"Well, just before the war, around 1917, old Rev. Atkins died in an auto accident and the church sort of went out of business, if you can say that about a church. Then some German society took it over, put in a lot of dough making it into a gym. Along comes the war and the place is shut down, then it burns, just part of the foundation and steps left. Lot of people think the fire wasn't no accident, you know how feelings ran high during the war. I never thought so, but..."

"What's this got to do with this Brown?" I asked.

"He was coming to that," Danny cut in. "One night this Brown comes in here and gets to talking to one of the boys— Frankie, come to think of it."

"Yeah, was him and Frankie arguing," Jimmy said.

"About what?" I put in.

"Nothing, really. Brown says he was born around here and remembered Frankie's father and mother, that he and Andersun was born a few days apart. Just bar talk, except he said he remembered when the church burned, only it wasn't a church then, and anyway it was before his time."

"And nobody ever remembered seeing him around," Danny added. "Why should a guy bull about junk like that? What got me, was his voice, had a kind of twang to it, funny way of saying 'r.' Nobody born here talk that way."

"Don't remember nothing odd about his voice," Jimmy said.

The blind man finished his beer. "But I did. I used to wrestle a lot upstate, around Elmira and Ithaca. People talk with that kind of a twang up there."

"That was the argument—about whether this Brown had been born around here?" I asked.

Jimmy nodded, as he washed and dried his hands. "That's all. Just remembered it because of his lying about the church burning."

"What did he look like? Recall his first name?"

The bartender examined a spot on his white apron for a moment. "Think he had some ordinary name like Jack, or Joe. As for looks—this was months ago—didn't make any special impression on me. I'd say he was around thirty, stocky, I think, and short."

"Dressed well?"

"Hell, I don't remember."

"Color of his hair?"

"Yeah, yeah, I remember that—red!" Jimmy said happily. "Yes sir, real red hair. I remember because not only was it awful red, but he was arguing a lot and I was thinking what they say about redheads being scrappers."

"He was a mean one, I could tell by his voice," Danny said. "I think he had a friend, another guy, with him."

Jimmy shrugged. "I don't remember nobody with him."

"Let's get back to the night of the killings—did Brown leave before Andersun?" I asked.

Jimmy laughed, showing a mossy set of uppers. "Jeez, mac, I didn't say he was in that night."

"But he was," the blind man said. "I been trying to remember where I'd heard his voice before and just now, when you was asking about strangers, it came to me."

"You only heard the voice twice, with a three-month time lapse between, and you're still sure it's the same voice?" I asked.

"Sure, it's been hanging around the back of my mind ever since the shootings. Like when something is on the tip of your tongue and you can't remember it. I don't mistake a voice. It was him all right."

"Danny, did you tell this to the cops?"

He shook his big blind head. "Telling you, I just thought of it."

I turned to the barkeep. "Did you tell the police about this Brown?"

"Of course not. I only saw him once before and as for his being here on the night of the murders, can't prove it by me," Jimmy said.

The clock up near the TV set said it was ten to four. I gave Jimmy one of my cards, said I'd see him again. I shook hands with Danny and neither of us tried the grip-of-iron shake, and I took off. There wasn't time to drive to the police station so I dropped into a drugstore, phoned Lieutenant Franzino. A gruff, impatient voice asked, "Yeah? Lieutenant Franzino speaking."

"I'm Barney Harris—the private detective Lieutenant Swan spoke to you about."

"Aha. What's on your mind, Mr. Harris?" To my surprise his voice became mild and polite.

"Maybe nothing, but I've been talking to the bartender and a big blind man in the Grand Café. They told me there was a fellow named Brown, first name something ordinary like Joe, Jack, or John. He's about thirty years old, bright red hair, stocky build, and has a slight twang to his voice. He was in the Grand several months ago, claimed he was born in the neighborhood, that he knew Franklin Andersun. But nobody remembered him, including Andersun. Also, from a mistake he made in talking about a church that burned, the barkeep knew he was lying about being born in the block. The…"

"What's this add up to, Harris?"

"Maybe just a lot of bar talk. The blind man claims he was in the Grand again on the night of the killings, before the shooting. The bartender doesn't remember him being there that night, but the blind guy is positive, says he's good on remembering voices. I figure it's too much coincidence."

"Yeah. Sure a better lead than we have now. A Tom, Dick, or Harry Brown with red hair. Be tough to locate, but we'll give it a look. Thanks, Mr. Harris."

"Danny, the blind man, said the twang in Brown's voice reminded him of the way people speak upstate, around Ithaca or Elmira."

"Good. We'll look into it. Guess Swan checked you out on what we know. Stay in touch, Mr. Harris. I realize you have to show some… uh… work, so I don't mind you looking about, only kind of keep out of my way. I don't like tripping over private dicks. Get me, Mr. Harris?"

"Sure. Don't worry, I never overwork myself."

I drove uptown and over to Audubon Avenue and parked outside the private school that was keeping me broke, but with the overcrowding in the public schools it was worth the strain. It wasn't four-thirty yet and I lit a cigarette, thought about the case, about the blind muscleman, and mostly about Betsy Turner. There was something phony about her, something I couldn't quite put my finger on.

Finally the kids came out and Ruthie came skipping over to me, looking good in the dress I'd bought last month. She was all long legs and arms as I opened the door and she climbed in, kissed me twice, said between kisses, "Hello, Daddy." Then she drew back and rubbed her lips. "You smell of beer."

"That a way to talk to the poppa?" I said, starting the car.

"How many beers did you have?"

"A million, Miss Nosey."

"Are we going to take a ride?"

"Maybe a very short one. Want chopped meat for supper?"

"Why aren't we going for a ride?"

"I have to go out this evening."

"Daddy, I don't like it when you go out. Where you going?"

"Have to work. Get May Weiss to stay with you."

"I don't like May, she's stuck-up. Always doing her homework, never wants to play. Why can't you stay home and read to me, or I'll watch you exercise?"

"Told you why, have to work," I said, running my right hand over her silky brown pigtail. Her hair was due for a washing.

"Not sneaking off to a movie, Daddy?"

"No, honey, you're the only girl I take to the movies. And what I'm working on sounds crazier than any movie."

We drove up to Yonkers and back, cutting over to Broadway to escape the toll bridge. Ruthie talked all the time as usual. She said she'd seen my cousin Jake Winston, the mailman, on the street. He'd stopped at the school to tell her he wanted us to come out to his place in Ridgewood on Sunday. Way all my relations kept after me, got me a little sore—I could take care of the kid okay.

I stopped at a super market and Ruthie went in with me, asked, "Can we make a Jello pie tonight?"

"Guess we have time for that. But I have to feed you, start your bath, take a shower and shave myself, and be out of the house by seven-thirty."

"Maybe you really aren't going to the movies... taking a shave at night. Here's the chopped meat."

"We'll get a thick steak. We're eating high on the hog tonight."

She looked up at me with big questioning eyes. "What does that mean, Daddy?"

"Means a person is eating real meat, instead of the pig's feet, the insides, or the tail."

Ruthie screwed up her pug nose. "But why do people eat the feet of pigs and the insides, Daddy?"

"Usually because they're too poor to buy the other parts," I said, knowing I'd started something.

The morning of April eleventh was the start of a pleasantly cool spring day, but the man rushing into a fourth-rate hotel off lower Eighth Avenue was sweating. His name was Martin Pearson and he was thirty-two years old, stocky, and of average height. He had a very ordinary face, except for his thick bushy hair, which at the moment was dyed a sandy blond. His worn tweed suit had been purchased in a Times Square store some six years before, the clean white shirt came from Amsterdam, the brown knit tie had been bought on the Rue de la Paix, and the shoes in Genoa. The old leather camera-gadget case hanging from his left shoulder had been ordered from a Sears Roebuck catalog many years ago.

Pearson was rushing and sweating because some twenty minutes before, while sipping his morning coffee and reading a paper in a Seventy-third Street cafeteria, he had decided to murder a man.

Nodding at the desk clerk who was still half asleep, Pearson ran up the single flight of wooden steps, turned into a dim hallway, knocked sharply on a door with a dirty metal eight nailed to it. There wasn't any answer and he knocked again, harder. After a moment a man's voice cautiously asked, "Yes? Who is it?"

"Me. Got to see you in a hurry, Harold." Martin was talking to his partner, Sam Lund, who was registered at the hotel under the name of Harold Bender.

"What's the rush, Marty? I'm... uh... busy."

"Damn it, open the door!"

Lund stalled some more because he had a girl in his room. Pearson kept pounding on the door and finally Sam climbed out of bed, after telling the girl not to worry, and partly opened the door, to explain the situation. But Pearson pushed the door open as the girl sat up in bed and tried to cover her meaty breasts with her hands.

For a second the room looked like a blackout tableau in a burlesque show: the dingy room, the nude girl on the bed, Pearson staring at her like an angry husband, and Sam Lund wearing shorts—calmly walking over to the dresser and lighting a cigarette. Lund was a large man in his early thirties and if his body was flabby it still showed signs of having been muscular at one time. His thin-featured face was overhandsome, but except for a fringe of hair above his ears, he was completely bald. His head had that hard polished look as though hair had never grown there.

The girl, in a statement she made at police headquarters several weeks later, said, "They both had the manners of a couple of bums, not even the decency to turn their backs while I dressed."

> *Q: You met Lund in a bar near the hotel the night before and agreed to spend the night with him for fifteen dollars. Is that correct?*
>
> *A: Yes, sir. And I was surprised at the way Harold—that's the name he gave me—acted, because he seemed like a smart guy, a good talker. I loved the way he talked, his voice was so clear and smooth, like a ...*
>
> *Q: Let's get on with this—what happened after Pearson came into the room?*
>
> *A: I admit I'm a hustler, but I still ask for some respect as a lady. I bawled them out and finally the smaller one, Pearson you say he is, turned his back and told me, "Look, sister, get dressed and take*

a walk. We have things to do."

I remember, I told him I sure was glad I wasn't his sister. He was getting steamed and then Harold said to me, "Sorry to rush you, honey, but we're salesmen and Marty is anxious to hit the road with our new line." I got my bra and stuff and...

Q: When you met Lund the night before, did he say what he did for a living?

A: No, sir. I never got around to asking. But I figured he was a salesman—had the voice to sell and liked to gab. And he didn't have much dough, I could tell. Yes sir, I remember, I thought he was a small-time salesman.

Q: Did you see any guns in Lund's room?

A: No, sir. And if I had I would have called the cops at once. I know better than to fool with hoods. Although I sure would never have suspected Harold—or the other one—for any rough stuff. No, sir.

When the girl had gone and Lund had locked the door, Pearson cursed him, asking, "Are you crazy? This is the one thing that can foul us up! Bet you were drunk, too."

"Relax, I wasn't drunk, merely in the mood for a girl," Lund said, yawning. "Anyway I'm checking out of this dump today. 'Mr. Bender' got his registered letter yesterday. Why all the ...?"

"You dummy, she heard you call me Marty!"

"So what? That was a slip on my part but you got me rattled, barging in like... Cool off, Marty, our luck's been riding high all these months and..."

"Has it? Remember this one?" Pearson took a neatly folded but hastily torn part of a newspaper out of his pocket, flung it on the bed. Lund walked over and raised the shade, read the paper, while Pearson saw a heel of a whiskey pint on the dresser, finished it with a single gulp. Sam sat on the bed, his face going pale, as he looked up from the short news item and said softly, "Damn! Damn! Of all the miserable breaks! How could we possibly foresee a thing like this, the dumb jerk winning the money?"

"We couldn't," Martin said. "One of those things, a break we have to meet."

"Throw me that pack of butts on the dresser. What do we do now, chuck the whole deal?"

Pearson, who had been studying the empty pint bottle, put it down and threw the cigarettes at his partner, watched as Lund lit one and began puffing on it nervously. After an awkward silence Lund asked again, "Now what—we chuck the deal?"

"We can't chuck it. Once they start investigating, in time everything will point to us. And I don't see why we should give up anything. There's another out, if we act quickly. Before this guy gets his passport application in."

"I don't get it."

"Yes you do, you know exactly what I'm talking about, Sam."

Lund jumped off the bed and said fiercely, "If you're talking about what I think you are—forget it. For Christsakes, that's murder!"

Pearson nodded. "Yes, that's what it will most certainly be. I've tried to rationalize it, call it other names. It's plain murder."

"Marty, talk sense! We've pulled a lot of... of... angles, but I never thought of myself, of us, as real criminals. My God, Marty, we can't murder a man!"

"Don't talk so loudly. I don't see what choice we have. These things build up, grow. A petty crime, then a bigger one, and finally the big leagues— the biggest of them all. We have a ..."

"No! I don't even want to discuss that!"

"Sam, you've had a big night, you don't understand our situation. We never thought of ourselves as criminals because a criminal is one who gets caught, just as a murderer is one convicted of killing. We've been very good, the perfect... criminals, and we still will be the..."

"Damn it, Marty, stop talking! I won't go for murder and that's final!"

"Cut the acting and keep your voice down. And listen to me. Sam, besides our boat tickets we have a little over two hundred bucks left. If we try to ditch the whole business, we're flat broke. Also, as I tried to tell you, if we let him go through with his trip, our game is exposed whether we chuck it or not, and we'll never know when they'll catch up with us—even in Europe. Once he makes out that application, we're finished. I don't have to remind you that we've broken several Federal laws, that the least we'll get is five to ten years. Is that what you want, to be broke and running the rest of our lives? To finally end up in the pen?"

Sam stood up, staring at the wall and seemingly so deep in thought he didn't answer.

Martin pointed to a lipstick smear on the pillow. "You want to be sleeping with cheap whores in a stinking room or sunning yourself at Juan-les-Pins with Gabby? Would you rather be hustling for small change here as a handy man, or a famous actor with your own motion-picture company?"

"Don't paint no pictures for me—you know damn well what I want. But murder—no!"

"These aren't pictures, Sam, these are facts." Martin pointed around the room. "It's a fact that a flea bag like this, or worse, will be your home from

now on—if you can afford a room. It's also a fact we can still wake up at ten and have a swim and a big breakfast and before it gets too hot, ride over to Nice or Cape Ferrat or San Remo. You always liked San Remo the best. Sam, the main fact is this: we have over forty thousand dollars waiting for us if we continue to use our heads."

"Think we'll be the richest jokers to ever sit in the electric chair!"

Martin smiled bitterly. "Your stupid jokes. Sam, killing was never a part of our plans, and we're not a couple of goons, we won't be caught."

Sam crushed his cigarette against the wall. "We have been smart, the best ever. But using a gun is where we start being dumb."

"Killing is a last resort, but can you think of any other way? We could try robbing him of the money, but that might not work, and it's too risky."

"And murder isn't?" Sam snapped.

"Look, Sam, the police are efficient because most killings fit one of several patterns. But this—be no motive anybody but us could possibly know about and... Look, I once read where some police authority said the perfect murder would have to be an insane act where a man suddenly shoots a total stranger on the street—no motive, no connection, no possible clues. That's the first thing came to me when I read the paper—we're shooting a stranger."

"He saw us—you—before," Sam said, lighting another cigarette. "Marty, there's things a man can do and can't do. I can't go through with a murder. That's all!"

"Merely saying 'That's all' doesn't solve anything for us. I'll do the actual trigger pulling, if that will make you feel any better. Yes, he saw us. He spoke to me once, a casual conversation in a bar some three months ago— and I was using a phony name. Who can remember that except him, and he'll be dead? For all practical purposes we're walking up to a total stranger and shooting him without rhyme or reason. Unless we're nabbed at the scene of the killing—and that we'll work out carefully, of course— the police will have to be lucky, downright stupid fumbling lucky, to even get on our trail."

"Murder is out."

Pearson walked over and shook his partner. "Stop talking like a goddamn parrot! If we get rid of him we're safe, have money, the good life. I'm back with Thérèse, you're a big actor. If he lives we're bums the rest of our lives and end up serving a lot of time. Killing is our only out. As you said, we couldn't foresee this, but we're in it and getting in deeper is our only escape."

"But... Marty, you talk so calmly about... murder!" Sam said, pushing the smaller man away.

"I'm not calm. I'm scared crazy, but not that frightened I've stopped

thinking, can't realize what has to be done. Be simple, we come upon him alone in the street today—it has to be today—best tonight. One quick shot and we're gone before anybody finds the body. Then we keep on with the cases we have cooking. Another month or two, we leave the country."

"Why not leave at once after, I mean... if... we do it?"

"Because we haven't got enough and what difference will it make? If they're on to us, they can extradite us from Europe. No, we keep on going as usual, like nothing happened. Sam, I've thought this out, racked my head till it hurts. How can they ever connect us with it? How can the police possibly stumble upon us? What can go wrong?"

Sam looked for an ashtray, finally thumbed his cigarette out the one window. "Marty, up to now it's been like a game—the whole works: outsmarting the army, the French cops, the stuff we've been doing here. It worked smooth because we never hurt nobody, worked our own angles... but now, a deliberate cold-blooded murder, I can't go that, I just can't!"

Pearson said coldly, "And I can't think of living without Thérèse. We've put in over five months on this, we already have about twenty-five grand set for sure, another fifteen thousand in the works. I'm not throwing all that over because this kid gets lucky. Get this through your dumb head— there's little risk—he himself won't have the slightest idea why we're killing him."

"As you said, the cops can be lucky."

"Luck has been riding with us, all down the line." Pearson opened his camera bag and dropped two Lugers on the bed. "Look how lucky it was I never sold these, held on to them."

Sam stared at the guns, his thin lips moving. Finally he pulled himself together, asked quietly, "Threatening me, Marty?"

"Killing you would be a wrong move, leave too many trails. But I want Thérèse so badly I considered it. Think it over, Sam. It's rough but we've been living on cream so far, can't complain. Get dressed, take a shower, take a walk and get the air... start thinking. Have a good breakfast. Think, then tell me what else we can do but kill him. Show me any other out, even a cockeyed one, and I'll be the first to take it. But you know killing is the only way. Think about it, Sam, think real hard... we have a couple of hours."

CHAPTER TWO

She had four very large rooms in one of these old, high-ceilinged apartment houses that never look like much on the outside. It was a front apartment overlooking the Hudson River, and full of severe modern furniture that looked uncomfortable—or maybe it was the violent colors. Everything was a patch-quilt of brash red and blinding yellows and mysterious purples. And somehow the effect didn't quite come off—it was as if she'd copied a room and overdone it. One wall was lined with books—in colorful jackets too—but they all looked too new, as if she joined every book club out and stacked the books away as they came.

Betsy Turner was wearing a Chinese-like outfit—tight red pants and a loose yellow house coat that should have given her an exotic look, but her kid's face was an almost comical contrast. Her face reminded me of the Kewpie dolls that used to be so popular—her nose and eyes and lips took up all her face, almost seemed to be overcrowding it.

Frankly I didn't get the play—the carefully made-up face, those tight pants showing off her strong legs, the teasing outline of firm breasts whenever the coat touched them. Either Mrs. Turner was expecting somebody after I left, or she wanted other kinds of work for her thirty a day.

To keep my eyes off her, I said "Hello" and glanced around at the several amateurish oils on the wall—like those pre-sketched canvas deals where you fill in the colors by number. In one corner of the living room there was an easel with a half-finished painting of a river scene—and without numbers. Near it was a large TV set, and near that one of these expensive record players. I said, "Nice place here. You paint much?"

"I play at it. I also decorated this apartment. Do you like it?"

From the tone of her voice it seemed important to her that I liked it. "Rather unusual. Yeah, I like it," I said. And the canvases, the books, the stacks of records—they could mean a lot of things, including loneliness. But hell, the fine ebony wood cabinet of the TV was easily a cop's salary for a month, or two, and the high-fidelity record player wasn't anything you found in a box of Cracker Jacks.... No wonder Ed Turner walked around with his hand out. And considering the short time he'd been on the force, he was a joker with a talent for letting people see his palms.

"I made this Chinese house coat too," she said, turning like a model for me to see it—and her. She sure packed a healthy figure. Only she still gave me this Kewpie-doll feeling—an expensive one.

"Looks wonderful. Very becoming."

She smiled faintly, like a kid with a good report card. "Please sit down over there, Mr. Harris." She pointed to a veneer bucket chair with dainty wrought-iron legs.

I sat down on a pigskin hassock, said, "Doubt if the chair is guaranteed to hold 248 pounds."

She sat down on a banana-yellow contour couch.

There was a moment of silence and I studied her legs, which were worth studying. She motioned toward a bottle and several glasses on a marble table with driftwood legs. "Noilly Prat, Mr. Harris?"

"No thanks, Mrs. Turner. And what is it?" We sounded like a soap opera.

She smiled and her lips were thick and red and girlish, and my temperature shot up. "Vermouth—French. I'm not much of a drinker, but this place has been giving me the jitters ever since Ed... died. It's a jinx apartment, and it caused our first real fight."

"That so?" I said politely. People who always brag how little they drink are usually in the lush class.

"Yes, I never really enjoyed this place," she went on. "After Ed passed the police exam, but before he was called, he was head of the shipping department and I was a steno in the front office—that's how we met. After we married we couldn't find an apartment and lived in a room for several months. Then Ed found this apartment and insisted we take it, even though the rent was more than our combined weekly salaries. I didn't mind scrimping because I wanted a place of our own, and this even had furniture—not this stuff—and we didn't have to pay anything under the table. Then I found out why it was vacant—a man had hung himself with a tie from the bathroom door."

Following her over-red fingernail I saw a white door off the cocoa-colored foyer. "Must have been a small man to do it with a tie," I said brightly.

She hesitated, not sure if I was kidding her, then decided I wasn't, said, "I didn't want the place then, it gave me the creeps. And using *his* furniture too. But Ed insisted. I didn't know till then how unhappy he'd been in our room, making coffee on a hot plate, using the window sill for an icebox. Oh, Ed always liked to live so big. He even hinted we'd part if I didn't take the apartment. I nearly had a fit when we moved in. Ed had to stay with me while I took a bath or I'd get to staring at the door till I saw a body swinging there. Ed said I was a baby but I couldn't help it."

"Able to go to the bathroom alone now?"

She sat up, face flushed. "Mr. Harris! Don't get fresh!"

I almost slipped off the hassock—Mrs. Turner was out of this planet— I hadn't been called "fresh" since I was in knickers.

"It may look... odd, asking you to my apartment, but don't get any ideas, Mr. Harris. Nor do I like you making fun of me."

"Merely asked a question, Mrs. Turner," I said, afraid I'd smile myself out of a job. "Only wondering if the place still spooks you."

She sort of pulled herself together, leaned back on the couch. "It was bad till... One morning several weeks after we moved in I was feeling... uh... unwell... had to stay home. Ed couldn't be with me, we'd have both lost our jobs. I was going crazy, imagining all sorts of things when a woman came to the door, said she had worked as a maid for the suicide and did I want to hire her? Of course we couldn't afford that but I was so happy to see anyone I asked her in for coffee and we talked about the dead man. When she told me he'd been a pansy, I don't know why, I was no longer afraid. Till now. With Ed a suicide everything scares me. But that's enough about me. What have you been doing, Mr. Harris?"

"Checked with Lieutenant Swan on the details of the case. By the way, Mr. Turner ever mention a man named Brown?"

"No. And we haven't any friends by that name, or..."

"Have many friends?"

She popped her eyes open like I'd jabbed her in the belly. "Why do you ask that? As a matter of fact, we didn't. I'm not the outgoing type and Ed— he liked to roam around alone, always looking for what he called suspects. As for his friends on the force, frankly I hated his being a policeman. It changed Ed. When a man makes his work hunting down other men, that's not good."

"I suppose cops are necessary."

"Mr. Harris, doctors are necessary too, but suppose a doctor limited himself to handling cancer cases all day, day after day—in time he'd probably become infected himself. A cop, always working with criminals, I think he becomes infected too. After a time the cop and the criminal blend, the hunter and the hunted become one." Her voice, which had been full and strong, went small again as she slipped me a smile, added, "No offense, Mr. Harris. Oh, I can't keep calling you Mister Harris. I'll call you Barney and you may call me Betsy."

"You call me what you wish, I'll keep using Mrs. Turner," I said, annoyed at her "... you *may* call me ..." I was really annoyed because whatever there was about her that troubled me... still troubled me.

She shrugged—a very sexy movement. "As you like. But I didn't mean to be personal when I said police work was a dirty profession."

"Can't offend me. I only stumbled into the... eh... profession myself. I'm an auto mechanic. My wife was in the insurance business and she got me a job checking on stolen cars for insurance companies. Usually the engine numbers are filed, other changes made to disguise the heap. It was my job to identify the cars, also check into phony auto accidents, and the title of private detective went with the job. I did that for five or six years and when my wife died I went into the private-eye business because of the irregular hours—gives me a chance to call for my daughter in school, be around the neighborhood."

"I'm sorry to hear about your wife," she said, in the proper sad tone. "Did you raise the girl by yourself?"

"Yes, and quite well, too."

"How old is she?"

"Ruthie will be six in two months from the twenty-fifth."

"Barney, I don't mean to be personal, but did your wife die in childbirth?"

"No, we adopted Ruthie. My wife was too old to have kids." I saw the puzzled look come into her eyes and wondered if she'd come out and ask me. She did.

"But you don't look more than thirty-four."

"I'm thirty-seven, Mrs. Turner. I was thirty-two when I married my wife and she was forty-one. I was her second husband, and I was infatuated with her beauty. You see she never tried to look younger than she was, rather she was always a beautiful forty-one-year-old woman. Maybe that's a beauty secret. Now let's get back to Ed."

Betsy nodded. "I'm crazy about children. Ed was too, till he became a cop... then he always wanted to wait."

"How long have you been married?"

"About four years," she said, pouring herself a taste of vermouth, sipping it as though it was hard stuff. "I'm from a small town way out on Long Island. I had always looked forward to New York City, but I found it such a lonely place. I met Ed on the job, my first real beau, and after a month we were married. It was like a dream, we were so happy, so much in love. Ed was tender and considerate, full of laughs. But he changed from the moment he entered the Police Academy. He became ambitious."

"Most wives like that. My wife tried to inject some ambition into me, but it didn't take," I said, wondering why her words sounded false although she said them straight, as if she meant them.

"Ambition made Ed tough and cruel. A few days after he was appointed to the force, we were in the subway, going to a movie downtown. Ed kept staring at a man across the aisle, told me, 'He looks like a guy I saw on a Fed-wanted flier. Dope case. Except his hair is black and this fellow was a blond.'

"I told him to forget it but Ed was always talking about making a 'good' pinch, jumping to a detective. All he did at night was to read those wanted circulars. Well, he kept studying this man, going over his face feature by feature, the way he'd been trained. Finally he said, 'That's him!' and went over and showed his badge—made a scene. The man denied he was the criminal but Ed yanked out a fistful of his hair, waved the bloody hair at me and shouted, 'The roots are blond!' Then he punched the man in the face and he was all blood."

"Was the man the one wanted?"

She nodded. "But how I *hated* that badge, the gun, the handcuffs, the blackjack!"

"Mrs. Turner, a rough world makes for rough people. The worst cop hater squeals the loudest for the police when he's in a jam. True, there are incompetent cops, nightstick happy. Also, in this corrupt world, if crime doesn't pay—being a cop doesn't pay much either. Now that I've finished my sermon for the day, let's get down to cases—this case. You have any boy friends, past or present?"

She jumped to her feet with cat speed. "How dare you say that?" Her big soft eyes were big and mad now.

"Take it slow, Mrs. Turner," I said calmly. "I'm working for you, remember? I have to sift through everything. A jealous boy friend could cause murder, or suicide."

"How dare you... I never looked at another man! I never... what sort of a mind have you?"

"A detective's mind—maybe. Look, stop the how-dare-you line. Mrs. Turner, you asked me up here. I don't mind a lot of social chatter, but at the moment I feel ill at ease, a bit like the rear end of a horse. I don't mean to be crude, or maybe I do, but the point is, I have to ask questions and I'd like some answers—without frills, if possible."

"You're crude, rude, and... and...!"

"Let's start over again," I cut in. "How about Ed, any other woman on his mind?"

"No! No!" Her face got so red I thought she was going to scream.

"Mrs. Turner, being a busybody is my job. You said in my office that you and Ed were very happy, yet all you've done tonight is carp about his job, his..."

"We *were* very much in love and happy! Get that through your thick head, you lummox!" she shouted in my face. Then she caught herself, sat down on the couch again, said in a normal voice, "I didn't like what his job was doing to him, but that doesn't make us unhappy."

"Have a job, Mrs. Turner?"

"No."

"This apartment, the furniture, your clothes—a detective's salary wouldn't make it. You knew your husband was keeping his hand out, but..."

"Ed wasn't dishonest!" she snapped.

"What did he do, win a lot of prize money like the Andersun kid? This case is tough enough, has the cops on the ropes—if you really want results, don't hold out on me."

"I told you, I never knew much about his job—never wanted to hear about it. He gave me money for the house. I never asked questions. Ed didn't like to be questioned about money matters. My God, you must think I'm some cheap, little ugly tramp that..."

"Don't know enough about you to say if you're cheap or not, or a tramp. But you're not little, or ugly. Now let's put the gloves away and get down to..."

Her eyes became soft again—that kid look—as she said, "Thanks. I do want to find out if... Ed was a suicide. It's so terribly important to me. I'm sorry I blew up, but you are a bit abrupt... and crude."

I wondered what the "thanks" meant. "One more crude question, Mrs. Turner. Why do you keep harping on this suicide kick? You say Ed was happy, and ambitious, hard—that's not the picture of a suicide."

"But if he was shot in the back without...?"

"Suicides are upset, depressed. You keep raising the suicide angle.... What was Ed upset about?"

She stared at the floor, finally whispered, "We had a fight that night. Something very personal."

"Like what?"

She raised her head and glared at me, said, "None of your business! I said it was personal!"

"But you hired me to find out the most personal thing a person can do— kill himself. What did you fight about?"

She sighed, leaned back against the couch, said in her small voice, "We were... incompatible. For months Ed hadn't slept with me."

I didn't say a word, didn't know what to say.

"I think he... he got some sort of... thrill... out of beating men. He once told me that. Maybe that was why he stopped... having relations with... me. On the night he was killed we... had a scene and I accused him of n-not being a man. He got so angry I thought he was going to hit me. He ran out of here. Less than two hours later he was dead." The words were forced out, dull little sounds. She added, "This has to be confidential. Don't even tell the police, please."

I stood up.

"Now you see why I must know—for my own peace of mind. I feel as though I killed him."

"If that's all you have to go on, Mrs. Turner, I still think you ought to save your money. Let the police handle this."

"I'll be the judge of that," she said, and her kid's voice was cold and snooty. "What do you plan to do tomorrow?"

"If you're going to tell me how to operate, then you don't need me."

"I'm not telling you your business, but I am interested, of course."

For a moment I wanted to walk out on the case—but only for a moment.

Then I said calmly, "This Brown lead might be something, although it's a long shot and doesn't make much sense. Takes me months to check on all the Browns in the city, but the police will do it quicker, so I'll leave it alone. I expect to talk to members of the Andersun family. I'm sure his slaying will explain everything. Sound like a good day's work?"

I walked to the door and she followed, without speaking. At the door I turned to see her looking at herself in a wall mirror, moistening her lips, straightening her bangs. "You'll be here tomorrow at eight?" she asked.

I nodded and opened the door.

"Barney, have you a picture of your daughter?"

Taking out my wallet, I showed her Ruthie's laughing face. She said, "What an adorable child."

"Thank you, Mrs. Turner."

"I wish you'd call me Betsy. Mrs. Turner sounds so... jarring."

"Best we keep it jarring, for the time being. Good night, Mrs. Turner."

"Good night, Barney."

In the lobby downstairs I asked the hall man if there was a public phone and he showed me one back of a door that led to the service entrance. I kept the door open as I dialed, had a clear view of the lobby. I told my baby sitter, "This is Barney Harris. Looks like I'm stuck for a brace of hours. May, can you do me a favor and sleep over on the couch? Sure, ask your folks if it's okay. How's Ruthie doing? Oh, I'll probably be home around... three or four in the morning. You bet, overtime is double pay. Look, you go downstairs and ask your folks and I'll call back in about five minutes."

I hung up and lit a cigarette, wondered if it would be smart to chat with the hall man. But he wouldn't tell me anything about Mrs. Turner. Probably the first thing the cops checked was what she was doing on the night of the murder.

An old couple came in and talked to the hall man as they waited for the elevator. I finished my butt and called back and May said her folks didn't like her staying out all night. I told her I'd phone them. Instead I phoned Cy O'Hara, asked him if he could baby-sit. He told me, "Look, Barney, it's near nine now and I'm to hell and gone across the Bronx. Besides, I'd have to wait till the wife came home from the movies. Probably wouldn't get there before 3 a.m. myself."

"I just thought maybe you could leave now. See you at the office."

"Sorry, Barney."

"Forget it. I'll get somebody. See you tomorrow, Cy." I couldn't blame anybody for turning me down—being single I could never return the baby-sitting favor. I got the Weiss number from information and spent ten minutes convincing May's mother that this was an emergency and after all, the kid was in the same apartment house and what could happen to her?

She finally said all right, but just this once. Said she'd go up and see that May was comfortable.

I went out and sat in my car, got some jazz on the radio. It wasn't hard to spot the Turner windows—not with all those slashing colors. Waiting is the thing a detective does the most of and I killed time by going through the papers in my pockets, tearing up the ads, the old bills, a letter asking if I was interested in a "Perfect Man" and weight-lifting contest at a Brooklyn YMCA; I was way out of shape for contest lifting, and maybe getting too old.

Mostly couples went into the apartment house, and a few men who somehow didn't look like "lovers." At ten-thirty the lights in her living room went out, then I saw her pulling down the blinds of her bedroom, and soon that light went out.

At 3:20 a.m. I drove home. Betsy Turner hadn't gone out, nor had the lights been turned on again. She hadn't been waiting for a man. That meant she'd dolled up in that sexy outfit for me.

And like the rest of the case, that didn't make any sense.

The army didn't make Martin Pearson a hustler—the war did. In an interview in the Syracuse Tribune, *Pearson's mother, Mrs. Francine Pearson, blamed the army:*

> *I'll never believe Martin is a murderer. Our family has lived here since the days of 1776 and not a single Pearson has ever been in trouble with the law—for any reason whatsoever. My Martin was raised as a sober, hard-working boy, but after those three-and-a-half years he spent in the army, he came home different. He was still a fine boy but it seemed to me his eyes were restless, always searching for something. He never seemed to look a person in the eyes any more.*

But the army only taught a comparative few how to work an angle, while war made scrounging the main occupation of most of the world's population—scrounging for food, the fast buck, the fast lira or franc: hustling for life itself.

Pearson was born on a small farm some twenty-four miles from Syracuse, New York on August 25, 1920. The farm was four miles from the "town" of Bay Corners, which consisted of a feed store, a garage, and a general store run by one Andrew Marsh. The rear of this store was also the movie house with several rows of wooden benches. Twice a week (and every night during July and August) Mr. Marsh squeezed his barrel body into his homemade projection booth and ran his old 16mm projector. Farmers supported Bay Corners the year around, but in the summer passing motorists and the campers at a near-by lake gave Marsh a boom business.

Martin was the fourth child and received little attention from the rest of the family. As soon as he was big enough, he did his share of the farm work. When he was twelve years old a small incident changed his entire life. Mary Marsh—the plump ten-year-old daughter of the general-store owner—sported a new bike, the result of selling twenty-five subscriptions to a farm magazine.

Martin also wanted a bike and knowing she had covered all the people in Bay Corners (fifty-seven according to the last census) he spent the snow-free days of the winter tramping from farm to farm. By spring he had twenty-five subs and sent away for the bike. Two weeks later the rural mailman handed Martin a large package, although obviously much too small for a bicycle. An enclosed letter stated that there had been a misunderstanding on Martin's part—the bicycle was given for a hundred and twenty-five subscriptions. For his twenty-five subs they were sending him a box camera, three rolls of film, and a developing kit. The magazine sincerely hoped this would be satisfactory.

It wasn't. In a rage Martin accused Mary Marsh of lying. She said, "Honest, I thought it was twenty-five subs. Poppa sold them for me at the counter and I never did know how many he got. Gee, Marty, nobody here ever had a camera, except the summer people."

Martin was still angry but he took pictures of his father and mother on a sunny day, developed them in the barn at night—carefully following the instruction booklet—and his folks and brothers stared at the hazy snapshots with awe. Martin realized the camera made him a person of importance, began spending his extra dimes for photo supplies and booklets.

By the time he graduated from high school at eighteen, Martin had a second-hand press camera and was making a few dollars a week cycling from farm to farm, doing "portraits" of the farm families. Mary Marsh was about to enter Teachers Normal College at Oswego, and had grown to be a squat young woman whose only beauty was her "clear skin." There weren't many young people in Bay Corners and it was understood Mary and Martin were "going steady," mainly because Martin hung around Poppa Marsh's theater, seeing each movie over and over, trying to understand the technique of motion pictures. Martin suggested she ask her father if he could set up a "portrait studio" in the store during the summer months, use the theater for a dark room during the day. For rent Martin offered 30 per cent of the take. Mr. Marsh settled for 50 per cent and Martin was in business with some badly lettered signs in the store window.

Martin would hang around the summer campers, quietly taking candid shots of them swimming and horsing around, return the next day with enlargements in cardboard frames. The happy campers gave him from three to five dollars a picture and during the summer he made almost four hundred dollars. Mr. Marsh hinted Martin would be welcome as a son-in-law and it was decided they would be married as soon as Mary finished college.

Martin bought a second-hand roadster (In his confession Martin Pearson stated: "Until I was in the army I never had a brand-new thing in my life. All my clothing, shoes, and toys were hand-me-downs from my brothers.") and the photography business went into a slump; all the local people had photos and in the winter there weren't any tourists. Martin took pictures of a forest fire and sold them to a Syracuse paper, soon became a free-lance photographer for several small country papers. He would ride around the countryside, snapping weddings, accidents, church bazaars; returning to sell pictures to the people in the photos, to the local papers, and sometimes to papers in Syracuse, Ithaca, and Buffalo. Although he worked hard, had a good summer trade, Martin never averaged more than thirty dollars a week for a year.

When he was twenty-two, Mary graduated from college and was immediately hired to teach at the Bay Corners school. She and Martin were married and he moved into the Marsh apartment over the store. By local standards they had a decent income and Martin wasn't unhappy—he was bored. Nine months after they were married he received his draft notice and according to his own statement: "If I felt anything it was relief."

Martin landed in an infantry basic training camp in the South. Every Friday afternoon the soldiers were reviewed by the elderly colonel in command. One Friday, while he was barracks orderly, Martin took his miniature camera and photographed the parade grounds. Using the camera as an enlarger, he ran off a few prints, found the soldiers eager to get copies—they offered him as much as five dollars per copy. Martin immediately wired Mary to send him supplies and was soon doing a flourishing business. A camp newspaper was being set up and Martin was made a Pfc., kept on permanent cadre, and assigned to the paper.

A large and steady stream of new men went through the camp, each new G.I. wanting a picture to send home. Martin had a stock shot in which he lay behind a small hill and snapped the new soldier jumping over the top, rifle and bayonet in hand, a scowl on his face. This was the five-dollar special and every payday Martin's hands were full of money, and it was all profit as he was now using army film and paper. Mary wrote dutiful letters, sent him homemade cookies and asked when he was coming home on leave, but business was too good for Martin to take time off. The editor of the camp newspaper was an earnest young man who was transferred in 1943 to Yank *magazine. He wrote Martin the magazine might be interested in him too, but Sergeant Pearson wasn't the least interested in leaving his cozy deal.*

In 1944 the camp cadre was suddenly shipped to Camp Kilmer, broken up for overseas shipment. Martin spent a fast week-end with Mary in New York City and in a fit of tender love-making gave her eighteen hundred dollars he had saved up, told her he'd won it in a crap game.

Three weeks later Martin was hanging around a huge repple-depple outside Naples, seemed to be taking his basic over again. One day Pearson read an article in Yank *by his former camp editor and wrote to him, asking if it was still possible to be assigned to the magazine. The* Yank *man was stationed in Rome and to Martin's astonishment he spoke to somebody on* Stars and Stripes *and Martin was soon sent to Rome as a photographer on the army newspaper.*

Pearson learned a great deal about photography here, for the other cameramen had all been professional newspaper and magazine photographers. Martin covered the front lines, flew a bombing mission, and rode a PT boat to Yugoslavia. Life was exciting but he missed the money he'd made back in the States and Pearson was constantly searching for an angle. Black-market cigarettes were small time; a bigger deal was selling G.I. photographic paper to Italian studios, but that was risky.

Almost any sort of camera sold for several hundred dollars, while a good camera would bring a thousand or more from the G.I.'s. A Yank photographer had a map of Germany with the towns with camera factories circled and he often talked of coming into one of these towns with the troops and "grabbing off a Rolleiflex or a Leica for myself."

Martin saw bigger possibilities, copied the map when he was sent into France after D-day. Months later Martin was with an infantry company when they stormed a German city noted for its expensive reflex cameras. While the soldiers were mopping up snipers, Martin drove a jeep directly to the factory, walked in holding a carbine to find Polish slave laborers still at work.

They stared at him without much emotion, only a kind of patient beaten weariness, and stood at their benches as Martin carried twenty-seven cameras (each in a neat wooden box) out to his jeep. The Nazi factory manager, finally convinced Martin was alone, at last came out of his office, demanded to know what the hell Pearson was doing.

Martin answered by busting his head open with the carbine, then shouted at the Poles, "You're free! Understand—free! Take what you want and scram!" He waved his hands at the open doors, but they still didn't move. Martin had taken all the rations out of his jeep, to make room for the cameras, and he handed these out. When he left he saw the Poles gulping the rations, then trooping out with whatever instruments they could carry, and soon the factory went up in flames.

After giving cameras to the motor pool sergeant, the PRO captain, and several others, Martin still had sixteen cameras and within the following month he was able to sell these for an average of $800 each, giving him nearly $13,000.

When the war in Europe was over Martin was stationed in Frankfurt, then in Paris, and in both cities he lived well, for he was an American sergeant with money and a PX card that meant cigarettes, candy, and soap. He got into some big crap games, and at one time his $13,000 went to $21,000 and once it shrunk to $4,500. He had $11,000 in Allied currency when he was awaiting shipment back to the States. He managed to change this into $8,500 in American money and money orders.

In January, 1946, Pearson was discharged and returned to Bay Corners. Mary Pearson had carefully banked all his allotment checks, already picked out a house they would buy, with a garage that could be made into a studio. He never told her about his money. In his confession Pearson stated:

> *I really don't know why I kept the money a secret from my wife. But I did. It wasn't the money, rather it was something I knew I could never explain to her. She would think it wrong and well... to me it wasn't a matter of right or wrong. I'd merely been lucky.*

When they were married Mary, as the college graduate, had been the brains and Martin a simple farm boy. But the Martin Pearson who returned to Bay Corners knew all the angles, spoke French, Italian, and German, had slept with many women, seen bombed cities and dead men and women, sunned himself on Capri, the Venice Lido, the beach at Cannes. He looked at the plain, plump, country-school teacher who was his wife and told her he couldn't take Bay Corners any longer. He didn't love Mary, but she was his wife and he wanted to make a try at living with her.

Martin said he didn't know exactly what he wanted to do, but he wanted to live in New York City. Of course Mary Pearson thought this foolish: she had her teacher's job in Bay Corners, their families lived there, and "... I hear some Syracuse people plan to build motels out by the lake. Means plenty of picture work for you. I figure you should make fifty dollars a week at least."

She talked Martin into staying in Bay Corners and he remained there— for three months. The day they were to buy a house, he took a bus to New York City. Mary Pearson never knew what happened to him till seven years later when reporters swooped down on her with Martin's picture on the front page.

Pearson spent a restless year in New York, working in a photography studio. New York wasn't what he was looking for. He decided to study color photography under the G.I. Bill and while looking into the various schools, he overheard some ex-G.I.'s talking about Paris schools.

In June, 1947, he got passage on a clean little freighter and sweated out a hot summer in Paris, living frugally and taking it easy as he brushed up on his French, hunted for an apartment. In September he enrolled in a photography school, but there wasn't much they could teach him. When he said he was interested in motion-picture work, his teacher introduced him to Thérèse Veyron, a film editor.

No man had ever called Thérèse pretty. She was tall and slim, flat-chested, and had heavy ankles. Her long, lean face contained sad eyes, an overlarge mouth, and was set off by carefully brushed brown hair that hung to thin shoulders. The only child of a middle-class family, when she was twenty-two—and with the help of a dowry—Thérèse married a fifty-two-year-old man who managed a movie theater on l'avenue des Ternes. He openly spent her dowry on his mistress, made a point of remarking about every large-breasted woman they saw on the streets. They politely hated each other and for lack of something to do, Thérèse took a job as a secretary with a concern that made short advertising movies. At the start of the war Thérèse was a film cutter.

Thérèse never considered leaving her husband but the war broke the pattern of most lives: for her it killed her husband, wiped out her family and home during an air raid, and left her mildly active working on underground movies that were never made, and lonely. With the war over she returned to the film business. There were plenty of jobs but no money, and although she worked hard she was always hungry and seedy looking.

Thérèse resigned herself to the fact that she was unattractive, that romance was out. Americans annoyed her and she only agreed to go out with Martin because it meant a good supper. He took her to a modest restaurant and she stuffed herself as he talked about photography. Over coffee and hot rums he carefully listened to her ideas about movies. And when he walked Thérèse to her three-room flat, he politely asked if he could sleep with her. She wasn't certain whether she was angry, amused, flattered, or astonished.

They turned out to be ideal lovers; each not only aroused a sincere passion in the other, but each of them was fanatically interested in the same subject—motion pictures. As soon as Thérèse could evict a girl roomer, Martin moved in. He made no secret of his money and they decided he would continue with school—to get the subsistence money—and in time they would open a small studio, produce the clever two-minute commercial used in French theaters between the showings of the regular feature.

Pearson had about seven thousand dollars left and they carefully hoarded this, living with moderate ease on his G.I. school money. They moved on the fringe of the movie crowd at Joinville, spent their spare time hunting for a studio, looking at equipment—and buying nothing but a cheap 16mm movie camera Martin used for practice.

Life was leisurely; they were sure of each other and their future: they were very happy. Pearson was one of the few fortunate Americans who wasn't searching for the Left Bank of the 1920's in post-World War II Paris. Martin loved the Paris he found. It made no difference to him if he ate in a swank tourist restaurant or had supper in one of the student places for eighty francs. He wanted nothing more out of life than to sip coffee and eat croissants in a café each morning, racing through the Paris Herald in a few seconds, then slowly stumbling through a French morning paper over his second cup. He would play the pinball machine and finally go to school. In the afternoons he roamed the city, taking pictures of the people, the wonderful old dirty buildings. He was amused by the tourists and never lonely for the States. In fact during the five years he spent in Paris he claims he only went to the American Express once. At five in the afternoon he would sit at a sidewalk café and exchange small talk with the waiters as he waited for Thérèse to have an apéritif with him. He enjoyed watching her in the crowds, the eager impatient way she walked, as if there was absolutely nothing in the world as important as rushing to meet and kiss Martin Pearson.

One October evening in 1951, as they were having a late snack of mussels and snails in a cheap restaurant on rue Clichy, Thérèse asked, 'You remember Gabby, the little one who thinks she is an actress because she has a bosom like a cow?"

Martin nodded.

"She is now living with one of your compatriots, a smug, stupid man who claims he was an actor in Hollywood and on Broadway. He is as bald as an egg, and I think you should see him."

"Why? I can't grow hair!"

"My darling, always you must joke! He has just come from your army in Germany. He has a car and spends his money like a fool. But Gabby swears she has seen three reels of Nazi newsreels he has managed to steal, films never seen before. She says there are pictures of Hitler, Eva Braun, and others, including a parade of nude girls on floats, and horror shots of the beasts looting a Polish village. This... actor has ideas of making a full-length picture around these reels. It can be done, so I have arranged for Gabby to introduce you to this Monsieur Sam Lund."

CHAPTER THREE

At seven-thirty Ruthie got me half awake by the usual method of tickling my toes, then banging me on the head, which always brought me completely around. At first I'd thought this was cute, now I couldn't break her of the habit. I went to the bathroom, wearing only a pair of shorts. There was a short scream—I'd forgotten about the baby sitter. May was a skinny fifteen and wearing an old robe of her mother's that went around her several times. Her pimply face was a furious blushing red. I said, "What you screaming about? Haven't you ever been to the beach, seen men in trunks? Want the bathroom first?"

"I have already completed my toilet," she announced, so I went in and left her to her blushing.

After breakfast I drove Ruthie to the nursery school. I only had a few hours' sleep and maybe some private eyes can bat along on no shut-eye, but not me. I needed sleep to sharpen my alleged mind, so I went home and crawled back between the sheets, after setting the alarm for noon. Exactly twenty-three minutes later the phone rang, jarring me awake.

Jake Winston said, "Hello, cousin."

"Hello, Jake," I said, trying not to sound angry.

"Waited till you were awake to call you," he said pleasantly. "I saw Ruthie yesterday."

"She told me."

"Why didn't you call me last night? You know Grace, always fussing with her cooking. Wants to know if you're coming out Sunday?"

"Well... eh ..."

"Been months since we've seen you. The boys want to see Ruthie and Grace will make some fancy dishes I can't even pronounce."

Grace was Syrian and could cook Oriental dishes that made you stuff yourself like a pig. "Don't have to sell me, Jake. Thing is I'm on a case and not sure I'll be free Sunday."

"Let's settle it that you're coming out. If you get stuck, I'll drive in and pick up Ruthie. A deal, chum?"

"I'm buying. How's the mail?"

"Heavy, lot of damn magazines today. See you, Barney."

I drove over to the office to pick up my mail—a waste of time, stopped at the coffeepot for a second breakfast and a couple of Alma's old dirty jokes, then headed down to the Andersun home. All the time I felt in a daze, my brain still working on Betsy Turner. There was something sad about her. All that stuff about her late husband getting his kicks out of beating men—I didn't believe it, but I guess anything is possible when a joker goes in for thrills.

I only expected to find Mrs. Andersun home, but the father was there too. Their apartment was much like mine, a four-room walk-up in a house that was on the verge of becoming a tenement. The Andersuns were ordinary-looking people, both in their fifties—Mrs. Andersun a very pale and delicate-looking woman. Her husband wore a torn undershirt, old pants, slippers, and a hearing aid. He was stooped and thin, a plump face held up by a scrawny neck, his skin an unhealthy pale-white.

When I told them what I wanted, he told me in a tired voice, "We have been through this so many times, so many questions."

I gave him the old reliable, "Only doing my job, Mr. Andersun. And you want us to find your son's killer, don't you?"

He shrugged bony shoulders. "Yes, I suppose I do want the killer captured. But that won't bring Franklin back to us. When he came out of the war alive, I was so happy, and now..."

"The war did it," Mrs. Andersun said as I parked my king-size backside in a worn chair. "Took a quiet boy like my Franklin, had him ride the sky at three hundred miles an hour. He'd be in Topeka one morning, maybe here in New York the next, or in California for breakfast and going to a show in New Orleans that evening. Then they expect him to return to a normal, slow life."

"Frank wasn't... eh... nervous or anything, was he?"

"No, sir, he was a bright boy, a student," the mother said. "Took three years of college under the G.I. Bill. Studied business. Always said how with the right methods and a little cash, a person could make a fortune these days. Had so many schemes—all legitimate, of course."

"What sort of schemes?"

"No sense going into that," Mr. Andersun said. "Other detectives asked us the same thing. Franklin never got started, you need capital and we're poor people. He managed to save a few hundred dollars and played the market with that. At first he made a small profit, then he tried some wild stocks and lost it all. He went to the big concerns with some of his merchandising ideas, but they wouldn't even see him. Then he got a couple of jobs, thought he could work his way up. They beat him down, broke his spirit."

"Nonsense, Franklin would have been a rich man some day. He had the spunk," Mama said.

Mr. Andersun shook his head. "No, he lost his drive. That's why he was going to take a trip with this money, instead of investing it."

"Where was he going?"

"No place special, maybe Paris, he just wanted to travel."

"Were you in favor of the trip?" I asked.

Mr. Andersun turned so that the hearing device hooked to his belt faced me. "Was I in favor of it? Oh, travel is a form of education. We hardly had any time to discuss it. Juanita, that's our daughter, she thought Franklin should spend it on new furniture. But far as Mom and I were concerned, the final decision would have been up to the boy."

There wasn't anything at the Andersun home, and the cops had already questioned them for several days. The old man had worked for the gas company most of his life, was taking time off now to pull himself together. They had never heard of any Brown, never heard or saw Turner before, hadn't a single idea why their son was shot. Juanita worked as a telephone operator and would be home late in the afternoon. She had a steady boy friend named Irving Spear, who was a hackie. Mom Andersun said, "A very good boy, going to evening college. Of course there's a difference in religion, but they will work that out. Franklin wasn't engaged, but he saw a lot of Cissy Lewis—lives in the house next door."

When I left them, I dropped in to see if Cissy was home. She was a silly-looking girl of about twenty-four, with curlers in her blond hair, and quite upset because I found her in a dirty housedress, cleaning up her folk's apartment. She talked in a shrill voice, said her folks ran a local vegetable store and made a point of telling me, "I never work there, of course. Wish I'd have known you was coming; I'd have got dressed. Lots of cops and men have questioned me. Gee, you sure look like a detective—so big and hard-boiled looking."

When I managed to get a word in, she said, "I was engaged to Frank and my heart is broken. As I told the reporters, I was so shocked at the news of his death, I fainted. I really did." She had one of these straight-up-and-down figures except for fleshy, quivering hips, and as she talked she walked around the living room, putting quite a movement into her hips.

"Frankie know any Brown?"

"You mean a colored man?"

"No, a red-haired man named Brown?"

"Not that I know of and I knew all his friends. We were going to get married soon as he got a better job. I'm a secretary—out of work, at the moment. I told Frank I was willing to work for a while, so we could get married now, but he wouldn't hear of it."

"What about the trip he was going to take?"

The-heel-and-toe strut stopped. "That was the dumbest idea I ever heard of!" Cissy shrilled. "When I read about it in the papers, I couldn't wait to give him a piece of my mind. Of course I never did. Poppa belongs to a checker club and I had to close up the store that night. Are you going to ask me where I was at the time of the killing, like the other dicks did?"

"No." I stood up. "Could have used that thousand dollars to get married," I said for no reason, except to watch her get steamed.

"Exactly what I was going to tell him. After all, I'm twenty-three, sure time I got married. One thing, I'm glad I never gave in to Frank. You know." This was followed by a giggle and a modest blush.

I thanked her and made for the door. She looked up at me, said, "My, you're a big big man. Married?"

"Six wives, honey. Good-by."

I drove over to the taxi-garage Irving Spear hacked out of, waited around—dozing in my car—till three when he drove in. He was leanly built, about twenty-seven, and had a pigeon-toed walk. His face was small and heavy shell glasses made it look smaller, and his noggin was on the bald side. From the way he moved and acted, he was a tough joker who could handle himself. I asked him if he'd have a beer. We got a booth in a crummy ginmill and he looked at my card, said, "Even private operators getting into the act. I can't understand the murder, Frank didn't have an enemy in the world. He was the mousy type."

"His folks said he was a pusher, business-tycoon type."

Irv laughed. "Frank wanted that but didn't have the guts. Actually he was a moody kid, like an artist or a poet. And he wasn't too smart. Surprised he had guts enough to even talk about taking off for Europe. Trip like that might have made him."

"Cissy Lewis, his girl, didn't go for the idea."

"That dumb tomato—she wasn't his girl. The way it was, Frank started taking her out a few times because she was always around. Bet in time she would have hooked him, too, even though he wasn't serious about her. Just a kid we grew up with."

"Frank ever know a girl named Betsy?" I asked, starting to describe Mrs. Turner, surprised at all the details I could recall.

"You're off base," Irv said, cutting in. "Frank wasn't a guy that chased. He didn't even have the nerve to talk Cissy into the sheets. Frank still had to pay for it."

"Where?"

He shook his head. "Now look, this gal is okay, I don't want to make no trouble for her. I never even told the real cops about her."

"Why should I make trouble? All I'll do is ask her a few questions. This is a rugged case, never know what will help."

"Okay, but I don't believe in knifing anybody. I'm strictly a live-and-let-live joker. Her name is Louise, you'll find her in the basement of a private house down the block—515."

"Did you know this man named Brown?"

"Who's he?"

"Guy with red hair who was in the Grand Café several months ago, said he knew Andersun, they were kids together—Brown said he remembered the church burning down."

Irv grinned. "Yeah, I remember that liar now. Never could figure what his angle was in bulling Frank. Had a guy with him who was giving me the bull treatment too. Handsome guy with wavy hair. Said his name was Smith, or Jones, something like that. He kept asking if I was related to a Spear he knew. Odd part was—and why I remember him—he said this Spear was an accountant; that's what I'm studying."

"What else did he ask?"

"Buddy, this was months ago and only beer talk then. He just asked about my folks being related to this other Spear, where I was born. That's all. I never saw him again. In fact I'm not swearing he was with Brown. But it was the same night."

"Did you see Brown in the bar the night of the murder?"

"Was he there? Like I told the other cops, I was in school that night. They checked. You people think Brown is the killer?"

"I don't think anything. Brown is merely a name that's come up twice. Going home? I'll drive you there. I want to see Juanita."

Juanita Andersun was alone. Her folks had gone for a walk, or in her own words, "Told them to get the hell out and air off." She was a wiry, sharp-faced young woman of about twenty-one, rather pretty, with clean thin features and eyes like twin judges. She dressed simply and smartly and looked like a pert college kid—till she opened her mouth, breathed acid. Looking me over, she said, "So you're the man-mountain the folks said was here. Come on in, if you can get through the door. Just crawled home from the job myself. Work is a bitch."

I sat in the living room as she went into the bathroom and said through the wide open door, "Be with you in a moment, got to exercise my bladder." When she came back she stood in the doorway, stripped to her bra and panties, watching my reaction as she showed one of those hard slender figures that never change much between the ages of fourteen and forty-four. She threw on a beach robe, pasted a cigarette to her lower lip, then kind of flung herself in a chair as she asked, "What's with your great big birdbrain, shamus?"

The "shamus" made me grin; the sale of detective stories must be sensational, and meeting Juanita was sure an experience—a lousy one. "Like to get your ideas on the killings, ask some questions. Ever see Turner, the detective, before?"

She gave me a shake of her poodle hair-do.

We split a moment of silence, then I asked, "What do you think of the killings?"

"What's there to think? Either the work of a maniac, or Frank walked into a fight. As I told the other dicks, my brother was not involved in anything—he didn't have the guts."

"Meaning?"

"In basic English it means he's the one that went to college. Me, I had to work after two years of high school—Frankie was a boy and in this family a boy is a Golden Boy. When Frankie came out of the army he was full of ginger, the old pep. Said any person with a little sense and willing to gamble, could make a pile—only suckers stayed poor. I thought maybe it was a break for us that he did go to college. He'd come home, tell me about the business methods he was studying—all the learned and fancy names for the old con racket. Frank and I would split a bottle of beer and he'd tell me how this and that guy started on the road to folding dough by putting a few bucks on some stock, parlaying the deal. Give you an example—Frank told me about some Englishman who heard about surplus U.S. Army supplies on an island in the West Indies—Trinidad, I think. So this guy bought all the stuff from Uncle Sam by cable, then sold them to the government of the island—by another cable. Made himself three hundred thousand bucks in less than a day, and all at the cost of two cables. That's operating. Sort of deal Frankie was looking for. On a smaller scale, of course."

"Was this Paris trip part of a would-be deal?"

Juanita gave me a full-lip sneer. "What deal? Frankie was all talk. If bull was electricity Frankie would have been a dynamo. Soon as he left school he dropped a few hundred in the stock market and that kayoed his spirit too. Part of the loss was my dough, but I didn't kick. Can't expect to win every bet. All his education, his books and big talk—Frankie ended up a stock clerk, another one of the beer hounds at the corner dump. Although I have to admit the kid finally came through, made good." She smiled at the blank look on my face. "We're collecting his ten grand G.I. insurance policy. You watch Irv and me hustle *my* share of that into some real salting money!"

"Ever hear of a man named Brown? Brother ever mention him?"

"Never heard of him. Should I have?"

"Guess not. What about Cissy Lewis?"

The lippy sneer again. "That drip. Frankie sure was lucky escaping her. Jeez, you don't suspect her, do you?"

"Just asking questions. Any other girls in Franklin's life?"

"Franklin—what a handle! No other dames—Cissy was for dancing and holding hands in the movies. There's a pro down the street who was hauling Frankie's ashes."

"Tell that to the cops?"

"They never asked me. All they wanted to know was what *I* was doing at the time of the shootings. In case you're thinking of asking me, I'll tell you... I was waiting right here, with the folks, to talk Frankie out of the trip junk when he came in. Any more questions?"

"Not for now," I said, heading for the door.

Without getting up she ran her eyes over me, asked, "How did you escape being a TV wrestler—big as you are? Well, I trust I've been of some help."

"You're a regular real live doll," I said, walking out.

I had over a half hour before I was due to call for Ruthie. I walked down the street to 515. This was a three-story brownstone; only now rooming-house fire escapes spoiled whatever beauty it once had. I walked down two steps to the basement, pressed the bell button next to the iron-gate door. After a minute, a man opened the inner door, asked, "Yeah?"

He was wearing sharply pressed slacks, a white wool shirt, and an expensive nylon sport jacket. He was tall and slim, long black hair carefully combed away from a face that was handsome in a kind of sensitive way, or maybe it was all the almost feminine mouth. One thing for sure—he spent a lot of time in front of a mirror. "Louise in?"

"Louise who? Whatcha want?" There was an uneasy whine to his voice.

"Louise."

"You a dick?"

I nodded and he opened the gate and I followed him into what had formerly been a dining room but was now a one-room apartment with a kitchenette behind a cheap screen. It was furnished in standard installment-plan furniture, including a new model TV set and a square Hollywood bed with a fancy red throw over it.

Louise stepped out of the bathroom, wearing a white robe, lot of lace on it. She was a chunky girl with solid breasts. She could have been in her late twenties, maybe older. Jet black hair flowed to her shoulders and framed her face. The face was exciting and would have looked even prettier without the heavy blackened eyelashes. She had a heavy lush mouth, painted a deep red. She looked sexy—a man would stare at her on the street, without knowing why he looked—at first. She glanced at greasy-hair, asked, "Cop?"

He nodded and I sat down without being asked. I didn't have to ask if she knew Turner—his picture was on her dresser in a cheap gold frame!

She asked weakly, "Pinch or shake-down?"

"Neither. I'm a private dick."

A big change came over pretty-boy. He put his hand on his back pocket, actually snarled, "Get out!"

The pocket seemed too flat for a gun. A knife. I said, "Take it easy, I'm not here for money or trouble. Only doing my job to…"

"Get out!"

"A cop has been killed, the police are looking for a fall guy. You'd rather talk to the police, all right with me."

"Ain't going to tell you again to scram!" the man said, advancing toward me. He took a switch blade out of his pocket, a knife carefully wrapped in a white silk handkerchief.

My insides got awfully chilly as I tried to say in a steady voice, "Use your head, the police get rough when one of their own is killed."

"Cliff, put that cheese sticker away," Louise said. "Put it back in your pocket." She had a nice voice, soothing. "What you want, mister?"

"Ask some questions about him." I motioned at Turner's picture with my hand. I didn't take my eyes off Cliff, who mumbled something about, "Comes barging in, like he was taking over." But he pocketed the knife, backed to the wall and watched me.

"Private badge—how are you in on all this?"

"I'm working for Turner's wife."

The tense lines in her face softened as she said, "What do you want to know?"

"Why didn't you go to the police when Turner was killed?"

"I have an alibi!" Cliff sort of screamed. "I can prove I…"

Louise said gently, "Baby, shut up." Then she smiled at me, that wonderful sensuous big mouth. "Why should I go to the police? I don't like cops, and I didn't do anything wrong. Sure I knew Ed Turner. He was a pest."

"He was an unbathed louse," Cliff put in.

Louise asked me, "What's your name?"

I gave her and greasy-hair one of my cards, said, "Let me get a few things straight. Turner was in here just before he was killed. That's why he was parked in his car down the street."

Louise nodded, looked around for a cigarette. I threw her my pack. She lit one and tossed the pack back to me, said over a cloud of smoke, "Here's the whole story: Cliff had me working a hotel, and Ed Turner was in on a raid. Whole thing was hushed up, a payoff. My Cliff has connections. But Turner got my address and the next thing we knew he was hanging around here, for free. He was a little nuts, I think."

"He was a miserable bastard!" the pimp said.

"Cliff, let me do the talking. I never had no trouble with cops, Mr. Harris. The hotel had its own protection and around here I just have a few local regulars. I play it smart, never let business get so big I attract attention. With Turner, at first all he wanted was to be on the free list. All that man had on his mind was bed, like a vitamin rabbit. It went on like that for a couple of months. That's all. As you say, I suppose he was leaving here when the fireworks started in the street. I don't know a thing about that."

"And Franklin Andersun?"

She chuckled. "A once-a-month customer, afraid to even nod to me on the street." She made a face and crushed the cigarette. "Cliff, cigarette me."

"Told you I was out."

"Go around the corner and get me a pack." She turned to me. "I can't smoke anything but mentholated ones." She turned back to her pimp, said slowly, "Gowan, Cliff. It's okay."

To my surprise Cliff slipped on a pork-pie hat and went out. When he was gone and we heard his steps on the sidewalk, Louise pulled a chair over beside mine, and she had an odd perfume or smell to her that my nose liked. She looked at my card, said, "I'm going to tell you all I know, so help me. But don't get Cliff in no trouble. In this racket a girl needs a man behind her and Cliff is tough, yet he's like a kid that needs a mother."

"A kid with a big switch blade."

"Sure, he's a mean kid at times. Know what we do? Sometimes when I knock off work, in the middle of the night, Cliff and I get into his MG and we race out to Long Island, or up through the mountains, going nowhere, but it feels fine to be tearing through the night knowing you're as good as anybody else, feeling like a big apple. Pretty hard in this world to feel like you're somebody. Anyway, Cliff is my personal business and I don't want to see him hurt. I used to hate Ed Turner's guts for his petty graft—a lousy free lay—but after a time I felt sorry for him. He needed mothering too. Trouble was, he fell in love with me. That was big trouble."

She lit one of my cigarettes. I didn't know what to say, so I said, "I'm listening."

"That's the truth. He drove me crazy. He loved me the way Cliff does. He wasn't jealous of any of my customers, they didn't count, but he didn't want Cliff around. Once he pulled a gun on Cliff and the poor guy had a nervous stomach for days. Believe me, it wasn't for me. Ed would have killed Cliff. I kept telling him I needed Cliff—hotel work is my main income—but Ed said he'd get me a better pad. But I didn't care for Ed like I do for Cliff, and anyway, his being a cop made me nervous—never know when a cop will throw you to the wolves. Ed began hanging around in his car outside this house, watching for Cliff. Got so I was afraid to go to the hotel some days, afraid he'd arrest Cliff, kill him. And in this business you can't hang up no days. They want you there when you're supposed to be there. That's the way it was on the night of the killings."

"What way?"

"Ed was in his car outside, mad as a boil, waiting to see if Cliff came in. Tell you, Mr. Harris, I know lots about men, and with whores they love 'em so much they hate 'em. For a time Ed used to get a bang out of slapping me around, playing tough. Then he started taking my money—got a joy out of leaving me just enough to eat. And that got Cliff so mad he wanted to take a knife to Ed. But after a day or two, Ed would show up with a gift worth twice the dough he took. A diamond ring once, then a watch. I still have the watch, but the ring is in hock. I'll show you the pawn ticket if you want."

"Not necessary. Tell me more about Turner."

"Not much to tell. Sometimes he'd be here every day, then I might not see him for weeks."

"When did you first meet him?"

"This has been going on for about... nine or ten months. He was so funny. Sometimes we'd go to bed and he wouldn't touch me. And at times he'd wake up in the middle of the night and start bawling, mostly about the deal he was giving his wife. Some guys enjoy two-timing their wife; with others, it tears them up. One afternoon he took sixty-two bucks I had and tore out of here to buy a modernistic lamp for his wife—brought it back to show me, as though I cared. It was some crappy palm-tree idea with an ebony trunk and lights where the coconuts should be, only it was all zigzag angles and funny looking. See, he thought he was hurting me, bringing the lamp back to show me, but I couldn't care less—except for the dough. Two nights later he was back with the diamond ring as a gift. Expensive, I got almost a hundred on it in hock."

She stopped talking and I sat there, trying to think, knowing I had something, but not sure what it was. "What's Cliffs alibi?"

Louise put a hand on my knee, said firmly, "Don't start talking or thinking *that*. I'm leveling with you, Mr. Harris, and you promised me no trouble. You got an honest face, level with me. Don't tell the cops about Cliff."

"You can't expect me to keep a thing like this quiet. Hell, Cliff has a motive, a ..."

"No, no, Mr. Harris. Believe me, Cliff didn't do it. He talks tough, but the sight of blood makes him sick. And he has a real alibi. Cliff is smart. Most pimps get sent away because they don't have no visible means of support. Cliff works as a waiter, from eight to midnight, in a downtown night club. He was working that night, honest he was, I checked myself. You can check too. You know what will happen, the cops will find his alibi holds, but in the meantime they'll work him over. And I'll be in a jam. I don't hurt nobody. I'm not a nuisance. I've never been sick. Only got in this racket because I was hungry. Now it's all I can do. If you..."

"But Cliff hated Turner, that's the missing motive. Probably shot Andersun by mistake, or maybe he was trying to talk Cliff out of killing."

"No, no, don't think that. Not so," she said in that low steady voice, her eyes on mine. "I trust you. I didn't have to tell you a thing. Cliff is a bunch of bluff, never cut or hurt anybody. Take him to a shooting gallery. I saw it out at Coney Island—being around guns makes him sick. The smell or something makes him vomit. Check his alibi. There was a wedding party that night and all the waiters were working. Believe me, if Cliff was the killer I'd be the first to blow the whistle on him, I'd run a million miles from here. If Cliff did it they'd throw the book at me for nothing. Cliff didn't do it, he couldn't have. I tell you because you look like a man who doesn't think I'm dirt, a freak, because I'm whoring. I can trust you."

Her dark eyes kept staring into mine until I looked away, felt uncomfortable. "Okay. I believe you, but I can't promise I won't have to tell the cops."

"If they would only check his alibi and leave us alone, I'd have gone to them myself, but you know what they'll do. Why must you tell them? Sure, Ed was here that night. He was here plenty of nights. But we have nothing to do with what he does, what happens, when he leaves."

I was still looking away from her eyes. There was no doubt what the cops would do to Cliff—hell, he was the only one who even *knew* both victims. They'd have to sweat him. I looked into her warm, intensely sincere eyes and asked, "Where were you at the time of the shootings?"

She sat up straight as though I'd turned into a rattlesnake. "Me? Why, you lousy... Don't try to pin it on me!"

"I'm not pinning anything on you. Look, as far as we know Turner and Andersun were complete strangers. Now we have two people who knew them both—two links—maybe the only two we'll have. You claim Cliff has an alibi. What's yours?"

"I was right here. Why else would Ed be parked outside?"

"Louise, right outside of *here* is where the murders took place. Puts you at the scene of the crime, as they say. Unless you have a ..."

"I had a girl friend with me. Ed'd come busting in that night, fighting mad. He'd had some kind of scrap with his wife and was all set for trouble. Said if he ever saw Cliff again he'd pistol-whip him. I wasn't feeling too well that night anyway—as though I didn't have enough troubles, that was starting. So when Ed left, I got the jitters, called this girl and she kept me company till one, when Cliff came in."

"What's her name and address?"

"Comes to an arrest, I'll give it, but she's in the business too and I don't want to bring the cops down on her. Mr. Harris, please swear you won't do anything to get Cliff hurt. This is a lonely racket. Every man you meet can't wait to leave you. When a Cliff comes along, even though I'm his meal ticket, or when an Ed comes by, despite all their nasty tricks, you want them around because they're about the only people stay around you. Promise me..."

"I can't promise anything. Ever know a red-haired joker named Brown? He's been in the Grand Café a couple of times, talked to Andersun once."

"Never heard of him. I'm no two-bit hustler working a dump like the Grand. Please, Mr. Harris, with Cliff..."

I stood up. "Honey, I don't hurt people, if I can help it. Not even a Cliff. I have to beat it."

"I like you, Mr. Harris, and that's no sales talk," Louise said, walking me to the door.

"You're an exciting woman—in a lot of ways. I like talking to you."

She gave me that big hot smile. "You're an all-right guy."

"What's the name of the place where Cliff works? And what's his last name?"

The smile fled.

"You told me to check his alibi, didn't you?"

"The Pigalle on West Forty-third Street. Cliff Parker. Don't make me any trouble. Please!"

"One more thing—take Ed's picture out of here. Been in the papers and somebody might recognize it, get curious. And if it isn't violating any ethical rules—how was Ed Turner in bed?"

"Lousy—kid stuff. What makes you ask?"

"Never know what makes for a clue," I said, as if I knew what I was talking about. "Maybe see you again, Louise."

When I drove up to the school Ruthie was waiting, with another kid and her Mama, and the mother gave me that you-poor-noble-bastard smile as she said, "I thought I'd stay around with Ruth till you came. I know how hard it must be for you to come here from business." This was followed by another sickly grin. I said thanks and Ruthie thanked her and rushed into the car and kissed me, whispered, "I didn't ask her to stay with me. I'm not afraid."

"Of course not. Only a few minutes late," I said, driving away.

"Where are we going for a ride—Yonkers or over in New Jersey, Daddy?"

"Downtown. Maybe we'll eat out. Like that?"

"Chinese food?"

"Okay."

"I like that. You going to train tonight?"

"No, darling, have to go out."

"Oh, Daddy, not May Weiss again?"

"Guess so. Daddy is on some case."

I drove down to the Times Building but had to park seven blocks away.

However Ruthie got a bang out of walking through the Times Square rush hour. We went downstairs to a back-issue newsstand and I bought a copy of the April eleventh paper. We drove up to One Hundred and Twenty-fifth Street and Broadway to a small Chinese restaurant that astonishes people by serving real Chinese food. First Ruthie messed up the table trying to use chopsticks. Then she had learned a story about a family of bunnies in school, and kept telling it to me till bunnies, Cliff, Louise, and Ed Turner's gold-framed picture kept blurring my mind like a runaway movie film.

May Weiss's father had to give me a lot of talk, wanted to know if this was going to be another all-night job, because if it was... I assured him I'd be home before eleven. Then Ruthie got sore because it was Friday night and she usually stayed up and I read to her. It was seven o'clock as I walked to a drugstore, wondering how come the movie dicks never are troubled with reading to their kids at night, making supper... or even having kids.

Over some orange juice I read the back issue of the *Times*—the little publicity plant about Andersun winning the thousand dollars—an item a person would miss unless they read the paper thoroughly. Turning to the marriage announcements, I got a break—there were only seven of them. I got some change and worked the phone book. I squeezed into a booth and called the first one—said I was the manager of the Pigalle and a green fedora hat had been left and I wondered if it belonged to anybody in their wedding party on the night of April eleventh. It was crude but on the third call a Mr. Worth assured me nobody at his party lost a hat, certainly not a green fedora, and if anyone had, he would have gladly sued the Pigalle since we were thieves and had grossly overcharged him. He almost busted my eardrum when he hung up.

I dialed the manager of the Pigalle, told him, "I'm Paul Worth, uncle of the Worth boy. Remember me, I was the one at the wedding party who had quite a toot on, did all the singing?"

"I remember you, Mr. Worth," the voice at the other end of the wire said, lying cautiously. "What can I do for you, sir?"

"Have a silly favor to ask. I have some pictures of the affair and I was just pasting them in our family album."

"Yes?"

"Well, in one picture there's a waiter in the background. In years to come I want to tell the children—and I hope they'll have a flock of little ones—exactly who was at the wedding. I have the names of each person printed under the photo. The waiter is tall, might say handsome, mouth like a girl, and shiny dark hair that..."

"Name is Cliff Parker, Mr. Worth."

"I'm very exact about these things. Spell that p-a-r-k-e-r?"

"Yes, sir."

"And you're sure that's the man, that he was waiting on us that night?"

"Yes sir, those lips belong to Cliff. And he's the only waiter we got with a full head of hair."

I thanked him and hung up. It wasn't airtight, but it was better than coming out and asking the manager—in case Cliff had told him what to say. Of course I was certain Cliff hadn't done it—if he had Louise would never have had Ed's picture around, or talked. If she hadn't told me, there wasn't a thing to connect her with Turner.

Still, the smart and safe thing to do was tell the police. They could put enough men on Cliff to tail every person he saw, know every time he breathed... could be some of Cliff's pals had done it. Maybe Turner was shaking down other pimps? After all, my *thinking* Cliff wasn't guilty didn't mean a thing.

But telling the cops would mean giving Louise a hard time and... The case was making less and less sense—now I was shielding a pimp!

I got to Mrs. Turner's house at exactly eight o'clock, but I waited around for ten minutes—didn't want her to think I was running around like her office boy—then went up.

She was dressed up again, a blue semi-evening gown that showed off her strong shoulders, the rise of her breast. The vermouth bottle was still on the table, but her breath said she'd been sipping stronger stuff. But she wasn't crocked.

"Good evening, Barney. You're late."

"That's right, Mrs. Turner."

I sat down on the hassock and glanced around the room. The coconut tree lamp wasn't much—a long ebony stem that made an uneven curve up to thin gold leaves, and the tiny bulbs arranged to give indirect lighting—if the whole mess gave off any light.

She took her seat on the couch, lit a cigarette, pushed the cigarette box toward me, gave me the half-closed-eyes look, as she asked, "Any luck today?"

"Glad you said luck—that's what we'll need in this case, all the luck we can stumble upon, the..."

"Find out anything?"

I nodded. "But I'm not any closer to the big answers. Talked to the Andersun family—nothing there to go on. But I did come across something... a little something."

She blew a good smoke ring which we both watched till it faded. As I lit a cigarette, she said, "Is this some sort of a game? What did you find out?"

"That maybe it is a game. Somebody has been holding out on me."

"Who?"

"You, Mrs. Turner."

Her cheeks turned a becoming pink, like a spreading drop of water color. "What am I supposed to say to that?"

"Anything you want," I said. "You came to me and you weren't too much concerned about your husband's being dead, but only if it was suicide. Then you've been giving me a series of small lies. Like you only drink wine now and then, only you stink of whiskey at the moment. That you were so very very happy with your husband, that you two were so happy in the hay. Then last night you casually mentioned that you and Mr. Turner had a little spat, in fact, you two were not doing so well in bed, but you had this pip of an idea that it was all because he got his kicks out of third-degreeing people. These were small lies, didn't detour me much, but I want to know why you've been stringing me. Hell, I work for you."

"Are you quite finished?" Her voice was pure ice and if her eyes were any sharper I would have been bleeding.

"I don't know. Am I, Mrs. Turner? You're paying me good money to find out the facts related to your husband's death. Yet, you've been giving me a bunko story from the start."

"If this is some kind of a riddle, I wish you'd come to the point. I said Ed and I were very happy when we married, that being on the force changed him some, but we were still happy."

I shrugged. "Okay, that's what you told me. I stumbled on something that will hurt, so if you want to skip it, go on playing..."

"What is it?"

"Mr. Turner has for many months been seeing a lady named Louise, a prostitute. The reason Mr. Turner was parked near the Grand Café on the night of the killings—he was jealous of one Cliff Parker, a pimp. This too seems to be a feud of several months' standing. Louise claims Mr. Turner was in her bed so often, he was something of a pest. End of report, Mrs. Turner."

She sat up, as though pulled by her head. Her eyes got very large and bright and she gasped, "I see, I see... Ed with a... a ..." Then the tears came, a flood of them. She bawled hysterically, her whole body shaking.

I waited for a long second—I can't stand seeing people cry. I went over and sat beside her, tried to dry her face with my torn handkerchief. She fell against me, sobbing on my shirt. I held her and liked the solid feel of her, the softness of her hair against my chin. "Easy, Mrs. Turner, easy. It's over and crying won't help. From what Louise says, Ed was a little... nuts about sex. If you didn't make a go of it, it wasn't your fault. Sorry this is a shock, but I had to tell you, know if ..."

She looked up at me, a face full of fat tears. "Barney, you think it wasn't my fault."

"'Fault' is probably the wrong word to use about something like this, but for whatever it's worth," I said, "I'm sure it wasn't your fault." In fact I was having a hard time holding my arms around her—in a casual manner. But I kept telling myself *that* would be the dumbest move I ever made.

She said through the tears, "Oh God, I was so happy when we were married. An end to the loneliness, the feeling of not being wanted. Marriage was so wonderful—at first—and then so awfully empty; and that hurt worse than being lonely."

"Perhaps you expected too much from marriage. It's a relationship, not a snake oil," I said, sounding like Dorothy Dix with whiskers.

"I only wanted a small share of happiness, but as time went on... you don't know what it was like, this always feeling guilty, that it must be my fault and going crazy wondering how and why. You've had a happy marriage, love..."

"Love is another magic word, a movie word."

"Didn't you love your wife?"

"We never tried to label it, that's why we got along. You've seen Lieutenant Swan, always bucking his way through life. Vi—my wife—had a lot of that too. Big career woman. She and Al, scrambling and pushing to 'get someplace'—more would-be magic words. They looked down their noses at me for being a schnook. Me, I believe in taking it easy; you only live to die, so make it an interesting ride. When Vi and I understood what the other was like, we didn't try changing each other; we got along fine. Maybe that's love—getting along."

"You never had any arguments?"

"Sure we did. Sometimes Vi would nag me and I suppose I wasn't any dilly to live with either. She'd call me lazy and I'd sneer at her stumbling over the fast buck. I even gave in and let Vi get me a job as a car dick with an insurance company. But the main thing was, we never tried to push each other around. When she called me a bum and I said she was a hustler, and when we could *both* laugh at that, we got married."

She stopped crying, was quiet. I began to feel a bit stupid, just sitting there, holding her on my lap as if she was Ruthie getting over a nightmare. "Mrs. Turner, why don't you forget all this? You were married and it didn't jell. That's a common sickness—90 per cent of marriages are two people with hot pants who suddenly find themselves married, and don't know how to get along. Why don't you go home to your folks, for a while?"

"Home?" She seemed to spit out the word and I could feel her body become heavy and tense. "I never had a home. My father is a carpenter, a good one, like his father had been. But he had to be a 'professional' man, didn't have enough money for med school, ended up as a pharmacist. Mama's older sister inherited the one drugstore in this small town when her husband was killed in the First World War. So we moved into her house.

Pop has been a clerk ever since and we've been 'guests.' Everything I did always brought a reminder from Mama, 'Now, Betsy, remember we're guests in Aunt Emma's house.' Only time I was ever spanked—and I've never forgotten it—was when Aunt Emma caught me digging in her rubber plants, told my mother I should be punished, and right in front of her, Mama spanked me."

"But that's over too. You're not a kid any longer."

"It *isn't* over. They still are 'guests' in Aunt Emma's house and Pop is still her underpaid clerk. My poor father could have made a good living as a carpenter, but he goes through life as a scrimping clerk. Whenever I needed a winter coat, Pop would do some carpentry on the side, make more in a few nights than he did all week in the drugstore."

"Well, maybe he was happier as a drug clerk than as a carpenter," I said, to say something.

"He was miserable. Nobody is happy in that house. Aunt Emma is one of those horrible women, gets a kick out of bossing us all. After a time nobody spoke to the other. Poppa, Emma, and Mom had a fight and for years everything was said to our cat. 'Pussy, tell Mama to kindly pass the butter.' 'Pussy dear, please tell Father to bring home some mineral oil tonight.' Or, 'Pussy, inform Emma the vitamin company insists upon payment of that old bill, and she'd best send them a check.' I couldn't wait to get away from them. Only... living alone, marriage to Ed, didn't turn out much better."

"Guess you can't go home. Got any friends?"

She tried to shake her head. "No. Not that I see now. And Ed didn't have time for friends; he had to be on the prowl twenty-four hours a day. Once I even took a course in art for a while and met a kid, boy of about nineteen. Sometimes we went around to the museums together. Ed knew about it. It was nothing. But when he saw us on the street, he got insanely jealous and beat the kid up. No, I haven't any friends."

Her face was near mine and as she talked her hair moved against my chin. I felt so damn sorry for her I almost kissed her, only I didn't want this to end up with my being paid off in kisses. I needed the thirty bucks per day. And at the same time I almost felt as if I was explaining things to Ruthie. I had a pretty clear picture of Betsy, or rather two of them. She was either a slick killer, which I didn't believe, but neither did I completely rule it out—or she was terribly naïve.

Everything went by rule with her: you had a neurotic home so you ran away and the first man you saw was Prince Charming and marriage *had* to be the solution to everything. And you faithfully copied the clothes in *Harper's Bazaar* and the furniture in *Home Beautiful* and you tried to take an interest in art, and if your husband's business had a sordid side to it, you simply forgot about that. And when things went wrong, your husband started two-timing you, why it was SOP to try to hit the bottle, be the sophisticated lady lush, the silent drinker. And of course it was also SOP to try your charms on the first guy that came along—me.

Under her smart clothes and beneath the skillful make-up Betsy was just a big Ruthie. Well, maybe not quite, but... She was sure the wrong type for a brash punk like Ed Turner to marry, or had he been a trifle backward under his toughness? I told Betsy, "You're young, attractive. In time you'll find..."

"Do you really consider me attractive, Barney?" The dull tone vanished from her voice.

"Yes, Mrs. Turner."

"Can't you call me Betsy?"

"Look, Mrs. Turner, most of the time you treat me like a servant or a..."

"I never meant to. It's just my way. I told you I can't make friends easily and of course since Ed's death... I've been so upset, unsure of myself."

"For now let's keep it Mrs. Turner. Perhaps when the case is over, when I'm not working for you, we'll be friends."

"What do you mean by friends? That you'll make love to me?" Her body stiffened again and there was a sort of horror in her voice that got me sore.

"Maybe. I might ask you to go to bed with me—sure."

She actually leaped out of my arms and off my lap; stood in front of me and shouted, "Now that I'm a widow I'm supposed to be a pushover!"

"You're a healthy-looking and pretty young woman, Mrs. Turner, and I'd be lying if I said you didn't attract me," I said patiently, picking my words carefully so I wouldn't talk myself out of the job.

"If you think just because you come here every night that...!"

"I don't think anything. When the case is over, if we want to be friends, then we'll both see how it shapes up—then."

"I thought you were warm and understanding.... You're just a man."

"I hope so," I said like a jerk, not sure what she was saying.

There was a moment of awkward silence, then she asked, "Want a drink?"

"No." She was back to her play-acting once more.

"You have the manners of a boor, Mr. Harris." She sat on the other end of the couch and reached down, came up with a pint of Canadian whiskey. She poured herself a small shot, tried to take the warm stuff down without coughing. Her eyes watered, but she lit a cigarette, like a hammy actress, asked in a cold new voice, "You're certain Ed was seeing this dirty whore?"

"I'm not certain she's dirty. She's merely selling what she can."

"I suppose you got this information as one of her customers!"

"I could easily be one of her customers, Mrs. Turner. You probably can't believe it, but Louise has a great deal of charm. But don't let it worry you, I wouldn't put *that* on the expense account."

She got to her feet. "I've had about enough of you, Mr. Harris."

"Okay. I'll send you the balance of your retainer on Monday."

"No, I didn't mean that. I want you to continue on the case. Only don't ever bring me any such gossip... this miserable woman with her false stories, her ravings about my..."

"It isn't exactly gossip. She had Mr. Turner's picture in her room—the same photo you have over there on the wall. She also told me about that coconut-tree lamp. Seems Mr. Turner took her money one day to buy the lamp for you—in a fit of remorse, I imagine."

"Did you find out if she killed Ed, or didn't you have time for that?"

"I don't think she killed Ed. Look, I only told you all this because if you still think Ed was a suicide, then I have to know exactly how things were between you two. There's not even a slight motive that we—the police—can find for either of these murders, but there has to be a motive for suicide."

"I've told you the truth—except that Ed and I didn't hit it off. It wasn't that we were unhappy, we just weren't happy. Can you understand that?"

"Maybe, after I think about it." I got up and walked toward the door. "Shall I report tomorrow night? It's Saturday."

"You work union hours?" she asked harshly. "Another thing, I demand some respect—comb your hair when you come to see me."

"Don't think I will, Mrs. Turner. That's my hair, and I don't consider combing or not combing my hair having anything to do with respect."

Her face turned pink with anger and as I opened the door I said, "Sorry I upset you, Mrs. Turner. Only did it as part of my job." I don't know why I had to say that, almost made me gag.

"Get out."

Out in the hall, as I was waiting for the automatic elevator and feeling lousy, I heard a small crash in her apartment. It hadn't been much of a lamp anyway.

Sam Lund was a hustler long before he enlisted. Orphaned when he was six, Sam was raised by an aunt and uncle who had a small hardware store in Boston. They were childless and adored Sam, but when he was thirteen his aunt had a change-of-life baby and after that Sam was merely somebody around the house.

He grew up tall and strong, an all-around athlete with the grace of a dancer. When he was sixteen he hitched a ride to New York City and landed a job as a chorus boy in a Broadway musical that staggered along for five weeks. After that Sam worked at whatever odd jobs would pay for dancing and dramatic lessons and in his off hours made the rounds of casting agents, lived in Times Square drugstores.

By the time he was nineteen he had danced in several shows, had bit parts in off-Broadway little theaters, and was trying to break into radio. Sam was crazy about the "theater," but it kept him broke. He was lucky to work two or three weeks a year as an actor or chorus boy and his other odd jobs never lasted, for as soon as he heard a show was casting, Sam would drop his bus-boy or stock-clerk job, to try his luck.

One afternoon he was in a dingy rehearsal studio on West Forty-sixth Street reading for a play due to open in the fall—if seventy-five thousand dollars could be raised. The producer was a middle-aged dapper ex-actor whose bleached-blonde wife took an interest in Sam. A day later she offered to set him up in a small Village apartment. Being supported by women wasn't anything new to Sam, but the lady was in her fifties, strapped her flabby body in a strait-jacket corset so she could wear a twelve dress, liked flashy jewels, and when she got drunk she thought it was tremendously funny to suddenly push her upper plate half out of her mouth and yell, "What's cooking, doc?"

Although Sam turned her down he let her buy him supper several times a week. She'd been around the theater all her life and she told Sam to really get among the people, study and understand them, instead of hanging around drugstores... if he was serious about becoming an actor.

He took a summer job as a barker for a sightseeing bus and a week later nearly died from scarlet fever. The fever left him completely bald. At first his bald dome was a great joke, but he soon found bald-headed young men were not considered for juvenile or lead roles, and that a decent toupee cost hundreds of dollars. He decided to take the apartment in the Village—till the play opened.

Sam admits the elderly blonde did a great deal for him. He told a reporter:

> *She really wasn't a bad sort, when sober. She bought me a remarkable toupee, a really terrific piece of hair, she had a custom tailor outfit me, sent me to a fine dramatic coach. But she would bust into the apartment in the middle of the night, drunk as a goose, then prance around in the nude under the illusion she was still a gay young thing.*

Lund couldn't take this, but there was another reading of the play in a ritzy Park Avenue apartment and he was assured of a feature role. By

October the show was still thirty-two thousand dollars short and the opening postponed till January. Sam was angry. While he had clothes, hair, and a charge at the corner grocer, he had no money. In November the producer signed to make a quickie picture in Hollywood and the play was postponed again, but Sam didn't mind, for the blonde went to the Coast with her husband and Sam had some peace and sleep. But she sent him a plane ticket, suggested he try the movies, and before Christmas Sam was rooming in a run-down house in Laurel Canyon. There was a vivacious nineteen-year-old red-headed singer also rooming there and Sam began sharing her room.

Aside from working in two mob scenes, nothing happened in Hollywood and Sam didn't care much for the place. He was glad to follow the producer and his wife back to New York in February, where he lucked up on a steady part in a daily radio soap opera. The play seemed almost certain to start rehearsals any day and things were breaking for Sam—especially when the redhead came East for night-club work.

But there was trouble finding a theater and in April the main backer switched his money to another play; the producer lost his option and announced the whole deal was off. The redhead was going to a Baltimore night spot and asked Sam to come along. The radio soap opera having folded weeks before, he was flat broke. When she was drunk the old blonde was careless with her jewelry, would often phone Sam the next day and ask him to look for a ring or pin she'd left in his place. So Sam hocked her earrings for two hundred and sixty dollars and went to Baltimore, where two detectives picked him up the following day.

Sam wasn't too alarmed. He begged the wife not to press charges, then threatened her with publicity about their affair. The lady merely stuck her false teeth out at him, said her analyst had told her that sort of publicity bolstered her ego. There was a line about the robbery in one of the columns, and Sam's picture made the tenth page of a tabloid when a judge gave Sam two to five years.

In the beginning prison drove Sam crazy, but for the first time in his life he read a lot, studied the men around him, and knew he'd really be an actor when he was released. Sam was finishing his twenty-second month in prison when Pearl Harbor was bombed. Several months later, when he came up for parole, he was told he would be set free if he enlisted.

After prison life the army was a snap for Lund, although the army didn't know exactly what to do with an actor. He was sent to a motion unit at Wright Field which was soon disbanded. Then Lund was assigned to special services and spent several months taking tickets at a Topeka air base theater. From there he was sent to England where he did guard duty, permanent K.P., and drove a truck. Lund spent some time with a touring

G.I. show, asked to be made an aerial gunner and was turned down for some unknown reason.

Toward the end of the war Sam was working behind a PX counter at a bomber base in France. It was easy to smuggle out a few cartons of cigarettes now and then and he began doing some minor black-marketing. However, when the war in Europe was over and the bomber outfits were being rushed back to the States, on their way to the Pacific, the bookkeeping was snafued in the general confusion and Lund sold cigarette cartons by the case. At his trial Lund admitted once selling an entire truckload of supplies, working with the driver and another soldier. Lund was fast becoming an "operator."

There wasn't anything waiting for him in the States, so Sam signed up for the army of occupation, went to Germany. Here he put on camp shows and engaged in various "deals."

> The new soldiers arriving in Germany were mostly kids, [Lund stated], all of them eighteen or nineteen years old. They thought it was a big deal to sleep with a Fräulein for a pack of butts. Me, I was now an "old army man." I didn't bother much with those kids. I put on a lot of corny shows—any blue line or raw joke had them in the aisles with laughter. I had plenty of time to look around. There were plenty of things worth looking into in Germany then, the black market was amazing, wide open, everybody was hustling. It was sensational.

He worked his angles carefully and when he suspected things were getting too warm, Staff Sergeant Sam Lund took his discharge in 1950 and headed for Paris. He had a new Dodge car, five thousand dollars in cash, and some jewelry said to be worth fifteen thousand dollars and which he was only able to sell for nineteen hundred dollars. Sam also had three cans of film he had stumbled upon in a bombed film office in Bavaria. He had vague plans about using the reels as the core of a full-length adventure picture about an OSS man parachuted into Germany during the war—the main role to be played by Sam Lund, of course. He felt this would not only make money but establish him as an international actor.

During his first week in Paris Sam stopped at the George V Hotel, went to Maxim's, the Lido, and Monseigneur nightly—only to find at the end of the week that he had spent eight hundred dollars. He quietly moved to a small hotel in the Pigalle section, where he met Gabby.

Gabby was twenty-two, small and trim, with a cute face and a jutting bosom. She was a movie actress, but her only roles were those of an artist's model, a native girl, or any brief part featuring nude breasts. She thought

Sam the greatest man in the world: he was handsome and tall, considerate of her, and he had money and an American car. Sam liked her because she worshiped him and because she was a part of the French movie crowd. Only, as he soon found out, acting jobs were few and the unions strong, and it was impossible for him to get a work card—a role—although as a result of living with Gabby he soon spoke French like a native.

One evening, after he had been in Paris four months, Gabby introduced to him another American, a quiet-spoken fellow named Martin Pearson, and his horse-faced girl, Thérèse. Sam was suspicious of Martin, couldn't see the percentage in letting anybody else in on the picture deal. But Martin was helpful. When Sam told him, "My ninety-day tourist stay is running out and I'm having trouble getting a carte d'identité. *How have you worked it all these years?"*

Martin told him, "Go to a school, under the G.I. Bill, then you'll get a student identity card. Be careful with this identity-card business. You may think the French police are slow, but they're good and they're sharp."

Lund became a student and in time became rather friendly with Pearson, although he still wouldn't let him in on his picture idea. Sam became a student in more ways than one—he learned there are angle men in every country and it's difficult for a foreigner to outsmart the native talent.

He lost five hundred dollars as the "manager" of a French boxer. After Sam had purchased a complete gym outfit for the pug, fed and housed him while the fighter got back into shape, he learned that a manager had to be a member of the French Federation of Boxers—which didn't admit foreigners. Then he paid six hundred and fifty American dollars under the table for the rent of a large house on the outskirts of Paris, only to find when he tried to move in that he hadn't paid the money to the owner; no one seemed to know exactly who Sam had dealt with.

He was swindled out of a thousand dollars in a black-market money deal—they slipped him counterfeit francs, and another American touted him out of several hundred dollars at the race track. But Paris was Paris and Sam was enjoying himself. In the summer of '52 he and Gabby, with Martin and Thérèse, drove down to Nice for an August vacation.

The main thing Sam disliked about Martin was the man's tightness with a franc—Pearson always let somebody else pick up the tab. In Nice when Sam wanted to play big shot and stop at the swank Negresco Hotel, Martin and Thérèse found a cheap pension in the center of town. At the casino Sam dropped a hundred and fifty dollars while Martin never gambled a franc.

One day as they were sunning themselves on the beach, the girls wanted ice cream. Martin didn't reach for his wallet. Sam gave Gabby a five hundred franc note and when the girls left, he asked, "The francs glued to your mitt, Marty? You never even offer to share the gas for my car."

"How much of your original bundle have you left, Sam?"

"What the hell business is that of yours?"

"Stop acting, Sam, how much?"

"About three grand. I hear you have something in your mattress, too."

"I have over six thousand," Martin said softly. "Sam, before you throw away the rest of your money, let's make that picture. We've already wasted two years. I'm off the G.I. Bill, need a source of income if I want to get my identity card, stay here. Thérèse and I have formed a picture company—in her name. I can trust her."

"And where do I come in?"

"You invest your three thousand and those reels of Nazi film. I'll put up six grand. I figure we can shoot most of the picture outdoors, around here, within the next two months. I've talked to a Paris writer who is willing to do the story and screenplay for a percentage. I'll help with the camera, Thérèse will cut and edit, you and Gabby will be the main actors. We won't have to hire too many people."

"About got everything figured, haven't you?"

"I think I have. Sam, I know you can sell the reels to one of the picture companies for about a thousand dollars, although Hitler is kind of old hat now. But you'll spend that and in a few years from now where will you be? Either back in the States grubbing for a job, or just another broke American in Paris. If you're serious about living here, about being an actor, let's get started."

"I'll think about it."

"Think all you want, Sam. Only remember the war is over—and so is the gravy train."

The next morning they all sat down in Sam's room and formed a partnership—in Thérèse's name with Gabby as treasurer, and Sam and Martin owning one-tenth of the company, as allowed by French law. They called in a lawyer to draw up the papers and Sam sent for champagne, but Martin said vin ordinaire *would do. Sam got a little high on wine and decided it was time to try his luck at the casino. Martin told him to save his money.*

"Let's get one thing straight. I don't like being ordered around," Sam said. "It's my money."

"No, it's the firm's money now," Martin said softly, and when Sam laughed and headed for the door, Pearson belted him in the stomach, stood over him and said, "I'm not playing rough, or telling you what to do, but it's time you wised up, Sam. Cut the overgrown-boy act."

At the trial Sam said he was afraid of Pearson. The transcript reads:

Q: You claim you didn't want to go through with the killing? Why did you? You're bigger than Pearson, knew he wouldn't shoot you?

Lund: I was afraid of Martin. I'm not trying to shift the blame on him. We're both in this. But I was afraid of him. Don't know exactly why, I'm not a coward, but there was something about the cold way he did things that scared me.

Q: You mean you were physically afraid of Pearson?

Lund: Yes sir, that's what I mean.

Within a day the four of them moved to a small hotel in Juan-les-Pins, between Nice and Cannes, and went to work. They had stationery printed with the company's name, and Thérèse started writing and calling directors, while Martin wired the Paris writer to go ahead. When they drove back to Paris in September, they had a shooting script of a story they all liked, but the minimum cost of the picture would be fifteen thousand dollars and they felt they should have at least another five thousand dollars on hand to cover extra expenses. They were eleven thousand dollars short and didn't know a soul in the world with that kind of money.

One evening Sam brought a beefy American with a plump baby face to Thérèse's flat, explained, "This is Eddie. He was a warrant officer in Italy, ran a PX there. He was in Germany for a while, too. Eddie is pulling a deal that can be the answer to our problem."

Eddie's plan was simple. He was driving his car into Germany with three thousand dollars' worth of penicillin and other drugs. He had the necessary contacts and expected to return with ten thousand dollars within a week. He'd made such a trip months before, shortly after he was discharged.

Sam told them, "Eddie is willing to cut us in—our nine grand will return about thirty thousand dollars. He takes ten grand for the risk; we get the rest. It's a cinch. He knows where to buy the stuff here, and the people big enough to swing a deal like this in Germany. We can't lose. Still be able to start the picture before winter hits the Riviera."

Martin chiseled Eddie's cut down to seven thousand dollars, then he and Sam and the girls talked it over through the night. The main factor was: could Eddie be trusted? In the morning Thérèse checked, found Eddie was interested in opening a Café with his French girl friend and her father— Evidently Eddie expected to settle down in Paris.

With the trunk of his Austin packed with two spare tires, which in turn were stuffed with drugs, they saw Eddie off on a Wednesday morning. He was to return by Monday at the latest. They spent a nervous, impatient week end and on Monday Eddie didn't show up. His girl was hysterical, said she had a feeling something was wrong. On Tuesday Sam phoned an army buddy stationed near the town Eddie had headed for. Eddie was in jail. He had overlooked one minor detail. He was still using old army plates on his car, forgot they were outdated. He had been stopped by German police one hundred and sixty miles inside the border.

Eddie returned ten days later—all charges against him had been dropped, but the German police had taken the drugs, probably to sell themselves. Even Martin was convinced Eddie hadn't double-crossed them.

Martin, Sam, and the girls got drunk that night in Thérèse's flat. She and Gabby passed out on the first bottle of cognac. Although he rarely drank, Martin managed to keep up with Sam. Martin said, to no one in particular, "Damn the way things work out. If I wasn't married, I could marry Thérèse and stay here, or take her back to the States. Now—nothing. No Thérèse, no Paris, no future."

"We can always sell our passports, five grand each, keep us eating here for another few years," Sam said, listening to himself, watching a mirror and thinking Orson Wells couldn't have said the line better. Sam always acted when he was drunk, and now he swayed in the center of the room and did a part he'd had in a little theater production years ago.

"You and your jerky hustling ideas," Martin mumbled, staring at Sam. Then Pearson staggered across the room to the couch on which Thérèse was sleeping. He said thickly, "You know... what you just said... rings lot of bells in my head. Gives me an idea, an out for us. Yeah. Listen. Sam, you goddamn ham, will you stop talking and listen? I have it... all so simple... and clear. Your car."

"What's the big idea, genius? And what about my car?" Sam added quickly.

"It's so simple," Martin said, as he tried to sit on the couch, rolled off to the floor, and passed out.

CHAPTER FOUR

Saturday started off badly.

I spent a restless night and when it seemed I was just about to knock off some real sleep, Ruthie woke up crying. It was a little after seven and she had wet her bed—first time in months—and by the time I'd convinced her it wasn't any great tragedy, it was half-past seven and I'd lost any desire for sleep. I just felt lousy.

I worked out with weights before breakfast, while Ruthie listened to radio music and watched. I took it easy, starting out with seventy-five pounds, and after doing a lot of curls and squats, I ended up pressing one hundred and fifty pounds, did some stomach work, and Ruthie was waiting for me to be flat on my back. She scrambled all over me and we "wrestled" and then took a shower together, which always gave her a big kick.

As I toweled myself I felt pretty sad. Even when I was in serious training I never had much hard muscular definition, like the musclemen you see posing for pictures. Now that I had cut down on my workouts, I was getting to look more and more like a tub of lard.

There wasn't much in the house for breakfast, so after toast and orange juice, we went down to the super market, and the place was jammed. I stocked up on eggs and bacon, bananas, bread and milk, along with some canned staples, then we got in line.

Waiting in line got me on edge. It seemed as if all I'd been doing the last few days was waiting, wasting time, or going around in circles. When we finally reached the cashier, he overcharged me two cents on an item. Although checking up on super-market cashiers is one of my hobbies, I didn't want to hold up the long line. Unfortunately the item happened to be Ruthie's cereal, and as the guy was putting our stuff in a bag, she said loudly, "Daddy, he charged you twenty-one cents for Shredded Wheat and it's only nineteen cents!"

"It's okay, forget it."

"But you always say these cashiers can't add—on purpose," she said in her shrill voice that cut through all the other noises of the store.

There were plenty of snickers behind me and the cashier gave me a pained look, started taking the things out of the bag. Somebody behind me in the line said, "Aw, for Christsakes, I'll give you the lousy two pennies!"

"Forget it," I told the clerk, putting a ten-dollar bill on the counter. He said, "Hold your money. If I made an error, I must correct it. Customer is always right—it says."

It took him about five minutes to check the items against the register receipt, and finally he found the error, then spent another few minutes making out a slip to put in the register with my money, and I finally walked out without daring to look at the impatient line behind me.

For a second I nearly bawled Ruthie out, before I told myself it wasn't her fault. She was highly satisfied with things. When we got back to the apartment and finished breakfast, she asked what we were going to do now, and I said we might as well do the laundry. I got her dresses and underwear, together with my things, and the towels. We had one piece of luck—one of the two machines in the basement was empty. While we were waiting for the clothes to wash, a couple of housewives came down and made the usual comments about how nice Ruthie looked, etc. All in this patronizing tone of, "You poor, poor bastard, so brave to raise a child all alone," which always got my water on.

We took the clothes up to the roof and hung them up. Ruthie suggested we go to Coney Island, but I wasn't up to that, and Betsy Turner was paying me thirty dollars to do some work during the day. We went down and changed the bed linen, swept and dusted, cleaned up the apartment, and by then the clothes were dry.

I usually spent the week end with Ruthie, so I took her to the office. There were two skip-tracing jobs in the mail and a request from an insurance company that I go out to Hempstead to identify the remains of a car wrapped around a lamppost. The wreck was now in a garage, so that could wait a few days. I sent out my usual first form letter to the guy who had moved with his unpaid TV set, and the family that took a deep freeze with them. It was Ruthie's day to investigate O'Hara's desk, and I yelled at her a couple of times, which didn't put either of us in a good mood. There was a phone message from the garage, reminding me to finish the wiring job on the foreign heap. I put that in my pocket and locked up.

There were too many cars on the roads for a ride, so we came back to the flat for lunch. The phone rang. My cousin Jake said he was working and Grace thought it would be an idea if he picked up Ruthie, took her back with him. "She can play with the boys, spend the night, and you'll be here on Sunday."

Ruthie was against the idea—violently against it. "I want to be with you, Daddy. I didn't see you much this week."

"But I told you I have to work."

"On Saturday?"

I nodded. "Tell you what, you go with Uncle Jake and I'll pick you up after supper, take you home. Then we'll both drive out tomorrow."

"Well... all right, but you're trying to get rid of me."

"Stop that kind of talk. You know I'm on a big case, have to work."

Over the phone, Jake shouted, "Give it to her, Dick Tracy. I'll be off in an hour. Want me to pick her up, or will you be at the P.O.?"

"We'll be outside the post office."

I made French toast with chocolate syrup for lunch and Ruthie felt better. Jake was sitting in his old Dodge when we drove up. As Ruthie got into the front seat beside him and said, "Don't forget to come for me after supper," Jake asked, "How come you're so busy-busy these days?"

"I'm on a m-u-r-d-e-r case."

"Well now," Jake said, impressed. "Who is it?"

"Gee, Daddy, you never told me you were working on a killing," Ruthie said, as I silently cursed TV and comic books.

"Nobody important," I said quickly as Jake winked and stepped on the starter, asked, "What time will you be over?"

"Eight o'clock," Ruthie said, and I nodded. "And I want to know all about the murder...."

As they drove off and I climbed back into my car, I remembered I was supposed to be at the Turner apartment at eight. I would have to phone Jake later and tell Ruthie to stay over, and she'd raise hell.

I sat in the car, wondering what to do, where to begin the day's "work." I needed to do a lot of straight thinking and I can think best when I'm working with my hands. Reaching for a cigarette, I came up with the message from the garage.

Joe, the garage manager, was glad and surprised to see me. I got into my coveralls, went to work on this low-slung job. I worked steadily for the rest of the afternoon and of course I knew what was wrong with me—I'd acted like a goon last night, slipping the dope on her husband like I was slugging Betsy. All things considered, she'd taken it pretty well, but I'd been too rough on her.

The truth was, I was giving her an all-around rooking. I couldn't solve the murders, was in way over my head. As Al Swan had said, there wasn't much any private agency could do here, but that wasn't any excuse for taking her dough.

Granted I wasn't much of a detective, but what little work I was doing was sloppy as hell. But what else could I do? It would take me months to check all the Browns in New York City, and that was probably a blind alley.

I could tail Cliff Parker, but I was convinced he and Louise were in the clear. That was sloppy—my being convinced didn't mean a thing. The Andersun family—all blanks. Betsy—? I didn't think she did it, but I couldn't rule her out. A man or woman feeling she was unsatisfactory in bed could snap her cap enough to murder. And hiring me could be a corny cover-up. Should check what the police had on her.

The police—I was playing the game wrong with them, holding out about Cliff. All told I was doing a good job of snafuing the works. It would be more honest to take Betsy's money by snatching her pocketbook.

I kept going over the possible angles, wishing I could come up with a motive—any motive. All I came up with was a headache. By four I'd finished and rechecked the car, drove it around the garage, and picked up twenty-five dollars. Joe tried it himself, and he was almost as big as I was and laughed as he squeezed into the small front seat. As I was washing up, I noticed him making out the bill. All told I'd put in nine hours and he wrote down, "Labor—two days." I didn't ask what he was charging the car owner.

He gave me the usual, "Barney, any time you want a steady job..."

"Yeah and thanks. Call me again, Joe, whenever you have something special."

I stood outside the garage for a moment, still restless, and finally I drove down to the police station, asked for Lieutenant Franzino, almost hoping he'd be out. I had to wait a few minutes, then I went into his office, which was as dingy as Al's.

Franzino was a surprise... a small man, shabbily dressed, with his suit wrinkled and a button missing. He had a thin face with a banana nose that had been busted a long time ago. An old hat was pushed back on his head, covering most of the iron-gray hair, and he looked serious, humorless, and very capable.

His voice was low and polite as he lit a fancy-looking pipe, sent out a cloud of aromatic smoke, asked, "What's on your mind, Mr. Harris?"

"Any news?"

"Not a thing. Put a dozen men on the Brown angle—no dice, so far. Running down one or two other things, but to date not a sniff of anything promising."

We were silent for a moment, and of course he didn't bother to ask if I'd found anything. "About Turner's wife, what's her alibi?"

"Says she was home alone. The super of the house was installing a lobby light between ten and midnight—he didn't see her leave. Got anything on her?"

"No."

There was another dull silence, then he asked in a mild voice, "What made you think your client might have done it?"

"Told you, nothing. Merely checking on all alibis."

He smiled and his teeth were a tobacco yellow. "You can be sure we've worked over every alibi. How's it feel to be in on a murder case? Swan told me this is your first criminal case."

His voice reminded me of the patronizing housewives at the washing machine. I lit a cigarette, let him have it gently. "By the bye, I found out what Turner was doing on the block, the night he was killed."

Franzino straightened up, like I'd stuck a pin in him.

"He was playing around with a woman named Louise who lives in the basement of 515. She's selling it and seems Turner was competing with her pimp, guy named Cliff Parker, a waiter. Ed Turner was a little sex-screwy and was waiting in his car, playing the jealous lover—or jealous pimp. Parker has a good alibi that checks, working a wedding at the Pigalle that night. Louise says she had a girl friend with her at the time of the bang-bang stuff."

"When did you find this out?" The voice was like a whip now.

"Yesterday. I was checking on Franklin Andersun—he was one of her customers—and she had Turner's picture in her room. Talked freely about..."

"Andersun too! Damn!" Franzino got to his feet and it was like pulling him out of a hole—he was over six feet tall, but all legs. "Why the hell didn't you tell me this yesterday?" he shouted as he strode to the door, yelled at the desk sergeant to bring in Louise and Cliff.

I reached over and grabbed his arm. "Now wait up...."

"Get your goddamn hands off me!" he actually growled, his eyes narrowing.

I let go of him and he went back to his desk, sat down and somehow got his long legs under the desk. He said calmly, "One thing I can't stand, anybody holding me. What's the idea keeping important info to yourself?"

"Maybe because I knew you'd act just as you did. Sure, they're a whore and a pimp, but they're still people, and you can't ride roughshod over..."

"Harris, this is a hell of a case. Everything ends up against a blank wall. Two people have been murdered, one of them a cop. In these tough cases, these impossible deals, one small break usually knocks everything wide open. We have the first and only link between Andersun and Detective Turner, and you sit there like a goddamn stuffed dressmaker's dummy, handing me some crap about a whore and a pimp! What's with you, sentimental over mudkickers? And what the hell do you think I'm going to do to 'em... cook 'em and serve 'em with apples in their mouths?"

"I think you'll beat the slop out of Cliff, make life miserable for the girl. I don't make any pretense of being a good detective, but I know this—if either of them had been guilty, or implicated in any way, they wouldn't have talked, or had Turner's photo around. I don't want you to push them about—I sort of promised her they wouldn't be in a jam for talking, and that Cliff wouldn't be made the fall guy for..."

"*You* made them a promise!" Franzino cut in, and for a thin guy he sure got a lot of power into his voice. "Who the hell are you to make promises? What makes you think we'd frame this pimp? Harris, what the hell do you know about the Police Department?"

"Not much, but everybody knows..."

"Everybody—everybody isn't a cop! Harris, that badge you carry is one degree above the kind they give out with box tops to kids." He yanked open his drawer, came out with a blue cardboard box which held a gold medal about the size of a half dollar. "I've been a cop all my life, even before I came to New York City. It's my profession and I'm pretty good at it, and proud of it. This medal was given to me by the Lieutenants Association for my general skill as a policeman. No matter what the hell you think or read, I don't go about beating people with rubber hoses, or busting their heads with a blackjack. We'll bring in this Louise and Cliff, question them. Maybe they won't like it, but I don't care about that. If they give me straight answers, and we don't have to hold them as witnesses, they can go. As for her hustling, that has to stop—in my precinct. Let her set up shop someplace else."

I shrugged. "That's a fair shake. I'll hold you to it."

He gave me an evil grin. "That's swell of you, Harris. And what else can you do about it?"

"Not much I can do," I said carefully. "Except this case has been good headline bait. When it breaks, everybody concerned will be interviewed. If Louise and the pimp are innocent, as I believe, and you give them a hard time... well, papers are always interested in police brutality—when they can tie in a sex angle."

"Son of a bitch—and you call yourself a detective!"

"Mainly I call myself a human being. I didn't have to tell you about Louise nor did she have to spill to me. Well, she did, and co-operation is a two-way affair."

He studied me for a moment and I could almost feel his eyes on my face. "Won't be any trouble for me to revoke your license."

"Don't threaten me. If you're so good at your job, then you don't have to resort to threats. Just be a cop—don't be a judge and jury too."

"That's all I ever try to be—a cop. An underpaid and overworked cop." He did that jack-in-the-box stunt again as he stood up. Walking to the door he said, "Wait here, I'm going to take a leak."

I picked up the medal—it was real gold. I was thoroughly steamed—but mostly at myself. I was doing things cockeyed and here I was sore at Franzino for playing it right. Only I wished he hadn't sent out the order to pick up Louise and Cliff. All they had to do was try to take a powder now and they'd be practically convicted.

Franzino returned and lit his pipe again as he sat down. "Sorry I blew up," he said quietly. "You're right. Under the law everybody is equal, even a pimp who operates on the wrong side of the law. Look, Harris, only a fool tries to give people a hard time. Sure, I'll admit I'm rushed and under pressure and there's a million laws we can't enforce and these petty lawbreakers in time make for the big crimes. Guy gets away with spitting on the sidewalk, he begins to feel a little above the law. We're living in a goddamn jungle and as long as it stays a jungle..."

"You have to use a whip?" I asked.

"I don't know. Mr. Harris, this morning a wino and his girl were in the grass on the Drive, juiced up. For no reason he suddenly stabbed her. She's in the hospital now. Two people saw him do it. Seems simple—a man has done an act of violence, he'll be punished, and the law is being upheld. But when they brought this drunken bastard in here, he suddenly says he didn't do it, starts screaming for a lawyer. Should I have argued with him politely for hours that I can't spare? Or do you blame me for belting him in the guts and telling him to shut up?"

"Lieutenant Franzino, you just said little crimes are the start of bigger ones. Same goes for a 'little' violence—like being a 'little' pregnant—ain't no such thing."

"Guess there's a lot to be said on both sides. If we had more men and the jungle didn't make winos, well... hell with all this. Swan tells me you're a crackerjack mechanic. Interested in motors and cars myself. Got a shack out on Long Island and an old Bugatti racer I picked up for a few hundred."

"Does she run?"

"You bet. Sometimes I take her out late at night—so not to attract attention. Clip off sixty or seventy miles an hour. You been out to the auto museum near Southampton?"

We sat around and bulled about cars for a while and it got to be five o'clock and we were arguing about the advantages of front-wheel drive when his phone rang, and he grunted into the receiver, "I'll be right out."

He stood up. "Excuse me, Harris, I'm wanted at the desk. Be back soon." He went out and I wondered if they had picked up Louise so soon. The door opened and Al Swan walked in, dressed all in blue. Dark blue serge suit, gray-blue shirt, deep blue tie, and a baby-blue fedora. I didn't dare look at his socks. He said, "Hello, brother-in-law."

"Hello, Al. When did they send for you?"

"Happened to drop in and Franzino just told me you've come up with something big. You astonish me, Barney. Could be you're a detective after all."

"Save that bull for the cold weather."

Al brushed off a corner of the desk with a blotter, then carefully sat down and looked at his nails, as if not sure they were all there. Then he said, "Barney, I put you onto this case because I knew it was easy dough. We got the police force of New York, Elmira, and Syracuse working on this, and all by your lonesome you've turned up the best lead we've had so far. Now maybe you're sleeping with this whore and..."

"Stop it, Al. All I'm asking is that she and this Cliff get a fair shake."

"Jesus—hell! A cop has been killed!" Al rasped.

"So what? He had a badge, not a halo. And this particular cop was part pimp. Also, there's a very ordinary young fellow named Andersun was killed, too. I want to find the killer as much as you do, only it won't be solved by the brass quieting the papers by playing tag with two innocent lives, making them 'it.'"

He shook his head. "We don't frame people, not even a whore and a pimp."

"Fine, then there's no argument. No reason to send for you."

He sighed. "Don't get you, Barney. If this turns out to be the break in the case, the publicity will make you a big-time agency. Instead of helping us, you start slopping over a pimp, talk like a cop fighter that..."

"Al, don't sell me, or put words in my mouth. You know I'm not a cop hater, and as for this pimp, I haven't any use for him, but that doesn't make him a murderer. Your side is raising the fuss, not me."

"You don't understand," Al said, trying to smooth his sandpaper voice. "The big boys downtown hear of your attitude, they can put you out of business. Barney, this can make or break you. Why, withholding evidence is damn serious, but you seem to think..."

"I'm not withholding a thing—came here under my own power," I said, and looking at Al trying to sell me this bum bill of goods, I thought of what Betsy Turner had said and how right she was—after a while the hunter and the hunted become one. "Al, these people have volunteered information—don't punish them for it."

"Don't worry, Franzino is a good man."

"I know, he's got a medal." I pointed to the box.

Al picked up the medal, said, "Never saw one of these before—they don't come easy. What's this stuff about Turner being a pimp?"

I told him and he put the medal down and shook his head. "And the way his wife is stacked. Hard to figure these young guys today. Take Turner, breaking his back to get to be a plain-clothes man. Big deal—why, a cop's best protection is his uniform. Not one in a thousand will shoot a cop, but by the time a dick gets his badge out—he'd better get his gun out first and... Hell with talking about Turner. I have to be moving. Say hello to Ruthie. She need anything?"

"Not unless you want to give her your new Caddy."

Al laughed too long. "Barney, you're not only getting good, but funny, too. Just remember, we're all on the same team. Franzino is a good cop. Take my word for it. When you coming out to the house?"

"One of these days. Visiting my cousin Jake tomorrow. Give my regards to everybody at home."

"Sure thing, strong man." Al slapped me on the shoulder on his way out.

Like in a one-set play, Franzino came in soon as Al left. He sat down at his desk, propped the chair against the wall. He didn't say anything, and after a moment I told him, "I have an uncle out in Philly. Want to send for him too?"

He smiled. "Not treating you like a kid, Mr. Harris. Called Swan because... I'm not used to arguing with people, especially people I don't have to argue with. Your opinion isn't worth a snowball in hell around here, but at the same time, no point in fighting you. Thought maybe Swan could tell you that better than I."

I glanced at my watch, stood up. It was six o'clock. A cop stuck his head in the doorway. "Got 'em, Lieutenant."

"Bring 'em in here—before you take 'em upstairs."

Three cops walked Louise and Cliff in. Her face was red and puffed—from crying—and she looked older than I'd thought. The lapel of Cliff's fancy sport jacket was torn and his glossy hair mussed. When she saw me, Louise sent me a look of hatred and contempt that turned my stomach. I was about to tell her she'd be okay, when one of the cops tossed a switch blade on the table, said, "He was packing this."

Cliff asked in a shrill voice, "Where's your warrant? I demand you release...!"

Franzino reached over and slapped him hard across the mouth. "That's my warrant! Take these punks upstairs."

Cliff's lips were bleeding a little as the cops walked him, and Louise, out of the office.

I picked up the medal, put it between my thumb and forefinger—it bent easily. Tossing it back on the desk, I said, "The gold's real—at least," and walked out.

There was a candy store across the street and I went in, started to dial New Jersey, tell Ruthie I wouldn't be out—when I got a better idea. I called Mrs. Turner, told her, "This is Barney Harris. Would you do me a favor, Mrs. Turner? I have to call for my kid over in New Jersey at eight. I thought we might have supper together, now, instead of my going to your apartment."

"I suppose this goes on the expense account?"

"I hadn't thought of that," I said, just as sarcastically. "Maybe it will, and maybe it will be on me. But if you'll have supper with me, I'd appreciate it."

"Call for me in twenty minutes."

She didn't dress up and the effect was good—she looked exactly like what she was, a rather simple and pretty kid of twenty-three. Her hair was in a horse's tail, drawn sharply back from her face. She had on flat ballerina shoes, a purple, pleated, swirling skirt, and one of these white elastic shoulderless things that look like an inverted girdle. It showed off her fine shoulders, the bold outline of her breasts. She had a purple knit stole over one arm, and as we rang for the elevator, she glared at me as if ready to bite my head off. I looked her over, said, "If I was younger, I'd sure whistle."

She suddenly grinned, the big red mouth splitting her face. "I can't stay angry at you, Barney."

"Glad of that, Mrs. Turner. I acted like a rough loon last night."

"Mrs. Turner, Mrs. Turner," she mocked me. "Going through that again? I could have killed you last night but now..."

"Easy on that kind of talk," I cut in, only half joking.

"... I realize you were right. I wasn't telling you everything and... What do you mean, easy on that kind of talk?"

"Anybody even vaguely connected with two unsolved murders might be... misunderstood."

There were other people in the elevator. We walked through the lobby and she nodded at the doorman and when we were in my car, she said, "That was a terrible thing to say. I'm getting mad at you again."

"Told you that for your own protection. What do you want to eat?"

"I don't care. Anything you want."

"I want Italian food drowned in melted cheese."

I drove over to the East Side and down to Twelfth Street, to a place called John's. Mrs. Turner was like me—a good eater— and we put away one of those satisfying heavy meals, from clams Casino to whipped-cream Italian pastry. I told her about Louise and Cliff, Franzino, ended up with, "Maybe Franzino and Al were right. I sure haven't come up with clue one. Only, Louise trusted me and I ..."

"You didn't ask them to."

"But still, I threw them to the lions. God knows what Cliff is going through right this minute."

"He's being beaten?"

"Maybe. And maybe I've just got the jitters."

"Ed once told me how they picked up a Puerto Rican boy for a knifing and they tied him to a chair. When they changed tours, every man entering and leaving punched him. It was after that I told him to stop telling me about his... job. But you shouldn't feel bad, you're only doing your duty."

I laughed. "Hey, that's my pitch, don't give it back to me."

She gave me a hot smile. "I like you, Barney. I liked you from the moment you tried to argue me out of hiring you."

"*Like* can mean anything, or nothing. I like this pastry. I like most people."

"Thanks," she said stiffly.

"Look, this case is complicated enough and... I couldn't be just a friend to you, corny as that may sound."

"I suppose you feel sorry for me."

"Yeah. I feel sorry and sort of tenderly curious about you, Mrs. Turner."

"Call me *Mrs.* Turner again and I'll scream!"

I nodded to the waiter for the tab. "A real scream would rip through that veneer you sport. Let's leave it at this. When the case is over, I'll drop around and we'll scream at each other."

"That will be so big of you," she said coldly. "You see, I don't know all the answers—like you do."

"I try to know them. It's a rough world if you don't know what you want."

"Barney, you're always so smug, so righteous. I... hate you!"

"Mrs. Turner, for now, whether you hate me or like me, that's not what we're here for. That's what I've been trying to tell you. First things first, and all that stuff."

She sighed. "Then let's get back to business—what do you plan to do next?"

"Wait around, see what the police come up with. I don't know what else to do. Seems to me either Andersun or Turner were killed accidentally. In other words, one of the killings was planned, the other was something one of them walked into. Since Andersun was killed first, would seem Mr. Turner walked into it. But that doesn't figure. I mean, there's more chance Ed was mixed up in a shake-down, like these vice raids he cut himself in on. Only thing Andersun ever chiseled was a cigarette. Still, the cops would, or should know all about Mr. Turner's deals. Perhaps I'll try going over Andersun's background again, *must* be something there we've skipped. About time for me to call for my kid. Shall I take you home?"

"Can I come along—for the ride?"

"Of course."

I paid the check and we drove over to the Westside Highway and up to the George Washington Bridge. Some fancy joker in a Packard roadster gave me the horn and passed me. I winked at Betsy and gave my Buick the gas and we whizzed by him, like he was standing still. I turned to her, asked, "How did you like that? This load can step."

She looked a little nervous, but she was thinking about something else. She said, "Barney, does your daughter—does Ruth—know she's adopted?"

"Sure."

"Why did you tell her?"

"Why not? She'd find it out sooner or later. We simply explained that anybody can be stuck with having a child, but to *choose* one, well, that's greater love. That was Vi's idea."

"Vi—she sounds like a nice woman."

I was amused at how everything was "nice," or Betsy "liked"... things. I knew what was coming next. It came.

"And I think you're very brave to raise Ruth yourself."

"What should I have done—tossed her back into an orphan home? For Christsakes, she's *my* kid. I'm attached to her— perhaps even more than Vi was."

"I didn't mean..." She stopped and didn't say a word till we turned into the bridge and she said, "This is a beautiful sight: the water, the lights of the bridge against the dark of the sky."

"Looks better when you're coming toward New York—more lights."

"Barney, you mean your wife didn't want the girl?"

"She wanted Ruthie, but it was like a fad, a hobby, to her. Vi had to work hard at everything. Reason she got along with a turtle like me was, she'd just recovered from a nervous breakdown when I met her. Realized she had to slow down, stop pushing so hard. Used me like a brake. She did slow down, gave up most of her insurance agency, but Ruthie took its place. Vi tried too hard with the girl."

"Do you mind if I ask what she died from?"

"You've already asked. Cancer."

She said she was very sorry—all in the proper sorrow-tone of voice. We drove the rest of the way in silence and when I walked her into Jake's place, Betsy was not only a surprise, but a sensation.

Jake has a one-family house, everything about it old and mostly homemade, because he's a handy oscar with wood. But it has the warm feeling of a house lived in by people who enjoy living. They were all grouped around the TV set—Jake and Grace, Ruthie and the two boys, one a string bean of ten and the other real big for his twelve years. The youngest, "the surprise baby," as Jake called her, a two-and-a-half-year-old girl, was sprawled half asleep in a big chair.

Soon as we entered, Betsy replaced the TV screen as the target of all eyes. Grace fussed with her apron, her hair, said, "Barney, you should have told me you were bringing a guest."

"This is my employer, Mrs. Turner," I said very formally, so they wouldn't get the wrong idea. I introduced Betsy around and when I came to Ruthie, Betsy bent over and said in that silly cooing voice adults seem to think kids want, "What a lovely big girl. Barney has been telling me so much about you, Ruth."

Ruthie gave her a polite smile, then asked loudly, "You the lady my Daddy has been spending all these nights with?"

Heavy silence hung in the room like a fog till Jake's oldest boy broke it with a snicker and I said lamely, "I'm on a case for Mrs. Turner and the only time she can see me is in the evening."

Grace said, "Of course," and glared at the oldest boy when he giggled again. There was more of the embarrassing silence till the little girl suddenly woke up, stared at me, then wailed, "Uncle Barney.... Present? Present?"

I tried to lift her up, but she pulled away and bawled. I told her, "I really didn't forget, Gloria, just left your present in my office. Next time I come I'll bring two presents."

That didn't silence her and finally Jake told her, "Go to sleep, Gloria. People don't have to bring you gifts all the time. I'll drive back with Uncle Barney and get the present. You'll find it here in the morning."

Grace said, "It's way past her bedtime, that's why she's so cranky," and took the wailing kid upstairs, while Jake made us some weak drinks and the boys asked if I cared to tear a phone book in half. I told them I was too full for stunts, and Ruthie immediately wanted to know if I'd eaten out and where. Betsy, who was sitting next to Ruthie, said we'd had a snack on the way out. Then Ruthie decided she must see the pleats in Betsy's skirt that made the swirling effect, pulled up the skirt and the solid thighs weren't missed by any male in the room, including the ten-year-old one. Betsy examined Ruthie's dress, and they started to talk about clothes, just as if they were two grown women. The rest of us watched some cowboy drama on the TV.

Grace came down—she'd changed into another dress. When she got herself together Grace was a pretty woman—only most times she dressed as if she'd just jumped out of bed. She said, "Turn off that darn set so we can talk. TV is making everybody antisocial. Jake, where's my drink? All right, sit down, I'll get it." She grinned at Betsy. "Jake's a postman so I try to save him steps." She headed for the kitchen, called, "Barney, see who needs a refill and help me."

Of course nobody needed a refill except Betsy, and the boys wanted some more root beer. Soon as I got into the kitchen Grace sprang on me and gave me a tight hug as she whispered, "Oh, Barney, she's lovely. And notice how she and Ruthie hit it off? I'm so happy for you."

"Aw Grace, stop it. I'm working for her—that's all."

"That's work? Even if you're only bedding together, good for you. But I think she's sweet and so young and..."

"Jeez, no wonder your kids are so sexy-minded. Look, it's only a job with me. Her husband was murdered a couple weeks ago."

That stopped her—for a moment. She made the drinks, including a double shot for herself, and as we headed back to the living room Grace whispered, "Well, she'll want a husband soon and no woman could do better than getting you."

"Now you know I've been waiting for Jake to fall into a mailbox so we two can get together."

"Barney, I'm serious. She looks like a fine, young..."

"You don't know how young, how much of a kid she is. I'm serious too—Grace honey, take the shotgun out of my back."

When I sat down again, Ruthie told me, "Daddy, Betsy has a sewing machine and knows all about making dresses. She's going to make me a peppermint-stick skirt, and let me run the machine!"

"Now, Ruthie, don't bother Mrs. Turner," I said, trying to give the kid the eye to shut up.

"It's no bother, really, I love to sew," Betsy said, and Ruthie gave me a I-told-you-so look.

The boys had turned on the set again and we sat around and tried to talk and watch the screen, and Grace brought out some sort of pastry that tasted like Shredded Wheat filled with nuts and dipped in honey, and after a while I said we'd better go and Ruthie said it was Saturday night and I said, "Come on, it's nearly ten, and take us time to get home."

I stood up and Grace told Betsy she must come out again, in the afternoon, to see her flowers, openly hinting I should bring her out. The boys came over and asked if I'd seen some 3-D private-eye movie, sort of recommending it to me as an instruction book—I think.

Jake said, "I'll drive to the drugstore, buy something for the baby. That kid, what a memory—Grace must have been frightened by an elephant."

"Oh, stop bragging," Grace said.

Ruthie and Mrs. Turner got into my car and we followed Jake to a drugstore. I got out and said I'd get the kid something and Jake said nonsense, it was his idea, and we got into one of those silly arguments. As I held Jake's money hand and bought a glass plane filled with candy, Betsy joined us, asked, "Is it all right if I buy Ruthie an ice-cream cone? I suggested it and she wants one."

"Sure."

While we waited for her, Jake said, "So you're on a murder job."

"Two of them."

"A double header," Jake said, awe in his voice.

"Fellow named Franklin Andersun and Mr. Turner were ..."

"Remember reading about that. I was interested. Turner was a cop, a ..." He turned and blinked at Betsy. "Gee, excuse me, Mrs. Turner. It was stupid not to realize you were... I'm sorry."

Betsy half smiled to show him it was okay. Jake added, "Reason I read about it, was this Andersun. Had a fellow on my route with the same name. Franklin Andersun, even spelled it with a *u*. But it wasn't him, of course."

I stared at Jake's moonface. "There was a Franklin Andersun on your mail route?" I repeated, that odd tingling feeling you get when you've finally found the break in a case welling up inside me.

"I even bought two morning papers to see the guy's picture. Didn't look anything like the one on my route. My Andersun had bright red hair. Odd way he spelled his name, maybe a relation to the dead one. See, when I was making out a registered receipt for him, I made a point of asking if the spelling was right. Nasty guy, too. Thought the mails ran just for him."

"A registered letter?"

"Passport, they always come registered. So damn impatient to get it. Kept asking, in this twangy voice of his, if the letter had come. I'd tell him..."

Grabbing his shoulders, I lifted him onto a fountain stool, said in a choked voice, "Sit down, Jake. Let's you and me chatter."

Martin sat up in bed, drinking his third cup of black coffee. Lund was sitting at a table, holding his head and nibbling on a thin loaf of bread. He asked, "Okay, so I can probably sell my car—so what?"

"Sam, it was your crack about selling our passports that gave me the idea—came to me clear and cold through my drunken haze. Your car brings fifteen hundred dollars. Between Thérèse's savings and my cameras I can come up with a thousand," Martin said, talking fast, the hang-over punishing his head. "We return to the States, hang around for six months— maybe less if we play our angles right. Hardly any calculated risk, the way I see it."

Lund gave him a bloodshot stare. "Marty, one thing at a time. About selling our passports, I don't like..."

"We're not selling ours. Too risky. Only mean ten thousand and we'd probably be thrown out of France anyway. Might get more if we sold them in Germany, but then we'd be stuck in Germany or sent straight back to the States. No, Sam, we're going to return here with a dozen other passports and sell them for sixty thousand bucks!"

"Aw Marty, we both have big heads this morning, or is it afternoon? How are we going to steal all those passports?"

"Steal? No, we'll get them all kind of legal—by applying for them! That's the idea that hit me. What do you do when you want a passport in the States?"

"How much do you want me to bet on this question?"

"Stop clowning, Sam. Know how one goes about getting a passport? You either write or visit an office of the State Department, with your birth certificate, two crummy pictures, a friend who will sign that he has known you to be a good citizen for several years—and ten dollars. In a few weeks your passport arrives by registered mail. Now, how do you get a birth certificate in a big town, like New York City?"

"Beats the slop out of me," Sam said brightly. "Wonder if quiz shows would go over big on the Paris radio?"

"Hard for me to talk with this head, so damnit, quit clowning! About a birth certificate—in New York City all you do is write to the Board of Health, give 'em the date of your birth, address where born, name of your parents and mother's maiden name. For a dollar you receive a birth certificate by return mail. Like the idea?"

"Marty, what the hell are you gassing about?"

"About the perfect swindle," Martin said, finishing his coffee, "except we're not hurting anybody, so there won't be any complaints." He got out of bed, wearing only shorts and socks, and his body was lean and hard as

he sat down beside Sam, broke off a piece of bread. "Hope Thérèse comes back with the charcuterie, *I'm starved. And stop giving me that blank look— Sam, the best rackets are always the simple ones. Listen: you and me—under false names—go into any bar or poolroom in a poor section of New York, Chicago, Boston—any large city. We each pick out a guy. Take a few beers, maybe a night or two, to make small talk about the neighborhood, pretend we're boyhood chums with the guy. Point is, we each learn where our guy was born, when, and the name of his folks. That doesn't sound difficult, does it?"*

"Sounds stupid. What do we do with all this great info?"

"Sam, you're really in a fog. Suppose the fellow you talk to is named Mark James and my guy is Edward Spero.... You rent a room in another part of the city as Mark James and I rent one under the name of Edward Spero—then we send away for their birth certificates. We take passport pictures of each other, hop down to the nearest passport office and make applications, as James and Spero, each being a witness for the other. In a few weeks we receive 'our' passports, as James and Spero, and move on. No possible traces left. Like it?"

"Think it will work?"

"Why won't it? Then we find a bar in another part of the town, say Brooklyn, start over again, only this time we go to a different passport office with our applications. Be easy to touch up the pictures and change our features with make-up. We work New York, Newark, Hartford, then go to Chicago, maybe even out to L.A. Within a few months, six at the most, we have a dozen passports, return to Paris on our own passports, sell the others. Show me a flaw?"

Sam stared at Pearson with open admiration, said, "Good God!"

"Dreamed about it in my sleep last night. Show me one thing that can throw us? All we need is time and living money and we have both. Still have to work out some details, be careful with the pictures and make-up, and most important of all, pick on the names of poor slobs like ourselves. Hell, nobody in my family, except me, ever applied for a passport. And be careful with Gabby, just tell her you're returning to the States to get your G.I. schooling straightened out. I'll have Thérèse keep an eye on her."

"Don't worry about her. She'll be faithful to me."

Martin stared at him for a long moment, then laughed. "I don't care about her sex life, I don't want her to talk. That goes double for you too. No more drinking, chewing the fat with strangers. Talk is the one thing that can jinx us."

"Marty, you know me. I ..."

"I know your big mouth very well, that's why I'm telling you. Sam, this means fifty or sixty thousand dollars. We make our picture, we're set for

life.”

“And in a couple of years, if there’s still a demand for passports, we can work the deal again, or...”

“No, just this one time. We’re going to be smart operators. Most jokers get caught because they work a good thing thin.”

Sam jumped up, knocking his chair over. “Where’s the paper? See when the Liberté *is sailing.”*

“Easy, Sam, my head won’t stand one of your bursts of energy. And we’ll go by a Dutch ship—they’re cheaper. First thing you have to do is start parking your car around the PX, and at SHAEF headquarters out at Fontainebleau. Pass the word that you’re selling the car. Only forget you’re an actor, don’t talk too damn much.”

CHAPTER FIVE

“What’s this all about, I say something bright?” Jake asked.

“Tell me more about Andersun.”

“Not much to tell. I remember him because I get along good with all the people on my route. They’re my friends. Andersun was living in a rooming house near Broadway and of course I don’t get to know roomers much, but for a few days he was always waiting for me, asking if I didn’t have a registered letter for him. When it finally came—I could tell it was a passport—I asked for identification and he said I knew him, but I said I needed identification and finally he came up with his birth certificate.”

“When was all this?”

Jake rubbed his nose. “Oh... at least three, four months ago.”

“Four months ago?” I repeated.

Betsy said, “If it’s that long ago, it would hardly have any connection with this...”

“It *has* to hook up.”

The cone dripped on her hand, onto Gloria’s toy and for some reason as I brushed the toy off I wondered if Louise had toys and attention when she was a kid. And what did that prove and why was I even thinking about it now?

Betsy said, “I’d best go out and give this to Ruth.”

I asked Jake, “Where’s this rooming house? Andersun still there?”

“Crummy joint on One Hundred and Second Street. I don’t think he’s there. Never get any more mail for him. Although he never put in a change of address card either. They come and go in these houses.”

“Can you remember any other letters you had for him?”

“Nope. Only would recall something special—like a reg.”

"Tell me again what he looked like."

"Can't exactly say, except his hair seemed too red. And his voice."

I wrote down the address of the rooming house, thanked Jake, and went back into the drugstore and phoned O'Hara, asked if he could baby-sit for me. Cy said, "Damn, you sure pick odd hours to ask! You know what time it is? Anyway, we got a bridge game going. Look, if you want, bring Ruthie here and she can sleep on the couch."

"No, that wouldn't work," I said. I didn't want her shoved around like a piece of baggage.

"I'm sorry, Barney, but if you'd only let me know sooner."

"It's okay. See you, Cy."

I went out and stepped into the car. As we drove off, Betsy asked, "What's all this mean, Barney?"

"What happened, Daddy?" Ruthie asked over her ice-cream cone.

"Look, honey, Daddy will probably be gone all night. Guess I can get May to stay with you—I hope."

"Oh, her. I heard her say she was going to see her uncle in New Haven for Saturday and Sunday. Said he was a rich uncle—always showing off."

I swore under my breath, tried to think of anybody else I could get to baby-sit on a Saturday night. "Ruth, would you like to sleep at my house?" Betsy asked. "In the morning we can start making some dresses."

I was about to tell Betsy to take it slow, but where else could I find a baby sitter? Ruthie asked, "May I, Daddy?"

"Well... okay."

Betsy smiled at Ruthie and said "That's lovely," then asked me, "Barney, because a man with the same name as Andersun gets a passport—months ago—what does that mean for us?"

"The red hair, the twang in his voice—that's Brown, the joker who was in the bar the night of the shootings. Still haven't any motive, but he's our boy. I'm going to see Franzino, go down to that rooming house tonight. After all this waiting around, I think we're finally moving in high gear."

I dropped Ruthie and Betsy off at her place, then drove up to the precinct house. It suddenly came to me that Brown's rooming house was just a few blocks from the Turner apartment and I wished I had some place else to leave Ruthie. The duty sergeant must have thought I was a salesman; he tried to brush me off for a while before he got Franzino on the phone. Within a half hour Franzino was at the station house, and a few minutes later Al Swan joined us, a bigwig from Homicide with him.

We raced down Broadway, the siren going most of the time, and it gave me a kick. Although when the siren was off, the engine made quite a racket—needed a valve clearance check. The rooming house was an ancient three-story affair and we promptly scared the night lights out of the old couple who ran it and most of their roomers, who were just coming in from their Saturday night elbow-bending.

The couple vaguely remembered Andersun—he'd lived there for about a month, paid promptly. They said he was a quiet fellow, didn't drink or raise any hell. No, he didn't seem to work, but he wasn't worrying about money either. Sometimes he carried a camera around. No, they couldn't recall any visitors he had except a tall handsome man who had also roomed there for a week. His name was Smith—they thought. He and Andersun were friends, moved in at the same time, but Smith only stayed a few days, although sometimes he came around to see Andersun. The couple kept sloppy records, didn't even have a record of when Andersun and Smith roomed there, the exact date, or Smith's first name. Andersun had moved months ago, left no forwarding address, and they'd never seen him since.

The letdown was pretty bad. We took them and some of the steady roomers back to the station. We also picked up Jimmy, the bartender, and Franzino got Louise out of the cooler. I had a chance to tell her how sorry I was, and what she told me I can't print. They all spent the rest of the night beefing about losing sleep and looking at pictures sent up from the rogues' gallery downtown. But we came up with a blank.

At four in the morning, over containers of bad coffee, Franzino asked me, "Got any more ideas, bright boy?"

"Why the sarcasm, Barney's been batting 1000 per cent," Al said.

"Who said I was being sarcastic?"

I asked, "Can we get the State Department in Washington to send us the passport application?"

"Already wired them. FBI is in the case now. They'll be here in the morning. We'll have to shake down the Andersun family again—why the hell should this Brown get a passport as Andersun? Maybe he's a relative, or ...?"

"At least we know why the real Andersun was killed," I said.

"Do we?" Al asked.

"Look, for some reason Brown gets a passport under Andersun's name. Then Brown reads in the papers about the kid winning the cash, heading for Paris. Meaning the real Andersun would need a passport, find out about Brown getting one in his name—so Andersun is knocked off."

"Too simple. For all we know there can still be two Andersuns, or maybe Brown and this other Andersun are the same guy, or again, Brown and our Andersun may have been working together," Al said, and in the early morning his voice was so hoarse it was a continuous whisper. "Still a lot of *ifs* we know strictly from nothing about. Like we haven't any idea how Turner fits into this."

Franzino yawned. "First thing we do is grab some shut-eye, see what those FBI glamour boys come up with in the morning. We might as well use the cots upstairs."

We finished our coffee and trooped upstairs and stretched out on some cots. The coffee, or the excitement, kept me awake. When I heard Al move, I asked, "Got any sodas in your car?"

"Yeah, got some cans of grape."

"With gin or rum? I need a shot." I sat up and put on my shoes.

"Certainly never appreciated your talents, Barney. A comedian, too. Find the cans in the trunk—here's the keys."

Dawn was starting to lighten the sky as I drank two warm grape sodas spiked with gin. I went back upstairs, hit the cot, and the next thing I knew it was bright sunlight, and I was alone.

I checked my wallet, found the can and washed my mouth out, ran cold water over my face. It was ten o'clock and Al and Franzino were downstairs, belching from a heavy breakfast. Nobody from Washington had shown up. I went out and ate, called Ruthie, who was bubbling over, having a big time. I told her I'd call back in a few hours and Betsy got on the phone and asked what Ruthie ate, and I heard the kid say, "I told you, Betsy, anything you eat. My goodness, what do you think, I still go for those sloppy baby foods?"

I was a little worried—Betsy was bubbling too.

A guy from the Passport Division of the State Department and two FBI men finally arrived, all of them dressed in natty banker's gray suits, white shirts and dark ties—like it was a uniform. They had the passport application, the duplicate picture.

According to the application, Andersun was five feet, six inches, had red hair and brown eyes. There weren't any "distinguishing marks or features," and the purpose of his trip was "Travel." One Irving Spear of a Bronx address had sworn on the application that he had known Franklin Andersun for ten years. Franzino had the address checked—it turned out to be another rooming house and "Irving Spear" had lived there months ago. Nobody knew anything about him except he was tall and "well spoken," and now and then drank in his room.

We all stared at the picture of Andersun—or Brown—the usual startled-looking passport photo of a young man with thick hair, quiet eyes, and a wide nose. The State Department said the passport had never been used, which meant Brown was still in the U.S.A.

The application was too old and smudged for fingerprints. All we really had was a sample of Brown's handwriting, and his picture. It was something, but it still added up to zero.

The State Department and the FBI said they thought it had the looks of a passport ring, and when Franzino asked what that meant, the State Department man said, "There are criminals here—but mostly of the international variety—who are stateless and want to travel. Other criminals, experts, can alter a passport once they have the seal, the actual paper. Depending upon the person who needs a passport, an altered one can bring as high as twenty thousand dollars. They probably were paying Andersun for the use of his name, but why this—uh—Mr. Brown's picture was used... well, I don't get the connection."

Al asked questions about passports, whether Turner ever had taken one out, and the Washington man said he would check.

A simple idea began to take shape in my simple noggin. The word "simple" was the key to everything... the names Brown, Smith, and the bartender said Brown's first name had been something like Tom or Dick or Harry. It wasn't any accident that Brown hung around an ordinary two-bit bar like the Grand Café, got into conversation with fellows who had simple lives, like Andersun, Irving Spear.

I asked the State Department man, "While you're checking on Turner, see if a passport has been issued to an Irving Spear and to a man named Smith—his picture will look like Spear's."

"Spear—that's Andersun's sister's boy friend," Franzino put in.

"I can check by phone," the State Department man said. "What's the angle?"

"Let's check first—I'm not sure it is an angle—yet."

"I don't like playing quiz games on a Sunday," the State Department man said. "What's on your mind?"

"If this is a passport ring, then there should be one in the name of Spear, because a fellow named Smith talked to him once in the bar. You see, this Brown got into a beer argument with Andersun about the block, the old neighborhood. Claimed he'd been born there. That's the can opener for us."

I collected an assortment of blank looks. Al Swan smiled at everybody, said, "Slow, Barney boy. Explain it to us again—in small words."

"Way I see it," I said, wondering if I was making a fool of myself, "is Brown learned from all this small talk where and when Franklin Andersun was born, name of his folks. Brown then gets a birth certificate as Franklin Andersun; do that by mail once he has the information, then rents a room under the name of Andersun. His buddy, Smith, is doing the same thing with the info he picked up in the bar from Irving Spear. With a birth certificate, a couple of lousy pictures—his nose, for example, looks out of shape, probably stuffed with cotton, and everybody said his hair was too red, so that was a dye job. Okay, with the birth certificate, the pictures, and Smith as a friend and witness under the name of Spear, Brown plunks down ten bucks, makes out a passport application, and in due time gets the passport, via registered mail, at his room. At a different address, with Brown as his witness, Smith gets a passport in the name of Irving Spear. The lads then chuck their rooms, dye their hair another shade, find a new bar, and start all over again." I smiled at one and all, as if I'd explained everything.

Franzino broke the silence with, "Wouldn't they be recognized when applying for a passport the second time?"

The State Department man shook his well-brushed head.

"We have two offices in New York City, others in Washington, Philadelphia, all over the country. Be simple and comparatively safe for them to try this five or six times, meaning they end up with a dozen passports, besides their own. Let me call Washington, check on Turner, Smith, and Spear."

We were sitting around the office of the detective squad, and the State Department man left to make the call as Al said, "Racket sounds too simple."

Franzino ran a finger along the beard stubble on his lean jaw. "Simple rackets are always the ones that work."

"If Andersun was in on a big deal like this, we'd have found some trace of it," Al said.

One of the FBI's asked, "And if this Brown has the passport, why should he kill Andersun months later?"

Before I could answer, Franzino said, "The thing is, Andersun wasn't in on any deal. The lead we've overlooked was the story in the papers about Andersun planning to use the prize money for a trip to Paris, which meant..."

"Why Brown and Smith operated in bars like the Grand Café," I cut in, determined to at least explain my own idea, "was because there was little chance of any of the boys in the bar ever taking a trip out of the country. Once Andersun applied for a passport, the State Department would investigate, and the whole deal would be cooked. They had to stop the real Andersun, and they did it with a bullet."

The State Department man returned. There was a passport issued to an Irving Spear, none to Turner, and they were checking all the Smiths and Browns. A photostat of Spear's application was being flown in, and handwriting and photo experts were checking Brown's face and writing against other recent passports.

There wasn't anything to do for a couple of hours, and I had some coffee with Al. Then we drove over to the Turner apartment. Betsy and the kid were mixed up in cloth and patterns, and we were in the way. The last thing Ruthie wanted was to leave, so I said I'd phone later, maybe take them both out to supper, and after that—no matter what—Ruthie was going home.

As we left, Al gave me an evil grin, croaked, "What a domestic scene—mamma, poppa, and baby," and started to whistle "My Blue Heaven," and I told him to shut his corny trap. We went for a ride and I put on some speed—with Al's badge beside me I didn't have to worry about a ticket. Al insisted his Caddy could outrun my car, but backed down when I offered to bet him ten bucks. I drove back to the station house and we waited around some more, before the Spear application came in.

Brown's buddy, Smith, was six feet tall, weighed 196 pounds, had a mole on the right cheek. From the picture he looked like a handsome, distinguished young man, but his bald dome made him look older than thirty-four. One of the FBI lads said the mole was probably make-up and his head had been shaved for the picture. Franklin Andersun had signed as his witness, and Franzino said, "These jokers thought of everything—there's some attempt to disguise his handwriting here. Tomorrow I'll have my men check every passport photo shop in the city with these copies. See what we come up with. Of course we'll have every dock and airfield watched, in case they try to leave the country."

"A passport is good for two years," one of the FBI men said. "They can lay low till the summer, when the travel rush is on."

"Another possibility—they could have skipped," the State Department man said. "They could have gone to Canada, Mexico, some of the West Indies—without passports—then use them shipping out down there."

Franzino sighed. "Or they could have taken a plane out the same night of the murder, for all we know. Hope this isn't another blank wall."

Al shook his head. "I got a hunch they're still here, playing it too cool. Also got a hunch this is it. Like shaking out a tangled fishing line—once you get the right line, it all straightens out."

There wasn't a thing to do but wait till Monday morning, while Washington checked, so we all knocked off for the day. I watched the cops line up before the desk as they were turning out a platoon, then I stopped into Franzino's office, asked, "How about releasing Louise now?"

"What did that whore do for you?" he growled, but had them both in his office within a few minutes. She looked bad, her face puffy and strained from worry and lack of sleep. Cliff looked okay, hair as slickly combed as ever. Franzino told them, "I'm letting you go as a favor to this big cluck. There's two conditions—break either of them and I'll toss you back in the can, lose the key. Don't move or become hard to find, in case I want to get in touch with you. And no hustling. Soon as this case is over, both of you get the hell out of my precinct."

Louise and Cliff hurried out and as I started after them to explain, Franzino called me back. He pulled his bent medal out of the drawer. "I'm afraid to hammer this—might crack. Think you can straighten it out again, muscle head?"

I got it fairly straight.

CHAPTER SIX

When it looked like we were really closing in, we fell flat on our collective faces. Not a thing happened Monday or Tuesday, except New York had one of those unexpected muggy heat spells. The air seemed to vibrate with heat waves, and as usual, the heat knocked me out. The passport photo places had never seen either Brown or Smith, and the State Department was "reasonably" sure nobody looking like either of them had used a passport since the murder.

On Wednesday Al Swan called for me and we went down to an office in the Federal Building on Foley Square. Franzino was there, along with two big apples from the Police Department, and an assortment of Feds. Except for me and Franzino, everybody was dressed like he'd been torn out of the men's fashion page of *Esquire*.

I was in fast company and I sat and listened. A State Department man made a short speech that added up to one thing—we were still no place. They'd found two other false passports, one issued to a light tan Negro named Alvin Hunt of Patterson, New Jersey, and one to a Richard Cohen of Brooklyn. Neither of these men had ever made an application for a passport; both vaguely recalled bar conversations some months ago about where they were born. In the passport pictures, Brown looked swarthy, his hair dark and close-cut, and he did something to his cheeks to make him look full-faced. Smith was sporting a heavy head of blond hair and didn't have a mole. A check on the rooming houses used by "Hunt" and "Cohen" gave us nothing—the guys had lived there for a few weeks, moved as soon as they got their passports. The talk ended with, "We have no way of knowing how many false passports these men planned to secure. But it is our theory that the killings will frighten them off the whole idea."

"Meaning the case is closed?" Franzino growled. "Why, damnit, a policeman has been murdered and we're going to find the murderer whether you guys play ball or not!"

One of the police brass curtly told him to shut up, asked, "You mean they'll stop trying for any more passports?"

"Of course we're as anxious to find these men as you are, but it is our theory they will destroy the passports, drop the whole scheme."

"Leaving us with Turner's death unsolved!" Franzino snapped.

The Federal man said, "These men are clever, and a clever man knows when he's had it. If they stop now, they're comparatively safe. Since their own passports may have been issued any time within the last four years—if they renewed them—it's almost impossible to check the thousands of passports issued during those years, so we can't find their real identities."

There was a moment of silence and I sat there, sweating gently and feeling sticky and uncomfortable. I asked, "What happens if a person abroad sells his own passport?"

"Usually they report it as lost or stolen, and unless we can prove otherwise, we issue them a special travel permit, good only for returning to the States."

"In other words, if they did get to Europe, they could sell their own passports and continue to live there, long as they didn't travel?" I asked.

"Yes. It's also possible for a man to travel about without a passport, once he reaches foreign shores. There are still soldiers who deserted during the last war, who are hiding out in France, Algiers, London. If a man tries to rent a hotel room, get a job, or leave a country, he has to show his passport or identity card. But if a deserter was living with a girl in her room, didn't work or travel, small chance of the local police catching up with them. And of course, there are such things as forged identity cards, too. Why do you ask?"

Before I could answer, one of the Police Department brass asked in a stage whisper, "Who the hell is that big guy?" and hit the ceiling soon as he heard I was a private badge. When Al and Franzino did a lot of whispering into his big ears, and this little storm died down, I cleared my throat, said, "Seems to me we still have a chance to take them. For one thing, *they don't know* we're on to their passport racket. And if they were going to chuck the whole deal, they wouldn't have shot Andersun, risked a murder rap."

The Fed said, "If you think they'll try for more passports, why of course we plan to keep a running check on that."

"What I think is this," I said slowly, trying to keep my voice from dancing. "They have four phony passports we know of. That means a big hunk of money if they can sell them—and don't sell their own. You say they're clever. Okay, they've put in a lot of time and patient work on this deal, and I can't see them tossing away all that dough. My idea is—why don't we try and decoy them?"

Another silence greeted me. I kept sweating like a pig, wondered if I was making an ass of myself. The thing seemed so simple to me; somebody else *had* to think of it too!

But they all sat there without saying a damn word. After a long moment I went on. "We plant two phony stories in the papers, give them a big play. First, that the police have the killer—this is all off-the-top-of-my-noggin thinking—but something about a guy who was brooding about Turner slapping him around months ago—thought Andersun was a buddy of his—

killed them both. Whatever the story, has to look good."

The silence was still upon me like a hot blanket. The Fed asked softly, "And where does all this take us?" Maybe there was sarcasm in his voice—maybe it was my imagination.

"It makes Brown and Smith feel safe, that they can go after the jackpot. Now at the same time we plant another story. Hunt or Cohen... no, best we make it Spear... Irving Spear is picked up in a big crap game and makes the papers on some legal point about the police have no right to the pot. That stinks. I don't know what the gimmick will be exactly, but Spear comes into a hunk of change, maybe because of Andersun's death, and announces he's going to Europe. As I said, have to be a gimmick that would make the papers. Believing they're safe, Brown and Smith will try to knock off Spear, only we'll have him staked out. That puts it up to them—either they have to dump the idea, or knock off Spear and take off for Europe, or wherever they plan to sell the passports.... It will make them move, jump."

You could still cut the silence with a blunt knife. I wiped my sweaty forehead with the back of my hand. The Fed man looked at the cops and the Fed said, "Granted it's a hell of a long shot, but since we don't have anything better, why not try it?"

"And if it doesn't work, we make the Police Department look like damn fools!" the police brass shouted.

"Who will ever know it didn't come off?" I asked. "The dummy we use will never come up for trial. Case will be forgotten—unless the Andersun family or Mrs. Turner make a stink, and I think we can talk them into co-operating with us."

Federal shook his head. "We can't have too many people in on this, too much chance of a leak. For all we know Brown and Smith are in touch with the family—I mean see them on a social basis, under other names. As for the reputation of the Police Department, no trouble there. If nothing comes of this, the D.A. will dismiss the case for lack of evidence, or an alibi comes up. All done quietly. More I think of it, better I like our chances."

"My client, Mrs. Turner, has to be in on it."

A Fed who hadn't spoken till now asked, "Afraid you'll lose out on a day's pay?"

"That's an idea," I said, fighting to sound calm. "I don't want Mrs. Turner to think I've solved the case when I haven't. Her interest—and mine—in all this is solely why and how Ed Turner was killed, and we're still a long ways from bringing that under the wire. Also, in my opinion—for what it's worth— you can foul things up easier by trying to hush this than by letting the people concerned know the score. That's why I've ruled out Hunt and Cohen. No point in starting with a new set of people. As for

Spear, he's going with Andersun's sister, so he'll tell her. Our best bet is explain it to them and…"

"We'll work out the details," a police bigwig said curtly. There was a little more chatter, and the conference was over. All the way uptown Al Swan kept telling me how, "…. Can't get over you, Barney boy. Just keep surprising the crap out of me. You been hiding a brain under that bushel of wild hair."

I felt uneasy, and when I left Al I went to the office, looked through the ads I called mail. I began to feel even more jittery. I kept telling myself it was the muggy heat, but that wasn't entirely it. I drove around to look up the last known addresses of a couple of deadbeats, then I went home to take a shower. I gave myself a stiff workout with the weights, ended in a river of sweat, and still restless. I finally got in the tub and cooled off, and of course started sweating again as I dried myself. I kept telling myself they had taken my ideas, yet I felt odd, on edge. I drove over to the school and when Ruthie climbed in beside me and I asked what she wanted for supper, she said, "Betsy said we can eat at her house."

"We're not eating at Mrs. Turner's house. And don't call her Betsy."

"Aunt Betsy?"

"Call her Mrs. Turner. That's good manners."

"Daddy, when you know somebody good, like I know Betsy, then you call them by their first name."

"Not little girls and big people."

"Well, why can't we have supper with her? She bakes swell and I want to see my new dresses."

"You'll see them some other time," I said, driving toward the super market. "We're eating home. Maybe a salad and…"

"But why, Daddy?"

"Because I say so!" I snapped and immediately wished I'd bitten my tongue.

Saying that made me jump back twenty-five years. The only real fight I ever had with my old man was once when I was eleven years old and he told me that, instead of giving me a reason. The old guy had raced with Oldfield—that's why he named me Barney—and as far back as I can remember he was always working on a garage on Sixty-fourth Street—a stoop-shouldered man, dirty with grease, an old skull cap pushed back on his big head. I was so mad I burst into tears and that got him; he made me explain what I was boiling about. Then he said, "Fair enough, a kid is entitled to a reason for everything—if I can give you one. Tell you what, next time I ever slip you that 'Because I say so,' you belt me." And I'd said, "But, Pop, I can't reach your jaw." And he'd laughed as he told me, "Don't worry, Barney, you're tall enough to belt me where it would hurt worse than on the kisser."

There was a group of chauffeurs hanging around—I always disliked them for being snotty know-it-alls. My old man's crack made them hysterical and when I asked Pop why, he said, "That's a reason I can't give you—yet. See, it's kind of a joke. Has to do with sex—something I'll explain when you're older."

About a year later, Mom overheard me arguing with a friend about Jean Harlow's breasts, whether they were "big" or not, and that night she told Pop it was time to "talk to him." Being a slum kid, I had a very clear idea of how sex worked, but I went for a walk with the old man, listened to him stammer it out. I remember he started with, "Barney, time you learned other people besides pimps and gangsters drive Cadillacs..."

Now I glanced at Ruthie as I parked the car; she was looking away from me, her little lips a tight line. I told her, "Honey, I didn't mean to jump you. I'm nervous today—maybe because of the heat. And—I'm working for Mrs. Turner, and we can't mix business and pleasure."

"Why not, Daddy?"

"I don't know, exactly. Unless because in business everybody is rooking the other fellow."

"What's rooking mean?"

"Oh—cheating, stealing."

"Why, Daddy, Betsy—Mrs. Turner—would never cheat you."

"Maybe I'm cheating her."

"Why, Daddy!"

I pinched her nose, said, "How would you like to buy cans of noodles and bean sprouts and water chestnuts, make our own chow mein?"

She got excited about that, but all during supper she kept asking me why? why? about everything, and when May Weiss came in at seven-thirty and I wouldn't take Ruthie with me to see Betsy, the kid started to whine and bawl, and I kind of lost my head and slapped her. I spent a hard ten minutes apologizing, and by the time I reached the Turner apartment I was hot and nervous and blue.

Betsy was wearing dungarees spotted with oil paints and a T-shirt, both of which she filled out nicely. She asked if I wanted a highball and I said no and sat like a lump for a couple of minutes, staring at the painting she'd been working on, but not seeing a damn thing. Finally she asked, "What are you thinking about, Barney?"

"Being a kid ought to be a wonderful deal; everything is done for you; no worries about food or rent or war. Yet it's probably the most frustrating time of our lives because adults act like adults instead of human beings."

She smiled. "Sounds like a profound statement—I guess."

"Maybe it is, Mrs. Turner."

"Will you please, please, call me Betsy?"

"Don't start that, I'm feeling nervous enough as it is. Here's my report for the day." I told her about the talk fest at the Federal Building and when I finished she actually clapped her hands, said, "You're a terrific detective, Barney! This is real news. Of course, so far it doesn't hook up to Ed, but I feel just as you do. When you find Andersun's murderer, you'll have Ed's."

"I'm the whizbang dick, the mighty private eye—who's smart enough to have a cousin Jake who was smart enough to be an observant mailman!"

"But you said—you've always said most cases are solved by luck."

"I know, but somehow all this makes me feel... a bit preposterous. Like I was being kidded. A mechanic like me telling the New York City Police Department, the FBI, how to solve a case! Doesn't make sense."

"To quote Mr. Barney Harris again—nothing about this case makes sense."

"Yeah, but somehow I feel this is all going to blow up in my face. Well, we'll see." I stood up. "See you again tomorrow night. Meantime, it's important you don't talk to anybody—including yourself—about this decoy idea."

"I won't talk. Would you like to take a ride, to cool off? I've been in the house all day."

"Well, I... eh ..." I didn't feel up to a lot of light gab.

"You don't have to!"

"I know that. I also know the cops still have Ed's car tied up. If there's any place special you want me to drive you to..."

"Yes, to the nearest movie, and I'll walk!"

The phone rang and she answered it, waved the receiver at me. "For you."

I was certain it was Ruthie and bad news, but it was Al Swan's hoarse voice. I asked, "How did you know I was here?" It was a dumb question and of course Al couldn't drop the ball. He said, "Why, I'm not only a detective in my own right, but my brother-in-law is a regular Sherlock Holmes. Some of the magic goofer-dust from his badge rubbed off on mine. I made a simple deduction, as we dicks say, after I phoned Ruthie. Say, the kid answers the phone like a grown-up young lady. 'No, Mr. Harris isn't at home. Can I take a message ...?'"

"What's on your mind, Al?"

"Having a little trouble with your decoy idea. This Irving Spear flatly refuses to be a sitting duck. And his girl friend, the Andersun tomato, she hit the ceiling too."

"Tell him to make out his insurance to her, then she'll go for the deal."

"Franzino is going to talk to him again tomorrow, maybe threaten to take his hack license away. Thought I'd tell you before you gave Mrs. Turner the big story about what a big hero you are. You having fun, chum?" There was an asinine chuckle and Al hung up.

I ran my sleeve over my sweaty face, lied to Betsy, "I have to go over to the station house, but I'll drive you to..."

"Oh, shut up!"

"See you tomorrow night, Mrs. Turner," I said, heading for the door.

"Mr. Harris, I imagine my retainer has been used up. If you'll tell me how much..."

I cut her off with, "Send you a bill when the case is over, Mrs. Turner." I walked out, wanting to make a crack about us sounding like Gallagher and Shean, except she was too young to have heard of them.

I took off my coat and my shirt was wet. I drove around, letting the car eat up the road, the wind drying my shirt off. But the car didn't give me a kick and I went home and told May to take off. I poured myself a good hooker and waited for the rye to loosen me up. All that happened was that I started sweating again.

I ran a bath and sat in the tub for a long time, chain-smoking cigarettes, thinking of Brown and Smith and their foolproof plan. All the time and patient work they put into it. Then one of those things happen—Andersun has to win a prize and decide to go to Europe. I could almost feel the way they must have felt, suddenly finding their perfect crime going up in the air, maybe the Feds on their tails, and murder the only out. Like a guy highballing along the highway, weaving in and out of the stream of cars— maybe just to show off for his girl. Then there's a car speeding the other way and showing off—a gag that in a matter of seconds becomes life or death.

And then, of course, the fantastic piece of luck—my cousin being Brown's mailman, and by another hunk of luck—telling me about it.

I took a shower and toweled myself, knew I wouldn't sleep much. I decided I'd have some talk with Irv Spear in the morning. I had another slug of rye and went to bed, feeling the tears of sweat rolling down my body as I waited for sleep to come.

It came fast—next thing I knew Ruthie was waking me and it was a bright clean morning, and cool. I felt pretty good and spent ten minutes swinging her in the air as she shrieked with delight.

I drove her to the nursery, headed for the office. As I got out of my car, a taxi gave me the horn and Irv Spear stuck his balding dome out of his cab, said, "Been waiting for you, Harris."

"Come on up to the office," I told him.

Cy O'Hara was busy reading the morning paper, but soon as he saw me usher Irv in, Cy said, "Going down for coffee," and went out after locking his phone.

Irv took a seat, cleaned his thick-shelled glasses and looked the office over. "So this is a detective's office? You're small time, but always smart business to keep your overhead down." He suddenly leaned forward as I was glancing at my mail, pulled out the bottom drawer of my desk, saying, "In the movies the private eye always has a bottle in the bottom drawer."

It was embarrassing; I *had* an unopened pint there. Irv looked startled. I asked if he wanted a drink and he said no, then studied my face with his solemn eyes for a second, said, "Hear this deal is your bright idea."

"And I hear you don't think much of it. Don't you want us to take Frank's killers?"

"Harris, let's you and me get straight. Don't throw me no curves or sales talks. Sure, I'd like to see the guy that plugged Frankie get his. And if it would bring the kid back to life, I might take the risk. But Frankie is dead and buried and I fail to see any point in becoming corpse three just to take the heat off the cops. I don't believe in making the headlines—feet first."

"Relax," I said, trying to make my voice sound light and easy. "Nobody is asking you to be a dead hero. Where's the risk? These guys have probably jumped the country already, so..."

"Crap. If you cops thought they had skipped, you wouldn't be pulling this stunt. Harris, I read someplace about an honest man being one who has a choice. I'm leveling with you—what's it going to get me to risk stopping a couple of slugs?"

"You'll be better protected than Fort Knox. There'll be..."

"Harris, don't crap me. You guys don't know for sure what these two killers look like. They aren't going to come up and make small talk—first thing that speaks will be the guns in their hands. I'm willing to gamble, but not when the stakes is me!"

"But you'll be surrounded by cops, FBI guys."

Irv slipped me a hard quick smile. "Frankie had a cop with him—they died together. Know what the cops want me to do? I'm supposed to go about as usual, hacking, school, see Juanita, and all the time they claim there will be cops 'someplace' around me. Sure, maybe the cops will nail the guys, but after I'm dead. This isn't a chance they're asking me to take, but sure death. Would you do it, Harris?"

"I don't know, Irv. But then Franklin Andersun wasn't my buddy, nor am I going with his sister."

"Juanita is against it—she knows this hero stuff is all for the birds."

"Sure it is, but we're not asking you to be a clay pigeon," I said, but I knew I didn't sound convincing. "After all, we have pictures of them and..."

"Sure, disguised pictures!"

There were a few seconds of silence, and an idea tickled my noggin. Irv fidgeted in his chair, said, "Funny, I feel like a louse. When they first came to me, I said, okay, I'd hang around the house for a few days, with some cops. But they said no, that would be a tip-off it was all a plant. I'm supposed to go about my daily routine—won't even let me have a gun. That might be a tip-off too. Hell, Harris, that's asking too much. These killers are sharp on this make-up stuff. I understand they even posed as a colored fellow once. How are the cops going to recognize them—in time?"

"I know somebody who'd recognize Brown, could act as a bodyguard for you."

"Who's that?"

"Danny Macci."

"But he's blind!"

"That's why he'd know Brown's voice at once—swears he'd remember that twang any place. Look, with Danny beside you all the time—and he'd never be mistaken for a cop—he could shout a warning to the police the second Brown opens his mouth."

"What makes you so sure these clowns are going to talk first? Hell, they don't want to chitchat with me. Might be only two sounds—the bang-bang of a gun and the plop of my dead body hitting the street."

I shrugged. "I'm not selling you anything, Irv. Sure, that's a possibility. But this is the *only* way we can ever get these guys—if they are still in the country. But with Danny with you and a flock of cops ready to close in and shoot at a split second's notice, I think you're reasonably safe. Also, we'll give you a bulletproof vest..."

"Got any bulletproof heads!"

I tried to give it a long laugh. "Irv, would you take me for a cop?"

"Well—no. Something about you, you're *too* big—look too tacky, down at the heels."

"Okay, you're a cabbie and I'm really a mechanic, and Danny, if they remember, is one of the boys at the bar. Suppose I tail along with you, and Danny—as our bloodhound? Buy that?"

He fooled with the few hairs on his head. "You guys are just trying to get me killed! All right, if I can have you and Danny with me, I'm in. At least I'll be surrounded by muscle."

"I'll talk to Danny right now," I said, getting up.

When we reached the street, Irv glanced around like a ham actor, muttered, "Haven't even started and I'm scared."

"Relax."

He took a deep breath. "That's the trouble—I might relax permanently."

"Long as you can joke about it, you'll be okay. Where can I find you in an hour or so?"

"I'll be at the garage by noon. Not in the mood to push a hack today.

Boy, this is how a bull's-eye must feel."

"Stop it. Tell you a trade secret. A guy has to be damn good to hit anybody with a pistol, unless they're right on top of 'em."

"Harris, you're the one making with the jokes. These guys have *proved* how damn good they are!"

"But they took Frank and Turner by surprise. This time they'll be the surprised ones," I said, and the words suddenly hit my brain like a hammer. "I'll see you at the garage at noon. And whether you believe it or not, the cops really don't want you killed. The... eh... publicity would be bad for them."

"That's a real comforting thought!" he said, getting into his cab. "Save those words for my tombstone!" He waved as he drove off. I stepped into the coffeepot, told Cy the office was his.

He made some corny crack, as usual, to Alma, and left. Alma gave me her best hard smile, as I asked for change of two bits, and asked where I'd been. "Busy, busy," I said, stepping into the phone booth.

When I got Franzino, I told him, "Got an idea. The..."

"I wish I could say to hell with your ideas, but so far yours have been better than mine. Hear about this jerk, Spear?"

"Just left him. I think he'll play ball with us." I told him about Danny and myself guarding Irv, and Franzino said, "I don't know about you—some guys assume *any* big slob must be a cop. But the blind man is a sweet touch. What kind of gun do you carry?"

"Gun? I don't have one."

"Sure be some guard. If I get you one, know how to use it?"

"Was checked out on .45 automatic in the army."

"Better learn—fast. Never know which way these guys will pump lead."

"Hadn't considered that," I said, wondering what I'd got myself into. "But this is the idea I called about. How does this sound for Turner's death? There were two guns involved in this. Turner was taken by surprise."

There was a moment of silence over the phone. The booth was hot and I kept opening and closing the door, trying to make the air move. Franzino said, "Okay, quiz kid, what's the answer? I'm not sharp this morning—what the hell you talking about?"

"Turner, the ambitious cop, was shot in the back—never even went for his gun. Up to now we've been figuring on one guy, and the same gun, killing both men. We know Turner was in his car, watching Louise's room. Now suppose he sees Brown shoot Andersun, steps out of his car—but Smith might have been standing a dozen feet *behind* Turner. Probably as Turner went for his gun, Smith shot him in the back."

"Well... Yeah, we might try that for size," Franzino said, his voice polite. "Because the slug that took Turner was missing we have assumed there was only one guy, one gun—although I don't know why. Harris, you're going to force me to go to the movies again—you private eyes aren't as stupid as you look. But that's as good a theory as any we've dreamed up. But see this blind man. We need action now, not theories."

"Thanks, I'll let you write a commendation for me to my correspondence course," I said, as we both hung up. I kidded with Alma for a moment, and she asked when I'd have some more calls for her "sexy voice." As I left she called out, "Be careful, Barney—I may try it out on you some day."

At five minutes after eleven I parked in front of the Grand Café. Jimmy, the bartender, wrinkled his nose as I entered, as though he smelled something bad. Danny Macci had a can of beer before him, while at the other end of the bar, a hungover joker was trying to taper off with an early morning shot and talking to himself in a low, soothing voice.

Slapping Danny on the back, I said, "Howya, Danny? This is Barney Harris. Remember me, the..."

Wailing "You miserable bastard!" Danny showed me his beer-can-bending stunt again, only this time he bent the can over my head!

I vaguely knew I sat down on the floor, that blood was running all over my head and down my face—cool blood. My head was throbbing like a jet plane trying to take off.

From a million miles away I heard Jimmy shout, "Danny! Want me to lose my license? Leave him alone.... Danny! you already hurt the louse..."

My head finally worked itself loose and took off from my shoulders as I blacked out.

CHAPTER SEVEN

I came to, still sprawled out on the dirty floor, although I don't know where else I expected to be. I touched my wet face, got my hands into focus. I wasn't bleeding—Danny had clouted me with an almost full can of beer and the stuff was all over my head and shoulders. I had an acute headache and even my wild hair couldn't hide the not-so-graceful, and throbbing, lump on the right side of my noggin.

I thought about getting up, glanced around. A few morning street-corner characters were staring in from the doorway, amused. Danny Macci was sitting in a booth, waving his white cane like a baseball bat, as he cursed. Jimmy, who was standing over me, said, "Warning ya, Danny, one more rhubarb like this and I'll banish your ass from here—for good!"

"That what this was, a rhubarb?" I asked, getting to my feet. To my surprise I made it. I guess I can't take it—this one belt on the head had me weak as a sick cat, made my stomach do push-ups. "What's the matter with

Danny?”

"He don't like you," Jimmy said.

"You're kidding." I walked over, stopped beyond the reach of his cane. "What's the beef, Danny?"

"You unwashed skunk, I'll break every bone in your thick head!"

Eyes are important in registering anger. A blind man can never look real steamed because his eyes are blanks. I said, "Guess you might bust my conk—in fact, you probably have. But why?"

Danny made some observations on the sex habits of my ancestors as he took a terrific swipe at me with his cane, almost busting it on the next booth. Jimmy came forward carefully, said, "Now Danny, goddamnit Danny, cut it out!" He turned to me. "Why don't you take a walk?"

"I'm only doing my job," I said, starting the old oil. "Doing..."

"Do it someplace else," the barkeep snapped.

"You must be tired of looking at your license. Remember, a cop has been killed."

"You threatening me?"

Danny shrilled, "Let me get my mitts on him, Jimmy. I'll tear his heart out!"

He swung again with his cane and I stepped in, grabbed the back of his wrist. He was strong, but I had the grip, and when he started to move his left hand, I grabbed his shoulder muscles with my left and squeezed. "Danny, you damn near busted my head—at least tell me what the beef is about?"

"I'll...!"

I squeezed harder.

"I'm a... The one woman who would let a blind old man sleep with her, sometimes for free, you got to make trouble for. Now she's moving, won't open her door to nobody!"

"She was good to Danny," Jimmy said solemnly.

"I didn't do a thing to Louise. Honest, Danny, it was the cops."

"It was you, you lying bastard!" Danny yelled, straining to get out of my hands. "She told me."

"I know how she feels, but she told you wrong. Danny, you and me, we're different from other guys. We're too strong to have to lie and cheat. I'm not bulling you. It wasn't me. It was the cops. And I can prove it."

Danny turned his sightless face up at me. "How can you prove it?"

"Come up to the police station, I'll let you talk to the guy who put her away. Only don't swing on him. He'll even tell you I got Louise *out* of the can."

"Bastard, you running me in?" Danny asked.

"Danny, musclemen are on the level. All I want to do is prove to you I didn't do her dirt. I've got to prove it because I have a job for you."

"Louise claims... A job?"

"What kind of a job?" Jimmy asked suspiciously.

"A job requiring muscle, so that lets you out," I told the bartender, and let go of Danny and stepped back. But the old man didn't try to cane me.

Danny stood up. "I'll go see this copper, just to find out if you're telling me the truth."

"Fine. Then we'll talk about the job."

Danny headed for the door, his cane out like a feeler. I followed and he asked, "What kind of work can I do?"

"Tell you later. Be a day or two's work. Ten bucks a day."

"Ten dollars? Who am I working for?"

"Me."

On the sidewalk, I took his hand but he said, "Keep your mitts off me. Keep talking, I'll follow you."

"My car is over by the curb. We'll drive up to the station, then over lunch we'll talk about the job."

"Why can't we talk about it now?"

"Because I have to be absolutely sure we trust each other," I said, holding the door open. He got in and I shut the door, went around to the wheel side.

As I drove, Danny said, "If this is a trap, if you're jailing me, I'll break your neck." Then he added in a sort of childish voice, "I haven't worked for... lot of years. Never begged though, either. When I first lost my sight, I traveled for a time with a crummy carnival, doing a lifting act. But they was always playing jokes on me, robbing me, so I quit. Ten bucks a day, you said?"

I nodded, then remembered he was blind, said, "Yeah." The nodding didn't do the pain in my head any good. I parked in front of the police station, got out and opened the door for Danny, told him, "Let me take your hand, lot of steps here."

Lieutenant Franzino wasn't in the best of moods. When I introduced Danny, and said he was *considering* working for us, Franzino said to the old man, "I've seen you around."

"Whatcha doing, spying on me?"

"This is my precinct. It's my business to know the characters in it."

I said quickly, "Mr. Macci wanted one thing straightened out. I was explaining to him that you decided to close up Louise."

"That's right. I'm running her hips out of here," Franzino said.

"Why?" Danny almost shouted. "She ain't hurting nobody."

"Because she's a whore and whoring is against the law. Maybe it shouldn't be, but I don't make the laws—just enforce as many as I can. And

I intend to run every whore I know of out of my district."

"Wasn't you getting your lousy two-bit cut? I got a good mind to wring your goddamn neck," Danny said, flexing his powerful arms. "And I can do it, too."

Franzino leaned back in his chair, said coldly, "No you can't, because I have a badge that gives me the legal right to use a gun or blackjack. You create a disturbance here and I won't hesitate a second to split your hard head open, or shoot you. Do I make myself clear?"

Danny muttered, "Man gets little enough enjoyment out of life without some snooper..."

"Stop slobbering all over my office," Franzino said, as if enjoying his own toughness. "If she gave you a dose you'd be the first one trying to kill her. As it is, she may be the cause of two murders."

"Louise is a clean woman, a law-abiding good woman!" Danny snapped.

"You law-abiding citizens give me a pain in the ass," Franzino told him. "You're always trying to see how many little laws you can break. Like smoking in the subways or littering the streets. When we come to you for help, you act like we were the crooks. Two of your fellow citizens have been murdered, and when we ask your help, you start sniveling about a whore. You and that other noble citizen, Irving Spear, make me want to puke. Crime isn't only our task—it's everybody's job. You don't want to help us, then stop wasting my time. Get the hell out of here!"

Before I could put in a word, Danny said, "You hide a big mouth behind that badge. Who doesn't want to help? What you talking about?"

"I haven't had time to tell Mr. Macci about our plan," I said.

"You—you got time to listen to this slop about a hustler, and guzzle beer. Smell like a gutter, Harris."

"Mr. Macci had to be convinced about certain things before he would discuss anything else. As it happens I haven't been drinking beer—I've been bathing in it."

"What's all this jabber-jabber about?" Danny asked. "If you and this snotty-voiced cop want something of me, ask for it like men."

So like men we told him what we wanted. Did he still feel positive he could recognize Brown's voice? Was he willing to take the chance, and the rest of it? He listened, his rough face even listening. Then he turned to me, "This the ten-bucks-a-day deal?"

"What ten bucks a day?" Franzino asked.

"Why... eh... I offered to pay Mr. Macci for his services. Come off my expense account," I began. "Thought it would be best that way."

Danny drew up his massive body as straight as he could, said with real dignity, "Frankie was a friend of mine. So is Irv. You don't have to pay me to protect a friend or find his murderer. Hell, ain't as if I'm losing time from a job, or something."

"Fine," Franzino said, his voice suddenly soft and polite. "I'll have Spear brought in and we'll get started. Lot of wheels to get in motion; maybe be able to plant the stories in the evening papers. Danny, you have to keep quiet about this. One leak and we could have a couple more stiffs on our hands—including you."

"You can't even tell Jimmy," I added.

"How will I explain to him about the job—my being away from the bar for a day or two?"

"The job fell through, and you got a sudden pain in your stomach, have to go to a hospital for observation," Franzino said. "Something like that. Only don't make it too complicated. Barney will think up something bright—he always does."

We were to report back later in the afternoon for further details, and as I drove Danny to a cafeteria for lunch, the old man said, "That cop sure had me scared for a time. I stole a traffic stanchion about a week ago— you know, one of them big ones with a concrete base—and I was sure he was wise to me."

"What did you steal that for?"

"To work out with—can't afford no bar bells," Danny said, as though I'd asked a stupid question.

They rigged out an elaborate setup to protect Irv—even he was satisfied. On the theory that the killers didn't know the cab company he worked for, the cops and the Feds took over a small garage on One Hundred and Fifty-fourth Street, overlooking the Harlem River, and across the street from a post office—which gave them a legitimate place to hang out, watch the garage. There were a couple of independent cabbies operating from the garage, but they were out all day and most of the night. Instead of having me ride around with Irv, I was to be the mechanic inside the garage, while Danny and an assortment of dicks would be Irv's passengers.

It was a dingy little garage, with a ramp leading down from the sidewalk, and an overhead door with a smaller door cut into it. During the baseball season they made some dough parking cars, and I figured the garage held about thirty-five autos when packed to capacity. Irv was given an old cab, but it had a small sending set under the dashboard which was in contact with police cars, and supposedly would pick up even a pin-dropping sound. I had a tow jeep and I was to drive Irv home at six, with Danny beside me. A couple of young cops were assigned to his classes in college, and two more were stationed around the clock in his mother's apartment where he lived. Three buttons had been installed in the garage—one push—and they'd bring the boys across the street on the run. They gave me a .38 police special to wear under my coveralls, but I wasn't sure I knew what to do with it.

The stories broke in the evening papers—broke in big headlines. A Tommy Wills had admitted shooting both Andersun and Turner, said he'd been drunk at the time and sore at Turner for roughing him up on a previous drunk-disorderly-conduct arrest. They had a picture of a ragged-looking guy, shielding his face from the cameras, and a lot of blah about the police commissioner being "highly gratified" at the excellent and relentless work of the Homicide Squad. At the end of the piece, there was a statement from the pudding company that they had given Franklin's one thousand dollars to his sister, who was going to use the money for a honeymoon trip to Europe with her fiancé, Irving Spear. There was a picture of Irv and Juanita kissing. It made good reading—two killings solved, and a honeymoon coming like a happy ending.

I immediately phoned Betsy and warned her that if any reporters called her, to say she was glad the case was finally solved and nothing more.

I still felt uneasy about things and when I called for Ruthie, she jumped up on my lap and gave me a great big hug and one of her little hands hit the bump nestled in my hair, and I screamed and saw stars—technicolor ones. Ruthie asked a million questions and insisted upon kissing it—which hurt like hell.

Then when I talked to May Weiss about picking Ruthie up at school for the next day or so, staying with her at night... May said she was behind in her homework and her folks gave me a speech about not sacrificing their daughter's future for a few bucks. I didn't get the connection, but the answer was a large no. Of course Ruthie immediately suggested Betsy and there wasn't anything else left to do but phone her. She not only agreed but said it would be easier if Ruthie lived at her house. For a while. I didn't bother to ask Ruthie if she was in favor of the idea.

Jake called as soon as I hung up, said he'd read in the papers about the case being solved and was glad, although it didn't seem as if his tip had helped much. He sounded disappointed.

Ruthie and I packed a bag, and I drove to the Turner apartment. Betsy looked properly domestic in slacks, a flannel shirt, and an apron. She had cake and milk ready for Ruthie, and yards of cloth all set beside the sewing machine. I started to tell her about not keeping Ruthie up late, what time she had to be at school, and Betsy cut me off with, "Oh, go look at TV or something, and leave us women alone."

Ruthie giggled at this coy corn and I told Betsy, "Going in a few minutes. I have to..."

"I really didn't mean you had to leave, Barney."

"Look at Daddy's lump," Ruthie said. "He got hit on the head."

Before I could stop her, Betsy gasped and stood on tiptoe and cached for my noggin. I saw the usual galaxy of stars as my dome seemed to crack. "What happened, Barney?"

"Nothing. Guy offered me a can of beer. Look, I have to go home because I got an early and long day ahead of me tomorrow." I gave Betsy the eye to walk me to the door. Then I kissed Ruthie, told her to be good, and I'd call her tomorrow night.

She planted a hard chocolate kiss on my mouth. The cake tasted pretty good, so I took a big mouthful of the piece she was holding, which didn't please Ruthie—I really have a *big* mouth.

At the door, Betsy stepped out into the hall with me and I told her, "If reporters call, play it straight. I don't know how long I'll have to stay with our pigeon. But I'll keep in touch with you by phone. Don't let Ruthie be a pest."

"She'll be all right."

"Look, I think I know what happened to Ed. We—the police—assumed it was the same gun that killed both men. Now that we know we're dealing with two men, seems logical to believe Ed was sitting in his car, waiting..."

"In front of that woman's place!" she cut in bitterly.

"Yeah. The killers didn't know he was there. One of them steps out of the shadows and plugs Andersun. Ed probably jumped out of his car, only he didn't know the other killer was behind him. He probably shot Ed in the back as Ed was going for his gun. More in keeping with Mr. Turner's... eh... ambitious character. Definitely rules out suicide. Might say Ed was just a cop trying to do his duty, lost his life at it."

She bit her upper lip, sucked on it for a long second. "Thanks. That makes me feel better."

"Now that you've found out what you wanted, about winds up the case—for you. From here on in I'm not charging you, but I want you to still retain me—gives me a right to stay on the case."

"I hired you to find Ed's murderer—you're still working for me. Only *that* will close the case for me. And be careful, Barney."

I said okay and nodded—and wondered why I still wanted to be on the case, for nothing started my bump acting like a midget buzzer.

When I got home the apartment was too quiet. I made myself a big bowl of Shredded Wheat and chocolate syrup and tried to listen to the radio. But when I finished eating, I set the alarm for 5 a.m. and went to bed.

A few days ago I'd thought of Betsy as the possible killer. Now I was letting Ruthie stay with her.... I thought about Betsy, the way she'd been throwing herself at me, and whether I was a dummy or not for turning her down. After what she'd been through with Turner, she felt she had to prove herself, and I was the first pair of pants that had come along. No, that was too simple, although she sure looked like mighty pretty proving grounds.

But I was a little too old and set in my ways to bother with a young girl's complexes.

I began worrying about tomorrow—that .38 they gave me. Irv sure had a couple of swell protectors—a blind old man and a would-be detective!

I fell asleep on that one, and the next thing I knew the alarm was ringing, each ring like a needle in my sore head. It was a cold, dark morning, and if there's one thing I hate, it's getting up early. I took a quick shower, got into a pair of coveralls, and drove to the garage. I got out the jeep—and it needed a ring job—picked up Danny in front of the precinct house. We had breakfast of wheat cakes and coffee—I quit when he started on his fourth stack—with Danny bulling me about the time he wrestled Strangler Lewis back in 1916.

When we picked up Irv, he was pretty gay. He said, "This is as exciting as my first mission in a B-24. Let's get moving—adventure calls."

"You crocked?" Danny asked.

"You've heard of punch-drunk slobs—well, I'm scared-drunk. Let's go before it all ends in one big scream."

We reached the garage at six-thirty and Irv took off in his cab, with Danny as a passenger. Across the street, in front of the loading platform of the post office, a couple of "mailmen" stood around and talked, while near the garage entrance, a small mail truck was parked. It would be monotonous for the two guys cooped up in there all day.

I had the garage to myself and I couldn't get the gun comfortable, kept switching the holster around under my coveralls. I decided I might as well really look the part of a mechanic, do some work. They had a '48 Oldsmobile on jacks and I took the motor apart, worked all morning on it. Except for a call from Franzino, to see if I was on the job, not a damn thing happened.

At noon Danny came in—in a cab driven by a city detective. The old man had coffee and sandwiches for me, and as we ate he said things were quiet. Nobody had tailed Irv's cab, although he had driven all over the city. At Times Square there had been a show for the TV camera—man-on-the-street interview—in which Juanita had kissed Irv, told the world how glad she was that the case was over, that she and Irv were applying for passports right away, and were going to be married at sea to save time. There were also pictures and stories in all the afternoon papers, or so Danny had been told, playing up the "romance." Brown and Smith should go into action— if they were still around.

I said, "Surprised Juanita is so co-operative."

Danny laughed. "Got me, too. She has her angles—figures all the hero publicity will help Irv when he gets out of college. She's probably trying to put her hooks into the pudding company to do something for Irv, too.

Think this sort of publicity sells pudding? Heard their publicity men are working overtime with the cops."

"Maybe—the idea of publicity is to bring the name of the product before the people," I said, going back to work on the Olds. Danny wandered around the garage, tapping with his cane. After about an hour, he was able to walk around without touching the cane to the floor. When asked how he did it, he said, "I can get the layout of a place down fast. All blind people can. In my room I walk around like I had eyes, but I had to keep telling my landlady never to move any furniture—that fouls me up. This is a snap, unless you should move one of these cars, or that jack over at that side."

At two, a cab with Al Swan as a passenger picked Danny up. I finished timing the Olds motor, found a battery, put some gas in the carburetor, and gave her a test run. I hadn't cleaned the oil pan and it must have been lousy with carbon specks; she stuttered and backfired till the gas gave out. I went out on the sidewalk for a moment, to get some fresh air, lit a cigarette. One of the "mailmen" came over, asked if I had a spare cigarette, then whispered, "Hear anything?"

"No. Didn't you guys hear the racket I just made with a car?"

"Not a sound. Old garage—walls are pretty thick."

"That makes things real ducky."

I went back inside the garage, gave the Olds a grease job, then washed up and read an old paper lying around. Being below the street level, the garage got dark by four and I turned on the lights. Danny returned a few minutes later, and the dick who drove him went back downtown. Danny had nothing to report except that there had been another TV interview, in which Irv told a group of "cabbies" he was applying for a passport in the morning, and the "cabbies" were talking about giving him a send-off in the garage.

At five I called Betsy and Ruthie was okay. As I hung up, a cab turned into the top of the ramp and stopped. Two men got out of the front seat and started down the ramp. They were both roughly dressed, hard looking. One was short and bandy-legged; the other was tall and heavy. Danny muttered, "Two guys coming."

I said "Yeah!" and my insides started turning over. They didn't look like what I imagined Brown and Smith would be— they were older—but still...

I called out, "What's on your mind?" and started up the ramp.

They stopped, not far from the door, and the small one asked, "This where they going to have the party for Irv?"

I nodded.

The bigger one looked around, said, "I don't get it. How come Irv switched companies all of a sudden? Yesterday he was working for..."

"Friends of Irv Spear?" I asked, thinking what a damn fool target I made.

"We know the kid," the short one said and for a moment I thought there was a twang in his voice. "Hear on the TV in a bar about the party, so we thought…"

At that moment half a dozen "mailmen" suddenly came running down the ramp, all of them with guns drawn. One of them snapped, "Keep your hands in sight, or we'll drill you!"

The little cabbie went pale, asked, "What the hell is this?"

They were quickly frisked and didn't have any guns. Danny came tapping up the ramp, said, "Neither of them is Brown."

The cabbies were explaining how and why they'd come, and the dicks herded them out, removed their cab. The last I saw of them, they were being hustled into the post office across the street.

One of the "mailmen" returned, said, "Don't be such a hero, Harris. This was a false alarm, but next time have your gun handy."

"You bet," I said, feeling for the holster. When the guy left I closed the overhead door, ran over to the Olds and picked up the holster and the .38 from the front seat.

I walked over to Danny and I was still sweating as I said, "That was almost it."

He started to laugh, deep belly laughter. "Jeez, them two hackies must think the world has gone nuts! Mail carriers pulling guns on 'em! What they going to do with them now?"

"I don't know. Have to hold them, or the word will get out that the whole deal is a setup. Damn, my heart is still beating wildly."

"I knew it wasn't them soon as I heard 'em," Danny said. "Hey, got any beer hidden around here?"

I said no and he asked for a cigarette, and we smoked in silence for a few minutes. The phone rang. An FBI guy with a crisp voice told me Irv would drive into the garage at six-thirty. Two cars would escort me as I drove Irv home in the jeep. I told him to honk twice, and I'd open the overhead door for Irv. When I hung up, I got into the jeep, had just about turned it around when there were two cough-like sounds, and then the light tinkle of glass as the garage lights went out.

For a moment I didn't realize what had happened, that the lights had been shot out with silencers. I switched on the jeep lights and for a split second saw the two men on the ramp, then the orange flame flashes, and the sound of the headlights breaking as they went out. Another flash and the windshield splintered, and I dived out of the jeep and nearly kayoed myself on the cement floor. It took me a long second to come to, get my wind back. I tugged at the .38, finally got it out. The garage was pitch black and tense with silence. I heard the small noise of somebody crawling toward me, and a terrible chill filled my guts till Danny's big hand squeezed mine.

Now I heard steps slowly coming down the ramp as Danny put his lips in my ear, whispered, "Stay put, I'll get 'em."

"The alarm buttons," I started to say, but his thick fingers closed my mouth and I could taste the tobacco stains on his hand. He crawled away and I swear I thought he was chuckling.

My head hurt; I was bruised all over—maybe that's why it took me a moment to get things straight. In the darkness we were all "blind"—all except Danny. His ears could "see." But even if he got his mitts on one of them, the other would be sure to plug him.

I tried thinking hard and fast, but for the life of me (and that wasn't any damn pun!) I couldn't remember in the darkness where the hell the posts were with the alarm buttons.

I hugged the floor as if I was trying to make a dent in the cement and waited. Then I told myself I *had* to help Danny—he sure couldn't take the two of them, and there was no point in my lying there like a dead duck. I got up on my knees—behind the jeep—found a wrench in my pocket that had cut my thigh when I dived on the floor. Gripping the gun, I threw the wrench with my left toward the far corner of the garage. When it hit I saw a spurt of orange over to my left and I fired at it and there was a shrill cry of pain and the sound of a body falling!

Two more angry flashes of flame split the darkness as the slugs struck the jeep, like two hammer blows. I hit the cement again, so surprised at my luck in hitting one of them I didn't know what to do. The last shots had come from a spot more to my right, but I wasn't certain exactly where and couldn't chance any wild shots. I might hit Danny. I could hear steps coming toward the jeep—the guy was off the ramp—slow careful steps. I got to my knees, got up in a half crouch, and waited.

The sound of the steps was slight but very clear in the heavy silence. The only relief from the blackness was the vague and dim squares that were the garage windows. The steps came nearer; the guy was walking very carefully and deliberately in the darkness. I raised the gun, pointed it in the direction of the steps... and then there was this terrible scream of agony that split the silence like painful thunder and Danny's yell, "Got the bastard!"

I stood up and fired three times at the garage windows—to call for help— and missed. The lights on the Olds should work—the new battery was still in—and I ran in that direction and fell flat on my face over something. I sat up, knew my arm and the side of my face were bleeding. My head felt as if somebody had sat on it. I yelled, "Looking for lights, Danny!" and climbed to my feet and limped forward. I walked right smack into the goddam Olds, cutting my right shin and knocking the wind out of my guts, but I got the door open, felt along the dashboard. Then the lights flooded the garage, washing out the darkness.

At the foot of the ramp a man was sitting up, a bald-headed man with blood running out of his right side, while a few feet from the jeep Danny had those tremendous arms wrapped around a little guy, who had the whitest face I ever want to see. I limped over, my gun covering him, told Danny to let go. The guy fell to the floor like he was dead.

Picking up his gun, I went over to the other guy, who was moaning softly, his legs kicking in pain. I got his gun. I fired at one of the garage windows again, my gun making a hell of a racket—although I hadn't heard it before—and missed. I felt awful dizzy, looked around wildly for the alarm buttons. Then Danny walked over to the ramp, and slowly started foot-tapping his way toward the overhead door. When he reached it, he jerked it up so hard he busted the door. He shouted once and a moment later "mailmen" with guns came running in. That was it.

I'd winged "Smith" with a lucky shot while Danny had jumped "Brown." Of the two, it turned out Brown was hurt the worst—Danny had crushed five of his ribs in that bear hug. The rest I guess you read about—it was splattered over enough papers. Their real names were Martin Pearson and Sam Lund, a couple of ex-G.I.'s who tried to make it the easy way, only it turned out they spelled easy h-a-r-d. These two had met in Paris, worked out this passport scheme. They had picked up ten birth certificates, three in Boston, two in Newark, one in Chicago, and four in New York City, and already had eight passports ready for sale. They confessed—there wasn't much else for them to do. Andersun's luck turned their scheme from a quiet swindle into murder. Turner had walked into it; they didn't even know he was a cop when he stepped out of the dark of his car.

I guess you've seen Danny's ugly face on TV. He was picked to be on a TV show the night the case broke and he stole the show with a couple of corny strongman acts—breaking chains and all that. He was on various TV shows for quite a while, and, all told, picked up several grand.

As for me, Al Swan figured he could retire from the force and we'd open a big-time agency on the strength of all the publicity I got. He slipped me the pitch the day after the case was over, when for the first time in my life I was cut and badly bruised, felt sort of beaten up. So I told him I was sticking to fixing cars and skip-tracing and if he ever pushed another criminal case my way, I'd break his neck, or maybe hurt him worse by ripping one of his fancy suits to pieces. The hell with this rough stuff.

P.S.

"Will we get married? I don't know. I don't think so. Now wait, don't stiffen up like that. Honey, you've lived too much by the so-called rules of life—but the phony rules, not the real ones. I mean, are you even sure you really want to marry me? Don't give me a quick answer—remember what you've been through. You got married; therefore according to the rules of soap operas, books, TV, and the movies, all your troubles were over, because people who get married are supposed to live happily ever after.

"Now that you're single again, the idea is to get married as quickly as possible, for deep down you still believe marriage must mean happiness. And I'm the first guy that came along, and also you feel sorry for me because I seem to be such a noble creature raising my little girl all by myself.

"No, Betsy, don't get me wrong. I'm trying to tell you this as calmly and clearly as I can, and that isn't easy. I don't want us to make a mistake, because the way I see it, a wrong marriage is about the biggest mistake two people can make. I know, I'm not an old man, but I am settled and not ready to go through growing up all over again. Baby, you're young and full of a lot of corny, and even younger ideas. Well—I can be dead wrong about all this, and I'd be eager to get a license tomorrow if I was sure it would bring us happiness. But this is marriage you want, not my bringing up another kid.

"Wait up, honey, let me finish. Maybe in time we'll know we're really meant for each other, trite as that sounds. Understand, I'm not running you down. I admire your courage in going through with this, insisting upon learning if Ed was a suicide and if you were responsible. In a way that was another of your phony rules, but most people would have taken the easy out, kept quiet, forced the suicide angle from their minds. Took guts to do what you did. No, 'guts' is one of the phony words. It took sincere courage and honesty to do what you did, and I admire that.

"And that's what I'm trying to do, be honest with you—and myself. As of now, I like you and you like me. Only 'like' isn't love. I don't even want to use the word love, because I don't exactly know what that is—maybe another of the phony labels we use. But at least you know—we know—that something was twisted in Ed's mind. That's another of your rules that don't work—a man and a woman don't hit it off just because they *are* a man and a woman. A ..."

Betsy was listening with her eyes closed and now sat up in bed and said almost sharply, "All right, Barney, but please, let's not argue about that now. May Weiss will be furious if you're not home by midnight."

THE END

ED LACY BIBLIOGRAPHY
(1911-1968)

Walk Hard—Talk Loud (1940 as by Len Zinberg)

What D'ya Know for Sure (1947 as by Len Zinberg; revised as Strange
Desires, 1949)

Hold With the Hares (1948 as by Len Zinberg)

The Woman Aroused (1951)

Sin in Their Blood (1952; published in UK as Death in Passing, 1959)

Strip for Violence (1953)

Enter Without Desire (1954)

Go for the Body (1954)

Exit 13 (1954; as by Steve April)

The Best That Ever Did It (1955; reprinted in pb as Visa to Death,
1956)

The Men from the Boys (1956)

Lead with Your Left (1957)***

Room to Swing (1957)*

Breathe No More, My Lady (1958)

Shakedown for Murder (1958)

Be Careful How You Live (1958; reprinted in pb as Dead End, 1960)

Blonde Bait (1959)

The Big Fix (1960)

A Deadly Affair (1960)

Bugged for Murder (1961)

The Freeloaders (1961)

South Pacific Affair (1961)

The Sex Castle (1963; reprinted as Shoot It Again,1969)

Two Hot to Handle (1963; two novellas: The Coin of Adventure and
Murder in Paradise)

Moment of Untruth (1964)*

Harlem Underground (1965)**

Pity the Honest (1965)

The Hotel Dwellers (1966)

Double Trouble (1967)***

In Black & Whitey (1967)**

The Napalm Bugle (1968)

The Big Bust (1969)

*Toussaint M. Moore series

**Lee Hayes series

*** Dave Wintino series

And for more twisted tales of obsession, we offer...

Douglas Sanderson

"There is more going on than you can believe, with backstabbing and double crosses galore."—Bruce Grossman, *Bookgasm*

0-9749438-2-7 Pure Sweet Hell / Cath a Fallen Starlet $19.95
"The plots read like a shotgun marriage between Jim Thompson and Mickey Spillane—on speed." Kevin Burton Smith, from his Introduction.

1-933586-06-0 The Deadly Dames / A Dum-Dum for the President $19.95
"One of those fast and furious novels with so much going on, so many dead bodies, and so many plot complications that you can't believe the author can pull it all together...but [Sanderson] manages just fine."
–Bill Crider, *Mystery File.*

1-933586-72-9 Night of the Horns / Cry Wolfram $19.95
"Exceptionally well written, action-packed, fast paced, and thoroughly entertaining...very highly recommended... the action is non-stop"
—*Midwest Book Review*

"Retro-crime fans will be clamoring for more."
–Wes Lukowsky, *Booklist*

Stark House Press, 1315 H Street, Eureka, CA 95501
griffinskye3@sbcglobal.net / www.StarkHousePress.com
Available from your local bookstore, or order direct or via our website.